Witchfinder

Sarah A. Hoyt

Cover Art background John Atkinson Grimshaw –Blackman Street, London
Figure cover © Flexflex | Dreamstime.com
Dragon©Algol | Dreamstime.com
Cover Design Marian Derby

Published by Goldport Press
Goldport Press
3570 East 12th Avenue
Denver, Colorado 80206

Witchfinder

Sarah A. Hoyt

... She had to see clearly. She made passes midair and tried to concentrate. Seraphim Ainsling. What was the foolish man doing? He worried Syddel far too much for it to be innocent. Syddel had a second sense about these things.

Seraphim Ainsling. She remembered his haughty expression, his aquiline profile from a party at which he had resolutely looked through her.

Her fingers ran through her hair again. Right. The Duke of Darkwater. I am beneath his notice. If town rumor was right, he was getting engaged to Lady Honoria Blythe of Blythe Blessings. The eldest daughter of the Earl of Savage.

His profile was now firmly in her mind, the green eyes looking at her intently in her imagining, and she stared at the water bowl again and saw him clearly, wearing the green jacket, and a pocket watch, and saying the final words of a magical formula.

Too late, she realized what the formula was. A transport spell. Far too late, she realized she'd let her mind get enmeshed in it and in his magic.

There was a flash, a magical blast that hit her like a punch mid-body. And then she felt the transport spell pull her through the Betweener and into a destination not of her choosing.

Her bowl of water fell and cracked apart, erasing all her careful chalk markings…

Sarah A. Hoyt

His Grace

If anyone had been looking closely at the duke of Darkwater as His Grace approached the double doors of the ballroom, he would have noticed the Duke held himself somewhat stiffly. Not as though he were injured or embarrassed, but more as though he were excessively careful of all his movements.

The two uniformed footmen exchanged a look before opening the doors. His Grace, the look said, had clearly been out drinking. Which explained his being so late to the ball.

Neither of them would have dared say it was just like His Grace, and – if it came to that – a lot like His Grace's deceased father, but it was plain that they both thought it.

As His Grace, Seraphim Ainsling, Duke of Darkwater, paused in the doorway, in the full glare of the brilliant mage lights positioned all around the walls, all eyes turned his way.

The attention was not due to the exquisite tailoring of his green evening coat, which showed off his muscular body to great advantage, or his commanding height and stately bearing. That he was possibly the handsomest man in the room, with his thick, raven-black hair, regular features marred only by an aquiline nose, and dazzling emerald eyes, was a part of it, as well as the fact that he was His Grace, Seraphim Ainsling, Duke of Darkwater, one of the oldest and most prestigious magical houses in the kingdom, not to say in the world.

No. The real reason his entrance gained the attention of all in the room was that this party was being held in his honor, and he was unfashionably late. His mother had almost given up all hope of his appearance, as had his betrothed, Lady Honoria Blythe.

The betrothal had as yet to be formalized, but everyone present expected the announcement to be made sometime approaching midnight.

After a pause that was so silent it was almost as if the orchestra had stopped playing – which it certainly hadn't — the conversation and dancing resumed.

Darkwater walked into the room, still moving with exaggerated care, reached for a glass from a tray held high by a passing footman, and tossed the champagne back in one swift move.

From across the room, his mother saw it and flinched. The Dowager Duchess of Darkwater was a petite woman. Her mother had been French, and Lady Barbara showed it in her small oval face, her dark eyes, her clearly marked, arched eyebrows, and in a certain air that denoted a quick temper, quickly tamped down.

She approached her errant son, maintaining every appearance of outward calm, even if her gaze couldn't help but reproach his lateness and his state.

"Really, Seraphim!" she said as soon as she could be sure of not being heard by other people. "After I have gone to such trouble putting on this ball for you, the least you could do is arrive in a timely manner. Dearest Honoria has withstood it all without a crack in her perfect demeanor, but I have been ready to faint from anxiety."

Darkwater glanced across the room to where Lady Honoria stood, pale, blonde, and beautiful, the picture of poise and elegance. She smiled at him, a calm smile that showed no emotion at all, neither anger nor relief, neither disdain nor caring. He sent her a stilted bow and a smile that gave as little away as her own. "She is to be commended for her good sense," he replied. "And you, Mama, are to be commended for not fainting. That would have set the tabbies' tongues wagging."

His mother clutched his arm and he winced and reeled a little, as though the force of her small hand clasping his sleeve were enough to unsettle his carefully guarded poise. "Seraphim – tell me you are happy with this match. If you are not, you should not go through with it. There is time to back out now, without injuring Honoria or the Darkwater pride."

"Back out?" he asked as he stepped away from her. "Why should I want to do that?"

"Because you are not in love with her. I have always wanted a love match for you, not to see you give yourself up to increase the family fortune. Our magic is still strong, and with your brother's new inventions, our fortunes will rally."

"Father expected otherwise," said Darkwater curtly. "An alliance between Ainsling's Arcana and Blythe Blessings was mentioned over and over in his diary as something that needed to happen before we could control our decline." He reached for a sparkling crystal glass from another passing tray. "Love is a fairy story, at any rate."

"So instead you drink yourself blind?" asked his mother. "You are making a good job of hiding it, but I can see you are unsteady on your feet."

"Hardly, Mother. Please do not fret." Almost reeling, he managed to visibly exert utmost control upon his rebellious body, bowed politely to his mother, and turned to cross the room. "If you will excuse me, I believe Honoria is entitled to at least one dance with me."

But before he reached Honoria, a figure intercepted him. Lady Barbara started forward, ready to stop the person she identified as Jonathan Blythe, the brother of the lady Honoria, a well-known rakehell, but Seraphim shook his head at Jonathan, and smiled, and proceeded to his affianced bride.

Seeing him bow to Honoria and offer his hand to be enveloped in her gloved one, his mother could but clench her two hands together. What she had endured from her husband – his careless disregard for her and her position – only she knew. She had exerted her discretion, her pride, the very last shreds of the love that had once drawn her into an unadvisable marriage, to keep her husband's missteps secret.

His debts at the gaming tables, she'd covered without a word; his frequent inebriation, she'd hid by talking of his "complaint"; his mistresses she'd paid off; his by-blows, she'd taken care to set in the way of good positions, his children she'd borne without complaint.

And all that time, her one consolation had been that neither Seraphim, nor his ten-year younger brother, Michael, nor even her single surviving daughter, Caroline, Michael's twin, showed the slightest tendency to imitate their father. Michael was perhaps the steadiest of them all – his mind given very early over to the perfecting of magic and the creation of magical engines to improve daily life.

But Seraphim, though a rather spirited boy, forever climbing trees and riding out on horses that were too impetuous for any other rider, had shown early enough a tendency to assume responsibility for the family, and to respect the worth and importance of his title and position.

Only, in the last year, it had all fallen apart. Rumors of his wild gaming and wenching, his haphazard living, his pride in his riding and shooting prowess – a prowess no one else could see a shred of – had reached even the ears of his mother.

No one had asked her to settle his debts. Yet. No one had laughed openly about his mistaken pride in his physical abilities. Yet. No light skirt or hedgeborn baby had sought her protection. Yet.

But in that ballroom, watching her son hold himself too stiffly and carefully, Lady Barbara Ainsling, Dowager Duchess of Darkwater, felt much like Sisyphus, who, having pushed the rock up the slope, sees it rolling back again.

Seraphim, his early character notwithstanding, was turning into a copy of his father.

Sarah A. Hoyt

Two Brothers

Darkwater lay sprawled across a low chaise in his dressing room. By the wavering light of two mage globes fixed on either side of the mirror above his dressing table, he looked like the picture of debauch. With his coat, tailored to a nicety to fit his broad shoulders and narrow waist like a second skin, unbuttoned, and his curls, in wild disarray, framing his pale, sweaty face, he looked like he'd spent the night in wild orgies.

He thought that no one who saw him now would doubt the rumors that he'd been drinking heavily before the ball at which his engagement to Lady Honoria Blythe was to have been announced. And no one would doubt that this was the reason the announcement had not been made.

By morning the tongues of the gossipers would spread everywhere the story that one or the other of them meant to cry off.

Right then, the Duke was trying to think the rumors, and how he looked to avoid thinking of pain. His mind was dark with pain, his breath coming in fast gasps, his brow creased with suffering he had not allowed anyone in the ballroom to suspect.

When he spoke to his attendant, who was rummaging through the drawers of the dressing table, his voice was little more than a croak, animated by no more energy than could be provided by extreme pain. "Penny, curse you. Can you not set about it?"

The valet spared him a look over his shoulder, gracing Darkwater with a frown that was much like the Duke's own. In fact, Seraphim knew Gabriel Penn – whom only His Grace dared call Penny – looked almost like Seraphim's twin and was well known to be a by-blow of His Grace the former duke, acknowledged as such, born a full year to the day before Seraphim's birth.

Seraphim knew that people said the fact that the two had been brought up together almost as brothers, and that Gabriel was now the trusted confidant and closest assistant to His Grace, showed Lady Barbara's forbearance and her unusual turn of mind. Or perhaps, some said, it just showed that she knew a high magical power, like Penn's, when she saw it, and thought it best not to have him run wild and untrained amid tenants and farmers.

"I'm shifting as fast as I can, Duke," he threw impatiently in Seraphim's direction. Though in public he called him His Grace and showed him every respect, in private he took liberties no one who knew Seraphim's stiff-necked propriety would believe. He called Darkwater Duke or

Seraphim, or occasionally, you damned fool. Right then he said the first as if he meant the last, and added, “Because if you think that coat is coming off without being slit, you’re a fool. And more of a fool for having squeezed yourself into it and gone to the ball, instead of calling me to you first.”

Seraphim gave a gurgle that might have been an attempt at laughing. “I couldn’t disappoint Honoria or humiliate her that way.”

“What I think of your Honoria…,” Gabriel said, turning with a sharp razor in his hand, and setting about cutting the sleeve of Seraphim’s coat with a skill that showed he’d often done it. “And that is more than I think of her brother Jonathan, who took a… ah…. stroll early on from the salon and behind the rose bushes in the garden with Mrs. Varley. I’m sure people going out for a breath of air must have heard them moaning and whimpering.” Gabriel turned very red. “What I mean is, no one could doubt what they were about. He’s very bad ton, Seraphim. If you ask me, the entire family—”

“No one has asked you,” Seraphim said, in the blighting tone that never worked on Gabriel.

This time, though, Gabriel did not answer him, as his cutting away of the coat, revealed not only a blood soaked sleeve, but a mass of ill-wrapped bandages – all of them equally tinted blood-red.

The stain, as he pulled away the remnants of the coat and tossed them aside, showed itself to continue all across the Duke’s shoulder and to over-spread his chest.

“Seraphim!” Gabriel said, as he cut away the shirt and the bandages, to reveal two jagged, irregular cuts, one extending all the way up the arm, almost to the shoulder, deep enough to show the glimmering whiteness of bones in its depths, and the other starting at the shoulder and stopping just short of the heart.

“My ribs deflected it,” Seraphim said. “It was my heart the villain was aiming for. Spelled dagger.”

Gabriel set his lips tight, in something that might be anger or concern. His countenance, always rather pale, had gone two shades paler, so that even his lips appeared to be glaring white under the mage lights. He swallowed and nodded, as if he were swallowing the reproaches he would normally have made. His concern showed in his creased forehead and in the depths of the green eyes both of them had inherited from their common father.

Turning, he rummaged in the drawers again, with a quick question of “I suppose you couldn’t close it magically?”

“No,” Seraphim said. His voice had devolved into a whisper. His good hand clenched the arm of the chair so hard that its knuckles shone white. "I told you it was a magical dagger."

Gabriel nodded and set on the dressing table certain articles that even the duke's mother would be very surprised to know were always kept in its drawers: needle; catgut thread; bandages and lint.

From a smaller table nearby, where it sat next to the annotated volume of Plato's Republic that Darkwater had been reading before the alarm had called him away, he grabbed the bottle of brandy and, as if as an afterthought, a large glass.

He splashed the brandy liberally into the glass and handed it to the Duke, saying with unwonted force, and complete lack of deference, "Drink."

"After all the champagne I had in there, my dear Gabriel?" Darkwater rasped. "I shall be sodden drunk."

"Good," Gabriel said.

Darkwater raised his eyebrows, but tossed back the brandy without further comment. Gabriel had kept the bottle of brandy uncapped, and now set the top down on the table. Possessing himself of Darkwater's hand, he stretched the duke's arm out, leaving his wound exposed and upturned.

"Must you?"

"If it's a magical wound," Gabriel said. "Magic won't close it or disinfect it. We don't need you being carried off in a fever. You take care not to alarm the house."

"Have no fear," Darkwater said, turning his head away.

Indeed, as Gabriel poured the caustic liquid along the open wound, then splashed a like amount into the chest wound, only a very faint complaint escaped His Grace's mouth. This was probably because he had taken the care of muffling any possible screams with his good arm. And, as Gabriel returned the now half-empty bottle to its stand, only the red marks of Darkwater's own teeth on his wrist showed what effort it had taken.

Gabriel said nothing as he set about threading the needle.

Only as he started to sew the ragged edges of the wounds together, did he speak. "I can," he said. "Put a pain-reducing spell on it. As soon as I'm done. Not before, or it will retard the healing."

Seraphim nodded, then spoke, in a bewildered tone. "It was a trap. There were, according to my…." He swallowed. "My foreseeing showed a boy and a girl, about six years of age, first coming into magical powers, and being condemned to death for them. I tried to… intercept… but there was a trap. And no children."

"What world?" Gabriel asked.

"Oh, the pyramids," Seraphim said and tried to shrug, before letting out a faint moan. "But I ended up in Betweener."

The pyramids was, if Gabriel remembered, the world where they sacrificed children with magical powers to their barbarous blood-gods. He didn't remember what the cartographers of their own world called it. Possibly something inspired like 435-65-A.

Most the Earths, spread out along the magical continuum of several universes, blocked from each other only by the thinnest of energy veils, called themselves Earth. And most of them thought they were unique – the only Earth in the only universe, inhabited by the only humans. Avalon, their own Earth, knowing there were many, had given itself that name. Legend maintained that it was the oldest of the Earths, the one from which all the others had fractured away, when Merlin had been captured and imprisoned in an everlasting magical trap. The occluding of his world-encompassing power had caused magic itself to fracture and the Earth to copy itself over and over – most of the copies retaining no magic, and those that did retain it often undertaking to forbid it.

Britannia remained the most powerful magical nexus in Avalon, and its citizens the most skilled at magic. Britannia citizens were not allowed to travel to other worlds. King Richard XVI had confirmed the prohibition first instituted centuries ago, but disregarded for most of those centuries. Even the kidnapping of the Princess Royal — the only child of the king — out of her cradle, when Seraphim himself was a nursling, though it was presumed to have been a plot from another world, hadn't lifted the prohibition.

And because the cartographers' designations didn't suit his mind, Seraphim gave those worlds to which he travelled routinely in an attempt to save from death as many magicians and witches as possible, names of his own coining. There was Pyramids and Swamp – which was not one, but a fetid world mired in superstition and covered in vermin – Slum and Desert and – for a particularly noxious world – Madhouse.

Gabriel frowned. "”An ambush! They know of you then!"

"Yes. No. I don't know. I suspect they don't know who I am, or where I came from. I suspect they were simply trying to stop the rescues…."

"Enough to set a trap? And interfere with your foreseeing? Take care, Duke."

Seraphim made a noncommittal sound in the back of his throat and, seeing that Gabriel had finished sewing his wounds, he sat up straighter. "Give me a shirt and a coat… the… green one," he said.

Gabriel cast a doubtful eye at him. "You can't mean to go back to the ball."

"Of course I can. I must. An announcement must be made by midnight."

Gabriel cast a curious look over the Duke. He looked pale but composed, but– almost without thinking, he raised his hand and cast a pain-dimming spell over Darkwater. He could see Seraphim's features relax almost immediately, and he looked easier as he stood.

"At least let me help you wash," Gabriel said. "You reek of brandy."

Darkwater chuckled. "So long as they think I'm such a desperate drunk as to come to my apartments for brandy before resuming the ball, they won't suspect what I'm really doing."

Gabriel clicked his tongue as he wrapped Seraphim's arm and shoulder in a thin layer of bandages. "Take care, Seraphim. One day you'll go a bridge too far."

But he helped Seraphim into his shirt and coat, and removed his watch and accoutrements from the pocket of his ruined coat.

As he passed them to the duke, Darkwater's pocket watch, his father's old watch, emitted a loud whine, which almost caused Gabriel to drop it.

Darkwater reached for it, swiftly, with his good hand, and flicked it open. He swore under his breath. "Swamp. Give me my crystal ball, Gabriel."

"Your Grace," Gabriel said, using both the title and the tone of deference he rarely used except in public, and continuing, in tight-lipped, scolding tones. "You cannot mean to go rescuing anyone right now. You could barely rescue yourself!"

"My crystal ball, Penn, and do me the favor of being quiet."

Sarah A. Hoyt

The Agent

There had to be worse things that could happen to a girl than dropping head first into a Regency novel. Nell Felix had no idea what they could be, though. A Regency novel with magic, at that. A world where she must mind her manners, curb her tongue, behave like a proper lady, and, oh, yeah, perform magic, too.

If you'd told her, back when she was a very junior programmer at Prince Management Systems – she could never make her bosses understand what was wrong with that acronym, either – that her use of the magic Grandma had taught her would attract the attention of an interplanetary spy and that, for his sake, she would end up living in another world where everyone still behaved as if the regency had never passed, and where America was just the colonies of dear old Mother England, she would never have believed it.

But it was true nonetheless. And in it she'd fallen in love with Antoine, somewhere between his telling her about other worlds and teaching her magic way beyond anything that grandma had known, magic beyond anything Earth would even dream about. And now she couldn't leave this particular world until Antoine was released. Which meant she had to satisfy Syddel's demands first. It had already been a year. How much longer would she have to work to ransom her lover?

The real Earth, or what she thought of as the real Earth, was so long ago and far away, and sometimes she didn't know if it felt like a weird dream, or if her current circumstances did.

"Miss, Miss," the cracked voice of the landlady called from outside the door to Nell's lodging.

It wavered, breaking on the high pitches and making an awful descant to the pounding of the landlady's impatient fist on the door.

Like cats mating inside drums, Nell thought, and her little, dark face, which was rather like a cat's itself, twisted in an expression of distaste, as she put her long-fingered hands over her ears. *Or like a car engine seriously out of tune.*

She repressed a longing for cars – and for flush toilets – and leaned forward toward the complex chalk drawings on her floor and the bowl of water placed in the middle of them. Lord Syddel had told her to find what Seraphim Ainsling was up to. But the duke must be using some magical protection, because it was easier said than done. So far the bowl had shown her no more than a murky fog with occasional glimpses of blood and cut flesh. And while this didn't reassure her that His Grace of Darkwater was on the right side of the law, it was hardly an indictment.

"Miss Felix. Miss!" The pounding and the voice, each competing – and somehow managing – to be louder than the other penetrated the ineffective barrier of her hands and shattered her concentration. The wavering image she'd been able to conjure in the water – of a green jacket seemingly bobbing about mid-air – vanished altogether, leaving nothing but water and cheap china. Cracked cheap china, Nell thought, noticing the chip out of the side and the wandering crack that descended like a yellow scribble towards the center of the bowl. "Yes, Mrs. Stope," she said. "I am coming."

The screaming did stop, but the pounding continued, if more subdued now, a tap, tap, tap, as though to remind Nell the landlady was waiting. Not that I'm likely to forget, Nell thought, as she got up and strode across the room to the door, being careful not to step on any of the chalk lines. On her Earth, she might get a peeved letter, but no landlady would actually be pounding on her door. Here, everything was so much more personal.

She was careful to make sure her body obscured Mrs. Stope's view of the floor. Not that witchcraft was illegal or even uncommon – though more uncommon in the lower classes, of course – in Britannia, but the landlady was the type of person to worry about the chalk on the floorboards.

Mrs. Stope stood squarely in the middle of the landing outside Nell's room. It would have been difficult to stand any other way, since the landing was hardly large enough to contain her. Not that she was fat. No, she was square. A short, blockish woman, with the sort of build that led one to believe that in a past life she had been a clock. The way she clicked her tongue also sounded much like a clock ticking.

She turned her watery-blue eyes up to Nell, then gave her a careful once over, from head to toe, taking in the well-tailored skirt and the irreproachable black jacket. "Dressed to go out, are you miss?" she said. "And I hope you're not intending to go for weeks, and the rent already overdue?"

"No," Nell said. "I meant to go out for a moment only." She regretted not for the first time that she couldn't tell the truth: *places to go, people to spy on.* If she said that in this world, it wouldn't even be a reference joke. It was still true. And it kept Antoine safe. Antoine… She swallowed and kept her mind from going down that path. The problem with loving someone is that it made it easy for people to hold him hostage and make you do what they wanted. "On some… errands. But I will have your rent for you when I return." *I'd better have it; at least Sydell is not so dumb as to forget it is unadvisable to delay paying your secret operatives, even your unwilling secret operatives.*

Mrs. Stope bent her head, momentarily, under the weight of this promise, but rattled back into it, game as a pebble, "Only last time you said that, you left for three weeks and then I–"

"I always pay," Nell said, pressing her lips together and allowing her face to show the mingled impatience and annoyance she felt.

"Yes, miss, but as I own the rooms, I need to have the pay regular, else how can I meet my own bills?"

"I will do my best," Nell said, putting on the airs she had learned tended to bring these tirades to an abrupt conclusion. And then, to reinforce the idea, "I was about to go see my father."

"Oh," The landlady said, and her face showed a cunning sort of curiosity. "His Lordship is in town, then?"

Nell only nodded, preserving the sort of distance and secret that the landlady would doubtless expect if Nell were in fact the by-blow of a nobleman. Which she very much doubted she was, since Earth had very few noblemen and few of them were likely to give even an illegitimate child up for adoption. But she was adopted, and so she couldn't say her parents weren't noble. Heck, it was weird enough she had magical power. She suspected most people back on what she thought of as Earth had had magic bred out of them. Since it didn't work very well or very reliably on Earth, it wouldn't confer any advantage. So maybe her parents were nobility from some other world. She couldn't swear they weren't.

Besides, Mrs. Stope had once seen Nell with Mr. Sydell and assumed that he was Nell's father and that their relationship a great secret. It always shocked Nell how little it was necessary to tell people lies. They much preferred to tell lies to themselves. Particularly in this world, where so much of society depended on convention and secrets.

She didn't exactly despise Mrs. Stope for assuming that Nell was of noble blood – she despised her for the reasons she gave for assuming so: That she'd seen Nell with Mr. Sydell, who was obviously a gentleman, and also that Nell's features were delicately formed, her hands and feet small and her ankles elegant. In many worlds, Nell had seen just those features in dirt-poor peasants. *And if I had a sovereign for every fat, blobby princess I've known,* she thought. *I'd be wealthier than the king.* But there would never be a way of convincing the Mrs. Stopes of any world of that fact.

"Well, if you're seeing your father, Miss…," the landlady said, with the sort of sigh more rooted in her despairing of knowing more than in her fear of not getting paid.

"Indeed I am," Nell said. "Now, if you'll excuse me and give me some time, I must write a letter to take with me." For some reason, in this world, writing a letter was accorded the same sort of privacy that the real Earth gave calls of nature. Perhaps because writing with a quill pen was one of the most undignified businesses in any world.

She added ballpoint pens to the list of things she missed.

Before the woman could say, *A letter, Miss?* and try to figure out what the letter would say and to whom it would be addressed, a query that Nell saw all too plainly in her eyes, Nell shut the door in her face, and returned to her work.

Perhaps I drew the right-reverse spiral too wobbly, she thought, doubtfully, as she stared at the drawing on the floor. She twirled her fingers in her hair, rendering it what Mrs. Stope would doubtlessly consider a completely inappropriate coiffure for a gently reared female.

Kneeling down, she erased part of the spiral, then drew it again, slightly differently. Then she picked up the bowl and stared, again, at the vague picture of a green jacket floating midair.

She had to see clearly. She made passes midair and tried to concentrate. Seraphim Ainsling. What was the foolish man doing? He worried Syddel far too much for it to be innocent. Syddel had a second sense about these things.

Seraphim Ainsling. She remembered his haughty expression, his aquiline profile from a party at which he had resolutely looked through her.

Her fingers ran through her hair again. Right. *The Duke of Darkwater. I am beneath his notice.* If town rumor was right, he was getting engaged to Lady Honoria Blythe of Blythe Blessings. *The eldest daughter of the Earl of Savage.*

His profile was now firmly in her mind, the green eyes looking at her intently in her imagining, and she stared at the water bowl again and saw him clearly, wearing the green jacket, and a pocket watch, and saying the final words of a magical formula.

Too late, she realized what the formula was. A transport spell. Far too late, she realized she'd let her mind get enmeshed in it and in his magic.

There was a flash, a magical blast that hit her like a punch mid-body. And then she felt the transport spell pull her through the Betweener and into a destination not of her choosing.

Her bowl of water fell and cracked apart, erasing all her careful chalk markings.

Sarah A. Hoyt

The Lion, The Witch and The Pyramids

Seraphim looked at his watch, and then at his crystal ball. Neither was strictly necessary. It was possibly to use one or the other. But the one thing his father's diaries had taught him was that it was never a good idea to rely only on one method. And Seraphim, rushing to the last alarm, had found that relying only on the watch might be the last thing he did.

The Others were perhaps no more cunning than he, but they were infinitely better armed, and there were more of them and they would have more magicians who could fake better alarms. And that was without counting the legitimate agents of his majesty, whose job it was to enforce laws forbidding citizens of Britannia from traveling abroad and who had once or twice come close to catching Papa. They too must be looking for Seraphim.

Seraphim got the coordinates of the talent at risk from the watch he'd inherited from his father, then tried to raise an image in his crystal ball to corroborate it; but all he could see was the shadow of his valet, standing determinedly between the light and the crystal ball. He obscured the light magic must use to form images.

"Penny, for the love of God–" Seraphim said, half in exasperation.

"No. You are in no fit state. You should not be standing up, much less going on a rescue mission where you might get stabbed again." Gabriel squeezed his lips into a thin line. "Or worse."

Seraphim clenched his lips tight. He wanted very much to answer, but he tried to avoid being rude to Gabriel. Gabriel could not answer in kind, and that made it churlish of Seraphim to abuse him. "We were not put in this world… in any world," he said, "to take our ease while innocents die." Realizing he'd just repeated something his father had written in his diary, and that shortly before committing suicide, Seraphim suppressed a shudder.

"There is a dire difference, Seraphim, between taking your ease and risking yourself foolishly. I beg you to consider what will become of your mother, your sister and your brothers should you–"

Before he could finish, a scratching at the door was followed by Lady Barbara's voice. "Seraphim? I would have a word with you if I might."

Seraphim looked at the basin filled with bloody water, the discarded, blood soaked garments, the evidence of his injury strewn around the room, and then his eyes met Gabriel's, and he realized that

Gabriel's thoughts had followed the same trend. "No," Gabriel's lips formed, though he didn't say it aloud. "I will make your excuses."

The valet went to the door and opened it. Seraphim heard him speak in a low voice, and could imagine what he was saying. *His Grace is indisposed* and other such rot designed to make Mama think that Seraphim was passed out, drunk, within. He heard Mama say once, impatiently, "Penn, he can't be that–," followed by a renewed flood of Gabriel's words in a sensible, persuasive tone.

What Seraphim should be doing was clearing the room of evidence of his injury and then attending to his Mama. But there was someone in need. He looked at his watch. It was very definite about someone in need of his help on Pyramids, someone with a very high magical talent and too ignorant to shield it. He didn't think it could be a trap this time. He didn't know how the watch worked. It had been created by his papa, possibly before Seraphim's birth. But he did know that it was rarely wrong. And that The Pyramids was a horrible world to have magical talent in. They put to death anyone who revealed talent or shape-shifting ability as soon as it was detected, and their thaumaturgic police were ruthlessly efficient.

But sometimes the alarms had a safety margin built in. Even in Pyramids, a few hours, a few days might pass before the new talent was spotted, and a couple of hours would give him enough time to go to the ball, announce his engagement, plead fatigue, and return to his room. Then he could go to Pyramids at his leisure.

He looked at the crystal ball, taking advantage of Gabriel not being there to obscure it, and he concentrated all his attention on it and on seeing the person at risk.

A breath, two, his eyes crossed and the lights and shadows arranged themselves into coherent images: a young boy running, pursued by … Royal Thaumaturgic guards in their dark green uniforms. They carried magic sticks, the discharge from which would severely wound or maim anyone with magical talent.

Seraphim cursed under his breath. Then, with Gabriel's murmurs growing more urgent by the door, he started to say the transport spell that would take him to Pyramids, hurriedly as he must perforce do if he was going to be out of here before his mother forced her way in the door, or before Gabriel realized what was happening.

Just as he said the capstone word that closed the spell and activated it, he felt some other magic touch his.

With the awful feeling that this was yet another trap, he tried to unsay the last word, but its echoes in the air could not be called back.

He heard Gabriel scream, "Seraphim, you bloody fool!" and his mother gasp, "Seraphim," and then he was hurtling through the cold and burning hot of Betweener and landing on his face in hot sand.

Breath was knocked out of his body. He blinked, hard, at the bright light of sun on sand, and thought that at least this looked and felt like Pyramids.

And then someone fell on him.

She must have knocked him unconscious. At least, later he would think that, because all he remembered was the horrible pain to his chest and arm, and then – some indefinable time later – being aware of soft feminine hands pulling at his arms. It renewed the infernal pain in his injured shoulder and arm, but he concentrated on her face, which was small, dark and panicked.

"Oh, please, don't tell me I killed you," she was saying.

Pain and dizziness warred in him. He felt as though he would throw up, but controlled it with all his might, and managed to say in something that passed for a creditably steady voice, "Don't be ridiculous. I'm not that easy to kill." And then, somewhat more sharply, "Please stop shaking me."

"You must move," she said. She glanced over her shoulder. "Or the lion will get us."

"Lion?" he said. The surprise carried him into sitting up and looking in the same direction she'd glanced. And there was a lion. A young lion, whose huge paws and skinny sides betrayed it as nowhere fully grown. But the tawny eyes looking out at Seraphim betrayed intelligence and fear no lion had ever known. And the light around the animal's head was the magical glow of a magical creature. The boy, Seraphim realized. He was not a witch, but a shape shifter. Of course, those were even more feared.

"It's not a lion," he said. "Merely a boy in lion shape." And standing up, he extended a hand, hoping the child was enough in control of his feelings not to act like the wild animal whose shape he'd taken. He spoke, clearly, loudly. "I am here to rescue you. I mean you no harm."

In the tawny eyes confusion and fear played out against a strange sort of hope. The lion lowered its head and looked poised to walk toward Seraphim, when a voice called out, "Stop in the name of the king. You are harboring a dangerous fugitive and our instruments indicate you are practitioners of illegal magics yourselves. Surrender now and we will be merciful."

Seraphim barely had the time to jump out of the way as the boy dove to hide behind him. As for the woman, she tried to take a step in front of Seraphim, even though her eyes showed panic and fear. "Who are they," she said, as Seraphim gently pushed her out of the way. "What do they want?"

"What passes for law in this miserable land," he said, pulling from the pocket his own magical, charmed stick. "And they want to kill us."

"What? Why–"

"No time to explain," he said. He looked around. They were on a parched red plain, strewn with boulders and intercut by pyramids. The pyramids, built in steps, were temples to the gods that forbid magic, the same gods to whom magic users were sacrificed.

The soldiers' promise of clemency was a hollow one. Whether they were shot multiple times with the painful magic-blighting weapons of the soldiers, or the soldiers captured them and bound them hand and foot to take them to a pyramid and sacrifice, there was no way to avoid pain. Except, perhaps… "Can you say the transport spell?" he asked. "Have you enough power on your own, without attaching to mine?" He glanced quickly over his shoulder at her. "Yes, I can see that you have. Start saying the spell for Avalon, and center on the point I departed from. Include me and the child-shifter."

As he heard her say the first words of the spell, he looked around, and found – by the magical brilliance – a soldier hidden behind a nearby boulder. He shot towards the soldier, then towards another one near him. The magical power found its mark, once, causing a man to scream. As long as he had charge, he could keep them at bay.

He wished the stranger would hurry up with the spell. And that she wouldn't betray him and take him to captivity.

At the last moment he wondered for whom she was working. Hitching on his spell had been no accident, that much was sure. But was she an agent of the Others? Or of His Majesty the king?

Sarah A. Hoyt

The Trouble With Heroes

Seraphim Darkwater could feel the spell assemble behind him, tendril by tendril. The woman's magic was odd. From Avalon in origin. He'd swear to that. He'd known enough power from other worlds to identify the markers of Avalon. But the magic had odd overlays, as though she'd learned it in some barbarous, ignorant place and had reinvented the whole discipline from the ground up. Then he realized that might be the only reason her spell was working. Something around them blocked normal magic. This time he'd come to Pyramids, right enough, but whatever spell had trapped him before had followed him here and had a blighting effect on his magic.

A part of him, the part that had been a studious young man, rivaling the knowledge of many of his tutors at Cambridge when it came to the history and theory of magic, wanted to turn around and watch the strands of magic being woven in the air. But he could not. Seraphim had been trained – born – to protect those who couldn't protect themselves. And right now, he was the only one in possession of a mage-charged stick.

He shot at a soldier running towards him from behind a rock. Then he shot again. And again until he hit the man, who screamed and fell, twitching a little as the magic charge hit him.

The soldier wouldn't die. Seraphim never charged his mage sticks a lethal amount, mostly because he never knew when the people he might defend himself against would not be the agents of His Majesty the king, enforcing the just laws of Britannia in his native world. A lot could be forgiven a high-born and high-spirited young man, even minor assault on an officer of the Empire. But, should he let those high spirits carry him so far as to commit murder, that would be a trespass too far.

As the man fell, twitching, Seraphim stepped back. And all at once he realized two things. The man had been a decoy, likely a volunteer sent to run at Seraphim's mage stick and keep him fully occupied as a party of guardsmen sneaked behind and around the rocks to his left. Now he caught a glimpse of golden braid on the gaudy uniforms, and realized they were too near, and there were too many of them. And one of them was pointing a magical gun at Seraphim, a weapon of the type that could disable witches and warlocks, but could kill shifters.

The boy-shifter. Seraphim must protect him.

He turned around. There were too many of them for his stick to be an effective defense, so he must take himself and his charges out of here, and take them out fast.

The woman behind him had set up almost the entire spell. Only the capstone lacked, and the coordinates. Perhaps she couldn't have set the coordinates from his arrival. Perhaps her odd learning hadn't taught her that. Or perhaps it was all part of a plan to trap him. Seraphim didn't know, and, right then, he couldn't care. Instead, he poured his own magic into the working, and set the capstone on it, with the coordinates of his bedroom, coordinates as familiar to him as the back of his own hand, or the sound of his own voice.

The portal opened, gaping, and Seraphim, realizing the impossibility of throwing a lion through it, poured more of his magic at the young shifter to make him shift back into human, out of the lion form. The child shifted and twisted, writhing and moaning in the pain of changing bones and flesh, all at a speed that would never happen naturally.

Barely had his form stabilized when Seraphim was grabbing his skinny arms and throwing him, bodily, through the portal. Seraphim knew, in doing so he was hurting his own shoulder and arm, but he couldn't feel pain. He could not feel anything but the urgency of getting them all through the portal and onto safe territory. Through the portal he could glimpse Gabriel and hear faint echoes of his talking to the boy.

Seraphim reached for the woman. She stepped back from him. "No," she said. "You go first."

"They have magic guns," Seraphim said, keeping his voice restrained, but letting urgency leak through. "They are near-lethal. You go, then I after you."

But she shied away from him, tried to step in between him and the moving ambush. Stupid on her part. She wasn't armed. He took a deep breath and mentally apologized to his mother and to his nanny who had taught him that a woman's body was sacred and not to be touched without permission. Then he grabbed her by the waist and, deftly avoiding her kicking feet and ignoring her voice saying, "Let me go," he tossed her into the portal and – as far as he could see through his sweat-stung eyes– more or less on top of Gabriel.

The portal wouldn't stay open much longer. But it didn't need to. Seraphim took a step towards it.

The ray of the magic gun hit him in the shoulder. Pain shot through his body, seized his mind. His body shuddered, one long shudder, as his heart seemed to lose the rhythm of its accustomed beats. He heard a hoarse scream, and was sure it was his.

The fall across the threshold of the portal, one half on either side, jarred his shoulder further. He gritted his teeth against the chattering that threatened to bite his tongue in half. He forced his shivering, shuddering body to obey him. He ignored the pain that coursed through his veins like fire and bit at his nerves like the edge of a well-sharpened sword.

The portal was going to close. He must get into one world or the other, or his body would be sliced in half and end up one half in each reality. He must crawl across the portal and to the safety of his room.

For long moments, his body did not obey him. His hands made frantic motions, but failed to push against the ground, his knees wouldn't stay under him. It took a superhuman effort to get them under control, to get them to pull him along the floor. He pulled himself forward one step. Two.

He felt hands at his ankles, and heard a triumphant scream from behind. He didn't turn to look. He could feel the portal starting to close. He keened with frustration and told himself he would not cry. He would die like a man.

From the fog clouding his senses, somewhere ahead of him, he heard a woman's voice say, "Oh, please, you must help him."

And he heard Gabriel's familiar voice say, "Damn you Duke," then. "Here, take this mage stick. Lay into them at will."

Seraphim tried to reach for the mage stick, but he couldn't even see it, and his hand would not obey him, and he could feel the mage-field of the portal pressing against his middle.

Strong, warm hands grabbed his hands and pulled. Seraphim screamed as the pain to his shoulder increased a hundred fold.

Then darkness engulfed him.

The Price of Heroism

Nell hated heroes. Years ago, when he'd first rescued her from Earth, Antoine had told her that he despised heroes who were men who would give themselves airs, and throw themselves in the breach with great pomp and circumstance, for the pleasure of pinning medals on themselves, no matter how many people died for their glory.

Her fury and surprise at Seraphim's taking the spell from her and putting his own capstone on it was nothing compared to her fury at his insisting on her stepping through first and on protecting her with his body. Her entire upbringing on Earth rebelled against letting a man, any man, protect her. And her months in Britannia, chafing against the arrogance of noblemen and gentry, made her want to scream at his assumed gallantry.

None of this was improved by his throwing her bodily across the portal and on top of a tall man in neat, understated attire. Disentangling herself from the man, who was blushing furiously and who looked past her at the portal with a horrified expression, she didn't see Seraphim get hit.

But when she turned around, there was no doubt he'd been hit by a magic gun.

She'd never seen one of these in action. They were illegal in most nations in Avalon, and of course, of no use at all on Earth. Or at least not that anyone knew. But she'd heard of them, and Sydell had once shown her a confiscated cache of them and described their effects. She could still hear him in her mind as he told her how the gun's discharge would kill a shifter at the barest touch, but was survivable to a mage, provided he or she was in good shape and got treatment immediately.

Only Seraphim wasn't getting treatment. He was fallen half across the portal, whose shifting light indicated it was about to close. Around his body shimmered the blue-yellow lights of a disturbed magical pattern, as clearly visible to her mage-sight as his outstretched hands scrabbling in vain at the oaken floorboards.

He made inhuman grunts as he did so, grunts that seemed like the result of effort beyond his capacity. All the while – and it seemed forever to Nell – the man on whom she'd fallen, was standing there, his arms akimbo, staring.

Seraphim's hands found purchase at last, and he pulled himself, a minute amount into the room, and then the men on the other side reached him, grabbed his ankles, and pulled him back far more than he'd pulled himself forward. She had heard of those step pyramids in that world. She'd heard they performed sacrifices there. And besides, they'd shot him.

She found her hands were beating frantically at the impassive arm of the motionless man near her, "Oh, help him. You must save him."

As though her words had rushed him to action, he stared at the scene before him and said in a tone of true rancor, "Damn you, Duke."

When he reached into his vest and pulled out a mage stick, Nell had a moment of frozen certainty that he was going to shoot Darkwater. But the man handed her the stick instead, and said, even as he bent down to grasp Seraphim's hands, "Lay it into them, good and hard."

She obeyed, almost without thinking, mowing down the soldiers grabbing Seraphim's ankles and feet, while the stranger pulled the duke into the room by his hands. A guardsman from the other world tried to plunge in just behind him, but Nell shot him with a bolt of magic, and he fell back twitching. None too soon, as her mage stick was spent. And the portal closed.

She let the stick drop from a nerveless hand and turned– to see the stranger taking a knife to the Duke. The sound of his voice saying, "Damn you Duke," came to her. She didn't pause to think or to consider the consequences of her actions. She raised a foot, high, and only slightly hampered by the dress and under dress, kicked with all her might at the knife wielding hand. The knife went flying, and Nell dropped back, hands raised, ready to grab furniture or books or something to defend herself. Or to send a magic spell against the man, when he came after her.

He didn't come after her. He didn't even seem to notice her at all, though he looked dismayed when the knife went flying from his hand, and he shook his hand, once, twice, as though to rid himself of pain.

But then he took his hands to the duke's coat, and pulled. The coat tore down the front, to reveal a shirt all covered in blood. And Nell realized the man had been about to cut Seraphim's clothes away from him, so he could minister to the duke. At the same time, the realization hit that this stranger looked a great deal like the duke and might very well be one of his brothers, though Nell had believed his brothers were all much younger.

She walked to where the knife had fallen, by a blue-velvet covered table stacked high with books, and noted without giving it much thought, that the covering was a little lifted and anxious eyes were peeping from under it. The eyes were familiar. It was the boy-lion.

Without a word to him, she retrieved the knife and walked back to the man kneeling by the duke and now trying, ineffectually, to tear the blood soaked shirt. She handed the knife to him, handle first, and he said, "Thank you, Miss," as though this were an everyday occurrence. She watched him cut the shirt to reveal, beneath it, a chest crisscrossed in blood-saturated ligatures. The man said, under his breath, "Oh, the damn fool," and Nell found herself agreeing. Only a fool or a madman would take it upon himself to go into another world and get into a fight when he had suffered what appeared to be very serious injuries. And most injuries were serious in Avalon, whose magic could at the same time perform healing feats that would startle Earth, and be totally ineffective against infections. People might regrow an amputated limb, but they would surely die of the infection, if the instrument used in amputating hadn't been properly sterilized. And she doubted the implement had been properly sterilized before it had made those gashes, now revealed on the Duke's chest and shoulder, as the stranger cut his ligatures off.

"I… Is there anything–" she was about to ask if there was anything she could do, and then she realized that the stranger was muttering under his breath, a steady stream of arcane words. As those assembled in her mind, she realized what they were. A resurrection spell.

Her eyes opened wide, as she stared at the duke with her mage sight. He wasn't dead. But the force of life around his body had ebbed so low it was like a flame that a careless breath might extinguish. Used in these circumstances, the resurrection spell, forbidden otherwise, as after death it only brought life to a soulless body, was much like the paddles with which, on Earth, people tried to stimulate a failing heart. Except that it took a massive amount of life-force from the one administering the spell. And she could do nothing but stand there, clutching her skirts, and watching as the stranger poured a not inconsiderable amount of magic into Seraphim Darkwater, in a desperate effort to save his life.

The stranger himself must be a considerable magician. Either that or he would end up in almost as bad a shape as Seraphim.

One time the spell was said. Twice. Its force flared and fizzled, pale blue against the dying flames of Seraphim's life which had ebbed down to a dirty sort of orange, like flames that have fed on oil and are almost spent.

Once more, and the force surrounded Seraphim's body, and it looked for a moment as though it would re-light the force of his life. But it died down yet again. The stranger's face grew stern, his features seeming to become all sharp planes and angles. He looked more than ever like Darkwater, a Darkwater determined to be brave and strong against all costs. Yet another damned hero, Nell thought, and it seemed to her she heard Antoine's derisive tone in her thoughts. And yet, she couldn't bring herself to dislike or despise this man who was pouring his magic and his strength so unstintingly into the dying body of … his master? His brother?

The stranger raised the spell yet a fourth time, and Nell told herself she'd take it next, rather than let the man commit suicide through generosity.

But this time, as the blue flare went out and surrounded the duke, the orange, dying flame of Seraphim's life, caught and sparked, then grew into a pale yellow-white flame. Not quite healthy life, but abundant, reigniting his vitality fully.

In the dead quiet of the room, she heard the Duke take one breath, then another. And then his rescuer took a breath, which curled upon itself in a sob, which, in turn, quieted abruptly, as if – hearing himself show a sign of weakness – the man had cut it off.

He lowered his head and shook, still taking painfully loud breaths, like a man at the end of miles of running, and Nell found that she, herself, had not breathed in too long a time, and took a gasping breath. Then she thought that the man looked very ill, waxen-pale and shaking, with the effort and reaction of a resurrection spell so oft repeated.

It wasn't even that it took a lot of magic, a lot of power, a lot of strength. No. It was more than that. When using such a spell there was always the danger that between sending it forth, and its hitting the target that the target might die. And if such a thing happened, then the mage's duty was to kill his creation immediately. In fact, in most of Avalon not to do so was punishable with death, though she'd heard that the law was rarely enforced. But it was certainly punished with exclusion from all society and magical association.

The stranger shook, and his dark hair was pasted to his head with sweat, and Nell surmised that he would not want her to see him in this state. Men were proud everywhere, but in this world more than anywhere else – particularly the gentry, which this man might very well be, as much as he looked like the Duke.

She fell back on the expected role of women in this time and place. Going to the wash basin set in a corner, she was relieved to find that it was supplied with an ever-filled ewer, the water magicked in – probably from the well of the estate – as soon as it was emptied, and kept warm in the container, by means of a spell.

She poured it into the basin, and grabbed a bar of soap and a pile of the folded linen towels left by it. With the towels under her arm and the soap caught her under her chin, she walked back carrying the delicate porcelain basin, with the pink and blue roses painted around the edge, and set them on the floor next to Seraphim, who still looked dead, but who was breathing regularly.

She dipped a towel in the water and, very gently, started swabbing at the Duke's blood-covered chest. She was relieved to find that he was not nearly as torn apart as it looked from the blood. His wounds were, in the main, two, one in his chest and one on his arm. Not that it mattered. In Avalon, you could die of a scratch if it were not sterilized in time. And the Duke's wounds were no scratch.

"Thank you, Miss," the strange man said, in the tremulous, breaking voice of a man pushed beyond physical limits.

She didn't look up. Instead, she smiled a little, while wiping the blood from Seraphim, and noting those wounds had once been sewn together, though the stitches had now been torn out. "My name," she said. "Is

Helena Felix."

"Miss Felix," he said.

"But no," she said. "You must call me Nell." And sensing, even without looking up, his shock at being invited to call her not just by her first name but by a nickname, she smiled again. "We have fought together. You would not call a comrade in arms by his last name would you?"

His breath skipped, showing a hesitancy. She looked up to see him open his mouth, then snap it closed. "I might," he said. "If he were well born. You see, I don't know what you– that is, you must know my name is Gabriel Penn, and I'm His Grace's of Darkwater's valet."

It was Nell's turn to be shocked. She fought having her mouth drop open in surprise, and instead managed to say in a creditable show of composure. "I see." But the truth was that she didn't see at all. Not only was the man an enormously powerful magician – she herself doubted she'd have the stamina to do the resurrection spell four times in a row – but he was undoubtedly trained. And while there was a chance of by-blows, men being what they were, and therefore of a servant having some form of magical power, bastards never – at least in Nell's experience – had as much power as this man had. And those who did were never taught. At least not the riskier spells.

Who were the Darkwaters? Seraphim went looking for fights in worlds where he had no business, in direct contravention of his majesty's laws, and this other man who looked so much like Seraphim, but who was a servant, used spells no one but a *gentleman* could have been taught to wield. Or have the power to manage.

"I see," she said again, and cleared her throat. "I shall call you Gabriel then."

He opened his mouth, then seemed to think better of it, and got up to go to the drawer in the dressing table. When he returned, he carried a box which, when set by the side of the Duke's unconscious form and opened, revealed needle and thread and what looked like a complete surgeon's kit.

"You might want to look away," Gabriel said, "Miss."

"No, I don't believe so," she said. "I've seen blood before. You'll want to disinfect the wound first, though." And realized he'd already laid hold of brandy and was pouring it over the Duke's wounds. She was about to tell him pure alcohol was better for that, when she decided the man knew his business as well, if not better than, she.

Instead, she watched as Gabriel sewed the first of the Duke's wounds closed, then started to slather it with a thick grey ointment that seemed to be infused with healing magic. "Give me the ointment," she said, firmly. "I will do that while you sew his chest wound."

He inclined his head, saying nothing. "You'll pardon me," Nell said at last. "But what business had he to go about like that when he was this seriously wounded?"

The man made a sound that might have been a hiccup, the beginning of a laugh, or a smothered sob. "None," he said. "But no use trying to prevent him. When he thinks something is his duty– a great one for duty is the Duke. If you knew how many times– oh, never mind."

But Nell had caught both the exasperated affection and the mingled admiration and anger in Gabriel's voice, and realized it was the feeling of an older brother for a younger brother who was inclined to biting off more than he could chew. The Darkwaters were unusual indeed. Clearly Gabriel knew these spells because he had been educated in magic. And given the aplomb with which he used them, he must have been educated at Cambridge, alongside his legitimate brother.

Because she knew better – had learned better over her time in this forsaken world – than to question legitimacy or the bond of blood between men of two such different classes, she said, instead, as she slathered the newly-sewn wound, and Gabriel finished cleaning the duke – or as much as he could clean him given his inability to submerge him in water – "The young man who came in with us is under the table there."

Gabriel nodded. "Good. I hope he'll stay out of the way till I can call the housekeeper to get him clothes and, hopefully, to take him to her cousin's cottage for a while."

Nell hesitated. "He… that is, he is a lion shifter."

Gabriel nodded again. "A lot of the rescues from that world are. Seraphim usually pays their way into a shifter seminar in Bath. There are two, one for young ladies, and one for young gentlemen. All the teachers are shifters and therefore equipped to train the young people in the ways of control of their magic, and in the ability to shift at will. But I understand they teach them other trades, usually as clerks or secretaries or the like."

Nell shook her head at the idea of a shifter secretary. Back in the day when she'd worked in computers, their group's administrative assistant had looked much like a weasel, but she supposed here it would be more obvious.

"And the housekeeper knows about this?" Truly the conspiracy to breach the sovereign shields of other worlds was extensive. And law said all of them were due death. She couldn't imagine denouncing Seraphim or Gabriel and seeing them beheaded and hung respectively. No. She had seen Seraphim almost die. But if she lied on her report and they found out, surely they would hurt Antoine?

"She's my godmother," Gabriel said, as though that meant something. "The housekeeper. Now, Miss, if you'd step aside."

Miss stepped aside, wishing in an annoyed sort of way that the proper Gabriel would call her Nell, a feeling that was dissolved into shock as that man who had just done four resurrection spells lifted Seraphim in his arms and carried him to the bed.

Oh, the bed was only three steps away, and Gabriel did totter under the weight of the duke, but that he could lift him at all – when both were well-matched for weight and height – much less after the ordeal Gabriel had inflicted on himself, was near-unbelievable.

Yes, the Darkwaters were an odd family. And they might be made of more-than-human stuff. In fact, she thought squinting, she'd swear that Gabriel Penn's magic wasn't wholly human.

Gabriel laid the duke down, and waved his hand at the mage light on the bedside bringing its glow down. "And now we wait," he said. "And pray if we remember how."

But if there was anyone listening to prayers at that moment, they must have turned away, because – before Nell could answer – the door to the room jiggled, then flung open. Framed in the doorway stood a small, dark woman old enough to be the duke's mother. It seemed to Nell that was exactly what the woman was, in fact. Nell had memories of seeing portraits.

But unlike the portraits, the woman wasn't smiling. She had her opulent dress clutched in either hand, lifting it away from the legs as women of this world did, when they must move swiftly. And she was saying, "Seraphim, I demand that you explain…." The words died, as she looked towards the bed and Seraphim, sprawled on it, unconscious. And then she said, "Oh."

The Coils of Duplicity

Of all the ridiculous situations to be caught in, Gabriel Penn thought. And then he wanted to laugh at the idea that he would call what had just happened – Seraphim almost getting killed, a strange woman in the room, a lion shifter under Seraphim's book table – ridiculous.

It was too mild a word and too inappropriate. It was like when, at some grand affair, the most ridiculous things would run through his mind while he leaned against the wall, all but invisible to the company. If he said half the things he thought, he would be … no, he wouldn't be turned out of the house. The dowager would never do that, and neither would Seraphim. But they might very well shut him up in the attics to which gothic novels would relegate insane relatives.

The situation was disastrous. The more so, as he saw the Dowager Duchess's expression grow grave, her eyes pinch, and her expression acquire that hint of dismay that used to accompany her looks at the husband she doted on, and who was never faithful to her. She looked at the bed, intently. Then back at Gabriel. "Gabriel," she said. Unlike Seraphim, unlike what anyone else would have done, she never called him by his surname. She never treated him as a servant. She treated him… not as her son, exactly, but not much different. "Gabriel. You will tell me what has happened to my son."

Gabriel opened his mouth, then closed it. The words had been more than a demand, a certainty. For a moment, the world shifted under Gabriel's feet. He couldn't remember what he'd told the Duchess before, to excuse Seraphim's using a transport spell, right in front of his mother. He didn't know how to justify Seraphim's near-mortal wounds or the presence of Miss Helena Felix.

And then he thought again how much like his father's imbroglios this was, and how if this had been the old lord, the reason would be something like he had to run out for an assignation with a married woman, whose husband in turn had challenged him to a duel and who–

And Gabriel had found his feet. When caught in something unlawful, he knew better than to try to make himself sound completely innocent. Unlike Seraphim, he'd had to learn to lie very early and lie very well. In this house, he, like Seraphim, had been told to speak only the truth. But in the years before the Duke had found him and brought him home, he'd learned well enough to survive by any means necessary. The advantage of not being legitimate, of not being the heir, is that you were to an extent free of the constricting bands of honor that imprisoned those of the lawful world.

"Forgive me, Your Grace," he said, and let his nervousness leak through, with his exhaustion. He intended to let the Duchess know exactly how gravely her son had been hurt. That way the best of care could be contrived. And Seraphim was going to need the best of care. Gabriel would risk both their honor and their reputations rather than his half-brother's life. "You will remember I told you that Seraphim had to go to London with all possible speed, to… to take care of a matter of business, and that he would be back upon the instant."

"You told me he had to go on a matter of gambling."

"It comes to the same for Seraphim, whose gambling is a debt of honor and who–"

"Cease. I know the excuses. But how come he–" the Duchess took a step to the bed, and stared at Miss Felix. If Gabriel hadn't stepped in front of her, she would have approached the bed.

"Well, it turned out the betting… well… it went wrong."

"You will not tell me that my son cheated."

"No, Your Grace. But the man he bested thought so. And challenged Seraphim to a duel, which– his opponent used a spelled knife and– and a magic gun."

The Lady Barbara reeled. She stepped backward, taking her hand to her lips, in a gesture of fear, then walked around Gabriel and to the bed. Now Gabriel let her. He would have spared her the pain of realizing how close to death Seraphim had come, but he must not. The Darkwaters were all magical talents, not like his own, of course, but very powerful for humans. And it would take all of their talent to get him through this.

He turned around and watched as the Duchess took her son's hand in hers. She looked, Gabriel thought, perfectly composed, serene. It was something he envied Seraphim. A mother who, without being cold, could be controlled.

Her magic working – which Gabriel was sure she was doing – did not show, nor could he read it by more than a feeling of magic in the air, a sensation on the edge of sound that energy had been sent forth and absorbed.

The Lady Barbara looked up. "Which of you?" she said, and looked from the young woman to Gabriel, then again. "Which of you used the resurrection spells? Four times?"

"Mister Penn did, Madam," Miss Felix said, with such disarming honesty that Gabriel didn't know whether to respect her for it, or to hate her for making his life yet more complicated. She must be gentry, he thought. And legitimate too. Only someone raised in the strictest bonds of respectability could be so stupidly honorable.

"Gabriel?"

He looked down and let go the willpower keeping his immense tiredness hidden. "I had to, Your Grace. I couldn't let him die."

"No," the Duchess said. "But you could have called me. I have…." She looked pensive. "…some experience in saving the lives of the foolish men close to me." And, before Gabriel could ask her what she meant, she looked at Miss Felix. "And you are?"

And here, Gabriel consigned his soul to perdition once and for all. He knew that if the young lady spoke, she would say something disastrous, such as that Seraphim had saved her from the Pyramid world. Or worse, that Seraphim had saved her and a young lion shifter. If she was in the habit of uttering the truth with no regard for the circumstances, likely she'd tell it now. And Gabriel could not allow that. Not even if it called for the most outrageous lie of his untruthful career.

His voice shook with the sheer enormity of it, but probably made it all the more convincing, as he said, "Miss Felix, Your Grace, is… a personal friend of mine. With– with the ball in the house, we'd expected to have privacy, you see, and … and we expected to be able to talk undisturbed."

The expression of shock in the Duchess's eyes, as she turned back to look at Gabriel, was only half that in the eyes of Helena Felix, and Gabriel felt unaccountably gratified that he had managed to pay Miss Felix back for the position she'd put him in. He gave her the hint of a restrained smile. If he was going to burn in hell for eternity, he'd amuse himself while he could.

The Duchess looked at him a long time. After the shock, a flicker of something in her eyes gave Gabriel the uneasy impression that she knew all too well all that was likely to have happened was literally talk, but then she cleared her throat and said, in a shaking voice, "Well… well… I'm sure that… that is, you wouldn't bring a woman of ill repute into the house, so you and Miss Felix shall let me know when I am to wish you joy." She gave him the once over, and there was the hint of incredulity in her eyes again. Or was Gabriel imagining it? He did tend to think that he was glass fronted and everyone could see right through him. "You've been very sly and kept it all from us, but I'm glad that Miss Felix was here, to help you save Seraphim's life." Her look at both of them told them she didn't believe a word of it.

"Now," she said, taking off the long gloves that had protected her hands and forearms during the ball. "If you and Miss Felix will leave, I will look after my son. Tell Martin to send for Doctor Wilson. And–"

And Gabriel, in a sweat of apprehension, thinking of the boy shifter under the table, and of Miss Felix, who, for all he knew, had nowhere to go in this world, plunged madly into the breach, armed with nothing but his knowledge of etiquette and his experience of living so many years amid the truthful and the honorable. "Your Grace cannot stay here," he said. "I beg your pardon," he added, to Lady Barbara's shocked expression. "But Your Grace cannot. Your Grace must see that if Your Grace were to disappear now, with the guests not having left yet, this would become the most astonishing rumor of the season, and no one would cease talking about it… oh, for a year perhaps. Particularly since the Duke didn't announce his engagement as everyone expected."

Lady Barbara favored him with a darkling look. It was not quite a look of reproach, it certainly wasn't a look of dislike, but it was the look that told him she knew very well he was manipulating her behavior for her own good, and that she didn't enjoy it.

"Whenever you start larding your speech with Your Graces, Gabriel," she said with the disarming frankness she had passed on to her son, "it is a sure thing you're trying to fool me. I have not forgotten the forcing house incident." She pressed her lips together, whether at the memory of that most spectacular mishap of his and Seraphim's childhood or at the present situation, Gabriel couldn't guess. "But much more the worse is that you're right. I cannot gratify my feelings by staying here, and thus risk humiliating Lady Honoria, who will be humiliated enough that Seraphim has as good as jilted her in our own ballroom." She sighed. "I shall say Seraphim is indisposed. They will understand he's drunk enough to be well and truly disguised, quite out of his mind. And no one will doubt it, considering the way he smelled and acted in the ballroom." She sighed heavily, and leaned over her son on the bed. Touching her lips to his forehead, she sighed again, then straightened. "Don't trouble yourself with sending for the doctor, Gabriel. I shall do so myself. Stay by Seraphim's side, until Doctor Wilson arrives."

She was out the door before he could get over the feeling she knew very well what manner of lies he'd imposed upon her.

"The forcing house incident?" Miss Felix asked.

"Oh." He took a deep breath and wondered if he could find the strength to talk. He was so tired that he felt as though this must be what it felt like to be ninety. Not that he expected to ever make it to that age. "I was … nine? Perhaps ten. I'm not… precisely sure of my own age, only that I'm older than Sera– His Grace. Probably a year or so older, and conventionally we consider my birthday the same as his only a year before. That was Sera– His Grace's idea." He saw she was looking at him in confusion, and tried to call all his strength to him and order his thoughts. "I arrived on his birthday, you see, and he wanted to share the party, which when you consider that I came into a dining room full of the children of the nobility in the rags in which… in which the old duke had found me–" He saw her eyes widen and decided he was going too far.

No need to tell this stranger from another world about Seraphim's longing for a brother, or how he'd decided that Gabriel would be that brother, even when they were both too young to realize they were related by blood. "Never mind that. His Grace was kind and generous even as a child. At any rate, he said it was to be my party too, and therefore it was decided my birthday was the same as his. And I was allowed to have a piece of the cake and the celebration… after the housekeeper gave me the most thorough bath of my life, before or since." He caught himself up again, knowing he was saying too much. Curse his weakness and his depleted magic. "I had lived here about a year, or maybe a little more than a year, when Seraphim and I decided to practice a growing spell we'd seen one of the farmers perform on the strawberries in the forcing house. We were both, you see, inordinately fond of strawberries, and it was March and the plants just set in the soil."

"And it worked?"

"After a fashion, Miss," he said. "We did grow strawberries, but we must have got something wrong, because they grew to astonishing size." Her gaze was interested. "And exploded. And we had to clean the inside of the glass with rags. For five days. But not for lack of my making up an elaborate story involving robbers. Her Grace was indulgent, because, I suppose, she feels sorry for me." And, plunging as quickly as he could away from that, he said, "But none of this matters, Miss. What matters now is to find you a place to stay before the doctor arrives."

She looked surprised. "I don't need a place to stay," she said. "I need a minute's calm to put together a transport spell."

"Miss?" Was she not aware that she'd been brought to a different world.

She blushed, from the neck up, till she looked the rough color of a turnip. "I beg your pardon," she said. "I suppose you assumed I was from that horrible desert world, with the pyramids? Well, I was not. My magic simply got entangled with the Duke's and it pulled me into that world and… it was why I was so distraught and half out of my mind. I went out of the world and back into it again in less than a few minutes. And, as you know, magical entanglements are painful and confusing for both people. It cannot have helped His Grace's reactions, either."

"What didn't help His Grace's reactions," Gabriel said, aware that his voice colored the honorific in irony, "is that he'd already lost too much blood and was in a considerable amount of pain besides." Which was the only reason that Gabriel could think of why Seraphim hadn't realized that his magic had become entangled. But it made no sense. "The thing is, Miss, that entanglements don't happen, unless– "

A knock at the door, and a voice called out, "Doctor Wilson is here, Mr. Penn." It was the voice of the housekeeper. "He's coming up the stairs."

Gabriel felt both relief and annoyance. Relief that he could now get the young shifter out of the room and into the capable hands of Gabriel's Godmother, and annoyance that he would not be able to question this young woman till after the doctor left. But there was no time to lose. He lifted the table covering, and offered the boy his hand, which the boy took, allowing Gabriel to lead him to the door.

The housekeeper, a kind woman of middle years, who still treated Gabriel as though he, himself, had been an urchin, looked from him to the boy when he opened door. "I thought there was as good a chance as any that there was someone," she said, "if the Duke is took ill." She looked at the boy. "I shall put a damping spell on his shifting, shall I, until he learns to control it? And the poor boy as naked as the day he was born. No worry. I'll get him into the lilac room and bring him clothes."

Since the lilac room was right next door, the empty room reserved for the wife Seraphim would eventually take, Gabriel knew it was safe enough. The relief of it must have made him weak, because he leaned against the door frame to recover his breath.

When he opened his eyes again, Doctor Wilson was saying, "And what have you been doing with yourself, Penn? Don't tell me it is nothing, because you look in need of my services, though it was the Duke I was called for."

Gabriel managed a weak laugh. "It is nothing, compared to His Grace's wounds, sir," he said. And as he led the doctor into the room, he realized that Miss Felix was no longer there. He felt vexed he'd not prevented her transport spell, which she'd told him she would use, then relieved she was no longer there, and he didn't have to worry about what she might say. It didn't matter if she'd gone somewhere. He wasn't fooled into thinking her presence accidental.

And there were always ways of finding out who she really was and where she'd come from. Many of those ways would have to wait until Seraphim recovered consciousness. But they would work. And he and Seraphim would discover who this woman was who took so much interest in the Duke of Darkwater.

A Step In The Dark

Nell concentrated on the coordinates to her room and stepped through. There was the moment of bitter cold of the Betweener, the sense of winds howling around her, even though in fact wind could not exist in this dimension that was wholly devoid of air or any other element needed for life.

And then she was stepping into the familiar confines of her room, almost on top of chalk drawings and a bowl shattered on the floor.

She surveyed the chalk drawings, with dismay, noting that the water had splattered out to mark the floor indelibly with the chalk dust. This was going to be very hard to clean, and before she was done she might very well need to scrub the entire floor and wax it, lest the landlady get upset. Which she would. Particularly since Nell had also broken one of the bowls.

It had taken Nell quite a while to truly believe that common belongings were considered precious, or that they were as expensive as they were. A simple glazed bowl, a platter, anything like that would have been thrown out on Earth the minute it became cracked. Here, even when broken, the shards would be collected in the hopes that the plate mender might fix it when next he did the rounds of the neighborhood.

She picked up the shards of the bowl carefully and stored it in the cupboard in the corner, hoping to mitigate her landlady's annoyance by telling her she'd saved the shards to be mended.

Nell couldn't understand it, and couldn't work it out logically. On Earth she'd had plenty of friends who read fantasy and it had been assumed in almost any novel that a society with magic was by necessity prosperous and clean and all the other things real, pre-industrial societies hadn't been.

But this one wasn't. Though Nell wasn't sure if it was in the past in relation to the world in which she'd grown up and which she still considered the real Earth, this Earth seemed to be stuck somewhere around the regency. Time was hard to pin down exactly, because this England didn't seem to have any of the same monarchs. Or rather, it had the same monarchs up to a point, that point being around the time of Arthur, who in this world was a real documented king, with his prime minister and court magician, Merlin. In fact, Seraphim, Duke of Darkwater, was supposed to be descended from Merlin and Morgan le Fey.

The thought had brought her right back to the subject her mind had been hoping to avoid.

Having come to it, she realized she couldn't avoid her obligations another moment. Taking a pocket watch from her desk, she looked at the time. Yes. She had to see Sydell. For one, he would be expecting a report.

Which would mean that he would be in the park down the street, standing by the lake and scaring the mothers and nannies and the children they supervised by glaring at all of them, taking out on them the fact that Nell was now three minutes late.

Sydell counted punctuality a virtue, one of the many things upon which he and Antoine seemed to disagree violently. Antoine had told Nell, very early in their acquaintance, that the only appointments worth keeping were those to which both heart and mind concurred and that if an assigned meeting didn't inflame your heart with wild excitement it wasn't worth keeping.

The appointment with Sydell, so far from inflaming her heart with wild anything, gave her a strong feeling of having been encased in ice and wishing to run away. But if she had to hazard a guess, she would imagine that Antoine would actually wish her to keep this one. Else….

Else, she wasn't sure exactly what, but she was sure it wouldn't be pleasant. Antoine had been arrested the night they'd first set foot in the islands of Britannia in Avalon. She'd never been told why or what he had done to deserve that fate, but she thought it was no criminal matter so much as something between Antoine and Sydell – some old vengeance or some unfinished game – because Sydell hadn't told her that Antoine would be going to trial, or that he would have to serve some sentence for some determined set of time. Instead, he'd told her that he, Sydell, was holding Antoine D'Argent at the pleasure of the king. Which pretty much meant, if Nell understood properly, what used to be called in France, in her world, before the revolution, a lettre-de-cachet, that is something that was used to apprehend an individual, keep him indefinitely and tell no one where he was.

At the time she hadn't realized this, and she'd been too numb, too confused, wondering why Antoine would take them to a world where he was likely to meet with such a reception, to be able to even ask how to free him. Fortunately Sydell had told her, unasked. *You'll work for me*, he'd said. *Three years, three days and three hours. You are a competent witch and, as the king's spymaster, I am always in need of one such who can nose out illegal use of magic, crimes against the innocent of unprotected worlds or other things against our law. You serve me well and you and your paramour will be able to leave Avalon in peace.*

Am I arrested then? She had asked.

Detained, you mean? No, you are not. You can leave this very moment, if you wish. But then your paramour cannot go with you. And his freedom will be entirely dependent on my benevolence, of which I have very little towards Antoine.

Nell sighed. Yes, Antoine would definitely want her to keep this appointment.

She picked up her cloak and wrapped herself in it. It was, like most of her clothes, serviceable. It had looked Romantic and interesting when she'd first arrived here and all their clothes seemed to be like something out of a fairytale. Now it was just a cloak, a little threadbare, bought second-hand because Sydell's stipend rarely extended beyond the bare necessities of food and lodging.

Clasping the cloak in front, she picked up her reticule and headed out the door, closing it carefully behind her lest the landlady discover the damage to her floor and decide to throw Nell out without ceremony.

On the way to the park she tried to set in her mind what to say. Normally, when Sydell had asked her to find out what someone was doing, she found things she didn't mind telling him about. Like that woman a few months ago who was sacrificing newborns in order to use their hearts in love potions. Nell had felt absolutely no qualms about turning her in to Sydell's justice even though she suspected Britannia had horrible penalties for her kind of crime. No.

She hoped Britannia had horrible penalties for her kind of crime.

But then there was Seraphim. His crime was terrible by Britannia standards. Because, from what she understood, Avalon was such a strongly magical world, the king of Britannia had made doing business in other worlds strictly forbidden. And doing business could be interpreted as merely visiting for some minutes. But taking people or things out of those worlds – or bringing them in – definitely fell within the definition. The penalty for that sort of infraction was death. And the death penalty for Dukes might be beheading, supposedly a quicker and more dignified death than hanging, but someone who was beheaded was still very thoroughly dead.

Yet Nell could see, in her mind's eye, the boy-shifter pursued by those horrible men with the magic guns, and Seraphim risking his life to save him. Risking his life to save her. And then Gabriel Penn…. She shook her head. She couldn't imagine turning either of the men in. But then, she couldn't imagine not turning them in. What could she tell Sydell that would satisfy him? If he thought she hadn't fulfilled her part of the bargain, what would Sydell do to Antoine? At various times, the King's spy master had intimated that only Nell's good behavior kept Antoine alive.

"Ah, Nell, in a brown study, I see," Sydell said. Even before she looked up, she knew he was in one of his moods. It was in the voice which had the biting edge of a chill wind.

Looking up only confirmed it. Sydell was a man of maybe forty, with black hair, carefully combed back from his forehead, in the style at the moment fashionable for men. His clothes were as exquisitely tailored as Seraphim Ainsling's had been: tight coat of blue superfine, so carefully fitted to his powerful torso that she thought it might require a spell to get him into it, and butter-yellow breeches, so tight that wearing them in public should constitute an offense against morals. His cravat, tall and arranged in graceful folds about his neck, was a thing of beauty.

But the face of such a carefully attired gentleman was pale and at the moment peevish, his lower lip slightly advanced, his eyes darting daggers in her direction. She thought of everything she knew, surmised, and had heard about Sydell. He was called a snake and worse, and that was by his friends and admirers.

Cold, dangerous, deadly.

The other things she'd heard about him included that he disdained female companions and preferred his men young and helpless. This didn't shock her as they would someone from Avalon. They only inspired in her pity for any men who might fall in his clutches, and relief that he was not interested in her in that way.

The park, filled with mothers and nannies and children, from those so small they were in carriages, to the ten year olds chasing each other around the lake or feeding the ducks, was a place of life and sound, but everyone seemed to avoid Sydell's periphery. Everyone but Nell, and she only because she couldn't avoid it.

She bobbed a curtsey by habit and with no thought. It was amazing how quickly such habits developed. "I beg your pardon, Sydell," she said. "I got myself… accidentally enmeshed in a spell, and it took a while to extricate myself from it."

He frowned at her, then his lips curved quickly upward, not in a smile so much as in what seemed like pleasure at her having suffered a delay. "Well," he said. "Well. What workings did you get involved in? Was it Darkwater? What has the Duke been up to? Tell me without delay."

And that was Sydell all over. *Tell me without delay* was his version of "please make a report" and delivered with even less ceremony than that would have been. Unspoken and hanging between those words was the sense that what it all actually meant was "Tell me or else."

But she could not tell. She thought of the Duke on the floor, his life-force ebbing away, and of Gabriel Penn desperately pushing strength and magic into the duke with his resurrection spell. She could not let them be arrested. Oh, they'd broken the law. They'd assuredly broken the law. But it was for a good cause, was it not?

She had a notion her argument was slippery, yet looking at Sydell's pale face, his frosty glare she couldn't imagine that he would be on the side of right in this. Instead, she reached, desperately, for the story that Penn had told the Duchess. She'd tell the same story. Something that juicy would be about town in no time, and the two lies, meeting somewhere in the middle, would corroborate each other. Sydell would never suspect, and it would give Nell a little longer to study Darkwater and to find out whether, indeed, anything nefarious hid behind the Duke's seeming benevolence.

She put a smile on her face and told Sydell, "Nothing of consequence. It's so diverting. I don't know what you thought Darkwater was doing, but what he is doing is what you expect of a wastrel of his kind. You see, he left in the middle of his own engagement party to meet with a ... a married woman. And I got pulled into his transport spell, and fell atop the lady's husband, who was hiding in the bushes, and the whole thing got blown out of proportion... or perhaps into proportion. The offended husband demanded satisfaction, and the Duke got wounded, just as you would expect, and then he transported into his room, and his valet tended to him, and I took the opportunity to return here before anyone asked my name."

Sydell brought up the cane he'd been playing with, an elaborate affair of varnished mahogany, topped with heavy silver, in the shape of a wolf's head. What he said was "I see." But what he did was twirl the wolf's head, as though absently. "And what was this lady's name? Or her husband's?"

Nell forced a laugh that she hoped sounded like an amused giggle, "How would I know? You are very well aware I know nothing of the fashionable of your world."

Suddenly Nell felt dizzy and swayed on her feet. She blinked, and had a sense that a lot of time had passed. The small park, with its duck pond, had gone marginally darker and colder, and there were noticeably fewer children than just a moment ago.

"My dear," Sydell said, and the coldness in his voice belied the apparent meaning of that word. "You should know that when you travel between worlds, there is magical residue left on your clothes. You should also know that I am a very hard man to fool. Next time, do not make me resort to outrageous measures to get the information you owe me." He got out a small pouch and handed it to her. "Here is your stipend, Miss Felix, and do try not to give me difficulties next time. You will continue keeping an eye on Darkwater, for now. We need more evidence to leave the case."

It wasn't till Sydell walked away that Nell's mind cleared enough for her to realize he'd put a truth spell on her and got her to tell all. Truth spells were much more effective than any truth serum on Earth. They were also almost a dark art, something no honorable magician would use. Of course, she'd long ago realized that the king's spymaster might be an honored man, but he was probably not an honorable one. An honorable man wouldn't use her lover's captivity as a lever to move her in whatever direction he wished.

Then another thought came on the heels of that. A case against Darkwater. That meant that they were thinking of prosecuting him. And that Nell had just handed Sydell evidence against the Duke. She must go back to Darkwater. She must warn those two men of what was about to befall them.

Two Attacks and an Alarm

Seraphim Ainsling, Duke of Darkwater, woke up with a sense of foreboding. For a moment, floating on the edge of consciousness, he thought he was a child, in the nursery in the attics of the house, with nanny hovering by, and that he'd been very ill.

Then he moved in the bed, and the feeling of his body belied the illusion. Not nanny. And yet there was someone nearby singing, singing in a high voice. That was what had given him the impression that he was in the nursery. Nanny used to sing to him, in a high but not unmelodious voice. Only nanny had never used words that felt like fire distilled through his bones and woven through his nerves, raking his conscience like unsheathed claws. Words he didn't understand. Words that felt wrong.

The scream of "stop" tore itself from his lips as he sat up. The voice stopped, immediately, and in its place there was a scream, answering his, a voice much like his own, "Seraphim!"

He opened his eyes to Gabriel running towards him, and in less than a second, Gabriel's hands were on his shoulders, Gabriel's voice too loud in his ears, "Damn it, Seraphim. You're not well enough to sit. You–"

He was in his room, his adult room, of course, and it was the middle of the night. Or at least the window, directly in front of his bed, showed only darkness, which meant it was night. Though both the bed and the window were equipped with heavy brocaded curtains – somewhat faded since the old duke's profligate spending hadn't allowed expenses such as replacing furnishings – Seraphim never let either set be closed. He believed in the virtues of fresh air. He also believed in keeping an eye on his surroundings, both within and without the house. Perhaps if his father had done so–

And then he remembered what about his surroundings, just before waking, had caused such a violent start.

"Who was singing?" Seraphim asked. "What were the words?"

"What? There was no one singing. You were dreaming. It was a dream."

Seraphim shook his head. "No. Someone was singing. Working magic on me. A woman. Where's the woman?"

"The– If you mean Miss Felix, the lady you brought back with you, she left, presumably whence she'd come. I have a feeling we'll know all too soon." Gabriel Penn felt at Seraphim's forehead with the back of his hand, then did one of the minor passes that allowed one to evaluate the state of health of another, and frowned. "You have no fever."

"Of course I have no–" Seraphim would never be able to say how he had seen the attack, much less how he was able to react so fast. One moment he was looking at Gabriel, trying to decide if it was possible at all that Gabriel had been playing some sort of trick, and thinking to himself that if Gabriel had been singing in a woman's voice and performing such unclean magic as those words felt like, then it was time to take him to an exorcist and find which entity had claimed his half-brother's soul. The next moment he caught a reflection on the glass, behind Gabriel's shoulder. Something. He could never say more than that he'd been aware of movement. And he'd reacted.

Perhaps he would not have reacted so quickly, if he'd not wakened to unclean magic. He couldn't say. What he could say and do was cast a protection spell so quick his fingers smarted as the power left them, even as he pulled at Gabriel's arm, and made him fall, awkwardly, across the bed. At the same time, Seraphim rolled, so he was in a different place.

Through the confusion, and a sudden burning-feather smell, he was aware that his protective shield spell had failed and the pillow was now on fire. He was also aware of Gabriel across his legs, struggling to get up. But neither took up his thought, and certainly neither got his attention because he was drawing all his power, all his reserves, and sending them after the spell that had just come in.

There was a moment – he remembered well from his studies at Cambridge – when right after a killing-magic-spell, the kind banned in all civilized countries, it was possible to follow it with one of the same kind and potency, even if you didn't know from whence it came and certainly if you didn't know how to cast such a spell, as no civilized man knew, such spells being forbidden in all right-thinking lands. It was allowed too. The only time it was allowed to loose a killing spell that was not contained in a mage stick. It was right of self-defense, secured to the English barons by the Magna Carta, and to all English citizens by the Land and Men act of Richard XII.

None of this occurred to Seraphim, of course. His reaction was instinctive, as he seized the feel and magic of what had been hurled at him, and hurled it back as fast as he could.

The power washed out of him in a great wave, and the room swam before his eyes. He would have collapsed back onto his pillow, but the pillow was on fire, so he collapsed sideways, at the same time that Gabriel finally managed to rise, got hold of something from the bedside table, and flung it at the pillow, putting the fire out, but adding markedly to the smell of the room with an odd scent of cooked meat.

As Seraphim managed to draw himself up and catch his breath, something about his expression must have given Gabriel the idea that his action was disapproved of, as he said, "Broth. For your dinner. I'm afraid."

Seraphim, though his mind was on everything but his dinner, managed a smile. "Better that than the contents of the chamber pot!"

A quick smile flitted across Gabriel's lips, then he frowned, as though coming to himself and realizing the import of all that had happened. "Someone… did someone send a killing bolt of magic through your window?"

"I'm afraid so," Seraphim said, and, rolling off the side of the bed, managed to hold onto it, though barely. Confound it. He was too weak. The reason why came to him, in bits and disjointed pieces. The damn pyramids; the woman; the boy. How had he let himself be caught so off guard? Perhaps he should have heeded Gabriel. Perhaps he'd been too weak to go off world.

"And you sent a bolt after it! Seraphim. It's illegal."

"Not according to the law I studied at Cambridge. Self-defense, Penny." Seraphim tried to make his way to the window, by means of grabbing now onto a small occasional table, now onto the back of a sofa. But before he reached there, Gabriel had guessed his intentions and stood in front of him. "No, Seraphim!"

Seraphim took a deep breath, "Gabriel, we must find out who it was, and where the bolt hit. You know such killing spells have to be line-of-sight, so he was line-of-sight when he loosed it. Or she, if it was that infernal singer."

"No one was singing! And you can't mean to show yourself at that window when someone just tried to kill you." He had Seraphim by the shoulders again, which was a deuced stupid habit for him to have acquired, and was trying by main force to push the Duke down onto a rosewood-framed loveseat. Unfortunately, at the moment, the force was on Gabriel's side, and Seraphim had to allow himself to be pushed down.

He was not, however, so lost to all reason that he would allow Gabriel himself to go to the window. To prevent this, he held fast to Gabriel's sleeve and said, "Not you either, then, you damn fool. We don't know which of us that bolt was aimed at."

Gabriel looked exasperated. "Seraphim? Why would anyone try to kill me? I am not the duke. I am not–"

"You are your mother's son," Seraphim said, and suddenly something that had been bothering him connected in his mind. "And I have a very good idea that the song I heard as I was waking was in the language of your mother's people."

Gabriel Penn went so still his features might very well be carved out of marble. He stood straighter, and swallowed hard, so hard that it was audible in a room that seemed, of a sudden, so quiet that even the crackle of wood in the fireplace sounded as loud as an explosion. "My mother–" Gabriel said. He shook his head, looked towards the window. "Impossible." But all the same, Seraphim saw his hand move, and from the very faint tracery of light visible only to mage sight, he could see Gabriel setting a protective spell in place. Nothing like what Seraphim had done in the haste of the moment, but something stronger, harder. Something odder, too, all angles and askew logic. Something not human. And Seraphim knew that despite that "impossible" Gabriel found the threat possible enough to guard against it.

"I'd swear to it, Gabriel. I don't know the language, as you … curse it, I never thought of it, but you must know the language. You were not an infant when…."

"I know the language," Gabriel said. He looked wary and tired. Very tired. So tired that ten years at least appeared to have fallen on his features. He dropped to the rosewood seat, next to Seraphim. "Blast it all, Seraphim. It is impossible. The treaties and the binds are unbreakable."

Seraphim cleared his throat. "I don't know the language as you do," he said slowly, deliberately. "But I know the sound and feel of it. When your mother's people came, shortly after you came to live here, remember? When they came to the door–" He stopped.

"Yes," Gabriel said. And how was it possible, Seraphim thought, that Gabriel seemed to be quieter than silence and more still than stone, and so convey a sense of urgency so great that it could not be expressed in word or movement? A sense of urgency that pressed on Seraphim like the knowledge of a life-and-death trial?

Seraphim took a breath. "Well, this language had the same feel, and I can't very well imagine any other language, anything at all else in the world that would sound like that."

"No," Gabriel said, and then, as though recruiting strength, "but perhaps you remembered and dream–"

"It wasn't exactly the same words, Gabriel. This time there was a spell being said. An unclean spell."

"Imp–"

Seraphim said two words he remembered from what he had heard, two words so odd and so powerful they seemed to burn his tongue with saying them.

"Stop," Gabriel said. His hand shot out and covered Seraphim's mouth. "Stop. No more."

"What are the words?"

Gabriel shook his head. "Unclean. And dangerous." He waved a hand, again, setting some form of cleansing in place. A form that Seraphim had never seen. Then he took a deep breath, loud in the room. "Two attacks then," he said, in the same tone as he might use to inform Seraphim that his carriage was ready or that, alas, the boot boy had ruined Seraphim's best boots. "Because that kill spell through the window was all human magic and none of ou– theirs. Two attacks. Aren't we the lucky ones. And they are after you, not me. For two days, Seraphim, you've been not only unconscious, but shielded under so many healing spells not one would be able to get a spell on you. Or to find you with one. But today, as the healing spells slid off two enemies found you. It was you they were aiming for."

Seraphim shrugged. "Or perhaps you were close enough to me while I was under healing spells, to make you less noticeable also."

Gabriel rose, "I shall send some footmen down to see whom you killed. There will be trouble over that, mind, self-defense or not. Death must stand examination and trial. And the King's court, because of your damned rank."

"Tell them to go armed," Seraphim said. He let himself fall back upon the sofa. "There might be more than one out there."

Gabriel nodded, as a matter of course. "As for the other matter, duke, those words you overheard, if they were part of an attack aimed at you, would indicate that they think you too have my mother's blood. And if they were aimed at me…." He shook his head. "Did you ever tell anyone? About me, I mean?"

"Which of the many things about you?" Seraphim asked, suddenly cautious.

"Any of them."

"My dear Gabriel, I don't tell your secrets to anyone. Oftentimes not even to myself."

A Mother's Heart

They were keeping secrets again. The Dowager Duchess knew this, though she couldn't tell about what exactly.

For the two days of her son's illness – of his lying beneath healing spells, swaddled in blankets and force fed broth – she'd wondered how it had come to this. And she'd wondered what Gabriel knew that she didn't know.

Something it was, that she could be sure of. For one, Gabriel's face was always easy for her to read. Had to be, as much as he resembled her own son. The reasons for that, though she'd tried to forget them, couldn't but confuse her feelings towards the boy. She both loved him, almost like her own son, and hated him as a reminder of a dark time in her own childhood and of the misadventure that had almost lost her to the world of humans.

It had been the same since the moment her husband had brought Gabriel in, and the truth was that if Gabriel hadn't been a year older than Seraphim, and a few months older than their marriage, the dowager would have insisted on claiming him as a son and brazening the world and the ton with some excuse about one of a pair of twins stolen by magical beings. But Gabriel was the elder, his age could be found by magical means not too difficult to employ, and there was no way to make that lie convincing. Not when at the time of Gabriel's birth the, then, Lady Barbara Hartwitt had been dancing the night away at various soirées and balls, slim as sylph and still unmarried.

Also, they couldn't risk Gabriel inheriting. Not with the blood in him. Most other people would not have been sure about allowing him into the house. She remembered her husband asking her, "Are you sure, Barbara? We don't know, after all, how he will turn out. There are some who say–"

But all she'd done was nod, because he'd told her what he'd taken the boy from, and what fate waited him if his mother's people got their hands on him, and Gabriel looked so much like Seraphim even then, that Barbara could not imagine consigning the child to death, or worse. So she'd taken him into the house, and raised him as a fosterling, letting everyone know he was her husband's son and that some provision would be made for him in the fullness of time.

They'd been more than ready to make provision, too, despite their straitened circumstances. They'd sent him to Cambridge with Seraphim, and were ready to stand him his beginning in a small magic business, or, perhaps, in law. Even the church, if he had a bent for it, though considering the magical trouble the boy got into, that seemed like a forlorn hope.

But now, standing in her room, pacing, Lady Barbara realized that had been the first sign of trouble. Gabriel had been sent down from Cambridge, for an offense that her husband would not speak about, that Seraphim claimed to be sworn not to disclose, and that Gabriel himself turned pale but refused to speak of.

Something had happened there. For a time, the Duchess had nurtured suspicions, but not if Gabriel was in a fair way to being engaged.

The problem was that she didn't quite believe he was in a fair way to being engaged. Not to Miss Felix, at any rate. She didn't know who the woman was, but she would bet she was not who she'd said. For one, the Duchess could feel Miss Felix's magic quite well. And it was not the kind of trifling magic that would fall to the lot of an illegitimate daughter or the daughter of a poor family. A woman who brought that kind of magic with her could aspire to the highest families in the kingdom. She would not be considering Gabriel, such as Gabriel's position and expectations appeared to be, and she would not be meeting with him on the sly.

No. The girl was something to do with Seraphim. And Gabriel was hiding what he knew of it, and what he knew of Seraphim's injuries, too. And it was no use at all denying it. She'd marked how Gabriel stinted sleep to stay by Seraphim's side and listen for any stray word, any casually dropped hint that might have told the dowager more than they wished her to know.

She took a deep breath. She was afraid for the boys. This time, whatever trouble they'd managed was far more severe than the forcing house.

A scratch at the door called her attention. It was the sort of gentle scratching that she'd taught her daughter to employ, instead of the far more brash knocking. "Come in," she called.

Caroline came in. She looked like a younger replica of her mother, her features small and well placed in her oval face. Only her eyes were the same as her brothers', the large, intensely green eyes of the Ainslings. Right at the moment, they were wide open, and her skin, which tended towards a more golden color than that of the boys, had gone pale. The dark hair which she wore in demure braids had become loose, and she was clutching the skirts of her white muslin dress in great handfuls, probably as a result of having run up the stairs. "Mama," she said, without preamble, "there was someone…." She swallowed hard. "There is someone killed in the garden."

The Duchess clutched at her skirt, in an involuntary reaction. "There's been an accident?" she asked, and then as it occurred to her that, the hour being late, her sixteen-year-old daughter, barely out of the nursery, and certainly not out of the school room, should not be up. "And pray tell, where were you? And why are you not abed this late at night?"

But Caroline only looked at her as though the dowager had taken leave of her senses. "I was looking for Michael," she said, as though that were of little or no importance. "But Mama, there was a death. Seraphim killed someone."

"Impossible! Seraphim is in no state to–"

"Pray, listen, Mama. Just listen." The girl was far too high-spirited, and now she would carry her point in the face of her mother's disapproval. "I went out to the garden, to look for Michael, because he is not in his room, and I thought he might be in his workshop. You know how he can get absorbed in his magical machines, and forget the hour. He didn't come for dinner, either, so I thought I'd go and drag him indoors to eat and go to bed." She paused.

The dowager nodded. Her daughter's attachment to her twin was well known, though why she should fancy herself as the boy's mother, Barbara Ainsling would never understand.

"He was not in the workshop," Caroline said. "And I thought perhaps he'd come in and was in the library doing some research. So, I came in through the side servants' entrance, and that's when I heard the footmen going out there. They went by me in the second floor landing, and have no fear, Mama, they never saw me, for I knit myself with the wall, but they were talking, and they said His Grace had sent out a killing bolt. That they'd felt it. And it was no use at all Mr. Penn saying it had been in self-defense, because how could it be, when it must have sought out the poor bas– the poor victim at the bottom of the garden, as the cook had seen it fly, true and fiery all the way there. It had to be a targeted murder, and His Grace probably had done it while out of his mind with fever and knowing no more what he was about than he'd known in his ramblings these last two days."

"And you came to tell me of what you heard?" the Duchess asked.

Caroline looked faintly shocked at the idea, "Oh, no, Mama. Nothing so cow-hearted. I followed them, of course, in the dark. No, Mama, don't scold, I promise they did not see me."

At any other time, the Duchess would have scolded her for this hoydenish behavior, but now she could only say, "And then?"

"What do you think? They got a man from the bottom of the garden. A very well-dressed man, Mama."

"Alive?" the Lady Barbara asked, on a sudden impulse of hope.

"Oh, no, Mama, very dead." Caroline pulled back her hair, which had loosened completely from her braid and fallen in front of her eyes. "And I'm sure it was done with a killing bolt, Mama. It had that feel." For the first time fear superseded excitement and she added, "Only… Mama, Seraphim can't have known what he was doing. They can't hold him responsible, can they?"

Only the Duchess wasn't sure that her son wasn't responsible. There was the something he and Gabriel were holding secret. But the time for hesitating was over. "I don't know," she told Caroline. "But I intend to find out. You go to your bed. You did well in telling me, but not well in wandering about the house at this hour. Go to your room and to your bed, and leave me to find out what happened. I'm sure your brother wouldn't do such a thing unless there were a legally defensible reason for his actions." At least, she very much hoped so. As it was, a problem of this magnitude, legal or not, might be the end of all his chances with Honoria, particularly on top of the shamefully delayed engagement announcement. The unworthy thought that perhaps this was planned crossed her mind. But no. Why would the boy insist on the engagement, then seek to escape it by dangerous means?

She kissed Caroline's forehead and said, "Go to bed now, child."

The Duchess was out of her room and halfway down the hallway to Seraphim's before she heard her daughter's voice at her back. "But Mama! I still have not found Michael!"

Sarah A. Hoyt

The Spider And The Web

Nell woke up. She woke up with no consciousness of having been asleep, or any time having disappeared.

It was rather like waking, or dreaming she'd wakened, and not being sure which. Had she slept before, when she'd imagined herself in the sunlit park with Sydell? Or did she sleep now?

Now she was in the same park, but it was the dead of night, and the park was deserted. Strangely, it was winter, too, though it had not been cold when she'd been there during the day. Now there was frost on the trees – or at least something white frosted the branches. The lake stood motionless like a mirror. There was no sound, either, though the park was not that large and from where she stood she should be able to hear the noise of carriages trundling through the night, or at least the noise of swans splashing in the lake. Any noise. Anything, even the rustle of leaves or grass blades.

Instead, everything was very quiet. It felt as if she were trapped in one of those dreams where silence has a physical presence and can envelop all.

She took a step forward, and that too was like walking in a dream. *I don't like it,* she thought, but the truth was that she didn't have to like it. She didn't have to give consent to it.

"I am asleep," she said, but the words came to her oddly, and she knew she wasn't. Each step she took seemed to weigh too much and take too long, and she walked all the way to the edge of the lake, slowly, very slowly. Every step seemed to take a million years. Each moment was unnaturally prolonged.

"I must think," she told herself. "I must think where I am and how I came to be here, and what I must do."

"Sydell. I met with Sydell and he rifled through my mind and took from it all the matters pertaining to Seraphim Darkwater and to whatever it is he's doing with the other worlds. All of it." And that was bad, and she knew it was bad, but she didn't count on the surge of panic that followed those words, on the feeling that there was more in her mind than pertained to the fate of two very nice, but let's face it, somewhat hapless young men who had broken the law in pursuit of justice as they saw it. No, there was more there. Enough, she thought, that could tilt the universe on its axis and make the world a very dangerous place indeed. Antoine had told her–

But when she tried to pursue what Antoine had told her, it receded before her mind, and she couldn't pin it down. Something about her mind and its memories. Something about locking them from prying eyes. "But you should have taught me how to do it, Antoine," she said, talking to the still air, the silent night, the cold-frosted trees standing, their pale branches gleaming in the moonlight like lost souls begging for mercy. "Because without you, my mind has got rifled through and picked, and whatever Sydell found in it caused him to send me to–"

To send her where? She'd reached the edge of the lake and looking down she saw the water. It was water, but it was unreally smooth, like a mirror, so smooth that it might well be solid, like glass calm and unreflective.

And from a place a long time ago, when she'd been just a young computer programmer, who seemed to have fallen into a fantasy novel and in love with a powerful wizard, she heard Antoine's voice talking. "Sleeping Beauty," he said. "Why do you think she slept a hundred years? And never woke? And never tried to fight her enchantment? Why do you think all those around her slept? The brambles never grew. That is a silly invention in your world. And no mice nested in the cupboard, no rat nibbled the sleepers. Do you know why? There are worlds in between the worlds that exist anew each ticking of the clock. Each time the clock ticks, reality hesitates and wavers, as many possible futures rush in and solidify into one. Just one present. Unending futures. From such unending worlds, though a magical accident, the multiverse's many worlds were created. But in each of these worlds, the infinity of futures coalesces to just one second of present.

"And between those many futures and the solidified present lies a unit of time. It's so brief that in it your heart would not have the time to beat once. It is so long that, to someone caught in it, it will last forever and the future will never arrive.

"A strong enough magician can spin another human – usually just one. One shudders at the thought of what it would take to really spin an entire castle and all its inhabitants into that space.

"– into that time. That time between future and present. That time that will never be present nor future nor past, but a place apart from time. In them no one dies, though it could be said no one really lives, ever. And you can stay forever, imprisoned. Alone."

Alone, Nell thought, looking at the water still like glass. Alone.

But there was a way out. There had to be. Sleeping Beauty had come back. The prince had kissed her. But that would need a prince, would it not?

"So I'm out of luck, since all I have is a duke," she thought and wanted to laugh, which is how she knew she was really tired and really scared, because laughter was inappropriate in here. Laughter had no place in this land where nothing would change and where she would be a prisoner forever.

No. No. there had to be a prince and a kiss. There had to be a way of attracting him.

The problem of Earth, she thought, and the problem of growing up on Earth was that one never got to learn how to get out of these kind of situations. If you could believe the people of Avalon, the Earth and Avalon, and the hundreds of other Earths had all spun from the same unified Earth.

The theory of when it had spun apart varied, and some maintained it had happened well before human history begun, and others that it was as recent as a few hundred years ago. Yet others, saner, thought that it had taken place at different times for different worlds.

But all of them believed they'd all come from common stock and had common legends. And that these legends, perforce, came from similar events, or encoded similar knowledge. And by and large that was true in Avalon, where one could learn from the perils of Cinderella – although mostly what one learned, at least according to Antoine, was not to perform love-spells involving one's own father and a nice-seeming neighbor lady, when one was a very young and inexperienced witch. And as for Little Riding Hood, that charming cautionary tale had prevented many a young girl from giving her pet dog characteristics of her human playmates in order to have him better play house.

But Nell didn't think that anyone had ever told her what the real meaning of Sleeping Beauty was. And in the world in which she'd been so fortunate as to grow up, the best-known version said that she should send bluebirds or something of the sort to call Prince Charming to come and get her out of this bind.

She snorted loudly. So much for Prince Charming. If he only answered to dial-a-bluebird she'd be lost in here forever, and he'd never know where she'd gone. Because, after all, nothing moved here. No bluebirds. No wind. Not even air. And she only remained alive because she couldn't die.

But she could move, her mind protested. She was an intelligent being and she could move, even though the rest of this world might be locked between past and future, never being present. And if she still had the ability to think and to move, then the only thing that she could use to call someone to her rescue was … her own mind.

Part of her wanted to rebel and to say that she needed no one for rescue; that she was a self-sufficient woman; that she'd been taught to rescue herself. But the old legends didn't work that way. They were older than mankind and certainly older than any vestige of self-determination, than any idea of females being embarrassed for being beholden to a male. The legends, and the puzzles they encoded went all the way back to the beginning, when a human without a tribe was lost, and when a tribe was often just a man, a woman and their offspring. In those times, in that place, you needed the rest of them to rescue you.

That meant… that meant, she thought, that if she had bonded with someone, preferably someone male, she would be able to now call her to him by magical means, and he would break through the frozen stillness of this nowhere place and rescue her.

But she had never bonded with anyone. Well, not that way.

"Perhaps Antoine," she said, aloud, and tried to take it seriously, but she knew it wasn't. Antoine was just a dream. He had been the dream of a young girl – the extraordinary, enchanting wizard who existed even though all the laws of the world said he shouldn't. But lately, just as they landed in Avalon, she'd started to wonder if he was truly all she'd thought, if he was as powerful, as urbane, as learned, but most of all if he was as good as she'd willingly dreamed him.

She didn't know the answer to that. She still didn't. But she knew that having doubts had severed the connection between them. If there had ever been a connection. Now when she tried to reach for Antoine's essence, for his magical strength, she felt nothing.

It was like pulling at one end of a rope that was supposed to be tied to solid rock, and instead feeling the rope come up, all of a sudden, slack and too light. It was like taking a step in the dark and finding nothing under one's foot.

Antoine would not work.

Gabriel, perhaps? Gabriel Penn had seemed a good, solid man. She'd liked his strength and his persistence, and his refusal to let his half-brother die. Given what the society was, and the difference in their positions, she could only imagine how many slights and insults Gabriel must have endured, and yet he was willing to risk it all for the legitimate heir.

Yes, he could be a rock in times of trouble, and though she'd not perceived any attraction from him to her, he had told the duchess they were engaged. Perhaps that was a sign of a wish he dared not express?

She looked at the lake, in the frozen not quite light of the not quite night. It wasn't she realized, that it was nighttime here, but more that the light that was here had solidified like water. It was light on the trees, not snow. And yet she felt colder just thinking about it.

Her mind, gently, carefully, quested in the direction of Gabriel Penn, thinking of him and of the power she'd perceived from him, and trying to establish a connection. Even if the connection was no more than a vague interest from him, that and her good will ought to establish a bond strong enough to–

To what? To have him ride up to her rescue? No. She didn't think so. She suspected it was more that establishing a bond would make it possible for her to pull herself up to where he was, to drag herself from this frozen never-was to the present. Wherever he was and whatever he was doing, as embarrassing as it might be, at least it was somewhere alive.

Her questing mind met with something. It wasn't like looking for

Antoine and finding nothing where his mind and power should be. Gabriel was a solid presence in her magical quest, taking up a solid portion of her magical map. But when she tried to pull up, to pull to him, to feel him – her mind careened into a blank wall.

No, not a wall, a gate. She could see it in her mind's eye – tall and made of something hard and cold. Metal, or perhaps stone. And locked.

For a moment she thought of shaking the gate, of rattling it, but realized it was less than a forlorn hope. The gate dwarfed her and loomed over her, and there was nothing in her human form that could open it. From beyond it came a disturbing song, in a language she couldn't understand.

She had the impression quite suddenly that the real Gabriel Penn was someone quite different, quite other than the servant he appeared to be. It was nonsense, but… She felt him as almost an alien being, someone she couldn't hope to comprehend.

That left…. She gritted her teeth and through her mind passed in review the many people she had met in her time in Britannia. Most of her meetings with men were less than inconsequential. Other than Sydell she'd had no constant male contact. And Sydell had sent her here. She was sure of it.

So that left… Seraphim. What possible contact could he have with her? Well, he'd risked his life to save her. But he'd risked his life, too, to save the lion boy, and yet she didn't think that he had any interest in lions. Or in boys, for that matter.

But he was kind and he was – if she guessed his character properly – hard put to resist the claims of someone in need. And she was in need. So, if not with her attraction, she could forge a bond with her need.

Thinking of her great need and that without him she would be locked in here forever, worse than a ghost, neither dead nor alive, till she went slowly mad in an eternity of solitude, she reached for the power she'd seen as Seraphim Darkwater's. At the same time, she called the duke's aristocratic profile, his laughing green eyes to her mind.

For a moment it felt like she'd met with the same wall that surrounded Gabriel, only if Nell had to picture this one, she'd picture it as those brambles grown around Sleeping Beauty's castle. A profusion of defensive thorns, things to keep others away.

"But I need help," she said, and cringed to say it, and yet – desperate – pushed her need at him, forcing him to see that without him, she was barred from life forever.

Whatever was holding her broke so suddenly that she had the impression of being picked up and lifted, then thrown bodily into the water.

She started to sink, under the weight of her skirts and petticoats, then managed to paddle enough to keep herself afloat as she struggled to remove the water-logged petticoats before they pulled her under. As she did, details sank in – the murmur of the wind in trees around this lake, and something else. The lake was full of boats, the boats filled with men who looked like gardeners or stable boys and who carried a lantern apiece. Each boat held two men, one of whom rowed while the other stood, the other holding the lantern aloft and trying to look into the murky depths of the lake.

There were two boats making for her as fast as the men rowing could make them. The man with the lantern called from the nearer one, "It is not him. Not the young master."

"Who is it then?" the standing man from the other near boat called.

"It's a lady," the nearest man called. "Someone tell His Grace there's a lady in the trout pond."

Lady In The Lake

Seraphim sat on his sofa, wrapped in a dressing gown which made no more than a pretense of keeping out the cold, but did so magnificently, in shimmering green silk with a pattern of flying dragons. He'd asked for his cane with the silver top. But even such an obvious means of support hadn't convinced Gabriel to let Seraphim get up and be about his business.

No, instead, Seraphim had to sit on the sofa, his hands atop the dragon-head top of the cane, his mind trying to follow, by sound, the very strange events in his household this evening and, more difficult, trying to make sense of them.

And Gabriel… Gabriel had entered what Seraphim, with the cruelty of an older brother, even if he was in fact the younger, had been known to call his housekeeper mode. He had marshaled the housemaids to remake the bed, he'd got someone to bring in a bowl of sweet and magically harmonious potpourri to disguise the stench of burnt feathers and scorched broth.

He'd threatened to have more broth brought in, too, but Seraphim had negotiated that distressing sentence down to a glass of cold milk, which he supposed must be making its way from the kitchens.

And Gabriel had sent the gardeners down to the lake, with crystal balls affixed at the ends of lanterns. The attack had come from near the lake, or at least the would-be assassin had been near it.

Seraphim should have thought, as Gabriel obviously had, that any body of water that large, around which serious magic was made, would have recorded the sequence of events and the strength of the attacks. And since it would come to a high court, the least Seraphim could do was make sure that there were crystal balls imprinted with whatever had been recorded in the water, to present to His Majesty when the time came.

But Seraphim hadn't thought of it, and Gabriel had, which was probably why Gabriel was the one to whom word was brought of whatever the new disturbance was.

The first sense of it the duke had was a shiver across the surface of his magic, as though someone had opened a portal between worlds nearby. But it could not be a full portal between worlds. It was something more attenuated and lighter.

Then there had come a knock at the door, and Gabriel opening it and mumbling something to a man outside, who mumbled something in response. And then Gabriel had started to close the door, and Seraphim had had just about enough.

"Penny, open the damn door and let the man speak to me." He understood well enough – perhaps better than other people in the household – Gabriel's penchant for taking charge, for being useful. He remembered – and wondered if anyone else did – what Gabriel had looked like when he'd been brought in, as Seraphim had then thought, as Seraphim's birthday gift.

Though older than Seraphim, and obviously very similar to the heir of the Ainslings, Gabriel had looked gaunt almost to the point of infirmity, his face had been bruised, and he'd appeared terrified. As though he'd been threatened with something even worse than the hunger and the violence he'd endured so far.

Seraphim had seen the look on Gabriel's face as he encountered each of the features of life at the Darkwater estate: regular food, toys, a warm and secure bed. He remembered Gabriel's delight at the roaring fires in the hearths that first winter, his amazed joy at the sweetness of fruit in winter. And he knew Gabriel tried to make himself useful, because at the back of his mind, somehow, he still thought the Ainslings would send him back where they'd found him.

He'd been afraid of being sent back after that bad business in Cambridge too, though if Darkwater had been asked – he hadn't – Gabriel had been more sinned against than sinning, and the fault lay with that damned Marlon fellow, who hadn't lasted much longer before crossing over to the dark arts, either.

Seraphim's own trouble at the time, his one and only serious love affair, had rendered him oblivious to the whole thing until it exploded, with Gabriel gibbering in panic at his doorstep. Something for which Seraphim would never forgive himself.

But as much as Seraphim loved and understood his half-brother, this was the outside of enough and he would not stand for it. He would not be treated as a cross between an excitable maiden aunt and an invalid grandfather in his own house. "Penn," he said, in a warning tone, as Gabriel hesitated, his hand on the door. "Let the man in, I said."

The man came in. He was one of the older gardeners, and Seraphim felt peevish annoyance that he couldn't remember his name and that Gabriel probably knew it by heart.

The man wore a crushed felt hat, a dingy coat, and pants that were obviously working garments, judging by the dirt adhering to them. To this was joined an overall dampness, and scraps of what might be aquatic plants here and there. He removed the felt hat – he should have done so on entering the house, of course, but even in a ducal house, the garden personnel was sometimes insufficiently educated in manners. Clasping it in his hands and turning it over and over as he approached Seraphim, he bowed, "As I was telling Mr. Penn, sir, it is the lady in the lake, and a right mess she caused with our recording of the magic, sir."

This speech caused Seraphim to wonder if the reason they were treating him as a doddering and senile grandfather was that he had, in fact, gone around the bend. Because none of this made sense. He had to admit ignorance, of course, but he admitted it in the most haughty manner he could conjure. "What are you speaking of?" he asked. "I do not have the pleasure of understanding you."

"The lady in the lake," the man said, as though the matter were obvious.

"Unless she brought a sword with her, then it is unlikely it is the Lady in the Lake as such," Seraphim said. "And even if she brought a sword with her, she would have to be an impostor, as I'm sure Arthur's sword is still where it resides, in the royal armory. So, kindly explain."

Gabriel huffed. It wasn't very audible, and the gardener probably missed it, or else, if he heard it he would have thought nothing of it. But Seraphim heard it clear as day and knew exactly what it meant: that "huff" was Gabriel's way of telling Seraphim to stop terrorizing the servants and being hard to please, and close upon it, Gabriel lost what patience he'd tried to summon.

As the gardener continued to twirl his execrable hat in his filthy hands, and stammer something that never amounted to a full word, Gabriel interrupted. "If it please Your Grace, what Marson is trying to tell you is that a woman fell into the lake, as they were using the magic recorders."

"Fell from where?" Seraphim asked, turning his inquisitive glance on Seraphim. "The trees? And is she a woman or is she–"

"She is Miss Helena Felix," Gabriel hastened, cutting what he presumed – truthfully – was Seraphim's question about the magical nature of the intruder.

"Ah," Seraphim said. "The capable Miss Helena. She stayed behind, then, while I was ill?" He was trying to imagine what Gabriel must have told his mother to justify such a thing. Good heavens, by now he might very well be engaged to the woman. He started to open his mouth, then closed it, because he remembered suddenly that he didn't even know if he was in fact engaged to Honoria. He had to get Gabriel alone and ask him a few home questions without being attacked by maniacs with bolts and spells.

"No. It appears she found occasion to come to us again, though," Gabriel said. "Marson has taken her to the housekeeper's rooms, to change out of her soaked clothes and get a cup of tea, while they finish the recording in the garden. And he's given orders that the gentleman who … ah… got unfortunately killed by the bolt you sent out in self-defense be put in the ice house, till royal officers can take charge of–"

"No," Seraphim said. And looked at Gabriel's surprised face. "No. I must see them both."

Gabriel's eyebrows shot up. "Both? Miss Felix and–?"

"The dead man," he said, and continued. "Penn, if you please, send one of the housemaids to tell Miss Felix I require her presence immediately. And Marson, kindly have four under-gardeners carry the deceased gentleman up."

"What?" the gardener said, clearly shocked. "To Your Grace's room?"

Seraphim allowed himself a smile. "If I were feeling more myself," he said. "I'd go down and look at the corpse myself. As is, though, I don't feel up to taking the flights of stairs down, yet. And the description I was given of his being a gentleman of average features, with dark hair, and richly dressed, you must understand, tells me very little about who he might be or whether I know him. As such, I'll thank you to bring him up. You can carry him down again, and fast enough."

"Yes, sir," Marson said, but left with the sort of haste that betrayed his suspicions about Seraphim's sanity. His haste did not escape Gabriel. As both the maids and the gardener left, he closed the door softly and turned to Seraphim, "I hope you're satisfied, Duke. Your servants will now think you have lost your mind, or perhaps that you intend to dabble in necromancy." But it was obvious it was just a joke, and, his face sobering, Gabriel told Seraphim, quickly, everything that had passed between the time of his coming back from the pyramids and the present.

"And you claimed Miss Felix was your fiancée?"

"You see how important it was to know what your mother knows about me?"

Seraphim sighed. "Knows, nothing. Understands, I suspect near all. You know she always detects you in falsehood."

"Perhaps," Gabriel said, trying to appear unconcerned, but biting the corner of his upper lip, something he only did when he was concerned. He opened his mouth as though to say something, but at that moment there was a knock, and on Seraphim calling "Come," the door was opened by two maids who curtseyed and then stood one on either side of the door, looking like statues. In between them, a woman walked in.

She wasn't ugly, Seraphim realized, now that he saw her without either anger or fear distorting her features. She looked concerned, she was soaked to the skin, her hair clinging to her head like a dark bonnet. And she was wearing a voluminous grey blanket draped over whatever clothes she'd worn when she'd fallen in the pond. But through it all, it was obvious her features were good, and that she had grace and poise worthy of a queen.

Miss Felix made that blanket seem like a trailing royal cloak, as she walked in to stand a few steps from him and curtseyed. "I was told Your

Grace wanted to see me," she said.

"I did," he said. "I would like to know how you came to fall in my pond. I presume it was not simply a matter of leaning too far over a branch."

Miss Felix looked over her shoulder at the maids by the door, then back at him. Seraphim nodded. "I believe, madam," he said, "that, inconvenient though they are, your chaperones must stay. You can't be in a room alone with two men."

She looked impatient. He'd swear she rolled her eyes, and he could not reconcile her air of obvious quality with this unconcern or ignorance of the social rules. "Very well," she said, at last speaking in an undertone. "But the thing is, Your Grace, that I don't know what to tell you. To own the truth, the secret I could tell is not mine, and on it depends the life of someone whom I once thought–" She stopped. "No. On my silence depends the life of someone who might have his defects of character, but who, I'm sure, has done nothing to deserve death."

Which, of course, was when the second knock on the door sounded, and on Seraphim authorizing entrance, as Nell stepped a little to the side and turned to look, Mr. Marson came in, leading four strapping boys, who carried, between them, a pallet on which was a form covered in a blanket.

The pallet was lowered in front of Seraphim, and the blanket pulled back at the same time a lantern was brought near that he might better examine the face of the deceased.

Seraphim saw a face that looked wholly unknown, and much as had been described to him: dark hair, regular features, a certain appearance of gentility.

And then Helena Felix leaned forward towards the corpse and gasped. "Antoine!" she said. She sounded more shocked than saddened. "It is Antoine."

Before Seraphim could ask her what she meant, and who Antoine might be, he heard running steps and someone burst in through the door, without asking. It was his sister Caroline, her dress rumpled, her hair in a mess. She curtseyed hastily, and looked around as if shocked at the mass of people in the room. Her gaze raked the corpse on the floor, but she seemed not to be at all surprised, more annoyed, as though all these people were here for the purpose of annoying her.

"Seraphim," she said, in a scolding tone. "Seraphim, it is the most unlucky thing for you to have everyone here, because you must come with me right away."

"Caroline," he said, and was about to scold her on her lack of manners. He had no time.

"Yes, yes," she said. "I know I'm being very shocking, and it's all very bad, but Seraphim, we think Michael was taken by the elves. They left a changeling in his place."

Changeling

Nell clutched the blanket tightly around herself and wondered what madness she'd fallen into. The entire night – indeed, the entire time since her interview with Sydell - had acquired a feeling of unreality.

She had to be dreaming. Antoine could not be dead, lying cold and pale on the floor, on that makeshift pallet, staring at the ceiling with unseeing eyes. Antoine had been....

In her mind she remembered the first time she'd seen him, dressed in jeans and a pale blue t-shirt and looking very much like a twenty-something-year old computer repairman. Which was what he'd said he was, that first time he'd taken her out for coffee. But then there had come the hints that not all was as it seemed, *you have great power* he'd told her, and, by the time he'd shown her how to open a portal, by the time he'd given her a glimpse of other worlds, it had become obvious to her that he didn't mean this as a metaphor.

Perhaps the dream started then, she thought. Perhaps if she closed her eyes and believed really hard, she'd wake up back at her desk, in front of a computer running some routine.

"Caroline," Darkwater said. He spoke very softly, his voice all the more terrifying for seeming so unnaturally calm. "What do you mean by a changeling?"

Nell didn't want to know what he'd been doing, or what had been happening in this household since she was last here. It was clear to her that though Seraphim had recovered from his near-brush with death – or at least this time Gabriel Penn didn't seem to be making desperate attempts at reviving his half-brother, he still looked near death. He was pale, his green eyes surrounded by dark circles, his lips looking dry and colorless. And the aura of magic around him looked faded.

This was all the more puzzling, since Nell gathered that more than a day had passed since she'd been here. His power should have recovered more, unless–

Unless something else had happened to make him lose strength. She remembered the talk by the lake, about how someone had made an attempt on Seraphim's life.

The gardeners, the under-gardeners, and for all she knew the stable boys, all those men who had been on those boats, in the lake, had been – if what she understood of their talk was right – trying to record the event, so that Seraphim would not be condemned for murder. But that meant that he had been attacked by Antoine. Or at least he thought he had.

She felt vaguely sick. She didn't know when she'd stopped being in love with Antoine, but she'd never suspected him– no, that was not true, either, over the last months she'd suspected him of perfidy often enough. She simply had never been sure enough of it to consider doing anything that would endanger his life. It seemed like a very foolish thing to condemn a man to death simply because he might not have been straightforward with her, or because he had deceived her by telling her he loved her.

But she had suspected he had lied to her, and more. First, because it seemed very unlikely that he'd come to Earth in search of her power, her aura of power, as he called it, guided through different worlds by the call of it. Since she'd been in Britannia, Nell had gathered that her power was indeed strong, and indeed large. But to call someone between worlds? That didn't even make sense. Even the stronger magicians, even with scrying powers, had to be looking for something specific before they homed in on a pattern among universes. Simply having a strong pattern didn't call anyone.

Second because she'd seen for herself that Antoine was strong and accomplished, and knew his way across the multi universe. And if that was true, how could he be so foolish as to transport into Avalon without a care, and let himself be caught in Sydell's trap.

No, there was more there than he'd told Nell. He had come here for some reason, and if it hadn't been to fall into the trap, still it had to be for some reason more important than that he found the world fascinating and wanted to show it to Nell.

But still– But still Nell didn't think that Antoine deserved to die, and now, she couldn't think or believe that Antoine was an assassin. Myriad ideas combated each other in her mind. What if this weren't real Antoine, but a clever simulacrum? What if this was all designed to make her break and tell all to Darkwater?

Except Darkwater wasn't even looking at her, but at the intense dark-haired young woman, who looked so much like the Dowager Duchess. "How do you know it's a changeling, Caroline, and not simply Michael in a trance?"

The girl they called Caroline shook her head. Her hands pleated nervously at the skirt of her robe. "It's not Michael," she said. "It can't be. Even in a trance he would wake up when I came in. He would react to my magic. Seraphim, he is all pale and his eyes are blank, and he looks… well, he looks more perfect than any normal human can look. And … And…" Her voice rose in a wail of distress. "Mama says it is a changeling."

After her outburst, she took a deep breath and exhaled forcefully, and thrust her head and chest a little forward, as though she expected her brother to challenge her. Darkwater didn't challenge her. He opened his mouth then closed it, then opened it again to say, in a voice that was little more than a whisper, "Mama?" He looked up and to the side, to where Gabriel Penn stood beside the sofa, seemingly keeping guard over his wounded master. The two men exchanged a glance that contained in it volumes of information Nell would give something to acquire. Both of them looked grave, and whatever wordless communication between them, it didn't dispel their fears, as both looked even more worried after it.

"One moment, Caroline," Seraphim said. "I will come with you, in a moment." He glared over his shoulder at Gabriel's exclamation, and Nell could see Gabriel making an effort to prevent himself from further outburst.

Darkwater turned away from his half-brother, and to the four strapping boys with the pallet on which Antoine lay. "Take him to the cold room," he said. "We must notify the coroner of the death. Send Jem, on a fast horse. Tell him I will be available for interviewing no later than tomorrow afternoon." He looked back at his sister, "And now, Caroline, I shall come with you."

"Your Grace," Gabriel said. "You are not well enough to–"

"There are duties," Seraphim said, ostensibly talking to no one in particular, "that one cannot delegate, no matter how tired or ill one is." He made an attempt to rise, supporting himself on his cane, then turned to look at Gabriel. "Give me your arm, Penn. I believe my strength is not equal to what I'd like it to be."

His strength was not in fact equal to much of anything, Nell thought, as she noticed how Gabriel Penn not only allowed the Duke to hold onto his arm to rise, but put his arm around the Duke's waist to support him. How ill was the Duke, and why? Had he really sent the killing bolt that had killed Antoine? She shivered at the idea, and, as the gentlemen who'd brought Antoine's corpse in prepared to take him out again, she realized she'd been forgotten.

The Duke and Penn were following Caroline Ainsling out of the room, and Nell thought she could stay here, until Darkwater had solved whatever problem had now visited his house, and came back to his room, and remembered Nell existed. Or she could go with Antoine's body and keep up some sort of vigil in the cold room – perhaps try to discover if that truly was Antoine's corpse or some contrivance that looked like it. Or… Or she could follow Darkwater and Gabriel Penn and find out what had happened to the Duke's younger brother and what else might be behind the turmoil in this household.

She pulled her blanket tighter about herself. It truly didn't make her any warmer, because her hair was dripping wet. But it made her feel somehow more protected. And then she started behind the Duke and his half-brother, as though she had every right to follow them.

The gardeners were waiting, with Antoine's body, but she thought that the maids, stationed on either side of the door, might stop her. So she threw her head back and looked very haughty indeed as she went by them.

The maids didn't move. They didn't even look at her as she walked past. She'd have suspected magic, only she'd learned in Britannia the value of a good pretense and that a good display of arrogance surpassed all logic.

The maids didn't even follow as she walked after the Darkwaters and Penn down a long, marble-paved hallway. Really, the one thing about this world that kept astonishing her was how the houses of the noblemen looked more magnificent than anything she'd ever seen on Earth. Take the way the hallway ceiling arched above, painted a deep blue and sprinkled with gold stars. It was like something out of a theatrical set, rather than something you'd find in real life.

It would testify in favor of this being a dream, except that in dreams one's feet didn't ache with cold and slosh in shoes that felt like they'd fall apart every time she took a step. And in dreams it was very rare for one's hair to drip down one's back in a disconsolate, icy dribble.

They walked down the hallway, then up a curving staircase, then down another hallway. As Nell tried to orient herself, she realized they were going towards the southern wing of the house, and, from what she remembered of the house's exterior – which wasn't much as she'd only ever seen it from the back, while approaching it, the other two times she'd magically transported into and out of it – to a little tower that protruded out of it at that corner.

She knew she was right when, ignoring the hallway to the southern wing, Seraphim, instead, opened the door to the tower.

The Darkwaters, followed by the quite disregarded Nell, entered a huge, circular room. The tower might look small from the outside, but that was, Nell judged, because it was dwarfed by the other elements of the massive Darkwater house. Inside, the tower was one vast room. Vast enough that on Earth it could have passed as the lobby of a very large hotel. Its architecture too resembled something one might find in a hotel lobby, being largely unimpeded: just one vast circular space, going up far more than one story to–

For a moment Nell looked up, disbelieving because it seemed to her as though the tower had no roof, but, instead, were open to velvety dark summer night sky, with naught but a golden spider web, of some sort, between them and the night. Then she realized the golden spider web was a framework for glass, and that the tower was one vast observatory or perhaps some sort of conservatory. And that roof had to be held together with magic, because with the technology of this world there was no way to keep that much glass up with so little metal.

Then she looked down and realized that there was more magic at work here than the roof. The space might be free of architectural obstructions, but it was filled with machines, and … contraptions, for which Nell had no name.

In the way of this world, these machines, no matter how utilitarian they tried to look, were made of polished brass and leather and wood, and their rounded shapes couldn't help but look pleasing. And they were animated. Arms moved, gears turned. Something that looked like a giant telescope pointed at the ceiling gyrated slowly on a frame, clicking gently in a steady rhythm, while a mechanical arm attached to it wrote steadily with a quill on paper.

In the middle of all this, perched on what looked remarkably like a high barstool made of brass, sat a young man, probably Caroline's age or a little younger. He was so young, one might still be able to call him pretty without offending too badly. He looked like a version of Darkwater, or perhaps of Gabriel Penn, made of clay that had yet to harden, or like a sketch of one of them done hastily and left too smooth and soft.

He didn't turn to look as the party approached. The Dowager Duchess, who stood next to him, looking at him, intently, as though he were an object that must be puzzled out, did turn to look at them. "Seraphim!" she said. Then she hastened towards them, hands extended. "You shouldn't have come. Indeed, you look very ill. And there is nothing you can do here, you see. Michael has been taken. They've left this in his place."

"Mama, are you sure–" Seraphim said, and stopped.

Nell was sure he had stopped because, like her, if he unfocused his eyes and brought his mage sight to bear, he could see that the thing on the stool was not and had never been a human adolescent. It was more akin to an animated sculpture made of ice, or perhaps intersecting nodes of light and power. Something that could only impersonate a human for those with no mage-sight.

Changeling. That was a thing the elves did, wasn't it? Was this creature an elf, then? Or merely a construct the elves had left behind?

Sarah A. Hoyt

The Duke's Duty

And now this. Seraphim stared at the thing on the seat. Were it not for his ability to unfocus his eyes and to look just so at that he would think it was Michael, but it was not.

The question was, how long had his brother been missing? Would this sculpture, this animated construct, always have been like this, listless and unresponsive? Or was there a way it could have acted like Michael and Seraphim not have known, or – more importantly – the household not have known, while Seraphim was unconscious?

He looked towards the Duchess and narrowed his eyes. "Mama, they've always told me… that is… I've always heard it tell that you knew about changelings, and that this related to something in your childhood, but no one ever told me what? It was all whispers and then 'well, you know, because of her childhood' and when I pursued the information they told me I was not to speak of it." He looked steadily at his Mama, hoping that she wasn't about to tell him this was not to be spoken of. He knew he was making poor Gabriel damned uncomfortable. He could tell without turning to look, without Gabriel saying a single word. He knew whatever the mystery with changelings in Mama's childhood was related directly to whatever and whoever Gabriel was. That Gabriel would not in fact be here today but for mama and whatever had brought her into the presence of elves in her childhood. "How did you know, Mama? What is it with changelings? Have you seen one of these before?"

The Duchess looked at the thing on the stool and sighed. "It is not," she said, "a changeling like the one they left for me, when they stole me to Fairyland as a child."

A long breath, with a sound on the edge of keening escaped Gabriel, but Darkwater didn't turn to look, and instead kept looking at his mother, who spoke like one in a dream. "This is a construct, animated. It looks like, and probably is, ice. Water that someone poured in the rough shape of a young man, and then left overnight to freeze, then animated and gave your brother's look by magic. It is not alive. It has no feelings. It–"

"Stop," Gabriel Penn said. And what was so strange was that Gabriel had told the Dowager to stop, something he'd never done before. "Stop, Your Grace," he moderated himself, and sighed. "It will not do. We should discuss it, yes, but not here. Not in … its presence." He waved towards the changeling, who remained, impassive, on his stool, looking blankly at the world.

"But Mother says it's not animated," Caroline said.

Penn sighed again. "No, but still."

"What should we do with it then?" Darkwater asked. It seemed to him foolish to leave the thing alone, as though it might get up to mischief on its own.

"Nothing," Penn said. "It is losing its magic and will presently melt. But if you feel better, Duke, we shall lock it in the closet." He took the creature's arm and led it, and it let itself be led, to a cupboard in the wall, where Michael kept his chemicals and his vials. Penn pushed the creature in there, closed the door and locked it. He closed the closet to sight and sound with a carefully aimed spell.

Then he turned to the room. "Shall we speak, now?" he asked. "This is one of the safest rooms in the house to discuss such things in, since Michael has hardened it against magical interference, so no rival houses could see his designs."

"But that thing got in," Caroline said. And Penn smiled at her. "Yes, Caroline, it did, but not through here. My guess is that Michael has been gone for days, perhaps before Seraphim was injured. These changelings have a certain programming and seem more real and solid initially, interact with everyone normally for a few days, and then wind down and become whatever material they were."

"Then why didn't you allow us to speak in front of it?" Seraphim said.

"Because sometimes they are rigged so as to transmit sight and sound to whoever made them. I have shut it in the closet and blocked all sound magically. We are safe now. And I believe," he said, "first I will let Her Grace tell us what happened to her in childhood."

It occurred to Seraphim, for the first time, that Gabriel spoke as though he knew what it was. He said so, and Gabriel pressed his lips together. "Indeed, Seraphim. Perforce, I know." And though Seraphim didn't know why, perforce, in fact couldn't think of any reason for Gabriel to know, save that, of course, his mother was an elf, and changelings were connected to elves, he kept quiet.

"I will tell," his Mama said. "But let us sit. Seraphim should not remain standing long." He allowed his mother to lead him to a little sitting area around a large, glimmering sphere whose purpose Michael had never succeeded in explaining fully, but which seemed to interest the heads of several magic houses. There were three straight-backed chairs, a chaise longue and a sofa. He refused to lie down on the chaise, but allowed himself to be led to the sofa and sat down on it, glad only that no one had brought an invalid's shawl to drape around his shoulders. Mama sat in one of the straight-backed chairs. Caroline half-reclined on the chaise. Gabriel remained standing, but Seraphim wasn't about to challenge him, suspecting it had to do with his idea of preserving the appearance of his position while in public.

Then he realized there was someone else with them. They'd been so absorbed in their conversation that he hadn't noticed her before. Miss Helena Felix had come with them, trailing her grey blanket. The woman must be freezing, even with the blanket, and indeed looked very pale and tired. He looked at her. "Miss Felix? Should we have private talk in front of you? To whom do you report?"

She gave something that wasn't a half laugh. "To no one, Your Grace," she said. "Up until this mor– no, up until the day I left here, whenever that was, I worked for Sydell, spymaster for the king. Then I would have said I reported to him. But all that was severed, first, by his betraying me, and then, by his killing the man he was holding hostage for my good behavior. I am now, Your Grace, entirely a free agent, and as a free agent, I confess I'd like to do what I can to bring your brother back."

Seraphim didn't know whether to believe her. After all, the king's spies were trained and paid to lie. He hesitated.

"She can hear my story," his mother said, quietly. Seraphim noted that the Duchess didn't protest that Miss Felix was Gabriel's fiancée. "It is nothing so secret that she can't find out the general outlines of it simply by talking to anyone old enough to have listened to gossip or practiced magic when I was a child. It is not normally spoken of, because people are afraid to give me pain, but not because it is not known."

Seraphim looked at Gabriel. "And you? Since I presume you'll be talking, also?"

Gabriel looked surprised, then glanced at Miss Felix and shrugged. "Oh, she can hear mine too. There is nothing in it that cannot be gathered with some sleuthing, and I suspect the king's secret services know it well enough. If I've kept it secret at all, it was to spare your family shame by association, but I judge in the trouble we face that that is the least of our worries."

"When I was five," the Duchess spoke, "I was stolen away to Fairyland. No one knows why." She spoke a little too loudly, a little too cheerfully, as though trying too hard to sound normal. And she'd barely let

Gabriel stop talking before she had started. "I had magic, of course, but no more than my brothers and sisters, and no more than a hundred other children in the immediate vicinity of my parents' estate. But whatever it was, and for whatever reason, it was a well-planned thing. You see..." She looked up at Gabriel, and her eyes unfocused. Not as though she didn't want to see him, but more as though she knew what she had to say would touch him very nearly and were trying to pull herself away from it, and not to dwell on the pain she was giving. "You see, the changeling they left in my place was not a construct, but a little girl. A little elf girl they had to have shaped from very early on to look exactly like me and behave exactly like me. For days – weeks – my parents didn't know I was missing.

"For myself too," she said. "It was hard to tell. I lived mostly in the nursery, with nanny and the nursery maids. My life was surrounded by toys and I was an imaginative child. As such…well, I thought simply that my toys were more alive than before. For a long time, I didn't notice that I was in another realm, and then…"

"And then?"

"And then I started to feel cold. Not physically. I don't think Fairyland is any colder than here. It is, after all, like another world in the multi-universe, just one that never fully separated. It has the same climate at the same time. But there is… everyone in Fairyland is cold." She shrugged. Gabriel was walking back and forth across the little sitting area, as though he couldn't sit still, but he nodded when she said that. "It's not that they don't show emotion," she continued. "It is that they don't know what emotion is. They are like humans without the…" She shrugged. "I'm sure Gabriel can explain it better than I."

"Yes," Gabriel said. "Yes. But not just yet, pray go on." He paced. She looked up at him.

"I realized that I was in a way absolutely alone, as… as a child raised by wolves would be alone." Gabriel shuddered, as though in response to her words. "But I was too young to know what had happened or to seek to escape captivity. I could not, and as such, I would have remained forever captive in Fairyland, but…but my parents had an hostage. And they did what has always been done when a real changeling, a living one, is left behind in place of the child taken. They tortured her. They subjected her to various discomforts, until I was brought back." She took a deep breath. "I'm sorry, Gabriel."

He paused in his pacing. For a crazy moment, Seraphim wondered if the changeling had been Gabriel, such was the tone of his mother's voice.

Could elves change their sex? He'd never heard tell of such a thing. And besides, Gabriel was around his age, was he not? Could he have been kept in some stasis, so he didn't grow? But no, Gabriel was Seraphim's half-brother. He had the Darkwater look, the Darkwater magic, and Seraphim's own father had recognized him as such.

"What is there to be sorry for, Your Grace?" he asked, pausing in his pacing to look at her. "Oh, perhaps, yes, perhaps it was that torture, which, though, from what I heard was very mild, at least for an elf, which led her to never quite fit in Fairyland again. But I don't think so. I never told you why we were thrown out, she and I, have I? I told my father when–" He shook his head. "I beg your pardon."

"You beg my pardon? For admitting the duke was your father? Or for mentioning it in my presence? Of all the things your father did, Gabriel, siring you was probably one of the most worthy. Don't scruple to admit it. He admitted you openly, even if he never changed the name your mother gave you, since nothing could be gained by saddling you with Ainsling, when no title and no fortune accrued with it."

Gabriel only nodded, though Seraphim wasn't sure to what.

"My mother was the changeling left in place of Her Grace," he said. "She was also the child of the deposed king of Fairyland. No, don't ask me how or why. There are revolutions in Fairyland, and civil wars, just as there are here. And I think at the end of the last such war, when my… I suppose, my grandfather, the then- sovereign of Fairyland, was deposed, he left behind his young daughter. It was thought that by sending her as a changeling to the world of mortals, it would dispose of her, I think – though the thinking of elves is not the same as ours and it is hard to fathom at times. However, in the time she was away, there was another revolution, and my… I suppose my uncle, became the sovereign of Fairyland. He could not allow a princess of fairykind to be tortured in the world of humans, and therefore, reluctantly – and I do feel it was reluctantly, though I can't explain why – gave Her Grace back to her parents and took my mother back. But my mother was ever odd. Oh, I don't think they did more than threaten her and make her uncomfortable, and perhaps make her work – the things that legend says one should do to changelings, though some people make the poor creatures sit on live coals or worse – and strangely, from what I know of my poor Mama, I don't think that's what changed her.

"Just as Her Grace could not survive in Fairyland, not without noticing the exceptional coldness of elves, and would have been changed beyond repair had she stayed in there longer, my mother had experienced the warmth of humans and it had changed her, so she no longer responded like a real elf.

"And she could not live in Fairyland, not fully. Instead, she would escape to the world of men. Which is how she met with Arden Ainsling, Duke of Darkwater. And she returned to Fairyland expecting me."

"And meanwhile, Darkwater found me, was enchanted by my resemblance to his vanished elf love, and started courting me," the Dowager said.

Gabriel hesitated, looking as if he would apologize, then inclined his head. "Only I fit in even worse than my poor Mama. I was more human, you see. There is… there is sport the elves engage in. They will capture some child out of doors on a dark night, or some lost creature, and they will torture it. When I was three or so, I tried to rescue a puppy that was being tortured for the amusement of the court. My mother and I were flung from Fairyland as unworthy." He was silent a long while. "When my father found me, we were living in a tenement and Mama…" A long, deep breath. "I begged to supplement our income. It wasn't until I had lived in this house for two years that they tried to reclaim me, and only because they couldn't allow me to live as a commoner among humans. They didn't want to keep me." He looked up, and a sudden fierce light burned in his eyes, such as Seraphim had never seen. "They didn't want me for me, or because they cared for me, or even because they honored me, or my lineage. They'd probably have killed me once they'd got me back to Fairyland. But they didn't want me to live among humans and perhaps come to value my human heritage over my elven one." Another pause. "I don't know why they took Michael or what for, but I swear to you, all of you, that I will do my utmost to bring him back, and – if I can – to bring Fairyland down with it."

Sarah A. Hoyt

The Fear Of Dark

Nell looked at Gabriel as he proclaimed his willingness to take down Fairyland if that was what it took to bring his youngest half-brother back. For a moment, for a brief breath, she caught a look in Seraphim Ainsling, Duke of Darkwater's face, as he looked at his half-elven sibling, nominally his valet. She didn't know what that look was. It might be surprise or awe or fear.

Nell knew, however, with absolute certainty, in that moment, that Seraphim hadn't known the details of Gabriel's ancestry. He might have known Gabriel was half-elf but not that he was what could be termed a prince of Fairyland, or why he'd left Fairyland. And he definitely hadn't known how strongly Gabriel felt about elves and the king of Fairyland.

It was just a moment, and then Seraphim looked away, his eyes half-lidded, hiding his expression, and his face went back to the impassive, reserved look she'd seen on it before.

Training, she thought, as though it were a novel idea. The man had been trained to hide his feelings. He'd been trained to behave impeccably in public. He'd been brought up to fulfill his role, and his role required that he follow a protocol in public and show nothing of his inner thoughts or feelings and, particularly, show no doubt, no fear, and no pain.

Having realized that, she could detect things in his expression: pain mostly, and tiredness. Though he looked alert and aware, she realized there were fine lines at the corners of his mouth, as if from holding his features unnaturally serene against suffering. And his shoulders were held too square and straight, as if he were afraid they'd sag under tiredness. And his hands held the head of the walking stick far too tightly.

She looked at him until she caught him giving her a long side glance, and then she looked at her feet. She hadn't yet decided what to tell him. What could she let the Darkwaters know about her origins, her work, and her involvement with Antoine, let alone her involvement with Sydell? What and how much did they need to know? And how much would endanger them? She didn't know enough to know what she could tell and to whom before they became targets for the secret service.

Now that Antoine was dead – something that didn't seem quite real, yet – she didn't even know how much of what she thought had happened since she'd landed in Avalon was true, and how much had been a lie perpetrated on her. The idea that Antoine would try to kill Darkwater made no sense. Certainly not when Antoine was supposed to be in a dungeon, his life dependent on her good behavior.

Once more, she caught the Duke of Darkwater's glance on her, and she looked down at her feet. The Darkwaters talked around her. It seemed as though they had little more thought than she did on how to rescue someone from the clutches of elves, and on this she had very little to hide from them. She'd had some idea that elves were real here, and their magic serious, as opposed to being – as on Earth – mere legends and rumors. But she knew nothing else. She'd heard of treaties between the two realms, but had never sought to inform herself of the details. Her assignments had been among humans.

It seemed as though the conversation was winding down when Gabriel said, "I will speak to my mother." From the way he set his jaw after saying it, it was obvious that this was neither an easy nor a safe task, but no one said anything to dissuade him. The Dowager Duchess said in the tone of someone who relieves her a mind, more than of someone who says something that needs saying, "We must get Michael back as soon as may be."

And Gabriel said, automatically, as though he'd been asked whether he intended to wear clothes outside, "Yes, Your Grace, of course."

Then Darkwater's voice rose, composed, forceful, "Miss Felix?"

She looked up at him. She remembered the charade the two brothers had played for the benefit of Darkwater's mother, and now she wondered if the Dowager Duchess had yet realized there was more to the two of them than they'd been letting on? Or if she'd known it all along? Or if she had just now noticed that Seraphim's wastrel ways, his dissolute living were, at most, a mask upon his real activities? Or perhaps not, Nell thought. Seraphim wouldn't be the first man to be both heroic and a libertine. The two were so far from being opposed character traits that it wouldn't even be that unusual. She must remember that when dealing with the two brothers, no matter how much she admired their courage and mutual loyalty. Until she could find a way to make it back to her native world, she must play by Britannia rules, and by Britannia rules her reputation was both valuable and easily lost, so she must keep undeserving males at bay. "Your Grace?" she said, a trace of reserve in her look.

Nell saw Darkwater's glance slide sideways at the Dowager Duchess. So either the Duchess didn't know of the two brothers' full adventures or,

Darkwater thought, she didn't know and wished to protect her. She watched as he frowned slightly, then shook his head as though to himself. "There is absolutely no reason for me to ask you questions tonight," he said, "though I will have to ask you much. I beg you to hold yourself at our disposal. It's been a very long… few hours for me, since I woke up, and I don't believe I can stay awake and speak with any semblance of rationality for much longer. I would enjoin you not to teleport anywhere. We would prefer not to fish you out of the trout pond again." He glanced at his sister. "Caroline, if you would take Miss Felix to the blue room, on your floor, and arrange for it to be made up for her use. Miss Felix, I shall see you at breakfast."

Nell understood it as what it was: dismissal. She didn't try to argue it. She knew enough of this world to know that Dukes weren't argued with. She guessed even that she was being got rid of so they could speak privately, which was probably the point, too, of having Caroline leave with her. As the youngest female, she would be protected by her older brothers, though Nell guessed that not much escaped Miss Ainsling's shrewd eyes.

The girl opened her mouth and said, "But Michael–" and must have read something in Darkwater's look, because she stopped her protest and said, "Yes, Seraphim," and bobbed a curtsey, then waited while Nell did likewise.

Nell followed her down a series of broad passageways and down two grand staircases, before Miss Ainsling opened her mouth to say, "I despise my older brother. My older brothers I should say, since it's no use their pretending Gabriel isn't one, as his story made perfectly clear."

"Despise?" Nell said.

"Oh, yes. They are so stuffy and full of their own consequence. And the way they try to keep me from doing anything, simply because I'm a girl and young, is not to be borne. Do you have any brothers, Miss Felix?"

"No," Nell said, and then sighed. "That is, I don't know. I was adopted, you see." And then she thought in terms this world would understand. "I was a foundling, I mean. Abandoned. I don't know my true parentage."

Caroline Ainsling sighed. "Oh, that's lucky."

Nell must have made some sound – some gasp – in reply. She wasn't aware of it, but Caroline Ainsling laughed, a brief burble. "I mean, you must understand, that growing up as the Duke of Darkwater's daughter, and then sister, I was forever being judged by what they did and how they behaved. I understand papa was terribly shocking, and Seraphim is in a good way to being so. And then when Papa… that is, after Papa died, everyone looked at us with pity and wonder, and you know, we were the center of attention, and we could not shed it. I often wished to just go somewhere and hide, but of course, there was nowhere where I wasn't known. Michael is lucky because he can hide out with his machines, as it were, and abstract himself from the real world, but I…." She shrugged. "I shouldn't be speaking of these things. I am conscious of my good fortune in having a family and a position in society. And I should worry only about recovering Michael, safe and sound. I am a wretch. But so I've always been." And she sighed again, though there was a theatrical element to her chagrin.

But wretch or not, despite her young age, Caroline Ainsling was competent at mustering the staff to make the room assigned Nell very comfortable indeed. It wasn't – of course – by any means a room such as she'd have had on Earth. There was no bathroom attached. The water-closet – Caroline said, blushing slightly as she pointed – was down the hallway. There was a basin and a ewer of water from which it could be filled, the ewer perpetually renewed, Caroline said, with warm water. And the bed was made with clean, freshly aired sheets, and the bedspread was velvet and soft.

Nell suspected that, were it seen by daylight and not soft mage light, the room would look shabby. She remembered stories of Darkwater financial difficulties, and she remembered shabby fabric and worn furniture. But by mage light this room looked luxurious.

When all was ready and the servants retreated, Caroline said, "And Seraphim will want to talk to you, of course, which is a great bore. But I'll have the maid wake you with tea in time to get you down for breakfast in the morning." And then, as though realizing for the first time that Nell remained in her wet clothes and was wrapped in a blanket. "What fools men are. No one gave you time to change." A self-conscious smile. "But then, neither have I." She gestured towards the closet. "There is a night dress and robe in there which should fit you. And there are many dresses from which you can choose, come morning. Mama used to keep many in different sizes in all the rooms assigned to ladies. I understand when Papa was alive, we had many house parties, and ladies would slip into the pond or tear their flounces or… there you have it. One of them should fit you. If not, ring the bell and tell the maid what you need and it shall be found. A maid will be sent to dress your hair for breakfast."

Nell started suspecting the Darkwater house was far more formal than she was prepared to endure. Then she thought that, perforce, it must be. After all the man was a duke.

A moment later Caroline was gone, saying, "I shall have hot chocolate brought to you. You must be very uncomfortable in those soaked clothes. Do you need a maid to help you undress?"

Nell assured the girl she didn't and, as soon as Caroline was gone, undressed herself quickly and laid out her clothes by the fire to dry. They were, of course, ruined, but she could wear them to return to London, she supposed.

She had just dressed in a nightgown and dressing gown, both of which smelled faintly of mothball, when there was a scratching at the door. The hot chocolate, Nell thought, and called out, "Come in."

The door opened, but what came in had never been a maid. She saw him first in the mirror, very pale, his eyes half-lidded, a lingering smile on his pale lips. She turned around and said, "Antoine!"

Sarah A. Hoyt

Bump In The Night

"You should be asleep," Gabriel said. And Seraphim knew that it was true.

He sat on the bed that had been freshly made and changed. The smell of burnt feathers and the broth used to quench the fire was gone from the air.

And Gabriel, with bright efficiency, closed curtains and did other things. He probably thinks I can't see his magical work, Seraphim thought. That I don't see him erasing the greasy feel of dark magic in the air, effacing any residual bad smell and making the entire room feel safe and secure.

It should be safe and secure, too. Gabriel knew his arcana, and at any rate he'd as much power as Seraphim, if of a different bend. He could not secure the entire house, but surely, now that he was aware of danger, he could secure this room.

But something still nagged at Seraphim, a sense of something gone very wrong, something unwinding, something… something he couldn't quite pinpoint. Making a stab at his feeling of uneasiness, he told Gabriel, "I'm not sure I can sleep with Michael gone." And realized he was being uncharacteristically open. It was not normal of him to talk about his missing brother. To think about it, surely, and to mind his disappearance, of course, and to be restless in his longing to find Michael and save him. But not to talk about it. Seraphim had learned long before he became head of the family that too many people depended on him – as opposed to his volatile father – to allow him to show weakness or excessive concern. He managed to discipline his face and say, "I beg your pardon, Gabriel. I must be more tired than I realized."

Gabriel nodded. "What is amazing is that you're not dead," he said. "As for Michael, we'll find him," Gabriel looked, in turn, very tired. "There are certain things I can do. And my mother might know something I can use as leverage to discover what has become of Michael, but most of all…" He pressed his lips close. "There is such a thing as single combat, and if it's needed I will challenge my uncle." He closed his mouth again, his eyes flashing menace, and Seraphim was shocked to hear his own mouth pronounce, "Would you want it, Penny? The throne of Fairyland?"

Gabriel's chuckle surprised them both. At least, it surprised Seraphim, and it was followed by such a startled expression on Gabriel's face that it would have been funny under other circumstances. He smiled, after the surprise, and shook his head. "You were not attending," he said. "There is this thing you mor– That people who have never visited Fairyland or never lived there, and who have no elven blood in their veins, think, this idea that all Fairyland is enchantment and beauty and effortless magic. You know that fairy kind does not work the land, and does not make machines, and none of the contrivances of everyday life for a human, and you assume that it must be beautiful in the land of fairies, where no one ever need work, where nothing ever need decay, where no one ever grows old.

"To me it seemed like a cruel joke from the beginning, to hear it talked of as the isles of the blessed or the summer land. It is beautiful, perhaps, as a naked sword can be beautiful in the sunlight, but it is…." He hesitated. He stood by the window where he had just drawn the windows closed, and now he turned to face Seraphim, and Seraphim noted how harsh Gabriel's eyes looked, and how glittering, like the eyes of a man suffering from a fever. "I can't describe it, but if you can imagine a very sweet poison, or a very beautiful torturer's chamber, you'll be closer to understanding Fairyland than most who never experienced it. King? I'd rather live forever among humans, cast off. I'd rather be a beggar in London than a king in Fairyland."

He shook his head and took a deep breath, and Seraphim got the impression that he was disciplining his expression and his emotions to the realm of what was acceptable. "Rest, Seraphim. Tomorrow will be time enough to worry and to try to find Michael. And that will be hard enough if you're well. With you ill and weak, it is hopeless. And I know you know your duty to family and house too well to allow yourself the uncertainty and despair that will render you useless to them. Someone is trying to kill you – and possibly me. Fairyland is somehow enmeshed in these plans, and I forebear to guess on which side, though I doubt it's mine. And Michael is missing. I thought, at first, that all of this, including getting you trapped in the Betweener was just a side-result of our activities in other worlds. I thought someone, perhaps the Others that we've detected in those worlds, had tried to eliminate us and stop our bothersome rescues. But now I think it's much more than that – something so big that the borders of it seem to reach everywhere, and the tangle at its heart seems too huge and convoluted to make sense. Still there is sense in it, and we will find it."

He came over to the bed and reached for the mage light on Seraphim's bedside table. It extinguished at his touch, but then, as though thinking better of it, he brought it back to a dim glow, just enough to see the contours of the room. Seraphim didn't comment, but he had not kept his mage light on, even this low, since the age of ten at least. So why would Gabriel think Seraphim wished it on now? Or perhaps Gabriel was trying to assuage his own fears. He turned to Seraphim now, "And the woman, Miss Felix, is mixed in it somehow?"

"On whose side?" Seraphim asked.

Gabriel shrugged. "Well, she knew the man who tried to kill you," he said. "But perhaps we shouldn't hold that by itself against her. After all...." He shook his head. "I sense no harm from her. And no fairy magic, before you ask."

Seraphim wasn't going to ask, but now that Gabriel had said it, he couldn't get it out of his head. He looked at his half-brother as he turned and said, "Well, enough, now, I too must get my rest, and then we'll see what we can do tomorrow in the light of day. I've put wards in place. Call me if you need anything." And then he was gone, which was good because for a moment Seraphim had feared that Gabriel meant to sit up all night by his bed, ensuring that another attack didn't find Seraphim.

And I might very well not be able to sleep with him in the room, Seraphim thought, and felt guilty about it. He didn't remember when he'd first found out that Gabriel had elf blood. Not that first day surely, and not the second. He suspected he'd discovered it either by listening to servant gossip – years ago, before they'd come to know Gabriel well, all the servants had been a little afraid of him – or by Gabriel himself telling him. It felt as though Seraphim had always known it, though surely that wasn't true, since at the very first he'd thought Gabriel was his full brother, brought into the family as a gift to him. All of which showed Seraphim's understanding of human reproduction had been both lacking and fanciful. But all the same, he felt as if he'd always known that Gabriel was part fey.

And yet, in his heart, he'd never thought of Gabriel as anything but his brother. Oh, his valet, too, he supposed, particularly as they'd got older and had to learn to act their respective positions in public. But most of all his brother and his friend.

So what had changed, now, so that Gabriel's presence in his room while he slept would feel less reassuring than vaguely threatening? Was it all due to Seraphim's memory of the chant in inhuman words? Or was it...? Yes, it was Gabriel's sudden slip of tongue, his almost referring to "mortals" to signify those unlike him, his talking about you as opposed to himself. As though he didn't consider himself human. Wasn't he? Was Gabriel Penn some form of immortal?

And what did he mean by telling Seraphim – who'd never thought of it before – that Miss Felix didn't have the blood of fairykind? Seraphim didn't like that preemptive denial. Was it true? Or was it part of that "me" and "you" that Gabriel suddenly seemed to divide the world into?

Oh, Seraphim believed Gabriel about the throne of Fairyland. At least, he thought he did. There had been too much loathing in Gabriel's voice to be false. But would he feel the same way about a creature like himself, half human and lost in the world of humans? And was Miss Felix such? There was something odd about her magic, Avalon born but learned by utterly alien means not even normal in any civilized world.

Seraphim stifled a groan as he sat up in bed. He knew he was about to do something he'd regret. He regretted it already, in fact, and yet it must be done. His silver-headed cane was resting against the bedside table.

He grasped the head and rose with its aid. Getting on his feet was more difficult, but he managed it. Putting on his dressing gown was only difficult because he must hold onto the bed with one hand or the other.

One of the advantages of having known Gabriel since they were both very young is that Seraphim knew exactly where Gabriel would have placed the spell that told him if Seraphim tried to leave the room. And also that, having learned the earliest spells together, Seraphim knew Gabriel's magical habits and how to disarm his traps. At least, he was fairly sure that if an alarm went out to Gabriel telling him his magical alarm had been rendered ineffective, it would be delayed.

He walked down the hallway as fast as he could. He must go to Miss Felix. Somehow, it all hinged on her. The world had been rational before her path had crossed his.

Sarah A. Hoyt

Trapped

"Antoine," Seraphim heard, as he approached Miss Felix's room. He heard it clear as day, sounding through the closed door, and he stopped, swaying a little as he balanced on his feet and his silver headed cane, and looking at the door in puzzlement.

She'd said the same word – and used the same tone – when she'd seen the corpse. Seraphim wrinkled his forehead. Was she talking about the corpse?

The next words "Oh, Antoine, no," made him wonder if she was lamenting the corpse's death. Stupid if so. Well, perhaps he was not in the position to judge. He'd never been in love. At least, he didn't think so. There had been that cook's assistant when he was twelve, but he rather thought that his interest in her had been predicated more on the currants that she had it within her power to dispense than on her own, very young and charmless, person.

However, he'd seen in his time how men – and possibly women, too – could become utter fools over love, or what they believed was love. Even Gabriel Penn, one of the people Seraphim knew best in all the world, had thrown over his academic career and the possibility of making his independent way in magic or law for the sake of love.

But at that moment words echoed through the thick oak door that might be related to love, but were not related to mourning a dead lover, "No, Antoine. Stop. You cannot do that." The last words were a scream, and there was real terror behind them.

Seraphim didn't think he could use enough magic to unlock the door. Not in his present weakened condition. And he didn't think he could put his shoulder to the door, either. He opened his mouth to call for help, but – this far, in the guest area of the house – he doubted anyone would hear him. Oh, of course when they had a house party, they staffed this part of the house, but not when it was merely a guest, and an unexpected one at that. There would be a bell in the room, but–

He put a hand to the doorknob. To his surprise, it opened at his touch. He threw it open, and stepped into the room before he realized he was staring at the back of a man, who loomed large, standing up, and cornering Miss Felix, who, in the corner of the room, held her fingers crossed in a gesture of aversion.

"Step away from the lady," he yelled, even as he thought that corpses were not supposed to be wandering the house in the night. The man was dead. Seraphim had made sure of that. The magical bolt he'd thrown at the creature would have felled anyone with even a particle of magical talent. And the man had magical talent. Had to have it, else he'd not have been able to attack Seraphim.

So, this man, Antoine, had to be dead. And dead men didn't walk, except in the fantasies of sickly old maiden aunts. Or unless, of course, someone had used the resurrection spell. And that would mean someone in Seraphim's house. And it would mean, of course, that Antoine, whoever he was, would still be dead, just an animated corpse.

The idea made Seraphim's hair stand on end. The man? Corpse? Hadn't reacted to his shout. Animated corpses were notoriously hard to deter. As Seraphim watched, the creature took one step closer to Miss Felix, whose whole face had drained of color, and whose eyes looked too wide as she stared up, in sheer terror.

Seraphim grabbed the nearest object – one of the decorative vases atop a nearby table – and threw it with force at the creature's head. The creature started to turn and Miss Felix ducked under its arm, and ran towards Seraphim. "I'm so glad," she said. It was almost a scream. "Oh, thank you," as she grasped his arm and almost toppled him with the force of her terror. "He's dead, you know. Quick. Let us–"

Before she could say what he should let them do, the creature who'd been threatening her had spun around, and Seraphim grabbed for his cane, and took in breath, horrified. There was no doubt that Antoine was dead. He looked exactly the same as he had while lying on the pallet which the gardeners had carried up from near the lake. His face was pale and immobile, his lips drained of color. His eyes, as far as they were open, showed only a sliver of white. There was no expression to the slack features.

Seraphim pushed Miss Felix behind him, with barely a qualm as he remembered she seemed to have objections to being protected. "Stay," he said. "What was he– it doing to make you scream?"

"Chasing me," she said. She must be mad with terror, because she made no effort to assert her ability to care for herself. "Trying to corner me. He should not be alive. Why is he alive?"

"Someone must have made a resurrection spell," Seraphim said, as the creature shambled towards them. "Someone in the house?" The idea was alien and obscene.

"Stay behind me," he said. "I won't let it hurt you. You must remember he is not your friend." He had no idea how he would not let it hurt her, considering that he felt as weak as a newborn kitten. But, he thought, though it was true that only the man who'd done the resurrection spell could undo it, it was also true he should be able to set a small magical restraining spell and stop this creature from coming closer. Once enclosed in a magical cocoon, it would be unable to follow Helena Felix, and Seraphim should be able to question her about how this situation had come about. More, he should be able to find out who, in his house, had dared use an illegal spell to reawaken someone who'd tried to kill Seraphim. And if Seraphim couldn't, Gabriel could for sure.

The thought of the circumstances under which Gabriel had last been involved with resurrection spells made Seraphim hesitate, but he shook his head at his own foolishness. Gabriel Penn might have been a fool for love. Gabriel Penn might be an idiot when it came to loyalty and friendship, even, but the one thing Gabriel Penn wasn't was a traitor to Seraphim. Half elf, perhaps, capable of his own designs and his opinions that would shock the polite world, almost certainly. Too smart for his own good, assuredly. But Gabriel Penn would not betray the Darkwaters.

The creature shambled towards them, and Seraphim put out his left arm, to keep Helena Felix behind him, while he raised his right hand that held the silver-tipped cane, and, using it as a magical wand to concentrate his power, said the first words of the cocoon spell, "Miras, enax–"

He got no further. The animated corpse facing him stopped at the first sound of the words, the first feeling of the power leaving Seraphim's body and flying forth. But that was only in the first second. A breath later, there was a feeling as though a line that linked Seraphim to the corpse had gone taut.

Later, neither he nor Helena could decide exactly what had happened. Each of them had different accounts, and both accounts were impossible. Seraphim remembered – he doubted he could ever forget – the thing's eyes opening fully and sparkling as though there were a fire lit behind them. Its mouth too opened, wide, wide, wider, impossibly wide, till they'd fallen into it, he and Helena both.

And that made no sense at all, because in his memory, either the corpse had grown very large, or they'd grown very small, both of which were impossible, and then he and Helena had stumbled together, falling into that dark vortex of a mouth, falling, falling, head over heels, like flying leaves or tumbling sticks, falling, falling, falling, falling, in darkness and cold.

He was so shocked it took him a moment to recognize the Betweener, and by that time they were past it, and dropped, head-first, into light and music and sound flailing and screaming.

As they landed on the ground, hard, he was aware of people all around and something ahead of him. He blinked… an elephant?

It was all the time he had before someone screamed, pointing at them. He was not sure where they were, or what had happened, but he knew one thing: in nine out of ten worlds, what they'd just done, falling out of seeming nothing, in a public place, was enough to warrant their death.

Barely able to stand, feeling as though the entire world had crashed in on him, he stood. His mind in turmoil, not knowing where they were or how they come to be there, he reached back and grabbed Helena Felix's wrist, and pulled.

He ran away from the elephant, away from the press of people, and into the first dark space his blurry and stinging eyes could find.

Sarah A. Hoyt

In Darkness And Despair

Gabriel Penn sat up at the feeling that his spell had been disrupted. He'd left an alarm spell in Seraphim's room, and it was supposed to trip and wake him if Seraphim left the room.

What he felt instead was the sensation that the spell had been tampered with, and that muffled and distant. Which meant whoever had interfered with his magic alarms had done it in such a way, and with such sure knowledge of how Gabriel set spells, that he could disable it and delay Gabriel's sensing it had been disabled.

Because Gabriel's magic was an amalgam of the human magic he'd learned in Cambridge and that elven magic he'd learned when very young at his mother's knee, only one of the human magicians in this house knew it well enough to disable it and to muffle the realization it had been disabled: Seraphim.

Cursing under his breath, Gabriel reached for his dressing gown, which he'd flung across the foot of the bed before laying down. He slipped it on by touch, then said the one word that brought the mage light on the bedside to full glow. It illuminated the full extent of his room – a tiny servant's room containing a narrow single bed, the trunk he'd taken to Cambridge and brought back again, and which contained all of his clothes, and a desk, pushed up against the wall and piled high with papers. From the mess on the desk he extracted his magic wand. He rarely used it these days, but he had a bad feeling over this whole situation – a presentiment of disaster, he thought, and he didn't like these feelings. Given his origin and avocation, they tended to be all too accurate.

Holding the mage light – fully lit – in one hand, and the magic wand in the other, he opened his room door and, not bothering to close it, pelted down the hallway and up the stairs towards Seraphim's room. He muttered under his breath, continuously, a word that would have shocked the ladies of the house very much if they'd heard it. It would to be honest, probably have shocked them, too, to see him running down the hallway in an ill-tied dressing gown over his underwear, which was all he'd worn to bed.

It didn't matter. He'd rather shock them, or the female servants, than have the feeling of dread in his mind be justified.

He ran up the stairs, two steps at a time, and down the hallway. But Seraphim's room was empty, the door open, the magic spell broken.

Gabriel stood in the hallway, his heart beating so loudly he could barely hear himself think. And then he felt it, coming from the guest wing, where they'd lodged Miss Felix: magic. A big discharge of magic.

He started running again, mindlessly, pleading with some nameless divinity to let him be wrong. Just this once, please let him be wrong.

But before he reached the room, he knew he wasn't. He felt the magical discharge of a trap going off, the pull and suck of a vortex opening between worlds – a portal not activated by the people thrown into it.

And turning a corner, he saw Seraphim and Helena Felix being sucked into a maw of darkness.

As the magical fog and darkness dissipated, he realized what was left behind was perhaps even worse than having lost your legitimate brother, the duke, to a magical trap that had taken him who knew where.

In the middle of the guest room stood an animated corpse.

"Shit," Gabriel Penn said, loudly and emphatically. And raised his wand.

Sarah A. Hoyt

A Strange Land

It was an alley, Nell realized, as she took a deep breath. An alley bordered by tall brick buildings, which could be an alley anywhere in Avalon, or – for that matter – in any large city on Earth. But the structure at the end of the alley was not something she'd ever seen either in Avalon or on Earth. It was purple – bright purple – and it looked like it was made of glass. It was also roughly egg-shaped, with a hole on top and an odd sheen to it.

Her first instinct was to think of it as a dumpster, but if so, these people kept the cleanest dumpsters in any of the worlds she'd visited while out with Antoine.

And on the heels of that, she tried to think of all the worlds she'd visited with Antoine. And not to think of anything else – anything else – relating to Antoine. Like, for instance, she truly didn't want to think of his livid skin, his staring eyes, his … no, she wouldn't think of it. Or of what type of horrible spell could make a man walk and talk when he was – when he should be – by all rights dead. Much less what kind of trap this might be.

At any rate, speaking of livid skin and staring eyes, she found that Seraphim too could fit that description. He was wearing a dressing gown. A very pretty dressing gown, she thought, though she suspected on Earth most men would be worried about wearing something that bright and silky. Never mind. She knew Britannia tastes, and for Britannia tastes, it was a very refined dressing gown indeed. He was also barefoot. And he was clutching the loveliest black-cane-with-dragon-head.

This looked completely out of place in what seemed to be a largish city in the middle of the day, but she put that out of her mind, because, really, how did she know what people here wore? One of the worlds she'd visited with Antoine, before coming to Avalon, had been apparently a nudist colony. Puzzling, since England at that time was really no warmer than England at any other time. And in another they seemed to wear vast rolls of shag carpet. For all she knew, in this world, men dressed for business in ankle-length white shirts topped with resplendent silk dressing gowns, and always carried canes.

What worried her more was the fact that Seraphim looked distinctly unwell. *No, really, let me think about this. In the space of a few days, he got wounded, then he got attacked with a mage gun, and almost died, or came so close to it that the resurrection spell had to be used. And then, not only did Antoine… Antoine…* She took a deep breath. *Not only did someone attack him again, but he had to perform magic to defend himself. And to defend me. And then he was dropped head-first into a weird world. He should look completely chipper and well!*

"Your Grace," she said. "Your Grace?" His eyes were trying to close, and she could hear noise coming from the mouth of the alley, a long way away. The kind of noise people would make if they were looking for two oddly dressed people who might be refugees from a mental hospital, and possibly dangerous.

"Seraphim?" This got her a little more response than *Your Grace* in that his eyes fluttered and he could be seen to visibly make an effort to wake up. But he sagged against the brick wall and made an odd sound like a sigh. And from the entrance of the alley came voices in an oddly accented English.

No accent could disguise the fact that someone said, "Is this where the witches went?" nor the tone in which someone else answered that perhaps they should call the police.

So, they were looking for witches, presumably the two of them. And Nell didn't think it was to wish them luck and give them a box of chocolates. If she had to guess this was one of those worlds where witchcraft was forbidden for whatever reason.

She and Antoine hadn't actually come across many of those. Possibly because Antoine knew the general lay of the land and what kind of worlds would be best to avoid. They'd come across worlds like Earth, where magic was disbelieved, ignored, or not used, but not too many worlds where it was forbidden, much less under penalty of death. And when they came across one by accident, Antoine got them out very quickly. But Nell had heard of them, aplenty, particularly in Britannia literature.

It seemed that the policy that Britannia must not interfere in other worlds, to the point of letting witches and wizards be killed in other worlds, was new. Or at least, literature from half a century or so ago talked about lots of rescues and derring-do in other worlds.

Seraphim Darkwater sagged further and started sliding down the wall, and she realized he had lost consciousness. At the same time, from the mouth of the alley came a voice saying, "Here, Gnarr, I'm glad you got the authorities. We'll now get those witches, right and proper."

She put out an arm to hold the Duke up and realized that the man was, in fact, very heavy, and that she wasn't going to be able to carry him. Hell, she couldn't even drag him behind the shiny purple thing. The best she could do was magic them somewhere. But where? And what if she got them somewhere worse?

There would be no time to open a magic portal to take them out of this world. Besides, she had a strong feeling whatever the magic used to bring them here had been designed so they couldn't return. She still made a halfhearted feel in that direction, but the Betweener felt as though shut tight.

In a panic, as voices came closer, she thought she should simply use the coordinates of her room in Britannia and take them to the equivalent location in this world. From there, she could take them elsewhere. How much worse could it get?

Blindly, her eyes closed, her arm aching from supporting the Duke, she heard someone say "Come on out and give yourself up and it will go–"

And she thought of the coordinates and pushed.

Magic flared like fire all around her. The purple thing at the back of the alley seemed to explode. And then she was falling head first into a body of water.

She had time to think, *Not again*, before she kicked up with her legs and came to the surface for a deep breath, which was when she realized that Seraphim hadn't surfaced.

Diving back down, she saw the bright dressing gown and dove for it. Grabbing it by the back, she dragged him to the surface, thanking the buoyancy in the water that allowed her to tow a weight considerably greater than her own.

Even so, and even after she managed to get his head above water and, hopefully, breathing, it took all her strength and concentration to drag him to the edge of the water. Fortunately it was not very far, or she'd never have been able to do it. Even more fortunately, the river – she didn't remember when she'd determined it was a river, but she was sure of it by the time she was pulling Seraphim out of the water – had a gradual, soft-sand bank, and she could drag Seraphim up it by stages by sitting on the sand and holding him up and pulling as she shuffled up the beach. Had the river had steep banks or even rocky ones, the Duke would have drowned.

As it was, when she dragged him all the way out, so only his feet remained in the water, and his body lay stretched on the sand like a great beached whale, she wasn't so sure he hadn't drowned. She was very tired, granted, and he was very wet, and also – she thought – very ill. He'd been very ill even before falling into the water. But shouldn't his chest be moving?

She felt the side of his neck, looking for a pulse, and couldn't find it.

His lips had a faint bluish tinge. She put her hand on top of his mouth and couldn't feel him breathing. A hand pushed between the folds of his dressing gown felt no hint of a heartbeat.

Her mage sight, brought to bear with much difficulty, seemed to show a faint glow of life and magic around him, but that often subsisted at that level for a few moments after the person had stopped breathing.

If I had a mirror, she thought. *I would be able to tell if he was breathing.*

Her own laughter startled her, as she thought that if she had the right machines, she would be able to tell if he had brain activity too.

She could use the resurrection spell. Arguably she should. But what if he were already dead? She risked making him like Antoine.

The tear that fell on his already-soaked hair surprised her because she didn't realize she was crying. She put up a hasty hand to wipe at her eyes, and in that moment, his eyes fluttered open and he looked at her in shock. He coughed, once, twice, then blinked. "Why…." He cleared his throat. "Why are you crying?"

"I'm not crying," she said, hearing the tears in her own voice and not sure why she was crying, unless it was tiredness and relief. And then she added, as justification, "You were dead."

"I was?" he said, surprised. And blinked again. "I don't think I was? Unless, of course…." He took a deep breath. "No. This is not the result of a resurrection spell. I'm not a reanimated corpse." He took a deep breath. "No. I see what it is. I… I went to your room, and then…" His eyes widened so far they looked like they were going to split. "There was a trap," he said. "He was probably set to reanimate after death, and there was a transport spell. Humans can't make that kind of spell, not at a distance. It must be fairy magic and that— that means— there was a song full of unclean magic— but that would mean fairyland must be—"

"Yes," she said, soberly. "That much I'd already realized."

He dragged himself up to sitting, though he swayed a little with fatigue. He looked at her as if she were a long way away and he had trouble focusing at that distance. "I drank an awful lot of that river," he said.

"I know," she said. "I dragged you out as best I could."

"Thank you," he said, but his expression remained distant, as if trying to think through a very difficult problem. "Miss Felix, please tell me that there wasn't a magic detector at the end of that alley."

"Magic–"

"Vast purple crystal egg? Detects magic being performed in the vicinity and imprints the pattern so the authorities can look for it."

She nodded, dumbly, and his eyes widened more, which shouldn't have been possible. Then he said something that sounded like "Muffin," which apparently was a bad swear word, because he immediately looked abashed, "I apologize. I'm sorry. I should never– Only… It's the world of the priest-kings, see. The Priest Kings of Okkar."

"Is that bad?" she asked. "Do they sacrifice magic users as they do in Pyramids?"

"No," Seraphim said. "They only execute anyone with magic who isn't related to the royal family."

Sarah A. Hoyt

After The Bird Has Flown

There was no worse feeling, Gabriel thought, than arriving to close the door of the birdcage a moment after the bird had flown.

Not that Seraphim and Miss Felix were birds, or that the odd portal – was it a portal? – to another world was a cage door. For one, Gabriel was almost sure that neither Seraphim nor Miss Felix had meant to go through it and into– where?

And then, in that split second after he realized he'd lost track of his legitimate brother, the head of his house on whom, in fact, his entire family depended, he realized that he had a bigger problem.

The corpse was shambling towards him.

He'd had some experience in Cambridge with reanimated corpses. He wouldn't say that was what had put paid to his one and only love affair, but it had certainly exploded the whole thing into the public eye and had forced him to leave Cambridge in disgrace.

Normally, the only way to kill a reanimated corpse was to get the person who'd first animated it to help. That had been the problem, really, back then, though perhaps Gabriel hadn't dealt with it as sanely as he should have.

But now, ten years later, he still had no idea how to deal with it. You couldn't put an animated corpse down without the collaboration and the help of the person who'd reanimated it. Who could have animated Antoine? It had to be someone in the house? But who would have done it and set him up as a magical trap to send Seraphim and Miss Felix– Where?

He backed up as the corpse shambled forward. He raised his wand.

And then, as if a switch had been turned, Antoine's corpse closed its gaping mouth, swayed, and fell, forward, with all the grace of a sack full of sand.

Gabriel realized he was shaking and sweating, standing alone in the empty guest room, staring at a dead man and wondering where Seraphim and Miss Felix were. Always, that question came back. What had happened to Seraphim and Miss Felix? And what would happen now?

Gabriel backed up, until his back hit the wall of the hallway, opposite the door to the room. For a moment – for just a moment – he thought he'd go back in and pull the bell pull and call for help. But what help could he call? The Duchess? Already fearing for the life of her younger son, and perhaps for his sanity, lost in Fairyland, what could she do about the loss of her older son? Caroline? Caroline was a mere child. Oh, precocious beyond her years, but how much help could she be? Worse, how much help should he ask of her. They were very likely to be dealing with forbidden magics here, before it was all said and done. Travel to other lands, for sure, and probably meddling in their affairs too.

Worse, he realized, with a feeling as though a leaden weight had settled on his stomach, some people – perhaps even the duchess, almost certainly not Caroline, but surely every servant in the house – would suspect him of having done this. The magic was so odd, the animation of the cadaver, the portal. Fairy magic, they'd say. They'd detect fairy magic and they'd talk about him behind their hands. He'd once again meet the odd looks that focused on him for a moment, then slid sideways, and know, know as he did in his first days in the house, that behind their backs they held their fingers crossed, an impotent attempt at stopping the evil magic he had no intent of using.

What could he do? He couldn't leave Seraphim lost. Or Michael. Or possibly even Miss Felix, if she was innocent in this. His mouth went dry in a panic, and at first he thought the loud banging was coming from his head or from his heart.

Then he realized it was coming from the front door. Someone was pounding on the door, loudly, and shouting something. Sounds of running feet echoed through the house, and distantly, Gabriel heard the front door open.

There were shouting voices, one of them almost for sure the butler's. Here, in the guest wing, where every room was unoccupied, there was a great silence, but the shouting voices continued, and now there were many people coming in, at least if Gabriel was interpreting the voices correctly.

Gabriel was the only son left in the house, even if he wasn't a son of the house, properly speaking. He must protect the dowager and Caroline.

He ran towards the noise, but before he got there, met with a maid running in the other direction, towards the family wing. He stopped her, daring – an unwonted familiarity in him – to put his hand out to her shoulder. He couldn't remember her name, though he was sure he knew it. Bessie or Annie or something like that. All their names swirled in his head, and what came out of his mouth was, "Please, you must tell me. Please, what is happening?"

If she was shocked at being touched, she didn't show it, though she did drop back and drop him a courtesy. It seemed to be unspoken etiquette of the house to treat Gabriel as an upper servant and to give him the deference they gave the butler and the house keeper, just short of the deference they gave Seraphim or the family. "Sir," she said. "Sir. It is the constables. And the king's magical police, and they want His Grace. They said as he done murder, and the murdered man, killed by magic, is in the house!" Her mouth worked and no words came out. "Sir. And they say as you helped, sir."

There are moments when a man's life hangs on a thin thread of decision. Gabriel was the only man left in the house, the only male descendant of the late Duke of Darkwater, who might protect the women in family. But he was also half fey, easy to paint as a villain in this tale that had spun itself out to ensnare his family. Not that he minded, or not too much. He'd grown used to it, if not easy with it, over the years of living amid the mortals. But in this case, what he was, who he was, could be used to taint all of the Darkwaters.

If they were going to argue that Seraphim had killed this stranger for no good reason, they'd need to get the closest witness out of the way, and that was Gabriel. Who also happened to be the only witness to the fact that Seraphim had disappeared against his will. And Gabriel would, on top of all, make people mistrust the family that had harbored him – his family. After all, people that took a half-fairy child into their home would surely do any sort of stupid thing, any sort of criminal thing.

Gabriel swallowed hard. He put his hand out again, and this time held onto the girl's arm. Given how leery he was, usually, of touching anyone at all in the house, it should have alarmed her but it didn't. Instead, Gabriel found her gaze fixed intently on him with a sort of puzzling expression. Was it hope? Did he add to all his sins the broken hearts of housemaids? He removed his hand slowly, and raked back his hair which somehow had fallen forward over his face, "Listen, Annie," he said, and in that moment knew her name was Bessie, but didn't want to correct it. "Tell Her Grac– No, tell Caroline, Miss Ainsling, that I've gone to… to avoid the… my presence can only hurt them. Tell Caroline that Seraphim was pulled into another world, and I'm going in search of him and find him or die trying. Tell her and then…," he thought, and suddenly realized that for the girl's protection itself, there was only thing he could do. He put magic behind his order, to make both parts a compulsion. "Tell her immediately, and then forget it. It never happened. You never saw me."

He let the girl go, and watched her walk – no, run – towards the family wing in that half-mechanical gait of people under a compulsion. And then he ran the other way, towards his room. He ran faster than he'd ever run. He ran as though the fires of hell were burning at his heels, the hounds of hell pursuing him.

He could hear the voices of strangers in the house. He could hear the tones as the butler tried to keep them from coming in further. He'd have to use a spell to leave. That would leave a signature, but never mind. He'd go to London, where the magical trace was harder to find, and then he'd transport from there. And then he'd stop long enough to figure out how to find Seraphim.

Blindly, he pulled his luggage from under the bed. Blindly, he threw clothes into it, both from the trunk at the foot of his bed, and from the peg on the wall. There were steps in the corridor, and his mouth was dry, and his heart was pounding. And now there was a knock at his door, and a voice calling out, "Mr. Penn?"

And the voice was not one he knew.

Without looking, without turning, he lifted his hand and threw a lock spell at the door. It wouldn't hold any sort of constabulary for long. Not if they had a magician with them, which they would. Surely, they would. But it would slow them down.

He looked down at himself and realized he was still wearing only his underwear and his dressing gown. His feet were bare. There was nothing he could do about that, and it was almost funny that he should leave this house as he had entered, grossly underdressed for the weather.

He lifted his hand and with a pass, opened a portal, and found himself, between one breath and the next, in the Betweener, and then, suddenly, again, in an alley in London. Nearby, a baby cried. Somewhere, farther off, a woman laughed, a full-throated laugh that reminded Gabriel of his mother.

London was a criss-cross of magical comings and goings, and it would take them a while to track him here, but how long was a while?

In his mind, the events of the last day had assembled. Someone had tricked Seraphim into committing what could be construed as a crime, and then they'd taken him away, so he couldn't demand king's justice. They'd taken Michael too. And now he, himself, had had to leave. Why? What did they want? Access to the house? Possibly. Or just to destroy the family? Possibly also.

But whatever they wanted, and whoever they were – perhaps the shadowy cabal he and Seraphim had encountered in distant worlds and nicknamed The Others – they would not be stopped by something like the difficulty of tracing someone in London. They'd barely be slowed down.

In his mind's eye, he saw his room's door smashed down. Now they'd be tracing him… now.

There was only one place he could go, only one place he could hide. Marlon, curse him, had a tight enough lock on his lodgings that in ten years of living outside the law, no one had caught him, nothing had emerged about his whereabouts.

And Marlon, curse him, would take Gabriel in, though the price would be more than Gabriel would ever pay for himself, by his own choice. But to save the only family he'd ever known? There was no price too high.

He lifted his hand and, loathing himself, loathing his necessity, opened a portal to secret coordinates he'd promised himself he'd never use.

Sarah A. Hoyt

A Rude Wakening

Barbara Ainsling, Dowager Duchess of Darkwater, woke up without a sound. Before she woke, she knew that something was wrong – very wrong.

Normally she woke with her personal abigail, Jane, bringing in a tea tray. It had become a ritual, and the Duchess's first consciousness came with the sound of the tray being set on the little table by the bed, followed by the sound of calm footsteps across the floor, which in turn was followed by the sound of curtains being drawn back. Then light filtered gently past the sheers and the Duchess woke, composed and ready for her day.

Today there was no light, no tray, no calm footsteps. Instead she had awakened to the sound of the door opening, then closing, stealthily. It was followed by the sound of someone panting rapidly, as though in a panic.

Barbara Ainsling had for many years been a Duchess, surrounded by both comfort and propriety, hemmed in by the precise politeness of her position. But she'd not forgotten her years as a child in a vast wooded estate in Derbyshire; her years of climbing trees and fishing with the tenant sons.

The much younger daughter of a large family, whose next youngest child was a full ten years her senior, she had learned to make her entertainment and had bid fair to become a hoyden, if not a tomboy, till the lure of her mirror, and how well she looked in ball gowns, and the effect she had on boys, had called her to more feminine pursuits and thence to marriage.

But even at forty-four, inside she often felt she was still that same wild girl she'd been. So she sat up, instantly alert, and reached, silently, for anything she could use as a weapon without moving much. Unfortunately the only thing she could reach without getting up was the coverlet over herself. It would have to do. It was Barbara's experience that very few people could be nefarious while trying to extricate themselves from a blanket.

She clutched at the coverlet with both hands. And then the person panting in the shadows gulped and said, "Milady?"

Barbara let go of the blanket, and, half careless, made the gesture for the spell that brought the mage light at her bedside to full power. By its unblinking light, she saw Jane by the closed door, both hands clutching at her apron, which, by the look of it, had been twisted between those clutching hands.

Jane was a most superior servant, abigail to milady and about Barbara's age. In fact, she'd been helping Barbara dress and arrange her hair since they'd both been fifteen or sixteen. Barbara trusted her so much that she had disdained to hire a dresser, as most ladies of her class were wont to do. No, for Barbara's purpose, Jane must do very well. And normally she did. And normally, on demeanor alone, anyone looking at two women would easily take Jane for the Duchess.

But now Jane looked discomposed and ill, her face blotchy as from crying, her hair disarranged. She had dressed herself, and even put on her largely decorative lace apron. But she hadn't combed her hair, and her cap was altogether missing. "Milady," she said again, and gasped, her eyes full of tears.

"What is it Jane?" Barbara said, trying not to sound as worried as she felt. The truth was that she'd never seen Jane this discomposed.

Jane swallowed again, audibly, and let air out, slowly, between her half-parted lips. "There are constables in the house, Your Grace, and men from His Majesty's magical enforcement force." She swallowed again, convulsively.

Barbara's mind flew to Seraphim and, with only a little delay, to Gabriel, to Michael missing, and thence, in a moment, to her husband's suicide, to that horrible moment they'd found him in his dressing room, his gun fallen from his nerveless right hand, his pocket watch clutched convulsively in his left, so hard that it had taken a wait for rigor mortis to pass and his fingers to let go. It clutched, aimlessly, at shadows and hints: at her sense that her husband had always been doing something far more complex, far worse, in a way, than mere affairs and infidelities – even if he'd done that too. And lately Seraphim had been secretive and Gabriel had, of course, been helping. And they were involved in something. And there had been a man killed by magic. And Michael was missing, perhaps kidnaped into Fairyland.

Oh, those boys, she thought, those careless boys, and surprised herself with thinking it, as though Gabriel and Seraphim, and perhaps Michael too, were about five and heedless, and not grown and almost grown men and playing with something very dangerous indeed.

She became aware that Jane was speaking, in between gulps and sobs. "It is the man as was killed, madam, you see. They say as His Grace done him in on purpose because he was the lover of that woman as– Well, they say His Grace done it for jealousy and not in self-defense, and they are– " she swallowed. "They're demanding to take His Grace before king's justice, and Mr. Penn with him, as well as Lord Michael."

"I see," Jane said. "And His Grace says?"

"Well, that's just it, Your Grace, as they say he's run and that's a sign of guilt."

"Run? Seraphim?" Barbara said. If there was one thing she couldn't believe Seraphim would do was run. Charge ahead foolishly, perhaps. But run, never.

Jane nodded. "I don't see how it can be, Your Grace, but they said as he and the young– the young person, Miss Felix, transported from the room where she– that they transported to another world, Your Grace, as is forbidden under the law."

Yes, Barbara could see how that story would assemble itself, in the servants' minds, and in the minds of the magistrates too. They'd think, of course, that Seraphim had been in the young woman's room, when he heard the constables come in, and had transported them both to somewhere safe. And she could well imagine the construction placed on his being in that room, in the night.

Barbara didn't believe it. Not for a minute. Oh, it was possible that Seraphim was romantically involved with the woman, though Gabriel had claimed she was his fiancée. For that matter the strange liaisons that men engaged in with a certain sort of woman were not something she wanted to probe. But something sounded very wrong in all of this, including the fact that Barbara didn't get the feeling Miss Felix was that sort of woman. Or not precisely. For that matter, though no one had ever told her exactly, she didn't think Gabriel Penn was the sort of man to be engaged to any woman.

The whole thing felt wrong, a sort of scene concocted to deceive the eye, but not very deeply thought out at all. A story to deceive onlookers. She heard herself say, hollowly, "Something is very wrong with that story."

Jane started, then nodded. "Yes. I thought so too," she said, slowly. "Because it doesn't explain how the corpse got to Miss Felix's room."

"The corpse?"

"The corpse of the man as the gardeners say attacked His Grace, the one His Grace … killed."

"Ah. Yes. He was in Miss Felix's room? No. That is not explained at all. I don't think that anyone would carry him there, would they?"

"No, miss. And he looked like he had fallen there, after walking, you know."

Barbara didn't know, but she could well imagine. "I see. And what does Gabriel say about all this?" Because if anyone knew anything, it would be Gabriel. Gabriel was and had always been Seraphim's willing accomplice, his faithful dog's body. Seraphim wouldn't do or know anything that Gabriel either didn't know or couldn't guess.

A deep breath from Jane foretold that the news there wouldn't be good, and Barbara felt a stab of foreboding. "He's missing, isn't he? Mr. Penn?"

"He's …" Jane swallowed. "Emma, you know, the kitchen help, well, her room is directly above Miss Felix's guest room, and she says that she heard him… that she heard him say something very loudly from… from the area of Miss Felix's room, just as the pounding first came on the door."

"What did he say?" Her Ladyship asked.

Jane colored and opened her mouth. "I wouldn't like to repeat it."

"I'm sure I've heard the word, whatever it is."

"Well… he said … *shit*."

"I see." She didn't in fact, see. She couldn't imagine Gabriel shouting anything of the kind loudly enough to be heard through the floor into the upper story. But she was sure Jane wouldn't repeat it, unless she were certain it had been correct and properly heard. "And what does he say to that?"

"No one can find him," Jane said. "His room… His traveling bag is missing, and his personal effects, at least some of them, and–"

"And?"

"Well, then, Mr. Penn locked the door on his room and… transported out. They are trying to sense where he went, but they haven't traced him beyond London and– " Jane stopped. She looked like she was holding back tears by an effort of will.

So. Seraphim was gone. And Gabriel had followed. She didn't know how or why Seraphim had left, but she was sure it wasn't because he had run. Not in any sense of the word. The only reason she could imagine for Seraphim to have left, at all, would be if his staying could only make things worse for his family. In that, he was like his father, who, despite his multiple sins against matrimony, had always tried to protect his family and his estates.

And Gabriel too, for all his sins, would never have left – would certainly not have left without leaving them word of where he was going –

without good reason. The reason being that his staying would make things worse for all of them.

Michael was missing.

That left the family house, the servants, and Barbara and Caroline to look after themselves.

Without Barbara knowing, the decision had made itself in the back of Barbara's mind. The constables and for that matter the magical enforcers would do nothing to the servants and the house. Nothing, that is, beyond ransacking the house and having the servants keep on here, as they were. At worst, if judgment were brought in against Seraphim, the house would be confiscated. The risk was to Seraphim, who would be beheaded, but not to the house or the servants. She shook her head. That part she didn't need to worry about. So, what was there to fear?

The only thing she could think of was that she and Caroline could be used as bait to bring Seraphim and Gabriel back. And to lead to their being executed. No. That couldn't be allowed. And so Barbara Ainsling, who, like her son, would not run from danger to herself, must put herself and Caroline away from danger.

She'd go to her brother. No one would dare penetrate her brother's estate in Derbyshire. "Jane, can you go to the stables? Are there… are there law… people, there?"

Jane's eyes grew large. "As of yet, no, Your Grace."

"Very well. Then go there, and wake Johnson, in secret if possible. Ask him to get the small traveling carriage together, with the match black horses, and to arrange for escorts for me and Miss Ainsling. As quietly as possible. Tell him… yes, tell him to get the carriage ready in the alley outside the walls. Without, if at all possible, arousing our… ah… illustrious visitors. Tell him – in the greatest secrecy of course – that Miss Ainsling and I will be going to Lord Hartwitt's in Derbyshire. Can you, Jane, and keep it quiet?"

"Well, of course," Jane said, and bobbed a courtesy. "What shall I pack for you?"

"Nothing. I shall travel as swiftly and as quietly as possible, and I'll acquire whatever I need on the way."

Jane blinked. "Oh, no. I must go with you. And, Your Grace– "

"No, Jane. This is likely to be very dangerous. I can't allow you to risk yourself. Go, and tell Johnson to have the carriage ready. I'll take a carpetbag with my absolute necessities." As she spoke, Barbara got up and started to brush her still mostly black hair and pin it back.

"Your Grace!" Jane said again, in a tone of shock. But Barbara was Barbara again and not just the Duchess of Darkwater. For years now, since she'd married the Duke, the bright, sparkling woman who'd been Barbara Hartwitt had been subsumed in the Duchess, the mother, the wife. Now....

"Leave it, Jane," she said. "I can take care of myself. And send Miss Ainsling to me, as quietly as you can."

"Your Grace," Jane said again, in the tone of one who doesn't quite believe what she's being told to do. She apparently, from her expression, could also not quite believe what she was seeing, as Barbara selected her most plain and sturdiest traveling dress and, with nimble fingers and hands still quite capable of reaching behind herself, started lacing herself into it.

"Now, Jane, there's not a minute to be lost, if we're to save something from this debacle. And should the magical... ah... gentlemen ask, you know nothing of where I went."

Jane moved then, bobbing another courtesy, and heading for the door. Before she opened it, though, the door opened, and Caroline came in, fully dressed. "Mama," she said. "Oh, I'm so glad you're up."

Jane hesitated, looking at Barbara, but at Barbara's quiet, "Go then, Jane, take care of that matter," she nodded and scurried out.

Caroline closed the door behind Jane, and turned to Barbara. "We must leave, Mama. And quickly too. You see, Gabriel sent me a message through a compulsion on a maid, and he said that Seraphim was pulled by a trap into another world, and Gabriel himself was leaving as fast as possible, so he couldn't be used to bring an accusation of magic malfeasance against Seraphim."

"Yes," Barbara said, gratified she'd reconstructed the situation properly and trying not to think of the cold feeling in the pit of her stomach, because of what the boys were risking, and because of the trouble coming down on all of them. "I realize that. And I thought it best if we left too, and could not be used against them. I've given orders to have the small traveling carriage prepared, in secret, so that you and I can go to my brother, in Derbyshire."

Caroline's eyes widened. "Mama! You must be all about in your head." And then, realizing how improper what she'd said was. "I beg your pardon, but you see it must be so. How can you think we'll escape in the carriage? Mama! They'll find the carriage easy enough. All they have to do is send a fast rider. And no matter how much you tell Jane or the coachman to keep the secret, they have magical compulsion and the right to use it by royal decree, and they– "

"Caroline, credit me with some thought. We shall leave, in the carriage, and then transport from it while it's moving. They will not be able to trace the transport spell, unless they can pinpoint exactly the place in space from which we transported."

"To your brother's? In Derbyshire?"

"No, of course not. I confess that was my first thought, but then I realized…"

"You realized?"

"While we might be safe at my brother's, it's too much like running away, and the Ainslings do not run away. It's obvious someone is trying to entrap your brother– your brothers, and bring this house down. And Fairyland is involved, which is …. We must find Michael. And Seraphim. And there's only one person who can help us."

She looked at Caroline's blank expression and almost laughed. "We shall go pay a visit to Mrs. Penn," she said. And by way of explanation, "Gabriel's mother."

Sarah A. Hoyt

A World of Hurt

They were in deep trouble. That much Seraphim knew, and he wished he didn't feel as though he'd very much like to sleep for the next several months.

He felt weak and vaguely ill, not to mention nauseated, as though he'd swallowed a good portion of this particular alternate of the Thames, which might not have as many houses around it, but probably was none too wholesome to drink. And they were going to be pursued. There was not the slightest doubt about that.

As though cued by his thoughts, he sensed magic groping towards them, the feel and gentle probing of the magical police in this world – he didn't know much about them, but he and Gabriel had once had a brush with them, and – he seemed to remember they were called the Imperial Pures. He allowed himself to mutter a word between his teeth and was amused to see Miss Felix's eyes open very wide and her cheeks tinge a dark pink color. So she was female and delicate enough to be shocked, was she? And what kind of insanity had possessed him that made her look devilishly alluring in soaked night clothes and with her hair plastered to her face?

On the other hand, the soaked nightgown was terribly revealing of her curves, and he almost wanted to laugh at the thought that perhaps he was his father's son after all: he couldn't be ill or tired enough not to react. But he tried to keep it from showing on his face, and instead he said, all propriety, "I beg your pardon, Miss Felix, but they are looking for us, and we must escape. I'm not absolutely sure what we can do, but I can think of only one place I can take us. Only one place they won't dare follow us. It's terribly dangerous, as it is a world where magic is absolutely disbelieved and, in fact, where only a very strange kind of magic works. I will be utterly helpless there, but the chances of anyone trying to find us there are close to none, and even if they try, there is a good chance they will not be able to find us, because the world is choked with iron, and therefore it is hard to find anyone there. In fact, it is dangerous to any magical pattern but the strongest."

Her eyes looked into his, and a small frown was forming, making a vertical wrinkle between her dark, arched eyebrows. "But–" she said.

"No," he said. "Do listen to me. I don't know how long I have, and I would have you understand what I'm trying to do. If I transport us there, it will use the last of my magical strength. If I should die–" He watched her opening her mouth and put his hand up to stop her talking. "No. If I should die, which is possible, though not probable, or not merely from the spell, I wish you to keep track of how I transported us, and use those coordinates, in reverse fashion, to take you back to Avalon. There you are to evade capture, and procure…"

He seemed to think for a moment. "...Gabriel Penn's help, but if you fail at that – as I think the concerted effort to bring down my house might include him – then you are to procure my fiancée, Miss Blythe, and tell her what happened to me, and to seek redress before the king's high justice. Trust me, she will be anxious to do so, as she will not want her name to be linked to someone who has broken the law by willingly traveling to other worlds. And then you are to convince the king to find who was at the back of the conspiracy and to do your utmost to recover my brother, Michael, from Fairyland." He recalled himself and, this time, gave a startled laugh. "Listen to me," he said, "laying down the law to you, as though I had the power to compel your obedience in the case of my death. I absolve you from all responsibility in following my wishes, of course, only beg you to consider that without me, or Michael, my house will devolve to a distant cousin, and the family will be left destitute. But of course, my transporting us and saving you," he added, urgently, "has absolutely no conditions. If we are captured here, my family will just as surely be disgraced and thrown into poverty." He inclined his head to her. "But I would appreciate–"

Something like a look of dismay crossed her features, and she protested, "Of course I'll do what I can to save your family. Only tell me why you think you might die, but not immediately?"

"In my weakened condition," he said, "being in a world with so much cold iron and so hostile to magic will–"

At that moment, he felt the probe again, and this time, felt the end of it fasten on them. Through the probe came a voice, unctuous and fulsome, as the voice of a functionary who has completed a difficult task, "I found them, O gracious one. The witches are–"

Seraphim took a deep breath. He called the last of his magical strength to him. He could feel his power fighting, his instinct of self-preservation attempting to keep him from doing such destructive magic, which could only result in his death, or at least, in serious damage to his magical power and his shields. It didn't matter. If they stayed here, she would have to fight for him. And that, he doubted she could do. Then they would both die. In this world, one of them at least might survive.

He reached with the last of his strength for the coordinates of the world he and Gabriel had called the Madhouse, the world he and Gabriel had sworn never to visit again, not since the last time when the sheer amount of cold iron had almost killed them.

At the last minute, as he was reciting the transport spell, he heard Miss Felix say, "Oh!" and felt reaching in, reaching right into his spell and… twisting.

It was still the Madhouse, he thought, frantically, even as the spell activated. But she had set different coordinates. What could she be thinking?

The cold of the Betweener hit him, and then he felt himself fall onto a hard surface, even as the sapping feel of cold iron leeched at his magic.

As consciousness ran away from him, he heard Miss Felix pound on something – sounded like a door – while screaming, "Grandmother. Grandmother. Please, help me."

Sarah A. Hoyt

Into The Lion's Den

Marlon had been reclining on a rosewood sofa upholstered in blue velvet, with a book on his knees.

Gabriel's first thought was that he'd changed not at all. His second thought was that he'd changed completely. And both were true. Marlon's hair remained that blond on the edge of red – the flame about to catch – and as unruly as it had been at Cambridge, wisps of it standing on end and forming a halo around the oval face. His body remained long and lean, and he wore – as he'd tended to do at Cambridge – blue pants of some serviceable material and a shirt that looked too large for him.

But at Gabriel's arrival, he looked up. And in that moment Gabriel sucked in air, remarking the difference in his erstwhile friend. Marlon had grown almost gaunt, and his blue eyes looked haunted, as though he'd looked too closely at horrors he couldn't forget.

Good, Gabriel thought. *He also didn't escape unscathed.* And immediately despised himself for it.

After the first start, the shock that widened his blue eyes, Marlon controlled himself and looked as though Gabriel transported into his house every day and twice on Sunday, and not as though they were seeing each other for the first time in years – and after they'd parted in anger and bitterness, in public scandal and private horror.

He stood from the sofa, with slow, calculated movements, as though he didn't trust himself to move fast, to lose control of himself. He kept his fingers between the pages of the book, holding the page he'd been reading. Standing, he came to a little above Gabriel's shoulder, but managed to give the impression of towering over him, and also of distant, cold dignity. As though he were the offended one, and not the guilty party.

"You honor me with your visit, Prince," he said, in extremely polite tones.

Gabriel opened his mouth to protest the title, then bit his tongue. When he spoke, he'd brought his own abominable temper under control, though nothing could stop his heart pounding, or the vague feeling of dread in the pit of his stomach. All the furniture here, everything, was what had been in Marlon's room at Cambridge, and it remained only the question: where was *it*? Where was that which had once been Aiden

Gypson? Gabriel took light breaths, feeling as though, should he breathe deeply, he would smell the faint scent of corruption in the air.

"I came to you," Gabriel said, with as much dignity as he could muster. "Because you told me I could always come to you if I ran out of places to go, and if I had no one else to help me."

Marlon's eyebrows went up. They were the exact same color as his hair, and when they rose like that they gave the impression of twin flames dancing above his eyes. "Nowhere to go, Prince? You astonish me."

"Don't call me that. You know very well I am not a prince. I gave up my dignity and my power long ago."

"Oh, I don't think you can give it up." A smile without mirth, an absolutely ghastly grin as unpleasant as a corpse's bared teeth, contorted Marlon's face. "I think if you're born to it, you will always be a prince. Not like the rest of us, who are born to less exalted positions."

"For the love of heaven, cut the tomfoolery," Gabriel said, impatient. "None of– None of what happened had anything to do with the fact that my mother was an elf princess or your mother a mere magical commoner. As different as those are, we still have more in common than with– than other people." Which had been more than half of what had thrown them together. The other half… Gabriel looked down, trying to discern any hint of the easy laughter that had once sprung between them, or that wordless understanding that had allowed them to communicate without the need for sound. He found nothing. All of that had shattered, years ago, when they'd last seen each other. "You told me I could come to you, if I were out of all other resources."

"Your high born brother abandoned you, then?" Marlon asked. His look was almost hungry. "The Duke's family has disowned you?"

In the face of that hunger, Gabriel hesitated. How much could he trust Marlon? If he told Marlon exactly the trouble he was in, would Marlon betray him? Run to the authorities?

But at that moment, he caught sight of it: the mortal remains of Aiden Gypson. In life, he'd been a tall man, and much of Gabriel's build. In death, his look remained the same, and he wore what Gabriel presumed were clean clothes – since the smell was not that obvious – in this case a serviceable brown suit. Above it, Aiden's face remained as it had been in life: the well-formed features, the dark green eyes, the narrow, high nose. Only the eyes looked lusterless, and the lips receded slightly to show the teeth. It took more than that, though, and the yellowish wax-like pallor to know the man was dead and had been brought back to life with a resurrection spell. You wouldn't know that he couldn't rest until the man who'd made that spell allowed it.

But if you were a mage you could see it and you could smell it: the not quite physical smell of the dead flesh that had not been allowed to decay and instead sparked and fizzed with unholy magic. And if you were a mage, you could see that more horrible thing: Aiden's specter, just behind the body, attached to it by a thread of spell, faded and impossibly-tired looking.

How could Marlon live with that ghost? How could he? When he'd met Marlon at Cambridge, he'd heard of Aiden Gypson and the odd, too-close relationship Marlon had had with Gypson until Gypson's death. But it had taken him more than a year to find Gypson, where Marlon had hidden him, in the attic room of his lodgings. And to realize what Marlon had done.

In sick waves of horror, Gabriel recalled how – in shock – he'd given the whole thing away and how the only reason Marlon hadn't been arrested and Aiden Gypson destroyed was that the two had vanished. Gabriel, himself, had been sent from Cambridge in disgrace, though nothing could ever be pinned on him. And weeks later he'd gotten the unsigned letter with the coordinates of Marlon's hideout and the line "when you run out of places to hide."

Well, he'd run out of places to hide, but Marlon could not denounce him or call the authorities on him. Or on Seraphim. Necromancers were at as great a risk as those who traded with unauthorized worlds.

In a rush, one eye on Aiden Gypson, who stood, knit with the shadows against the wall, half-immersed in them, he told Marlon a very brief version of the events. What he and Seraphim had found of their father's activities. How they'd resumed them, helping rescue witches from the forbidden worlds. And then the catastrophic cascade of events of the last few days.

Marlon showed surprise only once: when Gabriel mentioned the role that the elves appeared to have played in it. And that in a way was a relief. The thought of Marlon in league with the fairy realm was terrifying. And though his mother must have been a low-born elf – if she had been an elf at all and not another magical creature, one of the many thrown out of Fairyland – it didn't mean that Fairyland wouldn't use her son, and willingly too.

When Gabriel came to the end, he was quiet a while, and Marlon said, crossing his arms on his chest, "And what do you want of me, prince? Am I supposed to hide you?"

Gabriel shook his head. "I could have hid myself," he said. "That is, I'm not so witless that I could not have contrived to."

"Ah." Marlon said. "Then what am I to understand you to want?"

"Oh, curse you," Gabriel said. "Stop playing games. This is not funny. You know very well what I want. I want you to find where Seraphim went. I want you to find where Michael was taken. I want you to help me recover them and discover who is at the back of this, and why, and what they intend for my– for the Duke's family."

Marlon was very close now, looking up and somehow contriving to give the impression of looking down. "And what's in it for me?" he asked. His voice was harsh.

Gabriel felt a spasm of revulsion, but said, his voice controlled, "Whatever I need to do to convince you to save Seraphim and Michael and… and their mother and sister."

Marlon laughed, a short bark. "You couldn't *do* enough," he said. "It's more what you need to give."

"Give?" Gabriel asked, as his stomach lurched. And, uncomprehending, "Give?"

"My price, sweet Prince, is you."

"Me?"

Marlon was now so close, that Gabriel felt a though he couldn't look away, even as, by the corner of his eye, he followed Aiden Gypson's movement as he emerged from the shadow driven by who knew what random impulse.

"You," Marlon said. "Body and soul and magic too."

"You do have a penchant for trying to own people!" Gabriel said, before he could stop himself.

Marlon narrowed his eyes. "It's my price," he said. "Pay it or seek help elsewhere for your precious family."

Gabriel felt as though his throat had gone very dry, his mind lurching into horror, his body hovering on the edge of nausea. But Marlon was the only person he knew whose power was as strong as Gabriel's own. And Marlon was ten times as knowledgeable. And there was nowhere else Gabriel could go.

"Which one is it going to be, Prince? Yes or no?"

Feeling as though he had to force his body to obey him, Gabriel lowered his head and hissed through clenched teeth, "Yes."

Sarah A. Hoyt

Mirror Mirror

The dressing room smelled heavily of rose water, as though every surface had been scrubbed with it, every one of the frothy dresses hanging from a rod at the back dipped in it, every one of the ornate paintings on the wall painted with it.

The smell of roses mixed with other cloying scents: powder and grease paint, wax candles and a trace of the incense that climbed in a thin blue thread of smoke from the mouth of a dragon-shaped incense burner to the ceiling.

The Twin was in front of the mirror, applying makeup with quick, deft gestures. That's how Barbara, Dowager Duchess of Darkwater, always thought of her Fey double: as The Twin. She knew the woman had a name, something soft and liquid and running to excessive syllables, but she didn't know it, just as she didn't know Gabriel's elf name. Elves were born with their names, as attached to them and as much a part of their anatomy as a hand or a foot, and as important as their own heart. She knew, too, that in the human world The Twin went by the name Maryalys Penn, the last being the surname of her first husband, discarded a long time ago, but in Barbara's mind she was always and forever The Twin – that creature like herself and yet not whom she had first glimpsed for a few moments after she'd been brought back from Fairyland, and before The Twin was sent back to it.

Time had made differences between them, of course. The Twin hadn't aged from whatever age she'd been when she'd come out of Fairyland with Gabriel. Thirty? Somewhere around there, Barbara thought, though it was thirty in elf terms, which means she looked very much like the Duchess at seventeen, with pale, creamy skin, rose-touched cheeks, plump lips that rested in a smile, and midnight-black hair loosed down her back. Only their eyes were different. They'd always been different. The Twin might have been formed from birth to echo the Duchess, which one understood was how Changelings were created, but the eyes, though they might have the same shape and color and be nestled beneath the same dark, arched eyebrows, were not Barbara's. They managed to be both much, much older than those of any human who ever lived, and somehow not human. Like the eyes of a bird of prey, glittering and hard.

Had Gabriel had eyes like that, Barbara would never have allowed him into the house, no matter if he was just a child and had been living rough on the streets or had almost been killed just before Arden rescued him.

And now that Barbara thought about it, that was likely to be a point of contention between them. After all, Gabriel had been The Twin's to dispose of and to do with as she pleased. Or at least The Twin would think so. She could not have approved of the Duke's taking him away. And she would hold it against Barbara. No matter.

As The Twin's gaze met hers in the mirror, for just a second Barbara read surprise in them and then a thread of fear. There were many reasons The Twin might fear her human counterpart, of course, but the quick flicker, quickly subdued, gave Barbara a sense of hope. There was something there. And The Twin was involved in it.

Aloud, she said, "Good evening, Mrs. Penn. Are you preparing for a performance? I beg your pardon, interrupting you at this time, but I must have some information from you." She spoke casually, and adjusted her gloves on her fingers as she spoke, as though this were a social call and she were merely verifying a detail or two. It was probably all to naught. She had never fully known what elves could do – no human did – but she had an idea that Gabriel could smell much more acutely than normal humans, perhaps even smell magic. She'd seen him detect people in falsehood with no other indication. And she knew he could hear far more sharply than normal humans, since he'd used that talent all through childhood to cover whatever mischief Seraphim and he were engaged in at the time.

So this creature could probably hear the frantic beating of Barbara's heart, and surely she could smell the uneasy perspiration as Barbara hoped with all her might that Caroline would stay where she'd left her, at the door to the dressing room and behind some fantastical wheeled horse used in plays, where no one was likely to see her or bother her. Please, let Caroline not come in. Let her not be exposed to The Twin.

None of this mattered. Barbara's composure must be maintained, as much to keep Barbara from breaking down as to fool any external person.

The Twin's eyes glittered at her from the mirror. "I fail to see in what I might help you, my lady," she spoke, her voice also a perfect imitation of Barbara's at seventeen or eighteen, dulcet and cultured. "What of mine you wanted, you have already taken: my lover and my child. What more could you want me to give you?"

"My husband was never your lover," Barbara said, then caught herself. No use speaking half-truths around elves. They could always twist them. "No more than in the carnal sense, and there he was many women's lover.

He lay with you, sure. Desired you too, I am sure, since he married me, and I'm sure he saw in me an echo of you, but it is not love. If you don't know the difference between those, Mrs. Penn, you know not the least thing about being human, and all your time amid us has been wasted. As for your son, he was not yours when he came to us. From what I understand he had been living as a beggar in London and supporting you both. Something no child should do." She saw The Twin open her mouth to speak and said, "But that is neither here nor there, Mrs. Penn. What I wish to know is, where are they? And why?"

Again the stab of fear came. Again the sharp pang of something like panic, behind the hard, inhuman eyes. And The Twin's voice was a trifle too unconcerned, a trifle too light, as she said, "I have not the pleasure of having the slightest idea what you speak of." She tapped her chin lightly with a puff with some white powder, and said, brightly. "And now, if you excuse me, I have commitments which I must keep. I'm playing principal female in *One Thing And Another*, and I must–"

Barbara raised her hand and let the spell fly. And knew the moment she'd done it that it was a bad idea. It was a minor spell, not very strong, just a compulsion to tell the truth, with a hint of punishment to come. She'd never meant to use it. She'd never have used it, if she'd not got scared. Something she knew, which her husband had told her; yes, and her father too, after he'd recovered her from Fairyland. "If you go fighting elves, you must use all the force you can command and not an iota less. Because anything else they'll eat."

She'd not known what eat meant till this moment – only as her spell hit The Twin, The Twin absorbed it, swallowed it, and it made her alien elf magic shine more brightly around her preternaturally young form.

And then The Twin Attacked. There was a sense of rushing, and the scent of roses increased till Barbara felt she was choking on them, her mouth and nostrils and everything stuffed with cloying, redolent petals. As she gasped for breath, her body was slammed backwards against a wall, with enough force to rattle her brain. Into this, feelings poured into her, odd feelings: the feeling that she was nothing, that she had never deserved her husband or her children, that she had rightful stolen all those from The Twin, that she was old and useless and not beautiful, a speck of dirt on the face of the world, and one, moreover, that should be dead and gone a long, long time while the glittering creature before her continued to be vital and young and to inspire love and passion.

Barbara's grandchildren, and her grandchildren's grandchildren would be dead and long gone, and The Twin would still be beautiful and young and enticing.

Coupled with this came the strong suggestion that Barbara should stop cluttering the Glittering Twin's world, that she should efface herself, go, do away with herself.

The Duchess felt both the push and the desire to vanish, but at the same time, she clawed back with her own mind, that no, she had loved her husband and been his true wife, despite his infidelities and his frailties – none of them unusual in one who'd early been elf-touched. And she deserved her time upon the Earth which at any rate belonged more to her than to The Twin, a creature who'd never been fully alive and therefore could not be fully here.

She managed to choke out "No" through the cloying scent of roses, but she couldn't lift her hand to make any sign of protection, she couldn't command her mind to let a spell fly, and she couldn't breathe. Her heart strained against her chest, and she knew presently she would lose consciousness, and then the Twin could dispose of her as though she were an inanimate object. She would, too. Even if elves had qualms about murder, they wouldn't have those against killing humans.

The Twin stood before her, her hair standing in a dark halo around her head – beautiful like an angel and triumphant like death. For a fleeting moment, Barbara wondered if this was the last sight her husband had seen, then told herself it was nonsense. Darkwater had committed suicide. Killed himself over gambling debts and women. She had to believe it even if....

The door blew open. "Mama!" echoed in Caroline's most outraged accents, and Caroline stood there in the doorway, as young as The Twin looked, but a lot more vital, a lot more alive somehow. "Mama!"

Barbara tried to choke out a warning that Caroline should go, that she should hide, that this creature would get her too, but she had no time. Caroline's accents were frosty. "Well," she said, "this is a great deal of nonsense." Calmly, as though this were something she did every day, she spoke liquid, tripping syllables, which fell onto Barbara's ears like burning fire, but had an even stronger effect on The Twin.

The Twin tripped backward, like a ragdoll that has lost its stuffing, and fell into her velvet-upholstered chair, in front of her vanity, looking rather like she was indeed a ragdoll, arms and legs asprawl, mouth half open, expression blank.

Barbara, finding that she could breathe, took a deep, aching breath and stepped away from the wall. "Caroline," she said, in shocked accents, and was even more shocked as her daughter turned an admonitory look on her. "Not now, Mama," the chit said, looking and sounding for all the world as though she were the adult and her much-tried mother the child here. "Afterwards, I'll explain anything you might well want."

"Now," Caroline said, turning to the Twin. "Madam, if you please, and if you don't want me to use worse upon you, be so kind as to tell me where my brother Michael was taken and by whom and why, and also where Gabriel and Seraphim might be. And do not even think of lying." Another string of liquid, elven syllables. "There, that will prevent it."

The Twin flickered. It was like watching the flame of a candle, which now glowed yellow, now blue. She flickered, between the human form that looked like Barbara, asprawl on the chair in front of the vanity, to something glittery and hard and bony, like an insect, with an ivory carapace. It was only a moment, and she flickered back to human aspect, her eyes wide and terrified. They looked like a wounded bird of prey's brought down and about to be rent by dogs. Barbara wished she didn't enjoy the expression in them quite so much.

The Twin took a deep, raspy breath, and spoke in a deep, raspy voice that sounded somehow reedy and not quite human, and which had lost all its allure and glamour. "The– Fairyland wanted the young one. Your... Your shadow– no." She seemed to be struggling with the human language, suddenly, and pronounced with exaggerated care, "Your twin brother. My brother wanted him. I sent him there."

"I see," Caroline said. "What did they want him for?"

The twin made a hissing sound, and then another, and then – apparently unable to hold information any longer, and as Caroline moved her hand midair, in a gesture that her mother didn't quite understand – whimpered and said, "To mine. To pull from... to... to... eat."

"Eat!" Barbara said, outraged, and of course, one heard things, about elves feasting on human children, but she'd never believed it, and besides, Michael was not a child, not in that sense.

"Hush, mama," Caroline said. "You mean to mine him, like a metal source?"

The Twin nodded. "I see," Caroline said. She looked pale but steady. "You will kindly give us the coordinates and the way to reach him."

"Don't know... way to reach him. Coordina– yes." She let out a series of the words that could be used as magical coordinates to the location of another world.

Caroline seemed to run it through her mind, or perhaps to memorize it. Barbara, still shaken from her experience, could not concentrate on it, but she knew it was a place in Fairyland because of the truncated fifth locator. Fairyland was not a real place, a world like their own and separate from it. Instead it was a parasite universe, a flea riding on the back of the other universes.

She wondered, too, what they meant by mining Michael, and felt as though a cold hand tugged at her heart. They would find him. They would rescue him. But where had Caroline learned to do all this? Barbara was very sure it hadn't been taught at the Academy for Young Ladies of Distinction where Caroline had been sent for two years after the school room.

"And my brother Seraphim?" Caroline asked, coldly.

"He has escaped us," The Twin said, in a squawk of fury. "We sent him to the world of the priest kings, but he escaped. He… we cannot find him. Or her, the lost one. It was she who–"

Caroline had taken a deep breath. "And my brother Gabriel?"

"He's not–"

"My brother Gabriel, by virtue of shared blood, of shared upbringing and of shared fraternal affection. Where is my brother Gabriel? Where have you sent him?"

The Twin's laughter rang in the room, like a peal of bells. Before Barbara could recover from her shock at this, The Twin said, "He's gone where he's always wanted to go. Back to the necromancer."

"The necro–" Caroline said, and Barbara, who had an inkling that this was something she did not want Caroline to dwell on, who had a feeling in fact that this was at the back of whatever had got Gabriel expelled from Cambridge, said, firmly, "He is on his own, then? You have not sent him?"

"No," The Twin said. "And I cannot tell you his coordinates, because the necromancer keeps his location zipped up. But I'm sure he's very happy, seeing as he–"

"Stop," Barbara commanded. "No more. Caroline, I don't believe you wish to pry into Gabriel's affairs."

"No, mama," Caroline said, meekly. She made a gesture with her hand, and suddenly The Twin went limp, her face blank.

"You killed her," Barbara said, shocked, more shocked perhaps for a secret feeling of gloating.

"No, Mama," Caroline said. She put out a hand and held onto Barbara's forearm, pulling her. "She's merely in a trance state, where she will stay until she wakes, remembering nothing of our visit."

"Caroline!"

"Yes, Mama?" Caroline said, as she pulled her mother out of the Twin's dressing room and along a narrow corridor.

They'd exited onto a rather smelly alley when Barbara managed, "If you don't tell me how you learned this very strange magic, and what you just did to the… to Gabriel's mother, and with what power, I will have strong hysterics."

"Yes, mama," Caroline said, then giggled, as her irrepressible spirit took over once more. "You must forgive me. But it is so funny that I should know something you don't." She looked at Barbara and sighed. "It was Gabriel, when Michael and I were three. That," Caroline made a head gesture towards the back of the theatrical building they'd just left, "came prowling around. Not after Gabriel. After us. Michael and me."

"But–"

"Gabriel told us who it was," she said. "And he taught us how to defend ourselves. He said she often came prowling around because daddy–" she stopped abruptly.

"Yes," Barbara said, her voice raspy. Internally she thought of Arden. She rarely thought of him by that name, the name she'd called him in private, the name by which she'd fallen in love with him. Arden conjured up the name of the dashing young gentleman he'd been, looking a little like Seraphim and Gabriel, but oh so infinitely more dashing and daring and… everything a young man should be.

Thinking of him as Arden made her heart clench. It made her wonder if she'd ever truly known him, or had his love. Despite what she'd told The Twin, she wondered if in his heart it was The Twin he'd always loved. Elf love was like an illness, she'd been told. A fever that never fully passed.

It was almost a relief to hear Caroline ask, the prurient curiosity vibrating in her voice, "Who is the necromancer? Who has Gabriel always wanted to go to?"

"I understand he had an unsavory friend in Cambridge, who was… accused of some illegal magic. But as to his always wanting to go somewhere, I would place no credence on what the creature said. You know she lies as she breathes."

"I see," Caroline said, giving Barbara the uncomfortable feeling she very well did.

Before she could say any more, Barbara interrupted. They were now walking along a main street, well lit, but they were getting veiled glances from other passers-by. It was not normal for a well-dressed mother and daughter to walk along the street at this hour, unaccompanied even by a footman. And if there was a conspiracy of some sort – what else could it be that had made both Gabriel and Seraphim disappear, and which had stolen Michael from the home – then sooner or later someone would spot them. "Caroline," she said, in little more than a whisper. "We cannot go on in this way. Someone will notice us or recognize us."

"I know," Caroline said, with the greatest calm. "I'm just looking for an easy transition point to take us into Fairyland.

Sarah A. Hoyt

Madhouse

Seraphim woke up aching on a strange bed. Not only a strange bed in the sense that it was not known to him, but a strange bed in the sense that it felt odd beneath him, not like the feather mattresses and pillows he was used to. The blankets above him, too, felt oddly light but very warm.

He struggled from the shadowland he'd wandered into in his dream, and heard a moan escape his lips before being awake enough to control them.

"There, Mr. Ainsling," a voice said. It had an odd accent, and it sounded like that of an elderly woman. Then it said in a matter-of-fact tone, "You see, he's coming around. I told you he would. A good thing too. If he hadn't awakened we would have to take him to the hospital."

The voice that answered this first was familiar. It was Miss Felix's voice, though it sounded more relaxed than it ever had. "It wouldn't have been possible. In his state, he'd just have died there."

"Would he really? But why? He's not that ill, you know. A minor infection that the antibiotics will take care of, and very tired, that's all."

"I know. But their magic is not like that of Earth. They have, I think, a good bit of elf or fairy or something, or perhaps their magic is different and older. They react badly to what they call cold iron."

"But surely the Victorians used an awful lot of iron," the older voice said. "You can't tell me that they have that level of civilization without–"

"Oh, no. But they use spells in the forging so it doesn't affect them. Also, I don't think it's the iron that affects him. I think it's the machines. Too many machines seem to eat at their magic. A strong one of their kind can withstand it, but he's anything but strong just now."

Seraphim tried to pry his eyes open and to protest, but he couldn't, and presently, darkness overwhelmed him again.

He woke up being moved. This indignity puzzled him for a moment, because he was being bodily dragged by two women – he was sure of it by the hand size and the awkward way in which they pushed him this way and that. He could discern no rhyme or reason to the movement until he felt cool fabric under him. Then he realized they were changing the bed under him, and wondered why they hadn't called a man-servant to move him to a chaise or a sofa while that was done. And were the two women making the bed Miss Felix and… he remembered her calling as they landed in Madhouse – her grandmother? Had they no maids, either? Had he landed in a poor cottager's family? He must be giving them the devil of a time. He must awake and go home.

With a superhuman effort, he brought his eyes open, just as the two women pulled a sheet and something else – something that looked like a colorful patchwork quilt – over him, but that felt much lighter and warmer than any quilt that Seraphim had ever seen.

He was reclining against pillows – very soft pillows – in a bright room. It didn't look like a cottage, or smell like one either. The scents in the air were clean with a hint of flowers, and the room was as large as most workmen's cottages, and furnished, besides, in style, if sparsely. It had a dresser up near the window, and it was a vast, polished dresser, with a mirror above. The bed on which Seraphim lay wasn't curtained, but it looked well-made and almost new. There was also a bedside table, and what appeared to be a desk under the window. He blinked. "Where– "

"You're at my grandmother's house, Your Grace. This is my grandmother, Mrs. Lillian Felix."

He looked at the older woman and was almost shocked when she failed to curtsey and instead smiled at him, amused. "Your Grace, is it? What is that, a Duke? Well, we don't have those, so don't get all bent out of shape if I call you Mister. Nell says your name is Ainsling."

"Seraphim Ainsling," Seraphim said, while trying to figure out what she meant by their not having dukes. Surely it couldn't be … they didn't sound French.

She smiled. "Well. Seraphim is an odd name. It's plural, isn't it?"

Seraphim felt like he really had fallen into a Madhouse. Never had he and Gabriel bestowed a more appropriate name on any place. "My father named all his sons after angels," he said. "And his first legitimate heir seemed to demand something more, so he named me after a whole order of angelic beings."

"I see," the older lady said, cocking her head sideways. She looked nothing like Miss Felix, being very fair where Miss Felix was dark, and having brilliant blue eyes that reminded Seraphim of a certain kind of enamel. "I can't very well call you Seraphim, though, so you shall be Mr. Ainsling. I apologize, but I haven't paid any attention to forms of address to the nobility, not even when I was young and read an awful lot of very bad regency romances." She smiled brightly at these nonsensical words, then added, "I'll go get you some food, shall I? I bet you'll be very glad to eat something solid, instead of the milk and broth we've been tipping down your throat, and maybe you'll feel well enough afterwards to take a shower."

There followed the oddest two hours that Seraphim had ever lived through, and that included both trying to calm Gabriel after he found the still-living body of Aiden Gypson in Marlon's attic closet, and the hour that had followed that one, when Seraphim had tried to challenge Marlon to a duel and had it sternly pointed out to him that it would only fan the flames of scandal. And gone through with it, anyway, and wounded the bounder.

This time, there was nothing as shocking. It was more that all of life was both very familiar and completely odd. Take the meal they brought him: bread and broth with a little bit of cheese, followed, after some discussion, by a pot of strong, black tea.

None of the foods was alien or repulsive, like the fried bugs they ate in at least one of the worlds that Seraphim and Gabriel had visited.

But the bread was whiter and softer than any bread Seraphim had ever eaten; the broth was completely clear, as though it had been many-times strained, so that there were no bits of meat in it. It tasted of hints of garlic and spices, too, not normally something given to an invalid. The dishes, too, were odd, being fine and clearly new or at least very white and never mended. Yet, they were served upon a wooden tray, even if the tray was adorned with a lace cloth. He could not make sense of the signals he got about the Felixes' station in life. The house felt roomy and clean, but he had yet to hear a servant, much less to see one. The dishes were new, and very good quality, but they didn't seem to command silver or even pewter. It was like being caught in the middle of a puzzle he couldn't solve.

And then there had been the bathing facilities, which had completed his astonishment. The bathroom, next to the bedroom – which was odd by itself. What did the people in other rooms do when they wished to wash? – had a sink and a bathtub, but it also had a square enclosed in glass and floored in tile. That both the sink and the square – and the bathtub too – had running water and running water whose temperature could go from freezing to very hot with adjustments of two handles, shocked him to his core. He could not feel the magic by which it had been done. Then there was the toilet with the flushing mechanism. He'd heard of such, but he'd always thought they'd be inconvenient and smelly. Turned out no smell escaped.

However, he had his work cut out for him, making both women leave the bathroom and not help him use the appliances, or remove his clothes.

They seemed very matter of fact about it, and afraid he'd fall, so that what would have seemed gross indelicacy at any other time, now seemed an excess of quasi-maternal concern. Which did not make him feel any better. He felt an odd grievance that Nell Felix felt maternal about him. And he didn't have time to examine his feelings.

At length he'd showered, in gloriously warm water on the edge of hot, and washed his hair and body with the products that had been indicated to him.

He was dry and had put on a dressing gown, which they'd left for him – and which seemed to be a severe blue affair, made of the same material as the towels – when someone knocked at the door. At his call to come in, Miss Felix bustled in, bringing him something that looked completely alien, and which she handed to him with the look of someone who has completed a long quest, "Grandma says you'll want to shave. She'll pick up a cheap electric razor at the drugstore when she goes into town later. Such a small machine won't hurt your magic, surely. But for now this is the best I can do. Sorry it's pink."

The object looked like it was made of some sort of pliable shell, or perhaps hard jelly, and it was definitely pink, though it bore no resemblance whatsoever to a razor, Seraphim thought. As he looked at it, puzzled, she giggled and took it back, "I suppose you've never seen a safety razor." She pointed to the little glint of metal. "These are the blades. Here." She got something from a compartment behind the mirror, a cylindrical, metallic container, and sprayed a dot of white foam on her arm, then ran the apparatus over it, removing the foam and a little bit of the almost invisible hair on her arm. "Like that."

She'd stayed, surveying him and helping with instructions when he got confused, but perhaps he should be grateful that she didn't help him. By the end of it, he was exhausted, and all too glad to be led back to the bed, where he lay, recovering his breath.

For the first time, it occurred to him that not only Miss Felix but her grandmother too were very oddly dressed. They wore blue pantaloons of some sort, and light blouses on top, so fine that one could see the shape of their body, and the contours of what appeared to be a garment for controlling the bosom. Seraphim felt himself blush just at the thought. He was no halfling, but what seemed most shocking about these garments was the fact that the women wore them casually and not at all like they meant to seduce anyone.

"Miss Felix," he said, at length. "I see we came to the world I meant to come to, but you changed the coordinates. I presume it was because… I mean, you've indicated you know this world?"

"Oh, sure," she said. "I grew up here. I had to bring you here, because… well… because Grandma knows magic, and taught me some of it, so I figured she'd understand why you couldn't go to a hospital, because that's in larger population centers and there would be too much metal for you in your condition. But also–"

"Yes?"

"Grandmother is semi-retired, but she's a vet. A veterinarian, I mean. She treats animals. So I knew she could still get prescriptions for antibiotics, and I could tell you had a raging infection and fever."

"Antibi–"

"Tablets that cure infections," she said. And then quickly sketched for him the level of civilization of this world. She was clear and concise, and could have no idea how much she shocked him. The other worlds without magic that he'd seen were mired in the dark ages, with none of the comforts of civilization. These must be a very ingenious people, indeed, to have made all these changes to their way of life, and without magic, too.

"But…," he said, at last. "It sounds like a very comfortable arrangement. How came you to leave it?"

"I wanted to know where I came from," she said.

Sarah A. Hoyt

And The Dead

Gabriel felt as though he'd gone back in time. These new lodgings were not the ones at Cambridge, but they were not so much different. In fact, from sounds of children at play and the occasional carriage going past the shuttered windows, Gabriel guessed that they were in a city of medium size. Perhaps Bath.

The inside of the house, too – at least this floor – had the same layout as the house in Cambridge. The front room served as a reception parlor for visitors, perhaps not so much here, but it contained the same furniture, the rosewood sofa and chaise longue, the golden oak bookcases lining the walls, crammed with books that ranged from ancient falling-apart leather bound books to cheaply printed folios with no covers at all. They also ranged, Gabriel knew, from the most difficult books on the occult and magic to the latest novel making the rounds of young ladies' circulating libraries.

A great part of the attraction of associating with Marlon had always been the books. They were everywhere in the house; there was nothing Marlon didn't consider worth reading, and nothing he didn't consider worth discussing.

The parlor gave way to a smaller room, which could be cut off by shutting a pocket door. The pocket door was open, and this room, though in the same position as the dining room at Cambridge, did not have the same furniture. Instead, it was crammed full of furniture that had been in Marlon's offices at Cambridge: a workbench took up the entire length of the wall under a shuttered window. Above the workbench hung a stuffed crocodile. Against the wall to the right was a set of shelves with jars filled with magical substances. In the middle of the room, in the place taken by the dining table at Cambridge, was a massive golden-oak desk, at least twice as large as any other desk that Gabriel had ever seen. It was covered all over in papers and books with marks in them, in notepads with notes scribbled on them, in correspondence that, if Gabriel knew Marlon, might very well be the same correspondence that had remained unanswered when the desk was in Cambridge.

As Gabriel was turned when he answered Marlon's question – had he truly just agreed to sell his soul? It didn't matter. He owed Seraphim that and more – he could look at the desk and its papers and did look at them, rather than look at Marlon, as Marlon's finger traced the line of Gabriel's jawbone.

For a moment, with the tip of his finger just touching Gabriel's chin, the silence lengthened between them. Then Marlon stepped away. A quickly barked word seemed to have an effect on Gypson, who had been drawing closer and closer, and now stopped, and walked back, to stand against the wall, the scrap of soul clinging to it almost invisible in the semi-darkness.

Marlon looked Gabriel over and made a noise at the back of his throat. "Awakened in the middle of the night and no time to dress?" he asked.

"Not really awakened," he said. "I'd barely gone to sleep."

"Upstairs," Marlon said. "There is a room to the left. I just had a fire lit in it so it will still be chill, but the water in the basin will be warm. Wash and dress. I'll be in the kitchen," He pointed towards a door to the back of the house.

At least, Gabriel thought as he took the stairs two by two, he wasn't being forced to share Marlon's bedchamber. He wasn't sure how he felt about that particular detail. There were so many worse things one could do to someone whom one magically owned.

The room itself was tiny but larger than Gabriel's room with the Darkwaters. And the fire was burning cheerily in the fireplace. Gabriel could tell it had been set and lit by magical means and wondered what Marlon was playing at. It was dangerous to use magic in such trivial matters.

But Gabriel washed and then dressed, finding clothes in the closet and trying not to think they might have been Gypson's. When he went down to the kitchen he found Marlon himself just finishing making tea. The tea service was his old Cambridge one – silver and polished. Marlon used to say, joking – at least Gabriel assumed it was joking – it was a legacy from his mortal father. It had to be a joke, since Marlon's father had never acknowledged him and at least no one in Fairyland knew his identity.

He nodded to Gabriel as Gabriel came in, then carried the tray into the next room, where he set it on the table in between the sofa and the chaise. Gabriel stepped forward to pour, but Marlon waved him back.

It wasn't until Gabriel had a steaming cup of tea in his hand that he said, "You're using magic for household matters."

Marlon shrugged. "It wouldn't do otherwise, would it? I can't exactly hire servants. Or I could, but considering that every local magician knows who I am and that I'm a wanted criminal, it wouldn't answer."

Gabriel didn't say anything, but his eyes went involuntarily to the wall, where Gypson stood, immobile, save for the vague flap of his soul against the darkness surrounding him.

"As a servant?" Marlon said, answering the unspoken words. "One doesn't use the remains of someone one once loved as a servant. One doesn't use slaves, Gabriel. Drink your tea, Gabriel. I should have asked you if you preferred wine. I beg your pardon. I've grown quite unused to company."

"Not wine in the middle of the night and after all that's happened," Gabriel said. "I try not to tempt fate."

"Wise, that," Marlon said. "You said you want to rescue your… brothers. What do you wish me to do?"

"I want to take Michael from Fairyland," Gabriel said. "That is the first imperative. Seraphim…." He paused, to control himself. "Seraphim is an adult, and should be able to protect himself. Though he could very well be dead by now, as ill as he was when he fell into their trap."

Marlon gave him a look with raised eyebrows. "Prince, do you know what you're up against if you ever step foot in Fairyland again?" He shook his head. "Or I for that matter."

"I know what I'm up against. And that's why I needed you. I might have more raw power, particularly on the other side, but you know more."

The eyebrows raised impossibly more. "Perhaps," he said. And then, "And Seraphim isn't dead, not if what I sense is true. Though we might not be able to get to him." He sipped his tea, then lifted the cup, staring within, and Gabriel knew he was reading the tea leaves left on the porcelain. "He was sent to pyramids, but transported from there, very rapidly, to a world where magic is low. It must be an odd world, because there's a sense of… iron about it?"

"Oh. The Madhouse," Gabriel said. "Or one of the worlds in that series. I think, you know, they have magic, just a different type of magic. When Seraphim and I went there, it was full of animated carriages that went by themselves."

For a moment he thought Marlon was going to call him a liar, but instead the older magician shook his head. "Someday, Prince, you'll have to tell me what you've been doing with yourself these years. It sounds terribly fascinating and more than a little addle brained."

"My father committed suicide and Seraphim and I discovered–"

"Someday, Gabriel, means not now. I know you dropped out without finishing semantics, but I assure you that's what it means." Marlon stood up, with an appearance of unfolding. He set the tea cup down on the tray, and waving a hand to make the whole thing disappear, walked over to his work bench. "You want to go to Fairyland, we shall go to Fairyland. After all, you know, I hadn't anything planned for the next sixty years or so of life, so it makes no difference if it's ended prematurely. First, let's locate that tiresome youngest brother of yours."

Locating Michael proved far harder than it seemed. Working with Fairyland was always hard. Scanning Fairyland was harder. No one who had no elven blood could hope to do it, but even with elven blood there were easier things to do. Extracting blood from stones, for instance.

But more than that, after using his crystal ball and a not inconsiderable amount of magic, Marlon fetched a book from the shelves and tried another approach. At this point, Gabriel could tell his magic was running down and quite wordlessly provided his own to lend force to the endeavor.

He was rewarded with a brief, brilliant smile. And then Marlon sighed. "It is occluded," he said. "I can't see. OH!" The *oh* was loud and echoed dismay, and his hand went up to his forehead. "Oh," he said again. He looked at Gabriel, with a look of consternation.

"Tell me, Marlon, damn you."

"He's in the royal dungeons," Marlon said. For the first time there was a hint of fear in his voice. "They're strip mining his magic!"

"Well then, we must rescue him from them," Gabriel said, even as his heart thudded fast and he felt, incongruously, cold as ice.

"You're ready to face the assembled armies of Fairyland in the name of rescuing your misguided brother?" Marlon asked, with something like a hollow laugh.

"Yes, yes, I am."

The hollow laugh became louder. "Very well then," Marlon said. "We can die but once."

Sarah A. Hoyt

Dangerous Roads

In here, Mama," Caroline whispered, her warm hand on her mother's arm, pulling her close and into a dark space between buildings. For a moment the dowager saw nothing, then, in front of her like the landscapes one sees in a dream, a doorway opened, filled with something like twinkling lights.

The impression of twinkling lights held for a moment, nothing more, and then they were on a vast meadow, under the moonlight. It smelled like a dream, too, except of course one didn't normally smell in dreams. But what surrounded Barbara was a warm scent of hay and flowers and of water running nearby, all of it untainted by smoke or any sign of human habitation. Also, all the smells were heightened, stronger, the sort of smells one remembers from childhood, when the world is fresh and new.

She stood rooted to the spot a moment, as the warm breezes of the meadow wound around her, thinking that she didn't remember Fairyland being like this. Perhaps they'd come somewhere else altogether. But in her mind she was remembering what her rescuers had done to find her and bring her out – everything that she'd ever heard about bringing people out of Fairyland. She hesitated before speaking. If she told them to Caroline she risked offending her daughter.

It had become clear to Barbara over the last few moments that her daughter knew far more than Barbara herself about some things: those things being for instance how to go into Fairyland and how to defend oneself from elf magic. Crossing over into Fairyland was a major working. It required not only a susceptible location, where a portal could be opened, but also preparing the magical spell and working it for about half an hour, before the portal became obvious. Barbara realized that Caroline must have been saying the spell under her breath the whole while they walked down the street, and wondered if this too was something Gabriel had taught her. She wouldn't ask.

But there was a good chance, she thought, that neither Gabriel nor any of her teachers had taught the girl what she must do, to come safe out of Fairyland. She'd risk offending her daughter, then, because if they should get separated, what Caroline didn't know could kill her.

Just then Caroline pulled at her, but the first rule, Barbara remembered, was to stay on the road. And they were not on the road but on the grass next to it. She resisted Caroline's pull forward, upon the grassy rolling hill and instead spoke in measured accents, in a little more than a whisper, "No, my dear. The first rule you must remember," she said, while she in turn pulled Caroline sideways and a little back, until their feet were firmly planted on a brick-paved road. "Is that you must always stay upon the road. It will change as you walk, but the road is your only measure of safety. It exists only for visitors to Fairyland, and, as such, it is part of a pact between our people and elves. They cannot hurt visitors who are on the path and we, in turn, undertake not to deviate from the path, and to stay on it whilst in Fairyland. Do you know the other rules? I hesitate to ask, but what did Gabriel tell you?"

"That I should not eat anything any elf ever offered me." Caroline paused. "An elf other than himself, I presume, because that would make it very difficult particularly when I was little and he gave me candy."

"I don't think that Gabriel counts as an elf. Not a true one." She paused in turn, as an odd thought occurred to her. "At least not unless he wants to be one."

Caroline seemed to understand this, as she nodded a little. "I assume this applies to anything in Fairyland."

"Yes," Barbara said. "I very much believe so. But there are other rules."

"Such as?"

"You must help three people you encounter. You must remain loyal and pure and impervious to temptation, and you must do your best to help those who need you, while refusing to either leave the path or eat anything. This might include performing feats that would otherwise be impossible. In these tasks, you will usually find three helpers. These are not always wholly good, and usually they want something in return, but you must accept their help nonetheless, and count on being able to defeat their wiles later."

"And?"

"And you must under no circumstances accept an offer to live in Fairyland. Oh, it won't be presented that way. It's usually presented as great riches, a palace, anything you care to own."

Caroline looked at her mother curiously, her head tilted a little to the side, as though evaluating something. "How very odd. But you'll be with me and able to remind me of these rules, will you not?"

"I don't know," Barbara said. "What you have to understand is that Fairyland works in ways that our world doesn't. The same rules of logic do not apply to both. I wasn't with the people who came to rescue me, but I know that they got separated, and never found out how. So, if you get separated, do remember those rules. They should be enough to keep you safe. And now let us walk."

"Which way do we walk on the road?" Caroline said, confused, looking behind her, and then ahead.

"It doesn't much signify," Barbara said. "Direction also doesn't mean in Fairyland what it means in our world. Instead of north and south, they have deeper and out. Whichever way we walk in Fairyland, while in pursuit of our goal of finding your brother, we will be penetrating deeper into the lands of magic."

"But how do we leave, then?" Caroline asked, as the two walked the way they were facing, along the gently rolling road, amid a meadow so beautiful it looked like an illustration from a child's book. In fact, everything from the too-green grass, to the intense scents of summer, to the rolling hills gave the landscape the impression of being too beautiful to exist – something not even out of a real dream, but out of a story.

"We leave when we've found your brother and we've fulfilled all the conditions of our coming here, such as our agreeing to render help to three unfortunates. That is," she said, as another thing occurred to her. "When those are done, we are automatically ejected from Fairyland and into the real world. That is, unless…."

"Unless?"

"The king of Fairyland objects to our going," Barbara said.

"And then we're prisoners here forever?" Caroline asked, her eyes very wide and for the first time the hint of fear in them. "No. We're here," Barbara said, "until we can find a champion to fight for our freedom." She paused. Somewhere ahead, something or someone was crying desolately.

Mystery On Mystery

What do you mean?" Seraphim asked. "You came from Avalon?" He remembered the pyramid world and the feeling that she was a citizen of Britannia who had learned her magic in some far off and desolate place.

She blinked at him. "No," she said. "No. I simply knew I came from somewhere other than Earth." She turned around and paced towards the window, and looked out of it at the farm outside. He'd caught a glimpse of it when he was walking from the bathroom and had a vague idea of a broad plane drenched in sun with mountains in the distance. He had tried, of course, to place those mountains in his own world. Landscapes that existed in one place existed – after all – in the other and this was often a good way to guess where in this world corresponded with his own world. But the mountains were wholly unfamiliar to him. Yet, since Miss Felix and her Grandmother spoke English, he had to assume they were somewhere in the North American colonies. But he could not place it in any of the English-speaking portion of them. Not that it should matter. Sometimes different peoples occupied different places in alternate worlds, but it bothered him all the same.

"What would make you think you weren't from Earth?" Seraphim said, then cleared his throat. "Did you have a memory from another world? Or is the knowledge of other worlds that well known in this one?" There were a few worlds, he knew, where knowledge of magic and of magical alternates to the world they lived in were quite normal and in fact subjects anyone might discuss. But in the Madhouse, where magic seemed not to be used at all?

"No. I think I was brought over as a newborn or very little more," she said. "And no, belief in other worlds is not widespread. It's just that…."

She turned away from the window and towards him. He was struck by how beautiful she looked. And he shouldn't have found her beautiful at all, not in her outlandish clothes. In Britannia, the clothes she had struck him as comely enough, but not extraordinarily good-looking. But here in her native – or not her native – world, in those blue breeches that molded her figure, in a shirt so light and plain that a lady from Britannia would consider it too light for underwear, she looked magnificent.

He thought it might be that he was weak and therefore susceptible. Then he thought, no. It was that her small, delicate features, her dark hair, all of it lent itself to far simpler styles than anyone in Britannia would dream of wearing. He shifted in bed, lest his attraction should become obvious. But she was looking into his eyes.

"A little more than twenty-two years ago," she said. "My parents were childless and … well… very upset about that state. They wanted children, but there seemed no hope of conceiving one. Adoption in our world, in our region is, for various reasons, a complex and difficult process, or a costly one. You can't have one without the other. Also, father's income was irregular, as he was a classical musician, and… no, never mind that, it would take forever to explain. They finally managed to conceive, but the baby was stillborn. As a way of bringing mother out of a very deep depression, father took her to Paris when he went there to play.

"They were walking outside the convent of Holy Grace, in Paris, when they saw a basket appear on the steps. The basket contained a girl: me." She gave him a brief, brittle smile. "One of my father's friends knew a doctor in Paris, and they arranged to have it claimed mother had given birth to me, and for me to have a birth certificate, which allowed them to bring me home at the end of father's engagement in Paris six months later."

He tried to make sense of her story. "But surely," he said. "That doesn't mean that you are from another world. I mean, if your parents didn't believe in other worlds, surely–"

"No, listen, when they found me, they saw me appear on the steps."

"But–"

"They were walking under a steady rain, with an umbrella, you know? That's why there was no one around. But I and my wraps were no more wet than if we'd been under the rain for only one second. And that, you see, is why they thought I'd come from elsewhere. They didn't quite put it at another world, but the idea of parallel worlds is not completely alien here, and there are stories of people appearing or disappearing out of nowhere."

"I see. So you thought you might have come from elsewhere, and you wanted to find out from where?"

"They didn't even tell me I was adopted," she said. "Not till I was fourteen, and then they didn't tell me. Only they died in an accident, driving to a new job with a philharmonic in Kansas. I'd stayed behind, with Grandma, to finish out my school year. Anyway… when they died grandma told me. As you've found out, she has some magic, and she'd taught me some magic. It is of the sort that peasants do in Avalon, you know, healing minor ailments and such. I took what she gave me, and I built on it, and of course, my magic is much stronger–"

"Strong enough for a noblewoman in Britannia."

She flashed him a smile. "Yes, my landlady in Britannia has the persistent idea I'm some nobleman's by-blow." And then quickly, as he felt his cheeks heat. "Oh, I beg your pardon. I'm back on Earth, see, where no man would find it embarrassing to hear that, not even from a woman's lips.

Anyway, her illusions amused me, because surely… but never mind that. I don't even know if I come from Britannia. I might come from another world more magical than Avalon, where a peasant has as much power as a nobleman in Britannia does. No. But yes, I had more power, and after a while, grandmother thought, perhaps my origins explained it and so she told me. Therefore, I was … primed you might say, the first year I was living away from home and working at my first job when Antoine appeared in front of me, on a deserted street. And I was prepared to learn magic from him and to…." She blushed. "And to accept his invitation to go and see the other worlds. He said it would be fun," she said, wistfully. "And it was for a time. Gloriously fun."

Seraphim guessed at what she didn't say and didn't think much of the Antoine fellow. Even if he hadn't tried to kill Seraphim himself, and if his corpse hadn't been the reason that Seraphim found himself in these straits, Seraphim didn't hold with the sort of fellow who gave a respectable girl a slip on the shoulder.

And despite the odd clothes, and what he was sure was a very odd society, Seraphim would have put hands in the fire that Nell Felix was or had been a respectable woman. He chided himself on the "had been." It was different in Britannia. If a girl lived with a man as lovers, and it became known, the doors of society would close to her, and she would cease being treated as a respectable girl. But he wasn't sure at all this truth held here. In fact, just as a feeling, he had a sense it didn't. So she was still a respectable woman. And Antoine had lured her away. He was sure of it. But he wouldn't say it. Instead, he played with the edge of the blanket, and Nell, perhaps noticing no answer was forthcoming, said, "I know I was a fool, you don't need to tell me, but I… well… was very young. And I've been prattling on, and making you tired. You're not well yet. Sleep. Tomorrow, if you're feeling better, I'll show you around the farm."

But it wasn't till the day after that she showed him around the farm. Frankly, showing him around the kitchen had been a near fatal shock. He started to understand why these people had no servants. Who needed servants, when machines kept food cold, when stoves lit at the flick of a button, when machines even washed dishes?

After a while, he'd asked for pen and paper and started making notes. "For my brother Michael," he said. He sat at the broad, golden oak kitchen table and drew schematics on his paper, and made notes. "We can't hope to harness this electricity you speak of, or at least not fast enough to–"

"It's not that," she'd interrupted. "It's more that electricity interferes with magic. Even mine is not as powerful as it is in Avalon. I think, generationally, if you introduced electricity in your world now, you'd be devoid of magic in a hundred years. Or have it only at that low level Earth has it."

He nodded. "I suspected there was something like that," he said. "Some worlds have less magic naturally, but I didn't feel this as being true on Earth. And so I don't propose to introduce electricity to Avalon, something for which I doubt Ainsling's Arcana has enough capital, and that's supposing something terrible hasn't happened to my estates. I have a feeling…." He shrugged. "At any rate, my brother Michael is very inventive and gifted at designing magical machinery. I'm sketching the ideas for him, and hopefully he can design them to run by magic."

She tilted her head sideways, which he'd learned meant that she was thinking something she was afraid of saying out loud, for fear it would pain someone. He'd seen her look like that when her grandmother had said something about Nell now staying home where she belonged.

He understood what she wouldn't say and said, "I know, I know. You mean that Michael has been stolen away to Fairyland and that he might never come back. But…never fear. We will find him and rescue him." He'd looked at her, his eyebrows arched. "I keep getting the sense that there is something very bad afoot in Britannia, that I was got out of the way so something could be done to my family. Today I had a feeling Gabriel was trying to find me. I dreamed…." He made a face. "If I weren't still so weak and my power weren't still so impaired, I'd scry to see what is happening there and study where we can return."

"As to that," Nell said. "I can scry though the power is limited here, if you–"

At that moment her grandmother came into the kitchen, from the door to the basement stairs, "Nell, I was wondering if Mr. Ainsling, since you say he's been in so many worlds, would be able to tell us where the basket and fabric you were found in came from."

Seraphim submitted in good part to being shown a wicker basket – of fine manufacture, but nothing special, and two unexceptionable blue blankets. Wool, and fine wool at that, but it meant nothing. "It's very little to go on," he said, "unless I scry. She wasn't wearing any particular clothes, I gather?"

"Only a diaper," her grandmother said. "Linen, but no marks on it."

"Then I'm afraid there's nothing to tell me. It could be any of a dozen worlds," he said. "I think she's from Britannia, of course, but I would perhaps think that."

The two women exchanged a look. Her grandmother sighed. "Well," she said. "When my daughter-in-law pulled the blankets off Nell, something fell off. We don't know how it came to be there, but … when Nell was young she made up stories about her real mother putting it there to recognize her by, but it makes no sense, since every other identifying detail seems to have been removed."

"Something?"

Nell ran up the stairs to her room, which Seraphim had learned was next to his. She came back moments later with her right hand tightly closed. When she opened it, a gold medallion shone in it.

Seraphim's heart skipped a beat and his breath caught. But he didn't say anything till he picked the medallion in his palm, and saw upon it, on one side, a figure of a crowned lion, and on the other, a stylized apple tree. He tried to speak several times before he managed it. At last, after clearing his throat, he managed, in a thread of voice, to start in the most irrelevant place, "I bet this pendant managed to find its way into your clothes no matter where you left it, until you were about ten."

"How did you know?" Nell said. "I ended up wearing it on a chain because I could not get rid of it."

"Until you reach the age of reason, it's spelled to accompany you everywhere, in case you get lost, so you can be identified without doubt. I suspect someone thought they'd neutralized that spell, or perhaps didn't know about it. You have to be related to know, I think…."

"We're related?" she said, sounding shocked.

He let out a bark of laughter, which shocked him, because he didn't feel in the least amused. This added a complication he wasn't ready to contemplate. "Very distantly, Your Highness," he said at last. "I believe I'm your sixth cousin."

"Your–" she said, and blanched.

"Yes, Nell, I'm very sorry, but I believe you're the lost Princess of Britannia."

All The Paths

No matter how hard Marlon tried, he could not open a portal into Fairyland. Gabriel watched him do it, and watched him exhaust himself and at some level couldn't help admiring him for not giving up. It was much like watching a man beating against a closed door long past the point at which his beating had become feeble and his voice had gone hoarse from shouting.

Circles appeared beneath the dark-blue eyes, and the flame-colored eyebrows drooped, but Marlon kept trying.

But then, Gabriel reasoned, with a glance at Aiden, Marlon didn't seem good at giving up. After a while Gabriel slipped away to the kitchen, where he washed the tea things and made fresh tea and brought it out, and waited till a pause in Marlon's incantations to say, "Tea. With milk and sugar. You need it."

Marlon made a face. It was a face that Gabriel remembered. Marlon took his tea black. But he ran a hand back over his unruly hair, making it more so, and shambled towards the tea table, his walk no more lively than Aiden's. "There is no path," he told Gabriel. "No way to… to get to Fairyland. There is nothing I can do. It won't open to us."

"How not?" Gabriel said. "Though I believe I was thrown out of Fairyland with the specific injunction not to come back, I believe you weren't even born when you were thrown out."

Marlon set his cup down and rubbed at his nose between the eyes. "It's not like that. Not… specific to us, I mean, but to any magicians of a certain level of power, particularly those of mixed magic. And, Gabriel, I regret that I have to give you bad news. Something I learned through my scrying of the paths of power." He did look sorry, his tired eyes almost as lusterless as those of his animated lover's corpse.

"What?" Gabriel asked, and for a moment felt the dark, unremitting despair of waiting to have Seraphim's death announced to him. He didn't think he could live with himself if he'd allowed Seraphim to be killed, and his whole house lost with him. "Tell me."

"Your… The dowager Lady of Darkwater and her daughter Caroline have gone into Fairyland. They were allowed, or perhaps trapped, into going in. I don't know what they mean to do with them, but it can't be good."

"Caroline." Gabriel discovered he'd put his own cup down, and that he was clutching frantically at the sleeve of Marlon's shirt. "For the love of God, we must go and rescue her. She's just a child. She– I taught her some defenses but not nearly enough for what she'll meet with there."

"No," Marlon said. "And I did not mean to tell you until we could get in. But I don't think we can, or at least…."

"At least what?"

Marlon's face had acquired a pinched look, and Gabriel realized he was clutching the magician's arm hard enough to bruise the flesh beneath. He withdrew his hand and tried to compose himself. "I beg your pardon, but–"

"No. I understand. They are your family." A pause. "You know, I think part of what fueled my anger at you all these years, other than your incredible stupidity in alerting the authorities or your idiot brother's insistence on fighting a duel with me, after finding me through magical means he shouldn't be able to use–"

"Seraphim? He what?"

"Assure you. Fought a duel with me. For your honor. As though you'd been a despoiled maid–" Marlon shook his head. "At any rate, more than any of that, what fueled my anger at you was knowing that you had a family, and I never did. It was knowing you were loved by at least your father and not born of–" He shrugged. "And that they counted to you and on you." He looked up at Gabriel and gave the impression of being so tired he would presently sway on his feet. "And that you mattered to them. Foolish, I know, to hold it against you. It is not your fault I was not born in the same circumstances. But I was envious. Deadly envious. And it distorted all my feelings. It made me… never mind."

But Gabriel's mind was spinning dizzily over this duel, if it had happened. "Seraphim fought you? For my honor? But… what did my honor have to do with your practice of necromancy?"

He got back a level stare. "No. Idiot. Not the necromancy. Our… friendship."

"Oh. But–"

"Don't ask me to explain what goes on in His Grace's mind. I'm sure I couldn't tell you anymore than I can bring the moon down to Earth. I'm common as dirt, remember. He informed me in no uncertain terms that if I ever had any other contact with you, next time the bullet would go between my eyes."

"The bullet?"

Marlon pulled his shirt casually down to reveal a puckered red scar on his shoulder. "As you see." Then suddenly the tired blue eyes danced with devilish amusement. "As soon as I'd recovered enough, I sent you the letter with my coordinates. Because I was not going to let him win."

Gabriel had to cover his eyes for a moment, because it was impossible to think coherently through the desire to laugh and cry at once. "And yet, you'll help me rescue him?'

"Naturally. He's your brother. But for a price, remember?"

"How could I forget? Now to return to the paths into Fairyland."

"The famous Darkwater acumen returns!"

How could he, Gabriel wondered, at the same time admire the man and want to punch him unconscious within the space of less than ten seconds? How was it possible that Marlon would both be willing to help the people who had mistreated him, and yet not be able to keep from mocking Gabriel himself?

"Indeed," Gabriel said, keeping his own temper under control. "Now if you please, to speak plainly. You said there was no way in, only– only what?"

Marlon sighed. "Only there might be. I get a feeling what is keeping us out is not a shutting charm. I don't think they could do that against someone of mixed blood, anyway. Those with blood of Fairyland can always go back, can we not? I have the strong impression what is keeping us at bay is… a cat's cradle working."

Gabriel poured tea for both of them again. The cup he pressed into Marlon's hands was picked up without comment, and then Gabriel himself took a sip of his tea. The magical worlds – and Avalon was one of the more magical ones – all had lines of power which wrapped the world in a tight shroud of magic. Into these lines of power, smaller and more mobile lines of power were attached. Each magic user had his own, and through his life he wove a pattern upon the surface of the world. Those powerful enough changed the nature of the power with their design, and those powerful and active could even move one or more of the lines and alter the nature of the world's magic forever. This was why necromancy was forbidden. Because it could make the bright lines dark, and blight whole areas of magic.

A cat's cradle working was managed with the lines of magic themselves, which were intertwined and twisted in such a way that someone with normal magic could not follow them. "The major lines or the minor ones?" Gabriel asked. To twist the minor lines was what was called a fate work, not savory, exactly, but often employed by village witches making love spells, or by well-intentioned Hearth wizards making it so that a sailor would return from the sea or a soldier from war.

It wasn't good magic as such, because it restricted the will power and actions of others, and it could be dark magic, depending on what fates you were twisting or why. But to twist the major ones would take both an immense amount of power, which would snap back at any moment, without warning, and it would probably cause a deformation in the magic.

If the Cinderella story were true – and Gabriel doubted it, because it was far easier to lay a spell on coachmen to take someone to a ball in a borrowed carriage than to spell mice, and WHY pumpkins? – the change back in coach and mice would be what happened when lines snapped back. The question, though, was how long it would take to snap back.

Marlon squinted, as though thinking. "Both I think," he said. "And before you tell me how dangerous it is, remember I used to teach magic. But it's entirely possible it's only minor lines that are involved, just so many of them and so strongly bound that it feels like major lines."

Gabriel nodded. "So you are saying, if we can unwind the lines of fate – all the fates – we can discover a way to get into Fairyland."

Marlon made a sound that might be laughter, or else it might be a cough. "Indeed, but–"

"But?"

"The lines include those of the king. And my father, and your brother, Seraphim, who is in this other world we might not be able to access."

"Your FATHER?"

Marlon's face went blank, almost wooden in its lack of expression. "Indeed. My very honored father."

"But I didn't know– that is, I know he never recognized you, which is why–" Which was why the official name Marlon used was Elfborn, the name of every bastard kicked out of Fairyland, and attached to a certain stigma, to a definite untrustworthiness. That he'd managed to get an education, much less to become a tutor, despite all that, had been one of the things Gabriel admired about him. And perhaps that was one of the reasons that Marlon had been tempted into necromancy. If everyone assumes the worst of you at all times– But no. Damn it. He would not find excuses for the man. Marlon had chosen that one dark path of his own accord.

At that moment, Gabriel realized the expression on Marlon's face was ghastly enough that Marlon himself could have been many years dead. The smile that contorted his lips was closer to the grimace of a corpse. "Oh, but he did recognize me, Gabriel. I made sure of it, though it almost killed us both. Legally I have my father's name. For all the good it did me, since I had to go into hiding that same week. I had hoped– Never mind that. I chose not to publicize his name, though I owe him no respect and little gratitude. I had to force his hand to recognize me, to threaten to reveal that what happened to my mother was not consensual but the result of dark magic and of entrapping a Fairyland creature and then–" He shook his head. "My father would kill me, if he could. It is a good part of the reason I'm still so fiercely hunted these many years after, when my acts of necromancy amount to a resurrection spell said two seconds too late."

Gabriel looked towards the corner "Is that why–"

"Damn it," for the first time there was *fury* directed at Gabriel in Marlon's voice. "What did you think it was?"

"But– But then why didn't you–"

"Kill him again? Don't push Gabriel. There are things you should understand without being told."

And Gabriel, who understood nothing at all, could only take a deep breath, wondering what he should understand. That Marlon couldn't kill Aiden? But surely Marlon could see that tattered soul attached to the not-quite-alive body? Surely he could see its suffering?

Then suddenly he did see. If what Marlon said was true, then the magician had been born of rape. That meant his mother had gotten expelled from Fairyland, as well as Gabriel's mother had, but that she had never wanted to leave. He'd never asked Marlon exactly what his mother was. There were many creatures in Fairyland, from elves to centaurs, from the high-powered and princely sovereigns and noblemen of elves to the naiads and dryads and centaurs that the Romans had mistaken for minor divinities. Depending on what Marlon's mother had been, she might not have lasted long outside of Fairyland. And, regardless of what she had been, she might very well have abandoned her human child behind and gone back, to face whatever punishment would allow her to be part of the magic lands again. "Your mother...."

"Never met her," Marlon said. "Not consciously." He rubbed at the tip of his nose, and seemed to be oddly confused about the turn in the conversation. "I was raised in an orphanage for magical children." He made a face. "What does that have to do with any–"

But Gabriel's mind was still following its own thought. Orphanages for magical children ranged from the very good to the appalling, and he wasn't going to guess which kind it had been. Marlon had survived childhood, so it couldn't be one of the very worst ones. Unless Marlon had been *lucky*. Gabriel refused to pursue that thought. Marlon had never belonged to anyone. He'd had no family, no kin, and probably no friends either, because even weres were afraid of half-fey magic.

Gabriel thought of the fear that had met him in the eyes of the servants, the looks of dread, when he'd first gone to live with the Darkwaters. He imagined growing up with that, living with that, your whole life, unremitting. Then there had been Aiden Gypson, who had been– "You were friends with Aiden for a long time."

A face. "We were both charity pupils at his majesty's charity school for magically gifted young gentlemen. I think we were twelve when we became friends. What are you getting at, Gabriel?"

Nothing, Gabriel thought. *Nothing at all save that your foolishness has epic proportions to it. But then, why should I be surprised? Do you not do everything, always, larger than life?*

"I think we should sleep," Marlon said. "Because unraveling these fates will take us off into each of the places the people involved are. And you know, and I know, that we'll have to do a major working, which should not be undertaken as tired as we are. We'll need some hours of sleep at least. And you know time in Fairyland doesn't run at the same rate, so your brother's fate is not as urgent, or it's perhaps more urgent than–"

"Who is your father?" Gabriel asked. It had to be someone despicable, if he'd taken advantage of a female elf bound in a working, yet it had to be someone important enough to be enmeshed in this working – whether important in the human or the magical world.

"My dear Gabriel! What does it signify? We must rest and then we'll do our working. You are very odd asking me where I met Aiden, and then asking who my father is. It makes me feel like you're some girl in her first season, or else the girl's mama checking on my antecedents. I assure you when I said we should sleep I meant just that. There is strenuous magic to be done, and I–"

"And you speak a great deal of nonsense, Marlon. Who is your father? If he's involved in this working, we must understand how and why before we start."

"The fact he's involved has nothing to do with being my father. Far more to do with his being an ambitious man." Marlon tried to smile, but it didn't quite work and he sighed. "Has anyone ever told you, my dear Gabriel, that you have the most unpleasant habit of fastening on to irrelevant details and holding onto them buckle and tongue? First there was your calling the authorities merely because I lacked the cour– because I kept Aiden about. And now this obsession with my father. And you're not going to let me go up to bed until I tell you, will you?" He looked up into Gabriel's eyes, and whatever he read there made him sigh again. "Very well, Prince. If you must know, my father is Lord Sydell, His Majesty's spy master." And then, with a near sneer, "There, are you happy?"

Waking And Dreaming

Don't worry about it," Arden was saying, his voice very steady. "Don't worry about it, Barbara. The girl will be fine. She's full of determination, that one. The strongest of our children, and she had to be the girl. What a boy she'd have made." And then, with a smile. "Or perhaps not," he said. "Imagine all the duels he'd have fought and how many liaisons he'd have embroiled himself in."

Barbara, the dowager duchess, looked at her husband, walking by her side, in this path in Fairyland, and wondered what to make of his presence at all. He was dead. She knew he was dead. She remembered the study, and his corpse, and blood everywhere. It had taken them weeks to remove the blood stain from the floorboards, using all magical means available. She remembered the shock, and the pain at knowing she'd never see him again, in the flesh, no matter how much grief he'd brought into her life. He'd brought joy too.

The joy was now obvious in those green eyes, squinting at her with something like deep and secret amusement. It was the amusement that made her snap back an answer, as she'd so often done when he'd been alive. "Mind you," she said. "Your boys are not much better. Michael is, I suppose. He wouldn't get embroiled with anything unless it came with magical gears and perhaps a steam engine. But Seraphim!"

"I don't think it is what you think, with Seraphim," Arden said. "At least, I think he and Gabriel found my papers. I'm sorry, Barbara."

"Your papers… Yes, I've for some time now been worried that you were involved in something … something worse."

"Oh, I was, which is why I'm here," Arden said.

"You mean dead?" She asked, and her heart beat very fast, afraid he'd tell her, yes, he was dead and that she had now joined him.

But he frowned at her. "You know, I don't believe I am. No, no, it's true, this is not my body beside you. I'm not absolutely sure where my body is just now. It doesn't seem to matter much in Fairyland, and after a while…."

"But I saw you dead. I saw your body, I–"

"Surely, you of all people know about changelings."

"Oh," Barbara said. And then, "I am dreaming. I was just walking with your daughter, and we didn't turn, we didn't veer. Only we heard someone crying and…." She frowned, unable to remember when Caroline had disappeared or when Arden had appeared beside her.

"Yes. That's her path. Not yours."

"But we didn't part."

"In Fairyland, all paths are alone, Barbara, for those who don't belong."

Out Of Time

When Nell had been much younger and read everything she could get her hands on, she'd gone through an old suitcase full of time travel romances from the eighties, stored in one of the farm's outbuildings.

She now knew they were completely wrong. Forget the big things, such as the fact that in one of those the woman gets to take her tape player and tapes back to the middle ages, and since her music is the only thing she missed, lives there happily ever after – which had left Nell, even at eleven, scratching her head and wondering what they planned to use for electricity or batteries. No, what she hadn't realized before that what was wrong was how a person from the past would adapt to the present day.

In the books, there were one or two funny incidents, and then the dislocated person started behaving exactly like a modern-day man – it was usually a man – save for one or two run-ins with tech, which were more amusing than scary.

She knew from living in his time that His Grace, the Duke of Darkwater, was not a stupid man. In fact, she'd judged both him and his half-brother to be damnably acute. And she knew, because it had taken her forever to figure out how to navigate it, even though she had the advantage of having read books set in a similar time period, that his social etiquette was far more difficult than anything she'd ever learned. However, she'd never have known it by the way he behaved in this time period.

It wasn't even the puzzlers – like the existence of toilet paper, compounded by his archaic manners, which made him almost incapable of speaking of that sort of thing – or the fact that, in trying to be independent, he'd in fact managed to melt grandmother's plastic mixing bowl all over the stove, when he'd thought to boil water in it – it was the fact that he kept tripping over things so basic and fundamental that Nell had learned them before she was conscious of learning anything.

The result was that, over the next few days, she ended up being as much a nanny to him as though he were a two-year-old infant stumbling from peril to disaster. The worst of it, of course, being when he thought he was adroit enough to do for himself, or perhaps even help. She'd barely stopped him using clothes detergent on his hair, and shuddered at the thought of what the people in his world would think if he had to shave his head after turning his hair into a hay pile.

But that had brought her around, after four days, to thoughts she didn't want to have. She knew the royal symbol of the Royal family of Britannia – the local name for the British isles – in Avalon. And she knew it was the same as the symbol on her medallion. She'd just never thought about it. And besides, she thought, surely there were many such royal families in that many worlds. It didn't mean it was that one.

That in turn had brought her to what a coincidence it was that she should end up in Avalon. And then, with a sick lurch in her stomach, she knew it was no coincidence. It strained the limits of credulity that she'd both end up in the world where she'd originated and be involved in what was clearly an attempt to get rid of the Darkwaters. And the Darkwaters had been involved in something, too.

She looked over at Seraphim, looking startlingly modern and startlingly archaic, both, in a pair of jeans grandma had procured from town, sitting at the kitchen table, sketching the automatic shaver on a cheap note pad and making notes on how it worked. She didn't know yet whether the fact that his tongue protruded from the corner of his mouth as he sketched made her like him more or less. It was such a terribly undignified habit for a Duke to have.

And despite the jeans he managed to look like the cover of a romance novel, with his obviously well-muscled torso doing violence to one of her white t-shirts, and his dark hair severely tied back.

Instead of dwelling on how he looked, she cleared her throat. "Do you really think your brother will be able to reproduce a shaver with magic? I mean, one that works automatically?"

"It might look quite different," Seraphim said. "When he's done. But if he sees the principle of how it works, he'll probably have an idea for how to do it. And it would be no end of relief for Gabriel not to have to shave me."

She was briefly scandalized. "Mr. Penn shaves you?"

Seraphim looked as surprised as he had when the plastic had melted, then started burning with a merry flame all over the gas burner. "He is my valet," he said. "And besides… I don't know that I'd feel really confident with anyone else using a blade that close to my neck."

"But who shaves him?"

There was a moment of almost shocked hesitation. "Himself, I presume," Seraphim said at last and, once more proving to her that he was very far from stupid, he smiled, disarmingly. "I can shave myself too, Miss Felix, and I take your meaning, but he does it better than I can do it, and in my world there is the expectation that a person of rank–" A shadow passed over his face. They hadn't talked about her origins, not since he'd discovered them. Instead they'd skirted around them like a burned cat walking around fire. In a way they'd both tried to pretend it had never happened, and more often than not he called her Miss Felix, even if there was, sometimes, an almost palpable hesitation before the word. Grandma, too, had not mentioned it, but there was that look she gave Nell sometimes that made Nell wonder what she felt. Was she afraid of losing Nell forever? Nell was her only descendant and it had always been assumed, on Grandma's side at least, that Nell would inherit the farm, particularly since mom and dad had died.

But now Seraphim looked at her and sighed. "As you'll doubtless learn, once we reclaim your position."

"Are we going to reclaim my position?" she said, softly, sitting across from him.

He looked at her a long moment. "You are very wise, you know?"

"Am I?"

"You are. You're neither overjoyed at the idea of being a princess, nor foolish enough to tell me you don't need to go back, or you don't want to go back, and that you'd rather live your life out here, as it's been."

She sighed. "I'm not sure," she said, deciding confession was good for the soul, "that I am so much wise as cowardly. I've avoided discussing it, because I didn't want to think about it. It goes without saying that I don't wish to claim my inheritance in your world."

"Why does it go without saying? And it is your world too."

"Because… It's not my world. Not really. I was not brought up there. It feels uncomfortable, and odd, and I know enough, thank you so much, Your Grace, to know that at the higher levels in society there is even less freedom than in the other classes. I know that if I were to become your princess, I'd find myself married off to someone I don't love. I'd probably be bundled off to some country where I don't even speak the language, because the family I don't even know needs a treaty or something."

He looked at her a long time, his bewildering green eyes very intent. "Did you ever see the king, Your… Miss Felix?"

She shook her head. "There was," she said. "Some sort of ceremony once, and you could say… I mean, I saw him from a distance. Tall man. Grey hair."

"In family… even in the extended family, which we are, and in private, not in his capacity as king, he goes by Richard, though I believe my mother might call him something absurd like Ricky. They… my father and he were playfellows and when my father married my mother, she learned to address the king the way my father did."

"In family. You really are related."

He gave her the bewildering smile again. He seemed to have forgotten what he was sketching and instead, his pencil moving as if of its own accord, had started sketching a face on the side of the paper, shading it in. "Not really. No more than all nobility in the isles is at some level. If we didn't often import brides we'd all have two heads." He shrugged. "But we are distant cousins, and because my family is one of two important magical families–" He frowned a little, and she wondered if he was remembering that the other family was that of his erstwhile fiancée. Or were they technically still engaged? That particular bit of etiquette was bewildering beyond belief. "But because my father and Richard were friends, my father being one of a select group of youths allowed to play with the prince heir, they remained close. And given the status of my family, we were often invited over to … for family dinners, of a sort." An amused smile again. "It would still all seem unbearably formal to you, but to the royal family it is our version of winding down. I don't see how I didn't realize it before," he said, looking at her. "Except of course, one doesn't expect lost princesses to drop into one's lake… or on top of one. But you look a lot like your mother, Queen Cecily. Cecilia, I believe is her birth name."

"Cecily," Helena said. Useless to say she didn't want to know her mother or hadn't nurtured questions about her parents. "I… I never knew that was the Queen's name."

"No. Most people just refer to her as her majesty the Queen. But she looks like you, though in smaller point. you inherited some of your father's more substantial look. She is… was… a princess of Italy and married your father when she was barely a teenager. Or at least married him by treaty and came over to learn our ways and our magic. They married officially in their twenties, and had a long string of stillborn infants, before they managed to produce you. Their magic, you see, is somewhat incompatible, which is a danger when marrying far from home." He was now carefully shading the features. A woman's face, Nell decided. "But the advantage of course is that any infant who survives will be very magically powerful. As you are." He looked up. "Understand, they are a very happy couple. You are correct. At our level of society normally marriages are made for reasons other than mutual affection, but Richard and Cecily love each other. Lucky for them, of course. They're both of a quiet, bookish disposition, and on winter evenings they'll both sit in his office. She reads while he works. They could be any middle-aged couple. And of course, they wanted to have children." She realized with a shock that the face he'd drawn was her own and, having shaded it in, he as now busily giving her a crown. "They wanted to have children for the crown, but most of all they wanted to have children for themselves. I don't actually remember the princ– your disappearance, not as such. I was very young myself. But I do remember your baptism because there was a procession, and I was one of a few children allowed to carry your train… the… the edge of the cape attached to your christening gown." He sighed. "At any rate, I have heard from my parents how overjoyed Richard and Cecily were, then how distraught at her– your disappearance. How they tried to follow all leads in vain, only to find you were carried out of the world. And then, the king asked permission of parliament for an exemption from the prohibition of traveling to other worlds, so that he might send investigators to find you.

"It was denied, because it was felt it might upset the delicate magical balance of the universe, and… and my mother says that your parents aged ten years in a week. I don't know if it's true, but I know that–"

"Yes?" She said.

"That the two of them, though they're not actively unhappy, always look to me as though a part of them is missing. It's as though… as though they should be living a completely different life, one in which they have children and the hope of grandchildren, and instead, that part of them was taken away. It's as though… they are shadows of themselves."

"Damn you," she heard herself say, before she knew what she was going to utter. "Damn you. You know very well I could have refused the claims of the kingdom, but I can't refuse the love of my parents."

He didn't say anything. His pencil had given her an elaborate crown, and was now sketching a body in royal robes, a hand holding a scepter. After a while, he breathed deeply. "Understand, Your Highness, you do have a claim to the kingdom, too. Someone kidnaped you and sent you to a world where our scrying didn't work. Someone, too – maybe the same person – made sure to find you later, as an adult and bring you to Britannia for some time. And someone again, who knows how or why, sent you away, with me, to a world where you were likely to get killed quickly, had we not taken extraordinary measures.

"Unless the person doing all this is mentally ill, it can't be the same person. So the question is, who are the two forces warring over you? How and why was I pulled into this strife? What do these people have to do with my family? And how can we uncoil this confusion?"

Nell looked at him a long time. She wanted to scream and tell him his kingdom's problems were no issue of hers, or that she didn't care, or that she'd stay here and he could go back.

But in her mind was the image of the royal couple – her parents – who had mourned her loss for more than twenty years and yet had adhered inflexibly to their duty and the laws of their land, even when their position allowed them to impose their will. She thought of how Seraphim described them, as if a part of them were missing. She thought of Seraphim himself and his family, that bond she'd seen between the members of his family, even the illegitimate one.

She was close to Grandma, perhaps that close, but it was just them and had been since mom and dad died. But if she had more family, family who missed her….

"What if I go back? With you? We just transport into the palace and… find my parents…"

He tilted his head sideways, and looked at her through narrowed eyes, the way she'd learned he did when appraising magic. "You might have enough power to do it," he said. "And the commotion might even be worth it. But there might very well be traps set for you, should you return, and besides…." He sighed.

"Besides?"

"I'm fairly sure I'm wanted, and that a blade might have slipped into my back before you're even established…. Face it, we have a powerful enemy."

"Yes," she said, slowly. Then bit her lip. "How can we figure out… at least some of what is going on there? Sooner or later, you'll want to go back. You're almost well."

He pushed the notepad away. "I want to go back very soon. I've been having dreams about Gabriel, and I think he's in trouble. Bad trouble. But you are right. To go back blind might be death." He paused. "I could try scrying."

But she had a feeling that he couldn't scry very well, not from a world with so much iron and so little magic as Earth. She sighed. "No. I'll do it," She said. "I'm used to the magic here."

That got her the odd tilted look again. "Crystal ball?" he asked, as though this were somehow amusing.

"No," she said. "I'm self-taught, remember?" She got up, leaving him to ponder, and went into the dining room. On the drawer was the pack of cards her grandmother used for her occasional bridge nights. She came back and set it on the table. It amused her that his eyes widened. Playing-card scrying, in Britannia, seemed to be a parlor trick type of thing, almost a joke. "You cut or will I?" she asked. She was about to show him what she could do.

Cat's Cradle

Gabriel woke to the sound of curtains opening and of a tray being set on the table next to the bed. For a moment, for just a moment, before opening his eyes, he imagined he was back at Darkwater and that everything was as it should be: the intervening events had been some horrible, inscrutable nightmare.

Then he opened his eyes. Sunlight came through mullioned windows. The room was small, but not as small as his room in the Darkwater house. And the person standing by the tray, having just set it down, was not some benighted apprentice house maid, with her cap all askew, but Marlon Elfborn, his clothes no more rumpled than normal, his eyebrows raised as though someone had asked him a perplexing question, and a sort of questioning smile on his lips.

Gabriel squinted against the sun, stared at Marlon a moment, and then – somewhat to his horror – heard his own mouth say, "Rufus."

Marlon blinked at him. "I beg your pardon?"

"Your hair," Gabriel said and sat up, and even as he said it, he knew that it wasn't true, that Marlon's hair wasn't red. Not really. Nothing about Marlon was *really*. Not good, not bad. Not dark, not light. Gabriel groaned.

"Hardly," Marlon said, crisply, and sounding indefinably amused. "Not that it matters much, does it?"

"It might," Gabriel said, his mouth still independent of his conscious thought. "I wonder if your mother was a salamander."

And now Marlon's eyebrows went high, really high. "A fire spirit? Unlikely. It is not how my power trends, and besides, I'd like to see the human, no matter how magical, to impose himself on one of those." He shook his head. "None of which matters, does it? I have laid out the instruments we'll need downstairs, but I could use your help. I remember you can't wake without tea, and I remembered also," he looked like a school child caught at fault, "that you didn't like magic used around the house for chores. So I brought you tea and toast. There is food in the kitchen, should you wish for it. Stasis field, on the serving board. I'll be ready to work in half an hour."

And like that he was gone, so fast that he might as well have teleported. Gabriel ate his toast, with just a touch of the marmalade provided in a small porcelain dish, and he drank down his tea. It was strong and a little stewed, which, in his experience, was how Marlon had always made it. Not unpleasant, though.

There was a bathing room and a water closet next to his room, in between his door and what he presumed was Marlon's, Gabriel found it by dint of looking, and took care of his morning hygiene and hasty shaving. One thing that Marlon had never understood, Gabriel thought, annoyed, as he tied his necktie by touch, was that other people didn't spring from sleep fully awake and dress in next to no time.

But by the time he made it down the stairs, Marlon was too absorbed in disposing objects around the room to pay much attention to Gabriel, much less to reproach him on being slow.

The objects were objects of power, but an odder assemblage of them than this, Gabriel had never seen. There were stone spheres, vast and polished, swirling with metallic veins and crackling with barely-contained magic. There was one very large, very ancient shell that looked as though it had been corroded by the tides of an ancient sea. There was, too, an old crown, brown and worn down, that looked as though it had been buried for very long and had possibly been steeped in blood, besides.

Marlon disposed them as pieces on an elaborate game tray. He'd pushed all the furniture out of the way to arrange things, and as he pulled a particularly ugly little statuette of a wolf over one way, for just a moment Gabriel saw the thread of power stretching between objects.

Marlon looked up then, dusting his hands, as though to cleanse them from hard work. "There," he said. "Do you think that reflects the tangle, Gabriel?"

"I don't know what you're trying to do," Gabriel said. "I presume you wish to represent the tangle of magic lines, but … I never learned to do this."

Marlon made a sound of annoyance. "It's very simple, really. We're representing the world as it is – or rather, the mess that someone has made of magic lines as it is. And then after we determine that, we can twist them back – or at least to a less tense state. It's simple sympathetic magic, Gabriel and you must have learned it in grammar school."

Gabriel heard himself say, "We had a tutor, Seraphim and I," as though that explained everything, then walked gingerly down the stairs and into the magic field. Walking into an area where workings were being done was always dangerous, but Marlon hadn't completed a wall or a defense barrier, or anything of the kind, and other than a vague zapping at the bottom of his feet, Gabriel felt nothing else.

Then, looking around at the objects, he felt it and saw it, the tension that was built up in some of the lines being pulled out of position. "Oh," he said.

"Yes," Marlon agreed, as though he'd said a lot. "They are at high tension, at least some of them, but we have to reflect what they are, rather set them in the natural positions. I suppose the feeling of wrongness overwhelms you and you can't do that. Yet. It's difficult the first time. Very well. I think I have them right. Now, let's close the working, and then we can move the lines."

"You didn't close it to set it," Gabriel said. He'd just realized Aiden Gypson's body was nowhere around and wondered where it could be. At Cambridge, Marlon had kept it in a closet in an attic room, which seemed cruel, but somehow Gabriel would much prefer that.

"No. See you, I had to be open to the influence of the world and to the currents as they were. But now we can close it. Do you wish to do the honors of the knife? I shall call the guardians." He handed Gabriel his working dagger, a piece of ancient metal probably inherited from some teacher. Working knives had to be inherited or have another reason to be held in affection. They were supposed to be, in a way, a part of the magician's own self. Gabriel felt a pang at realizing he'd somehow forgotten his own dagger at home, at his work desk. It had been a gift from his father.

He took Marlon's, though, and walked a quarter circle, slicing at the air. "I cut this working from the world, into a space between the worlds," he intoned, in his best learned-ritual-voice.

Marlon stood next to the piece and called to the guardian of the North, "Guardian of the North, ice and cold, we call to you. Protect this portion of our working that no undue influence can intrude."

They repeated it at each of the cardinal points. Gabriel watched Marlon very carefully to make sure no strange magic crept in. Once a man had dabbled in necromancy – had he really said it was not intentional? – it was only a matter of time till other dark workings came into his daily magic. Or at least that was what Gabriel had been taught.

Finally the circle was closed, and within it, they turned and looked at each other. Neither would willingly break it, because doing so would endanger those who set it. Since they both had, it would be double jeopardy. The circle would need to be opened before it could be broached. For now, they were in this space, in some undefinable way between realities, which gave them the opportunity to perform magic that would be dangerous in any world.

"Right," Marlon said. "Now, if you please, we may start moving the lines. We'll start with that one there." He pointed at the wolf image. "My oh-so-dear father." He squinted at the wolf statue. "I think it should go here." Stepping nimbly among the lines, he tapped his toe on the ground.

Gabriel acquiesced, but, to his shock, it took his help for Marlon to move the statuette he'd casually carried around moments before. As they both pulled at the statuette with all their might, Marlon saw the expression on Gabriel's face and laughed. "We're dragging fate and magic with us. Did you expect it to be light?"

Once they set the wolf down, Gabriel reached for the crown. It was the next highest point of tension.

"The king, I presume," he said.

Marlon nodded and reached for the crown himself. But, before he could touch it, a flash of darkness came through the shuttered windows. That was the only way that Gabriel would ever be able to describe it. A flash of dark as strong as any flash of light, robbing the room of ambient light. It was followed by a rumbling, as from a subterranean tremor. With it came a smell, a feel. Gabriel wouldn't have named it before, but he knew it was elf magic. He made a sound at the back of his throat and stepped backwards.

Marlon grabbed his wrist and pulled him in. "Watch where you walk you fool. Don't step out of the circle."

"But… it's elves. They're outside," Gabriel said.

"I know," Marlon said, his voice annoyed and softer than it should be. "I should have known they would find us where humans failed. They have stopped my … they ripped the disguise from my home, and yes, they're surrounding us from outside, and I suspect from underneath too." This said, as another tremor started.

"Do you think…," he said. He felt his mouth very dry. "What can they want with us?"

Marlon shook his head. "This working can only be done with the help of elf magic. The working we're undoing. They won't want it undone. As for why – even I don't understand elves."

They reached for the crown again, and managed to move it to the right place, despite various rumblings. Marlon then pointed out the perfect green marble sphere near the north cardinal point. "Your honored brother next, and that will be hard, since he's off world."

"Will this move him back?" Gabriel asked.

"Not… immediately. But it will hasten his coming back. Or move things … to the place they would have been had he never gone away, is more accurate. The futures will merge, instead of diverge to the world where he never went away."

Seraphim's marker was heavier than the others. Maybe because he was in another world. It took all of Gabriel's and Marlon's strength to lift it two inches above the ground.

They were both thus bent to hold it when the rumbling hit from beneath, stronger than ever. The floor rocked, and lifted.

Gabriel realized he was going to fall across the line, and lifted his hand, letting it drop in one of the emergency circle breaks allowed.

It wasn't in time, and it wasn't careful enough. On the one hand, the jolt of magic as he fell across it was not a killing blow, which it would otherwise have been. On the other hand, as he fell backward and across it, he felt as though he were being sliced by a thousand knives, and his vision went momentarily dark.

When it cleared, he and Marlon were both on the floor on their sides, holding the stone that represented Seraphim between them. There was a trickle of blood from Marlon's forehead, and his eyes looked wild. "Are you … are you well?" Gabriel asked, since asking someone who is looking at you if he's alive seemed quite outside sanity.

Marlon nodded. "Not, well, no, but… They're throwing magic at us. They're…. Oh, damn."

The Betweener hit like an icy wall running somehow through them. It left them lying somewhere quite different and, as they strove to stand, Gabriel found they were kneeling in the middle of a field, and there was a strange horseless carriage bearing down towards them. No. A horseless cultivator. This could only be one world. They had their hands on Seraphim's marker and– "The madhouse."

Marlon looked demented as he grinned, a grin with no joy at all. "Where His Grace is? Splendid. He gets to try his marksmanship again!"

Straying

Caroline hadn't left the path. She was sure of it. She set her jaw in what a young man once had told her was a very daunting expression. Not that she thought it was true, only the young man had strayed from a ball held at Darkwater and had found her in the garden area just outside the nursery. Caroline supposed that this meant he had thought her an easy mark, since she was only fourteen and not yet come out.

Afterwards, Seraphim had told her the gentleman was a desperate fortune hunter, his pockets prodigiously to let, and had been trying to seduce a girl he thought was a naïf, and also had a pretty fortune. The gentleman had been wrong on both counts, and Seraphim and Caroline had ended the night by laughing over cups of hot chocolate in the governess's rooms, about the surprise the fine young dandy would have got, had he managed to seduce Caroline.

But of course Caroline was not a fool and knew better than to believe claims that she was the fairest woman this man of the world had ever seen, or that, in her plain muslin frock, with the ribbon trimming, she eclipsed the belles of London. She might have been fourteen, but she'd never been stupid. She'd set her jaw just like so, her teeth clenched against all his compliments, and she'd carefully set a don't-touch spell between herself and the young man. As it happened it had been the yelp he gave when reaching for her and meeting the painful barrier which felt rather like a bite, which had got Seraphim's attention, and Seraphim had escorted him off the grounds, with stern words, before coming to speak to Caroline.

Caroline wondered if Seraphim had fought the man. It seemed hardly worth it, as he had not in fact touched her, but he might have. The code of honor of men was a closed book to the young woman.

She scratched her nose. But the one thing that was absolutely sure was that Seraphim could not in fact fight a duel with all of Fairyland for having led her astray. Though doubtless he would try. He could be very foolish that way.

Caroline felt like she wanted to cry, and instead set her teeth hard and rehearsed her wrongs. She had not strayed from the path, nor left her mother. They'd heard a cry – from a woman they thought – and they'd made it a point of going to help her. This made perfect sense. What made no sense whatsoever was for her to now find herself alone, her mother nowhere in sight.

"Mother?" she essayed. And then "Your Grace?" just in case other rules applied here that didn't apply in the normal world. And then again, in a high, hopeless voice, "Mother!"

But her mother didn't answer, and Caroline set her jaw again and determined she would be brave. After all, Fairyland might very well be able to take her tears and do something horrible with them. She couldn't tell. She'd once heard a conversation between Gabriel and Seraphim. She'd been hiding – or at least not quite hiding, but in a place she couldn't be seen – in the library. She'd whiled a snowy afternoon away there, in a window seat half-hidden in the shadow of the fireplace. Wrapped in a woolen shawl, she'd read all afternoon, and then napped and woken to find that Seraphim and Gabriel were there and talking, and that neither of them had any idea she could hear them.

She supposed she should have said something; given the alarm in some way. But the truth was that listening to the two men talk, when they thought she wasn't about, had been like opening a window onto a vista that she'd never been allowed to gaze upon.

She supposed she'd always known that Gabriel was their brother. At least, she couldn't remember not knowing. He was the son of their father, and a fairy lady. The same scary fairy lady who'd come around when Caroline was very small.

But she'd never seen Seraphim and Gabriel behave as brothers, as they did that afternoon. There was nothing much to it. Or at least, most of their conversation went above her head. But it was clear that Gabriel was teasing Seraphim by making comments about Seraphim's magic that she supposed would be a terrible insult in anyone else. And Seraphim laughed at them and, in return, called Gabriel "Penny", a nickname that Gabriel said was utterly revolting. In the middle of the conversation she remembered, most of which might have been more understandable if it had been spoken in Chinese, she'd heard a sentence clearly uttered and ever afterwards remembered: "Fairyland feeds on emotion."

If that was true, she would do her best to control hers. Let them starve. She assumed that by some magic they'd taken her from one path and onto the other, and left her mother upon the other. She hoped her mother would be well, then smiled at the thought that she was worrying about someone who had far more magical experience and power than she did. Yes, she'd been helpless before her magical doppelganger, but that didn't mean that the Duchess didn't very well know how to take care of herself.

She continued following the path – difficult, as a rosy fog grew with every step. She had to feel about with her foot, until she found the edge of the path. At one point, for just a moment, the path cleared, and what she saw through the fog made her more determined than ever not to stray. Because what she saw through the fog was nothing. Not darkness, not a chasm, but nothing – a howling emptiness such as must have existed before creation.

And then the path veered and widened, and suddenly she was before the person crying. Person was a matter of speaking, in this case.

Caroline took a step back, hastily, barely managing to stay on the path, and gulped hard.

She was in what would otherwise be a charming clearing – a broad opening in between low trees that looked rather like a gardener had just got done trimming them. It was carpeted in soft, even grass. On the grass lay…. She blinked.

A dragon. It was enormous, and reddish-orange. Now more red, now more orange, the colors chased each other across its sparkling scales, giving it the look of a lake ruffled by the wind. Its huge paws were stretched in front of it, to accommodate a massive head. It was crying. From its fanged mouth came distinctly feminine sobs.

Caroline didn't even know that dragons could cry, much less that they could shed tears, and now, having found out, she was torn between empathy and fear.

After all, what would make a creature this size cry? And if it was one of the three she was supposed to help on her path, what could she do to help this outsized grief.

She stepped back and must have made a sound, because the dragon looked up, and its tiny, stubby wings fluttered upon its back. "Oh," it said, in a distinctly feminine and lady-like voice. "I did not mean to… I beg your pardon. I must have alarmed you."

Which was when Caroline realized that its wings were not short and stubby. Well, not naturally. Instead, they had been cut across, crudely, with some sharp instrument. The ragged edges still bled.

"Oh," she said. "Does it hurt?" The dragon had the most disconcerting violet-blue eyes, fringed by dark lashes which looked at Caroline in absolute incomprehension. "Your wings?

The dragon sniffed. "I beg your pardon," it said again. "I've forgotten myself." And then, like that, it sat up and… shifted. It was the only way that Caroline could put it.

In front of Caroline and completely naked, and seemingly not caring, was a very pretty young woman, her hair the color of the dragon scales, and rippling with color in the same way. She sat herself in the sort of pose one expected of mermaids waiting for wayward sailors, and smiled through her tears at Caroline. "I'd like to put a frock on, only I don't have one here, and I'm afraid I can't leave here."

"Why can't you leave?"

"Because of my wings," the woman said, and her voice went all watery again.

"Who cut your wings? And why?"

"For trying to leave Fairyland," she said. "The king said I should never do so."

"But I thought elves could leave and… and possibly elf dragons too," Caroline said, confused. Because the truth was that she'd never heard of shifter dragons in Fairyland. Most shifters were completely human, even when their forms were mythological. But she'd heard that there was such a thing as fairy horses, so perhaps there were fairy dragons, too. She refused to speculate further.

"Oh, yes, but you see, I… I went out and I became pregnant, and the king punished me by saying I couldn't leave Fairyland. And when I tried to leave anyway, he cut my wings and confined me to this clearing."

Caroline gulped. "Why would you try to leave, against the king's will?"

"To find my baby." The woman's arms made a cradling motion. He was thrown out as a newborn, and I thought I could find him, if … I thought I might find him before he died, abandoned, on the street. But now it's been two weeks and–" she gulped, "if he's not been found, he's dead." She sighed and the tears started again. "I just realized it and I…."

"Don't cry. Very few children are left to die on the street." Though homes for magical orphans were often not much better. "Don't cry. Tell me, instead, what help can I give you."

The woman controlled her tears with an effort. "I see. You're walking the path, then?"

Caroline nodded.

The woman bit her lip. "You can give me my wings back and then, before the king finds that they have grown, I can go out and find my baby and raise him. I don't care what I have to do. I don't want him raised by strangers."

And that at least was something Caroline could understand and approve of. "I can't take a look at your wings – or at your back, I suppose, in this form, without leaving the path. If you approach and turn around."

The dragon lady did so, facing away from Caroline. On her back there were two cruel gashes, just starting to scab over. And Caroline had a problem. She had used healing spells before. And she could make these wounds close and stop paining the woman. What she couldn't do – had no idea how to do – was make the lost parts of skin which she supposed became the dragon wings, grow back.

She started explaining her predicament to the woman, but the dragon-lady interrupted, "Oh, please. You have to be able to. There must be something you can do, or the paths wouldn't have brought you to me."

Caroline considered the possibility the paths had been wrong, but in her experience magic rarely went wrong that way. Instead, she thought, best think of what she could do that would serve.

A glimmer formed in her mind, something that she'd once watched Gabriel do to a still-live bird the cat had brought in. Gabriel had told her, then, that such a spell was dangerous, more so for full-humans, and that if he ever caught her doing it, he would give her the hiding of her life, even if the dowager Duchess killed him for it.

Caroline set her jaw and ground her teeth. Well, then, Gabriel wasn't here, and neither was her mother. She would do what she had to do to get Michael out of captivity in Fairyland.

Symbol and Sign

She cut cards like a card sharp, and it caused him to raise an eyebrow at her, before he knew what he was doing. Heaven knew she'd not be the first member of her family to have a wicked addiction to the gaming tables, but the disaster that had been her great great grandfather's reign didn't need a reprise.

But she looked up as she brought the deck back together and grinned at his expression. "You need not look so dismayed, Your Grace. I was not weaned on betting or card games. Please remember Earth is different. Mostly I learned to play Go Fish with my grandmother's friends when they visited. And one of her friends taught me to cut cards."

"Go … Fish?" Seraphim asked, wondering if she was trying to insult him in a subtle way. But no, it didn't have that tone.

"Oh. Yes. I imagine in Britannia even quite young children of good houses play Faro and loo in the nursery."

"Not silver loo," he said, in the hopes of making her laugh, and it worked. Her silvery laugh rang out, though she looked as though not quite sure he was joking.

He felt something, not quite a tug at his heart and he told himself he was all done with that and long ago.

"Well, in my world," she said, softly and seemingly unconscious of knowing this was not quite her world. "Children don't play for money. I think Go Fish is primarily designed to help you learn the suits." She disciplined her features, amusement banishing. "Now, if you excuse me, even my poor methods require me to concentrate before I scry."

She took a deep breath and steepled her hands over the playing cards. Elegant hands with long slim fingers, and Seraphim saw them bedecked in rings, and for a moment, wondered if he was having a premonition. Then he realized her hands resembled those of the queen, which he usually kissed, when he visited. The queen, of course, usually wore rings.

Something like a non-physical pain seized his middle, making his breathing difficult. After Nell went back to Britannia, after she was returned to her family, all he'd see of her were those evenings when his family got invited in to discuss important magic policy points. She'd give him her hand to kiss….

He realized his eyes wanted to fill with water, and he refused to allow it. Stupidity. Of course she was the princess of Britannia, and of course she had to go back. He might have used her parents' grief to get her to understand this, but her parents' grief was true nonetheless. And also, the kingdom needed her. Without her… he refused to think about it.

The king had refused to name a successor because, of course, naming a successor was the same as admitting his only, beloved daughter was either dead, or gone so far from this world that she might as well be dead, for all she'd never come back.

And neither the king, nor his father, nor yet his father's father had had any siblings. Four generations back, there was a numerous family of seven girls and two boys. All the girls and the younger boy had been married to royal houses in Europe. If the king died without descendants – or with no descendant able to come back and claim the throne – the isles would fall prey to the dynastic ambitions of a dozen ducal families in the kingdom itself, who would claim their distant relationship to the king – on the level of Seraphim's own, at least five generations back and more – was preferable to turning the kingdom over to strangers. Alas, the territorial ambitions of Europe would be unleashed, too, and he doubted that there would be a kingdom small enough not to send at least a second son to stake a claim. Even the Portuguese royal family were cousins, he thought. And the Low Countries too.

Behind his eyes, which closed in an attempt to block out his thoughts, images of armies descending on his beloved homeland and laying waste to it while killing its peasants and raping its magic passed like a blood-soaked painting succeeding another.

He was called back from these troubling visions by a slap of a card on the table. "This," Nell's voice said, slowly, "is the questioner, who I think for this purpose must be you, as you're the only other person present, and one involved in this matter." She lay down the King of Clubs, and Seraphim grinned at it, because he suspected half of Britannia would expect him to be the King of Hearts in any reading. But clubs was more like it. His was wealth acquired by work – or at least it would be, if he had his way. Right now the wealth was largely imaginary. Even his exalted position – before this adventure – was something precarious that only work could secure to him.

"And this," Nell said. "Is myself – since I'm also involved in this matter." She lay the queen of Hearts over the top of the King of Clubs, crosswise. That not-quite physical pain troubled Seraphim once more. The Queen of Hearts. A woman who represented home. As Nell must, being the rightful princess of Britannia. A woman who represented love– his brain skittered away from that thought. He was done with love. His one affair had exploded in his face just before Gabriel's liaison had become near-public. He shuddered at the memory of his hellish six months. At least he'd not been sent down from Cambridge, as poor Gabriel had been.

Over the last few days, he'd been closer to Nell Felix than he'd ever expected to be to a woman not related to or married to him. She'd helped him with details of everyday life and shown him the mysteries of zippers, among many others, which had required a level of closeness he'd not expected to have with a decent woman not betrothed to him.

Truth be told, before his discovery of her origins, he'd thought that he would have to do the decent thing and marry her. Where this would leave him with Honoria was not something he wanted to contemplate. It was quite possible that Honoria had severed her relationship with him in his absence, particularly since he was fairly sure he was now considered a fugitive from justice. If not, then he must perforce jilt her when he returned, and marry Nell.

He was fully aware that in either case this would cause a rift between the two houses, possibly for generations. Though he supposed, Michael being sixteen, he could be offered as a husband to Honoria, a sacrificial lamb in Seraphim's place. Michael, being who he was, and married already to his inventions, was likely not to notice a forcible marriage, anyway. He'd drift gently through the ceremony, then disappear into his workshop to sketch a magic powered ring-bearer.

The image made him smile, and then he remembered both that Michael was a captive in Fairyland, and might well be dead now, and that Seraphim could not possibly marry Nell. She was the princess of Britannia. The *royal* princess of Britannia. What talk had there been of her marriage, over the years, should she return? Something about Francis of France. Seraphim shifted uncomfortably in his seat. He hoped not. The rumors about Francis were almost as ugly as those about the fellow that Gabriel had taken up with at Cambridge. They were definitely as … odd. Such a marriage, royal or not, was not likely to result in the harmonious union that the current monarchs enjoyed. It would also probably not result in children. Unless the princess got bored with a loveless match and sought– he put an end to the thought, quickly, before it could fully form. He was not his father.

Nell was out of his reach by position and birth. And anything of an underhanded nature, anything disrupted of the vows of marriage – undertaken for love or by duty – would be beneath his honor. He sighed audibly, and realized that Nell had lay a row of cards above them.

He stared down at the ace of diamonds; the three of diamonds; and eight of clubs; a ten of clubs; an ace of clubs. He looked up at Nell and waited for her interpretation, knowing there were as many interpretations as readers, and it was important to know what the one scrying thought it all meant.

"These are the roots of the trouble," she said, her eyes troubled. The long, elegant index finger touched cards. The Three of Diamonds, "Legal trouble, or trouble with the law. I think this is a given, for you and me, both." The Eight of Clubs. "This trouble would seem to result from jealousy and greed – though I don't know whose." The Ten of Clubs. "Travel to distant lands." Her lips quirked. Then her finger pushed at the ace of diamonds, bringing it out of the row. "This one is troubling, because I have no idea what it means – I get a strong feeling it refers to a piece of jewelry."

"Perhaps it is your pendant," Seraphim said.

She inclined her head, though apparently not convinced. "And the Ace of Clubs. This represents happiness and wealth," she said. "And I fail to see how that can be at the root of our problems."

This time Seraphim inclined his head, acknowledging his own confusion.

"These," she said, rapidly slapping cards down, "are the people and things who can help us."

The Jack of Clubs, the Jack of Hearts, the Queen of Clubs, the Queen of Spades, and a Five of Spades. Nell frowned at this array at the feet of the two original cards then, rapidly, reached into the deck and covered the Jack of Clubs with a cross wise Jack of Spades, and then over the two, slanted, set the Four of Clubs and the Six of Diamonds. Then she seemed to regard this mess, and the whole row, with a look of utter bewilderment. "Uh," she said, and scratched her nose, in an endearingly young-looking gesture. "That, I think, Your Grace, must stand for your family, but…. Is your mother perhaps contemplating a second marriage?"

"What?" the exclamation was wrenched from him, uncouth bluntness and all.

Nell sighed. "Well," she said. "I'd assumed this," she set her finger on the Queen of Spades, "was your mother. It usually stands for a widowed lady. And this," her finger on the Queen of Clubs, "I assumed was your sister Caroline, who seems self-willed and intelligent."

"She is that."

"And this," the Jack of Hearts, "would stand for your brother…." She paused, seeming bewildered. "Either of your brothers, to be sure. Since it often stands for a male relative."

"To be sure," Seraphim agreed.

"But this," she pointed to the small pile, "is clearly someone about to embark on a second marriage that is fraught with perils and complications. And, as you know, the Jack can stand for either male or female. Usually for young, but not always."

Seraphim felt a sick lurch in his stomach. His mother had been widowed long enough and surely she was allowed to marry again. But what if she chose unwisely? He would go a long way to keep her from hurt. She had told him nothing of another relationship. What would she keep from him?

But Nell's hands were rapidly slapping down another row of cards: the Two of Spades, the Nine of Spades, Ten of Spades, the Three of Spades and the Four of Clubs. Her finger pointed as she said, "Gossip and intrigue; bad luck in all things, destruction and deaths; imprisonment and unwelcome news; unfaithfulness and broken partnership; changes for the worse, lies and betrayal. That seems to be at the root of our troubles."

"Intrigue me," he said. "I'd have thought that we had been plunged into this by loving kindness and a wish to help us."

"Don't be scathing," she said. "It is clearly trying to tell us there is a vast conspiracy underlying this all."

"That, too, we could have gathered."

"Undoubtedly." The finger poked at the Ten of Spades. "This one worries me. Whose imprisonment?"

"Michael's maybe," Seraphim said. "Or yours being sent to this world."

"Very possible, and in fact part of it, I sense," she said, "but I also sense that's not complete. There is more in this."

"The conspiracy."

"No, I mean, there are other people imprisoned."

Seraphim's stomach lurched again. "I've had dreams," he said. "It is very possible that even now Gabriel is in jail." He tried not to think of what the law thought of half-elves and how harshly it dealt with those unpredictable creatures. "It is my ambition to bring him out safely before they can do one of the curious things they love doing to half elves, like stripping him of his magic."

Nell almost let the pack of cards fall. "Strip him of– Is that even possible?"

"Very possible. If you don't mind destroying the mind with it." To her credit, she looked as sick at this as he felt. "That," she said, "must not be allowed."

She slapped a row of cards down. "These are the people arrayed against us." The Three of Clubs, covered by the Nine of Hearts; the Seven of Hearts; the Nine of Clubs; the King of Spades. After a while, and hesitating, she covered the King of Spades with the Eight of Hearts. "Someone who is making a marriage or attempting to make a marriage to gain advantage from his partner." Honoria. Seraphim's stomach lurched. "But it's covered by the dream card. This marriage is a key to all this person's hopes and dreams." Honoria. He really was an abominable cad, Seraphim thought. Well, he would marry her, then. It wasn't as though he could marry Nell. "An unfaithful, unreliable person who breaks his promises." Seraphim's mind lurched to that damned necromancer that Gabriel had got enmeshed with. Seraphim should have killed him. But at the last minute, the man's gallant deloping at their duel – firing into the air, which admitted his guilt in the matter – had touched Seraphim's compassion. At least the cad and the filthy necromancer knew he was a cad and a filthy necromancer. Seraphim's hand had deviated a few inches and not got him through the heart. A mistake that. He'd make sure the hunt to find him resumed. Yes, as a half elf, he was likely to be put to death for Necromancy. But then, better that than endangering Gabriel. "A new lover or admirer to whom you should not be resistant."

"Beg your pardon?" *Gabriel. On the other hand, Gabriel would kill Seraphim if Seraphim killed his—*

"I don't know," she said. "It's among the people or things that might either attack us or array to make our life difficult. How would I know? It's probably your mistress or something."

"I don't have a mistress."

"No? Gossip would have you keep any half a dozen of them."

"Indeed. Carefully laid gossip, m'dear. The truth is I can't afford a single mistress, much less six."

"Very well, then," she said, and pursed her lips, in clear disapproval of his morals, which made his having a mistress or not a question of money, not of heart. "It might be a relationship for someone else. I daresay it will become clear."

"I daresay, like most scrying, probably much too late."

"Indeed," she agreed. "And these." She tapped on the juxtaposed cards. "These are – or is, perhaps – an ambitious, authoritative man and a," she frowned, "an intruder. Someone from elsewhere."

"Covering the ambitious man?"

"Yes, not merely involved with him, which would be crosswise, but covering."

"Oh," Seraphim said. He shook his head. "Someone from.... An elf? A changeling?"

She started. "Yes. Yes. Definitely that."

Seraphim sighed. "Not a surprise. They are involved in this to their black hearts, I'd say. It worries me, because Gabrie–"

At that moment, they both felt it: like a tearing midair that indicated someone had opened a portal nearby. Nell dropped the cards and ran out the kitchen door, Seraphim followed more slowly, out the door, past the small patio, through the gate in the fence, to a field they'd watched the mechanical plows – Nell called them tractors – dig up the day before.

In the middle of the field were two men, one of them standing and swaying on his feet. "Mr. Penn," Nell said, "but who is it with him?"

Seraphim stared, "The damned necromancer," he said. "But why is he digging in the dirt with his bare hands?"

Sarah A. Hoyt

The Threads of Time

Caroline knew this was a dangerous spell, but she'd seen Gabriel do something like it. Not to this level, she thought, as she stared at the wounds on the dragon-woman's back. She needed to reach for a time when the woman's back had been whole, and superimpose it on it as it was now.

Of course, doing that in Fairyland might be more difficult than doing it in the human world. Or at least more dangerous. But Caroline had realized long ago that you didn't have a choice between something you really liked, and something you dreaded. Or not usually. You had a choice between two things that were both unpleasant, and you tried to choose between them for the less unpleasant one.

In this case, she could choose to ignore the woman's need and keep herself safe. But then it was unlikely she would be allowed to walk the rest of the paths of Fairyland till she found Michael. And even if she were, she wouldn't have the allies she was supposed to acquire through her journey. She knew the rules of Fairyland. Everyone did. They were built into the earliest stories told to the smallest children. In Fairyland, you had to help three people in desperate straits, and then – after you did that – you'd get where you wanted to go. Distance in Fairyland wasn't straightforward, or measured in meters. It was measured in feelings and the heart, and three good deeds were the sacrifice needed to get where she was going.

To rescue her brother Michael.

She pulled back a strand of her thick, curly black hair. It felt clammy. All of her felt clammy, as if the clearing had suddenly got very hot. The dragon woman turned back to look at Caroline over her shoulder. Her eyes were the oddest Caroline had ever seen, a golden-orange, as though it had flecks of fire burning in its depths.

"I'm going to do something…," she said, and looked into the woman's eyes, and swallowed. "I'm going to use magic that might feel odd to you. Please, bear in mind, I do it only from the best intentions. It is the only way to heal you."

The large, fiery eyes blinked. "Do it, then," she said, intently. "Do it and be done with it. I cannot bear to be captive here while my baby might need me. Do what you have to do, no matter the risk. You were sent to me by the paths, they must know you can heal me."

Caroline wished she could be anywhere near that certain. She put her hands up and recited the incantatory protections for when one worked with time. For all the good it would do her, here, in the heart of a place built entirely of magic, and while using the magic on a sentient being.

She was going to die of this. No. She banished the thought, forcefully, and lifted her hands, to let the magic flow through her palms, onto its destination.

Then she did what she dimly remembered watching Gabriel do. She remembered seeing it – and she might have – though it would have required her to link to his mind and look through his mind's eyes. Perhaps she had. She had been very young and very unguarded, and Gabriel, too, hadn't guarded against her.

Because of that, she could remember the mental vision of time as a tapestry. She'd once seen a tapestry weaving machine. Michael had wanted to see one of the new manufactories, operated almost exclusively by magic, where men did no more than feed thread to the machines, and clip the finished product, or clean around the working, moving parts of the machine.

She and Michael had escaped through the window of their nursery while their nanny was asleep and walked down to the village, where one of the manufactories was. It had taken them the best part of the day, and when they'd been found – through a spell cast – Seraphim had collected them in the carriage. She remembered being afraid he was finally going to give them the spanking that he and Gabriel so often threatened them with. In retrospect, though, she thought what he had done: sitting white faced and tight lipped next to her in the carriage for the full hour drive back home, had been far worse. As had the fact that neither Seraphim nor Gabriel smiled at or talked to Caroline or Michael for a good two months.

The manufactory itself she hadn't thought about till now. Michael had been fascinated by the gleaming, moving parts, the thread moving into place, all without the touch of human hands. Caroline had looked at the people cleaning accumulated lint from the machines, or feeding them the colored thread. They were children, little older – or perhaps younger – than herself. It was the first time she'd been aware of her good fortune and her station in life.

Now, though, as she reached for the threads of time, she saw it exactly as that machine in that long ago manufactory. There were threads – the life of each person, the path of each object everywhere – being fed into time, and what emerged was the completed tapestry. Reaching out, she touched the mind-seen strands mid-air. There were Caroline and Michael going to see the manufactory. There was Gabriel, coming in in the middle of Seraphim's birthday party, in that outlandish outfit, all rags, with the livid marks of whip strikes livid across his face and the exposed parts of his skin.

Caroline blinked at this. She'd been born after Gabriel had joined the house, and she was quite sure that, though she'd heard him described as filthy and covered in rags, she'd never heard of whip marks. Whip marks why? Who'd dare whip the child of the Duke of Darkwater – even if a bastard son? She blinked, and shelved the thought for another day. For a moment that thread, and the one next to it – Gabriel and... she blinked again – Seraphim's? gleamed with the bright blue of strong magic. It was tempting to see what was happening to them. But she could not. Not in the middle of this working.

Instead, she concentrated on the thread of the dragon lady – a thread of pure fire woven through the tapestry. It was tangled and twisted, and ran alongside two other threads, both of which seemed to merge with those of the Darkwater family. If Caroline had time–

Enough of this foolishness. She didn't have time. Instead, she ran her fingers along the length of the thread displayed by magic in front of her eyes, but in fact existing in dimensions humans couldn't see.

There. There was the last time this ... person had been whole. Now....

Carefully, Caroline took the time thread between two fingers. She couldn't cut it and retie it, as Gabriel had done to the bird's thread. The bird had just been injured, and, presumably, its thread had touched no one's fate but that of the cat who had dragged it. This woman's fate was enmeshed with various others' – men, women, and possibly elves. If Caroline cut the thread and tied it again, she would do damage to all those fates, and all of those people's magic and – by extension – her own. The recoil itself would kill it.

The recoil of this... she tried not to think about it. No point in it. Instead, she took the thread and carefully, deftly, looped it around her fingers.

Touching that much power, that much strength, gave her an almost physical shock. And as she grasped it to tie it together at the base of the loop, bringing the woman's whole body in close proximity to this moment, she felt as though her fingers burned with it. Her every instinct told her to let go, to let the thread fall into its natural position, to leave it alone.

The instincts were wrong. She must – she must – rescue Michael. She bit her lip against the pain and the burn that was forming welts in her small fingers, and forcefully tied the knot.

"Oh!" the woman said, and it sounded like some of Caroline's pain had rebounded on her. Her face flashed white and drawn, then for a moment it seemed about to change into a dragon's. But Caroline did not let go of the thread. She was not done.

Holding the thread of the woman's life and existence through time in her hands, she closed her eyes and forced those missing parts of her body – the clipped wings – forward through time and in existence in the present.

She would never be able to explain it, but it felt as though the wings, on their way to the present, passed through Caroline's own body, and her magic. Her body they could not have passed through. Not really. But her magic, they might have, and it felt as though every sharp bit, every rough surface shredded her magic on the way through, leaving it bleeding and torn, like skin raked by claws and teeth.

Nausea hit afterwards, a nausea so strong that Caroline felt she could neither keep her eyes open, nor focus, nor even stand. The threads fell from her suddenly lax fingers, and snapped into the tapestry, the loop still in place. Her fingers hit the grass of the clearing. She was aware of the threads vanishing from her magic sight, but she couldn't think, couldn't concentrate. She clutched her middle. She closed her eyes. Nausea ebbed and flowed in her like a tide, and she groaned with the feeling that her body was made of nausea, a sharp point of discomfort and uncertainty, dissolving and twisting through the currents of time.

I shall dissolve completely and be gone, she thought, and whimpered with fear, thinking Gabriel had been right. Of course he had. And it wouldn't be needed for him to punish her. She was going to die of this.

"Thank you," the woman's voice said somewhere, outside her misery. "If you need me, at anytime and anywhere, call out to the dragon of the fire lake. I am in your debt." And then there was the sound of wings and a feeling of unbearable heat.

Caroline opened her eyes, to find herself enveloped in flames. Looking up, she saw the dragon, flying just above her, and blowing flames from its – her? – nostrils, which surrounded Caroline completely.

No. I saved you, she thought. You're not supposed to kill me.

But the fire wasn't killing her. Hot, yes, but not lethal, it twined around her, an ocean of living flames. It seemed to move through her, searing. It was as though every weak place in her magic, every slow place, were burned away, leaving only the best, clear and glimmering in the firelight.

And then it was gone. There was the impression of words in her mind "A gift of gratitude" and then the dragon was gone, flying away and through, to another time and another place.

Caroline didn't know what the gift had been, and now she couldn't ask. She stood up. The nausea was gone, but she felt as though she'd run for miles and miles. Her breath came in short pants, her body was sweaty, the clothes sticking to her. And her eyes seemed to prickle with sweat that had run into them. And she was thirsty. But you can't eat or drink in Fairyland.

On shaky legs, she made to take a step towards where she hoped the path was.

She heard the sound of hooves from behind and before she could turn to look, a male arm twined around her middle, and a voice said, "We have need of you."

At first she thought it was a rider, and that he was bare from the waist up. Then she realized it was a centaur who had got hold of her and was carrying her, held only by his strong arm, while his hooves galloped madly into a shifting landscape of fog.

For My Lady Fair

The Duke took off running towards the field, and there was very little that Nell could do but follow him. She had, of course, understood that Gabriel Penn had just ported in from whatever trouble the cards might have indicated – and she could not even imagine what represented him – and that he had someone else with him. A necromancer.

The idea made her flesh crawl – an expression she'd heard before but never actually experienced. Only now she had something to associate with necromancy: Antoine's dead corpse walking. She remembered the blank look in his eyes, the feel that whatever and whoever Antoine had been was no longer there. Now, there was just a thing: an empty shell.

That in itself had always made her feel odd, the few times she had witnessed death – mostly of animals – but the idea that the dead meat should walk, move as if of its own volition was obscene.

Even now, the memory made her feel like her throat closed in disgust, and her flesh tried to crawl away beneath her skin. She took deep breaths of the cool morning air, scented with the familiar smells of the farm, and ran as fast as she could. If there were a necromancer come to the farm, she must defend the farm – and grandma – from him. More important, if there were a necromancer come to the farm was it the one who had been responsible for re-animating Antoine?

If so, she would have something to say to him. She was beginning to think, in light of what her true origins were likely to be, that she'd fallen in a neatly set trap, and that Antoine was part of it, but one way or another, and whatever he might have been, he didn't deserve what had been done to him. No one did.

She arrived in the field behind Seraphim. Impossible not to. His legs were much longer than hers, and besides, she'd been accustomed, for her time in Avalon, to be restricted in her ability to run anywhere. She was out of shape.

When she approached the group, Seraphim Ainsling was yelling something. The shock when she understood his words, and also what he was doing, was almost too great to permit her to react rationally.

Seraphim Ainsling, the proper Duke of Darkwater, of whom much was said, but not that he had fishmonger or carter ancestry, was screaming at the top of his lungs at the two men – one of whom not only was completely oblivious to him, but seemed to be attempting to dig to China with his bare hands, and burrow face-first into the hole.

Worse, the one standing was the Duke's valet and, Nell presumed, the Duke's brother and – from what she'd seen of them – one of his closest friends, but the Duke was holding him roughly by the arm and shaking him.

What came at her, shouted at the top of the Duke's voice, was almost impossible to understand, so loud and rapid it was, "– I should wash my hands of you. Are you out of your senses to be approaching this creature and to fall into his clutches once more?"

"Now, Duke," Gabriel Penn said, very mildly, but in a tone of worried distraction. He made as though to take a step sideways to pull his companion out of the dirt, or perhaps to succor him, but Seraphim held him fast.

"No, don't you go trying to cajole me. You know what coils this creature embroiled you in, and you know he can only bring you dishonor and grief. Even if he captured you by dishonorable means, you should know–"

Gabriel Penn's eyes flashed with a look not unlike Seraphim's own when animated with near-uncontrollable fury, and for a moment he showed his teeth, pressed close together. Nell thought he was about to slug the Duke, and for just a second, without thinking, moved to step between them. Then she checked herself. Even on Earth, stepping between two men about to engage in a slugging match was perfectly stupid. But, stepping between two men from Britannia about to engage in a slugging match might be crazier. Not only would they slug it out around or over her, but they would also hold each other responsible for causing her to step in. Their rules of chivalry were complicated, but that one was obvious.

As she paused, Gabriel reached out and got hold of both of the duke's arms above the elbow, "Your Grace, you bonehead, listen to me: Marlon Elfborn did not capture me. I went to him to ask for help when I had nowhere else to go."

"Well," Seraphim said, struggling to pull his arms away from his brother's gripping fingers. "that only proves you're not competent to run your own affairs. Furthermore–"

"Yes, I know, furthermore, he interrupted my education, raised the dead and deflowered the family goat. Give over Seraphim, you fool, do. Stop your vendetta and listen to me."

"He deflowered what?" Seraphim said, stopping mid-shout and frowning.

A dark-red blush climbed Gabriel's cheeks. His eyes darted at Nell, and he actually attempted to bow, which went to show that the training of Britannia men was quite past rationality or sanity even. "I beg your pardon Miss Felix, I–"

"Not Miss Felix," Seraphim bellowed. "Not Miss Felix. She is the Princess Royal."

"Oh, dear," Gabriel said, and his face looked as though someone had lit a candle inside his skull. He looked like he would presently join his friend in digging in the dirt.

Which finally triggered Nell's reaction. She couldn't do anything about the Darkwater brothers. She had a strong feeling whatever had been happening here had been going on for a long while – possibly since their births – and would go on yet longer. But right now, at this moment, there was a creature who was suffering from either insanity or some compulsion, and she must help him.

She looked at the digging man with her mage vision, and saw… Earth was near-lethal for a creature like Seraphim, even, full of magical power and not hardened from birth to the proximity of what they called cold iron, and which was in fact more what Earth would call technology. But this creature, the red-headed man scrabbling at the dirt, was at least three-quarts magical, probably with Fairyland blood – had to be. Gabriel had called him Elfborn – but with some other magical blood mixed in as well.

And while, unlike Seraphim when he'd been transported here, he was not ill, and while he should be able to defend himself from the hostile surroundings, he seemed to have been caught by surprise.

He hadn't intended to teleport here, Nell guessed, and therefore hadn't shielded himself from the surrounding influence in time. She would guess Gabriel Penn had had a second longer to shield, and that made all the difference.

Elfborn's unshielded magic was under attack on all sides, much like a glob of flesh thrown into strong acid.

Acting instinctively, she threw a protection veil over him. Not a spell. A spell wouldn't work for something like this, because it was not alive and would just get corroded along with everything else. The only protection to extend in this case was a veil of magic, an extension of Nell's own magic, fortunately hardened to the conditions of Earth.

It worked, to an extent. It stopped the creature's magic dissolving and disintegrating. It wouldn't allow it to regenerate, because she couldn't build a thick enough wall between it and Earth. Particularly not since – as the effect hit a second later – to be so linked with him meant that she could feel his pain too. It was somewhere between a migraine and a whole-body toothache. She gritted her teeth against it, and turned to the two men, who had stopped arguing and were looking at her, as though she'd just grown a second head.

Gabriel recovered first. "Thank you," he said. He let go of Darkwater's arms, and like a total idiot, attempted to throw a veil of his own over hers.

"No," she told him, using whatever concentration she could spare away from her task to magically block his attempt. "You're half-elf yourself, and you're not used to Earth. If you try that, we'll have you both in the same condition."

"Well, if you think–" Seraphim Ainsling said, to Gabriel. She could spare them no look, but something must have passed between them, some wordless argument, because she heard the duke draw a deep breath, and then she felt his power, like a barrier, interpose itself not just between hers and the influence of Earth's anti-magic, but between Elfborn's and her own.

The pain lessened, receding a pace, and Elfborn's magic pulsed, once, and reorganized into a coherent whole, if still fainter than it should be. He stopped digging and fell back on his haunches, looking dazed. Which, apparently, gave the other two men an opportunity to start screaming at each other again.

"What in the– Hades do you mean the family goat?" Seraphim started, at the same time that Gabriel said, at the top his voice, "You said she is the Princess Royal?"

"Please, don't start screaming," Nell said, thinking that hot tempers must run in the family. which made perfect sense, as both the men seemed over-controlled, which they would be, if they knew they were likely to lose control completely, once they unbent. "The Duke of Darkwater does believe that I am the Princess Royal of Britannia, Mr. Penn. I'm not quite sure why myself, except a medallion and some… some other indications, but he says I look like the Queen. And, Your Grace, I presume Mr. Penn said what he did in an effort to derail you so that we could attend to Mr. Elfborn. Is that so?"

Gabriel Penn opened his mouth as though to say something. He reddened dark again and shot his brother a glowering look. "Yes. Pardon me, Seraphim, but you– Oh, never mind. We must get Marlon's magic stable so he can survive here. Miss– Er… Your Highness, do you chance to know where there are any standing stones hereabouts?"

"In the United States?" She saw his blank look too late. "The equivalent of your American colonies, sir. We have no standing stones."

"Oh. But we–"

"It's a different world," Seraphim said, testily, and she thought that his tone was as much the result of whatever animosity he had towards Elfborn, and the not-quite-pain-and-worse-than-any-headache behind the eyes that protecting the man's magic caused. "They don't have openings to Fairyland here. Which, I suspect, is what makes this a safe world for all of us right now, because I suspect, pardon me, Gabriel, that your magical kin's stinking court politics are at the center of this mess."

"Yes, I suspect so too," Gabriel Penn said, and turned to Nell. "And this is why I wondered if you had something like standing stones. They would have provided a shield for him, even if they're not connected to Fairyland. They are places of refuge for magical creatures caught in this land, and they would allow him to recover. He was trying to dig in the dirt, because that would be protection of a kind."

Nell sighed. "So, an underground room would help?"

"Somewhat," Gabriel said.

"Very well. The house was built in the time of coal heating. There is a basement with an outside entrance. There is nothing in it now, but I used to play in it as a girl. If you'll follow me."

She led them around the house to the entrance. This part of the basement, which had once contained a coal furnace, now dismantled, had been cleaned out and outfitted as her own private refuge when she was a little girl. She'd always liked it, and liked hiding there to read. Now she wondered if it was because it had afforded her own magic a respite from hostile forces.

Whatever had driven her to it, her grandmother had aided and abetted it. The little refuge had not only bookcases, a small table and a microwave, but also a loveseat draped over with a colorful shawl that hid the tears in the upholstery. It also had a tiny powder room attached. It had been installed late enough – after Nell had claimed it – that Nell knew it had plastic piping. Just as well. Sometimes too much metal was a problem for magic in the literal sense.

As soon as she closed the door to the outside, she felt the pressure against her shield over Elfborn abate. It was like coming in from a raging storm to a place of calm. Seraphim must have felt it too, because she saw his features sag in relief.

Gabriel Penn had helped Elfborn to the loveseat and dropped him into it, and the man's eyes were returning to some semblance of understanding. He looked at Seraphim, and his eyes widened. Then he looked at Nell and they widened further.

"I beg your pardon," he said, his voice creaking. "I understand one or the other of you will wish to kill me. Might I–" He looked at his dirt-covered hands. "Might I be allowed to rinse the dirt from my hands and face, first?"

"Oh, Marlon," Gabriel said. "Stop the cheap tragedy. Seraphim isn't going to kill you, and I can't imagine why Miss– why her– why the lady would."

"Will they not?" Elfborn said, something like the light of battle and a rueful look in his eyes. "You only think that because you don't know the half of it."

Prisoner and Guards

Caroline couldn't think and couldn't focus. Not that she wanted to focus. As the ground seemed to speed beneath her, and she saw the clods and small stones struck up by the hooves just an arm span away from her, she was all too aware only the centaur's strong arm, its tight pressure beneath her breasts, kept her from falling down and being trampled.

She closed her eyes, but it was impossible to ignore her situation. She smelled horse and human sweat commingled, she felt the jarring pound of the centaur's hooves beneath. After a while she heard yelling, and then the hooves stopped and the movement, and the human arm let go.

Caroline opened her eyes in time to stumble a little then recover her balance. She stood on a clearing filled with dozens of centaurs, clustering round her on all sides.

The centaur who had brought her pushed her forward, a hand on her shoulder, and said, "I have brought her, you see. At the council's command."

Around her there were many centaurs. All of their human bodies were swarthy, heavily muscled, and her first impression of them was of a menacing group, particularly as they moved restlessly, their hooves stomping the ground, and calling out words she only partly understood.

"In the sacred ground of our ancestors–"

"The announced one–"

"In this dire hour."

They spoke now one and now the other, their voices louder and more resonant than normal men's voices, their heads tossing – just like horse's heads, she thought, in shock, even if they were atop men's trunks and necks – their long, dark hair sweeping and becoming even more disarrayed. They had overgrown stubble or outright dark beads. Some wore necklaces of what appeared to be human teeth.

Caroline wanted to run, but she could imagine this troop of centaurs following her – hunting her down. She swallowed hard and felt sweat prickle at her eyes. Her throat was so parched she feared she might not be able to speak, but she had to speak. If she couldn't run, she had to do something to prevent these creatures– to prevent the creatures from what?

She could remember, vaguely, from her classical mythology and history that drunken centaurs could get thoroughly unpleasant, in the way of unpleasantness that mama would say Caroline shouldn't know about until her wedding night – and perhaps not even then. But Caroline had heard the women of the nearby village talk, and some of the maids too. And besides, the home farm had livestock. And Caroline was no slower of mind than she should be. So she had a pretty clear idea of how unpleasant, and in exactly what way, centaurs could get.

Though she wondered if it was exact enough to fend it off. She should have asked Gabriel. Of all of the adults in the house, he was the only one not likely to tell her she was being unladylike or to turn her mind to more appropriate thoughts. Michael wouldn't have told her that either, but he knew no more than she did, and besides, frankly, Michael was not very interested in what went on between centaurs or women. Or men and women for that matter. If it didn't have gears, he was simply not much interested in it.

Which brought her to here and now, and whatever the centaurs meant to do, and the fact she was quite – quite – powerless to defend herself. Except by trying to do what mama called showing herself a lady and therefore beyond their touch. She looked at those large hands, at the end of bulging muscular arms, and realized not a few held knives or lances. She swallowed again, then planted her feet and spoke loudly, "I am Caroline Ainsling, the sister of the Duke of Darkwater, and I want to know what you want with me."

They moved. At first she wasn't sure how. There was just more stomping of feet, and more galloping, and sounds like a stable. Smells like a stable too, which made her wonder how human centaurs were, and how animal. Around the edge of the clearing where the centaurs were assembled, two of them galloped in circles.

"Quiet!" It was a clarion call of a voice, a voice such as, unleashed in a square in London, could have called the whole city to attention. Caroline trembled, thinking the yell directed at her, but then the voice said, "We are being rude to the maiden, and fools to seek her help but not tell her what we wish. Agapios, Thanos, cease your mad galloping. If you insist on behaving like colts, you shall be excluded from the councils of men."

To Caroline's surprise, the two madly galloping centaurs stopped, and one of them lowered his head like a schoolboy caught at fault. It occurred to her that despite their golden skins, the long, dark hair, they were very young. If they'd been horses, their horse-body would look like a colt's not fully grown into its height, and if they'd been humans, the human body would have looked too gangly, too thin, not muscular enough. The sweaty faces were devoid of stubble, and one of them wore his hair pulled back from the forehead with a bit of ribbon, an affection that, for some reason, made him look younger. She almost smiled at him, then remembered the situation, and that she definitely shouldn't encourage centaurs with untoward friendliness, and tried to make her face impassive.

"Caroline, Daughter of the Duke, Maiden," the man who had first spoken, spoke again, and then, to Caroline's eternal shock, fell on his front knees in front of her, and looked up at her with anguished eyes that didn't look any less scared for regarding her from under beetling brows. "We need your help. My son has fallen in a snare, and you're the only one who can save him."

Caroline looked again at the powerful bodies around her. "I'm the… only one? But you…."

The centaur shook his head. "No. It is not a human snare, nor one such that can be defeated by the hand of a centaur, or the force of our arms. It is a snare of the mind, a snare of the soul, and we are powerless against it. We felt your nearness, and we went to get you. We don't know if your potency will hold against the local magic, but we hope so."

Her … potency? Had they lost their everlasting mind? And where were the centaur women? Unpleasant ideas formed in Caroline's mind, and she drew herself up very tall – or as tall as her five feet would allow – and spoke in a way that, she hoped, would do the Duchess credit. "I do not have the pleasure of understanding your meaning."

"It is my son, Akakios," the centaur said. "He has been captured."

"Captured by whom? Where?"

There was movement again, this time towards her. No. The circle that had been all around moved, so in front of her there were only trees and no centaurs. The centaur who'd knelt before her – the same one who'd brought her here? – now stood beside her, his hand on her shoulder. Impossible not to follow as he walked forward, though he neither pushed nor pulled her.

He said only "Caroline, maiden!" and at that moment, they reached the edge and she could see through the trees. She'd thought they were in a large clearing, but the clearing ahead was twice as large. From the center of it, suspended on what seemed to be a silver chain that attached somewhere in the distance, was what looked like a crystal bird cage. For a very large bird. A very, very large bird. Only there was no bird in it, but a young centaur.

His hair was in more disarray than that of his congeners, the other centaurs. His hands were clasped on the translucent bars of his cage. And his human chest and horse body were crisscrossed with bloody slashes.

He raised his head as if sensing her scrutiny and looked at her with eyes that were as green as leaves in spring, and that looked like he'd been crying.

Then she saw them: Around the clearing, as though on guard, galloped many unicorns.

They were large, white, glimmering, beautiful. It took her a moment to realize that the tips of their horns were stained with blood.

The Coil Winds

I helped find you," Marlon Elfborn said.

Nell had got coffee, because she knew – both because Antoine had told her, and because Seraphim had confirmed it – that coffee was good for restoring damaged magic. Some people believed the only way magicians could survive on Earth was through vast infusions of coffee, and coffee shops were always a good place to find magicians porting between dimensions, stopping on Earth for a few hours or a few days.

Elfborn was holding his cup between both hands, with the sort of clenched-fist grip normally reserved for the proverbial straw and the drowning man. He took it black, and he'd drained almost the whole cup, which was fine, since she'd brought the pot down. What was interesting, as far as she was concerned, was that Gabriel Penn had gone to sit gingerly next to him, and was – as far as it was possible to tell from the outside – monitoring Elfborn's magical power. There was that odd, analytical look as he stared at Marlon's magic through half closed eyes.

It seemed for a moment, staring at Penn, that Nell discerned something else in those eyes, but … in Britannia? Besides, what she'd heard from Seraphim about Elfborn's character…. It seemed hardly likely, though she'd come to believe that people did the most stupid and out of character things when it came to their private lives.

Gabriel Penn glared at her as though he could read her thoughts, and she cleared her throat and looked back at Marlon, who was looking at her, with the sort of unfocused look of one not fully attuned to his surroundings.

"You… helped find me? What does that mean?"

Marlon shifted the cup so the fingers of his right hand curled around the handle. The left went up and raked at his hair. He darted a furtive look at Gabriel Penn, then looked at his coffee. "When Gab– When Mr. Penn… that is… he should not have–" He paused and seemed to collect himself. "When Mr. Penn discovered the reanimated corpse of my friend in my attic and… and was alarmed enough to… to… to let his– that is… when he let His Grace know–"

Seraphim snorted. He mumbled something that sounded like "If coming to my door in abject terror didn't let me know, nothing would."

But Gabriel put a hand out and grabbed Seraphim's arm, and Elfborn seemed to ignore the interruption and went on, "And His Grace laid information against me on two capital crimes, I had to disappear. I had to disappear fast. Contrary to popular belief, magic tutors that Cambridge… No. Magic tutors whose whole background is a foundling home, aren't paid princely salaries. We are- I was given a place to live and fifty pounds a year. It was not held against me if I tutored on the side to make ends meet, which I did."

Again Seraphim snorted, and Nell had the impression that Gabriel glared at him and squeezed his arm harder, but she didn't look at them. Instead she was looking at Elfborn in near horror. While house servants made considerably less than fifty pounds a year, they got not only a place to live, but also food and clothing and often used clothing or other side benefits that could be sold. But a governess might make a hundred pounds a year, and she too got not just a place to live but food and at least some furnishings and other benefits including – as she had found in Britannia – the not inconsiderable one of – in most decent households – coal for heating.

To live on fifty pounds a year, even with lodgings paid for, support the state of a gentleman which would be expected of a tutor, and buy the necessaries of his profession, including the extremely expensive tomes on magic research would have… been well-nigh impossible, even with tutoring on the side. She knew what tutoring paid – she'd known people who had done it. It was near to nothing. The thought that Cambridge, whose "regular" tutors got paid quite decently, took advantage of people whose tainted blood made them less than equal in society made her stomach clench. "Yes?" she said, trying to keep her voice indifferent. "I fail to see why you'd need money to escape. Magic yes, but–"

"Oh, magic too," Marlon said. "The police are not completely stupid, you know, no matter what popular fiction shows, and they do have some very competent magicians on staff. They would have found me if all I'd done was throw a veil over my magic. I needed to… I needed to go between-times," he said, as if bracing himself. "Between places. The sort of thing you read about in fairytales, where the door is only there if you're looking for it. As for money," he shrugged, "a magician in hiding still has to eat. I suppose if I'd grown up anywhere where one lays snares or hunts I could have done that, though I hear one can't live on rabbit without starving. Or I could maybe have kept chickens, or something. But I grew up in a foundling home, in London. And I never learned to hunt. I needed enough money that I could… buy food. For years. For however long… for as long as need be."

"But," Nell said, "surely necromancy pays well?" She'd heard rumors of fortunes paid for such illegal magic. "If you're a necromancer–"

"He is not. It was accidental. He raised Aiden Gypson through a resurrection spell applied too late. Stop glaring Seraphim, I believe him."

"Of course you do, you're very eager to believe–"

"Shut up, both of you," Nell said, reflecting only later that she'd ordered a duke around as though he were an unruly school boy. And he hadn't complained. Oh, very well, then. She might grow to like this princessing thing. "Mr. Elfborn, I still don't understand it. Oh, I understand your needing money, but you say until as though it would have an end."

He shrugged, "Oh, it would. But it might be ten or twenty years in the future. You see, they put an embargo on my leaving the world. I couldn't port out. I had to wait–" He paused and his eyes almost crossed. "I'm out of the world. They can't have removed the embargo. The minimum time is ten years. They can't have done it."

"No," it was Gabriel, assuredly.

"So… when we were ported out violently, it must be … someone with the keys…"

"That much has been obvious for a while," Seraphim said. "Now, if you would answer Her Royal Highness's implied question about whom you found her for, perhaps we can find out who ported us here."

Marlon's hand went up and made a worse mess of his hair, and he took a sip from his cup, only to find it was empty. Nell held his wrist to keep the cup in place, and poured coffee for him. He took a sip, then sighed. "It might be them. I always thought it was them. I don't know how they found I was in distress, but of course, I suppose they keep track of those of us like Gabriel and myself in your world, and from one or the other of us, they must have picked up my bind." He looked up at their blank looks. "Fairyland, of course. They sent envoys to my house, in between the time Gabriel left and before … and before the law arrived, while I was hoping… while I was convincing myself Gabriel would come back and I could expl–"

"You set a compulsion on him, did you not, you filthy bastard?" Seraphim asked. "It only activated now. I should–"

"Enough, Duke, he–"

"Compulsion?" Elfborn blinked at Seraphim as though he'd said a foreign word. "No. I just hoped he would come back. I thought if he car– I thought he'd come to his senses and come back and I could explain."

"An animated corpse in your closet, really? You could explain?"

Elfborn gave a short, hollow crack that might have been an attempt at laugh. "I could try. But I never got the chance, as the next person at my door was Your Grace, challenging me to a duel and informing me you'd set the law on me. But before you came, there were envoys from Fairyland. They offered me a place already turned in the magical way that made it hard to find and ten thousand pounds– As I said, I didn't know how they found I needed help, but my need was desperate enough that I took it."

"I went to my mother before I went to Seraphim," Gabriel said, not looking at Elfborn.

"Penny!" from Seraphim echoed, in tones of great shock. "Your mother?"

Strangely this made Elfborn smile at Gabriel and shake his head, his eyes amused. "You really were past thinking, were you not?"

"Well–" Gabriel said. "If you'd told me– If you'd explained– As it was I thought everything… everything I'd thought you to be was a lie, and possibly that you intended to kill me and keep me… I thought…." A red tide swept upwards through his skin, giving him the appearance of glowing red from within. "One reads of such things. Of people who… of people who are only… interested when someone is… that is, reanimated. It's one of the reasons it's illegal, and yet there are rings of them that they catch sometimes."

"You thought I'd kill you and reanimate you for sexual purposes?" Elfborn asked, and his voice sounded shocked but also as though he were on the verge of laughing.

Which didn't last long, as Seraphim grabbed him by the front of his shirt and half-lifted him from the sofa. "You will not speak of such things in front of Her Highness. You will remember your company and you will–"

"Let him go," Nell said, and was shocked to see herself obeyed instantly. She could really grow to like this princessing. Unfortunately, she was almost sure there were drawbacks. She sighed and turned to Seraphim who managed to look both embarrassed and vaguely confused about why he should be embarrassed. "Your Grace, I grew up on Earth. You have seen, and read, enough of our entertainment since you've been here to know I will not swoon at the mention of sexual practices no matter how vile. I hadn't thought of it, but of course, in a world where necromancy is possible there will be a sex trade for reanimated corpses – and yes, I consider that absolutely vile. But it won't make me swoon." Something had formed in her mind. It wasn't a suspicion, but more like a sudden falling of a jigsaw puzzle into place. It was as though a hundred half-seen looks, a hundred glimpses of expressions, a hundred half seen gestures had come together in that moment. She took a deep breath, aware she was going to poke her nose into a can of worms. But it had to be done, she thought, or the three of them were going to continue talking around things, and Seraphim would keep erupting at the worst times, trying to protect her, and making it impossible for her to piece together what Elfborn knew.

"You said two capital crimes," she said, and looked at Elfborn. "I am not fully aware of your laws, but I know that in our time, when society was close to yours, homosexuality was a capital crime, though rarely enforced and never for people of high birth."

"I'm not of high birth," Elfborn said.

"So you and…," she glanced at Gabriel Penn who was looking like he'd lost the power of speech. Also, like he would presently have a heart attack. She hoped Elfborn would be quicker with a resurrection spell if that happened. "...and Mr. Penn were lovers?"

The room went wild. She'd half expected it would. The thing she didn't expect is that it would be all caused by Seraphim, because the other two were completely speechless. Elfborn managed something that might have been a nod; Gabriel Penn had covered his face. BUT the duke made up for it in triplicate, by jumping up and yelling at her, at the two other men, at – possibly – the walls of the room. She couldn't make much sense of his yelling, but the gist of it, as far as she could tell, was that Gabriel didn't know what he was doing; that at nineteen he'd been underage; that Elfborn had used compulsion and magical tricks; that he was a more powerful magician than anyone else in Avalon, just about, and that he had no morals, as he'd proven by reanimating his dead lover and keeping him around; and that Seraphim would put a bullet in his head and soon. At which point Nell screamed for Seraphim to shut up. And it was absolutely ineffective, showing that there were limits to the princessing powers.

And then Gabriel spoke, very quietly, and Seraphim stopped, suddenly, and looked at Gabriel in complete shock. "He didn't use compulsion, Seraphim," Gabriel said. "I know, because I did."

There was a long silence, and the Duke of Darkwater swayed slightly on his feet. "You what?"

"I used compulsion, Seraphim. It was a stupid thing to do, but I was very young and I knew nothing of life outside Darkwater… Not really, not as an adult. But I knew THAT. How do you think I survived after my mother left her husband and before our father found us?"

"You…."

"I found gentlemen of certain tastes were willing to pay for a comely half-elf child. Yes, I know what is wrong with them. Yes, I agree with you that those gentlemen deserve death – or at least … no one should have to do that when they're only a child and can't understand any of it. On the other hand, without it, I'd have died of starvation. Crossing sweeping doesn't pay that much."

"But–" Seraphim dropped back onto the chair by the table, next to Nell's. "But… you never told me."

"You were younger than I. And besides, there are things one doesn't talk about. I was… just glad to be at Darkwater, and to have enough food, and not to have to… not to have to do that."

"Oh. Did father–"

"Of course. When he found me he knew. It was rumors that led him to me, and he knew how I'd been living. He was shocked, and… it overcame his reluctance to bring his half-elf child into the house."

"Did he tell you not to speak of it?"

"No. He… He let me speak of it to him, for a while. I had to. You don't understand, I think. If it's possible to have scars on one's mind or perhaps one's soul–" He shrugged. "I had to talk to someone, but it was hard to. It was easier to Father, because he already knew. I think that's when I came to love him as a father. Before that, he was just… a vague figure. And of course my mother said horrible things of him."

"But after that…." Seraphim looked from Gabriel to Elfborn. "After living through that— How could you– I mean, wouldn't it put you off men? Perhaps off all physical contact."

"For a long time, I thought I'd never want to do that – with anyone. When I got old enough that the scullery maid tried to show–" He coughed. "That is, when girls our age started showing an interest, despite my elf blood, I thought I'd been too wounded to ever feel that for anyone. I didn't even really like to be touched. I tolerated it from you and Father, but I didn't like it and I certainly didn't want any more intimate touching. But then…," He cast a look from beneath lowered lashes towards Marlon Elfborn, "we became friends. Both of us had elf blood, and…." He shrugged again. "We had a similar sense of humor. And around him I didn't feel like he was cringing, afraid of what my magic might do at any minute. I–" The blush came again, dark red, and Nell wondered if the duke also blushed like that. She must find an occasion to test it. "I fell in love. But he was… he didn't seem to care. So… I used a compulsion."

"It wasn't that," Marlon said. "It wasn't that I didn't want— It was just… Aiden was the one person I could trust. After he died…" He shrugged. "And since I didn't have the courage to destroy his corpse, I felt like I was too tainted to–" He paused as though something registered. "You used compulsion?"

"Only the first time," Gabriel put his hands up. "Only the first time, I swear."

"You *do* know that's legally rape, right?" Elfborn's eyes danced with amusement. "Three capital crimes. Only one is yours, princeling."

"He was underage!" Seraphim said, in the sulky tone of someone who has a feeling he's losing an argument.

"Right," Nell said. "Now that this is out in the open, and that the duke of Darkwater doesn't have to protect my ears from sullying–"

"You're very jaded, Madame," he said, disapprovingly.

"Rather," she answered drily. "But let me ask the important question – who came to your door? And why did they want to find me? You said people from Fairyland?"

"The centaurs," Elfborn said. "And they wanted to bring you back to Britannia. I didn't see any harm in that."

A Pure Mind

Caroline reeled at the sight of the caged centaur, the bloodied unicorns. A couple of unicorns, at the edge of the clearing, made passes at her with their bloodied horns, and she stepped back.

She thought she would be safe, and that's why the centaurs had called her. After all, virgins were supposed to be safe from unicorns, weren't they? And a virgin she was. But there was something else operating here, something that didn't seem to fit in with that idea.

For one, while she was willing to believe perhaps the caged centaur, Akakios, despite his name, was no more than her age – perhaps younger, it was hard to tell – he might very well not be a virgin. She had an idea that centaurs were more sensuous creatures than humans, and she was very willing to doubt that he was a virgin. But all the same. She bit her lip. All the same, it wasn't possible that among all the centaurs – and where were their females? – there wouldn't be at least one who retained his or her virginity. Why would they have let Akakios go anywhere near the unicorns, if he weren't safe? And if the trap had been laid for Akakios unaware and he didn't know there were centaurs about, surely they would have another member of their tribe who could free him?

So why Caroline? Other than that she was a stranger and they didn't care if she lived or died? But no, that couldn't be it, either. She could see the boy centaur was bleeding. They might not care for her, but they cared for their friend. If Caroline didn't succeed, she wouldn't save him.

She turned, rounding on the male centaur who had spoken to her. "You said he is your son. But who are you?"

The centaur, threw back his head, "I am Nomiki, King of Centaurs." He somehow managed to look beseeching and regal all in one. "And I ask you as a boon to my whole tribe that you save my son."

Caroline took a deep breath. Then she disciplined her face as she had learned in preparation for her season, when in truth the stakes would have been much smaller, even if not according to the lady her mother. She showed no doubt, no emotion, and conveyed the impression of being somehow above all these creatures, as she said, "Not until you tell me why you chose me and what you want."

She expected anger, or perhaps surprise. She didn't get it. Instead, the man – the centaur, got up from his knees and tossed his head in a way that made her think of a horse. "It is fair and proper," he said. "That we tell the champion what her weapons are before she goes into battle."

Had Caroline been less trained in the social graces, she would have asked him what he meant and if he were mocking her. But her understanding of etiquette stayed her tongue, and what she said, when she'd had time to take a breath and recover her composure, was, "I presume it is not just for my virginity you sought me. Surely some of your people have that virtue, too."

He made a sound. It might have been a chuckle, but it sounded like the sound a horse makes to clear its nostrils. "Akakios has that virtue," he said, "and you see how much good it has been to him."

Caroline looked at the boy centaur in his cage out the corner of her eye. "Yes," she said. "I see. So, what makes you think I can avoid the like fate."

The king of centaurs shuffled his hooves on the ground, and Caroline had to exert all restraint to keep herself from rummaging in her pockets for a sugar cube, as she did when her pony was impatient or restless. She had a feeling it would not be well received.

"It is like this, you see—we've heard tell, as you have, and as everyone has, from time immemorial, that the virtue of the virgin can stop the murderous unicorn. So when we needed… That is… When we wanted to rescue the–" He paused.

"When you wanted to rescue the—?" Caroline said, implacably.

"The duke your father."

"My what?" Caroline said, and on that, her composure broke, and her appearance of calm.

"Your father, Lady," Nomiki said, and frowned slightly.

"But my father is dead!"

Nomiki looked puzzled and opened his mouth, then shrugged. "It is not that simple, and I do not have time to explain it, though I promise to, once Akakios is safe and his wounds bound. But the unicorns guard your father, to whom we owe a debt of honor, and Akakios, brave and pure, made a vow to free him…."

"It did not go according to his intent," Caroline said, her composure returning.

Nomiki shook his head. "No. And we cast leaves into the fire and asked of the Pythoness–"

"Who?"

"It matters not. We asked of the oracle and received an answer for our confusion. Akakios is pure enough in his body and mind but not in his magic. His mother, you see, she is a stranger, and from her he gets another type of magic. He lacks the strength and the intent to… It is not the purity of body that counts…though that does too, with the uncounted possibilities of a future unset, but it is the purity of the mind, forged and ready, steel and fire. The way to keep the unicorn from tearing you to pieces is to keep him from piercing you by controlling his mind. And he'll take only the most clear, bright directions. Among our band, we have many who are pure in body, but none so pure in spirit."

"And you think I am?" Caroline asked.

"We know you are. It was the clear, fiery precision of your mind that attracted us." The King started to kneel again. "Lady, daughter of the duke, save my son."

It was crazy, foolhardy, full of unwarranted pride on her part. In her mind she could hear both Seraphim and Gabriel screaming at her that she couldn't risk her life in this way. The trouble of having older brothers is that after a while they started living in your back brain. But Caroline also knew what her duty was, and beyond all that, she'd come to Fairyland to save Michael, and she had to help three other people on the way. Even if the people were dragons and centaurs.

She reached out. She held the centaur's wrists. "I will, but get me a sword."

The king of centaurs hesitated. Caroline sighed. "If I'm going in there, I will not go unarmed. The sword might be pitiful, but at least it will make me feel safer. Your son has hooves and is stronger than I, and look at him. I must have something besides my supposedly strong mind."

Nomiki shouted something that sounded Greek, and a galloping centaur with a roan body brought forth a sword on his extended arms. It was iron, and almost as long as Caroline. She thought to herself that if all else failed, she could whirl around while holding it, because surely she couldn't wield it in any meaningful fashion. One more question, she had, as she lifted the heavy sword. "Why are the unicorns there, in that clearing, and do not attack us here?"

"That is their sacred territory. They cannot survive outside it."

"So if I get hold of their minds and send them to you…," she said, thinking of a plan.

But Nomiki was shaking his head. "No. You must not hurt them or kill them. Their force is part of what keeps Elfland in balance. If you destroy them, it will unravel and all the magical worlds with it. He knew that who set them as guards. We dare not kill them with our magical arrows, or we kill ourselves and all the worlds with us."

"He who set them as guards?"

"The King of Fairy."

Sarah A. Hoyt

A Blessing Of Unicorns

You must not hurt them or kill them, Caroline thought, on the edge of the sacred clearing, staring at the unicorns with their blood-stained horns. How could she defend herself from these magical creatures without doing either of those?

Her mind.... The force of her mind. She thought of the dragon touching her with the fire, the feeling that every impurity had burned away. Perhaps that was it. Perhaps.

One way or another, she thought, as she held the sword in both hands, she'd have to do it. One way or another, she'd have to step into the clearing. If she could not figure out how to use her mind force, or whatever her virtue the centaurs talked about was, she would just be a smear on the floor of the clearing. This might be ultimately the end of it, but she must at least try.

She stepped over the threshold into the clearing. There should have been a magic shock, a sense of having violated a boundary. There wasn't. She was between two trees and on soft grass.

Five unicorns were running towards her at once. She raised the sword, hoping to stop them. They didn't even slow, but rushed....

One of them, nearer, plunged his horn into... She thought he'd plunged his horn into her thigh, but she couldn't feel it, even as a flower of blood bloomed through her skirt.

It seemed to Caroline that time had slowed down and that everything was happening very slowly. It seemed to her that she stared for hours at the blood seeping through her skirt, even though she knew it must have been less than a breath, because the seemingly-frozen-in-mid-leap unicorns were still approaching her.

They would pierce her multiple times with their horns. She would be a smear on the clearing grass. She–

No. The voice came out of nowhere, very clear. No, not a voice because it wasn't someone else's word, or someone else's decision, but her own, coming from within. No. Just that, forceful and serene.

No, she would not be a smear on the grass. No, she was not going to die. No, she was not going to let the young centaur, Akakios – didn't that mean no-evil? – die. No. These beautiful, ethereal death instruments could just think again.

She twisted around, the sword heavy in her hands, and pushed the unicorns away with it, trying not to bludgeon or smite, but merely use the sword as a shield. Meanwhile, her mind reached, her magic searching for a strong mind.

There would be a strong mind here. Horses were, after all, herd animals. That meant someone, probably a stallion, was the leader of the herd.

She found him, to her surprise – a tall white creature standing by the cage. He was three hands taller than the others, and his horn gleamed like pure gold. He must have felt the touch of Caroline's mind, because he lowered his head in an aggressive gesture and looked as if he'd charge.

She never gave him time. She remembered the dragon and the words that everything that was weak and impure in her had been burned away, and she threw her magic – all of her strength and her will power – at the creature, pushing at its mind.

The mind of a unicorn was not – as the legends said – pure magic, or pure anything. Or perhaps it was, except that its purity was the purity of clear animal impulses, not muddied by reason or thought.

The mind she touched was an animal mind – a magical animal, but an animal nonetheless. She pushed into it forcefully, finding the mind that controlled it – an older, stronger and definitely human mind. It controlled the unicorn not directly, but by being its master, the way Caroline controlled her pony's actions at home, because she was the one who carried sugar lumps in her pockets which could cause the pony to prance and nuzzle for the reward.

Very well. It was time to break that control. She seized the animal's mind and made it known to him that she would not – now or ever – be hurt by it or its stallions. She let it know she was the master, and gave it just a touch of the pain she could bring to bear, should it continue misguided attacks.

For a long time, she thought nothing would happen, then the head came up. The unicorns that had been mid-charge in her direction averted their jump, sometimes falling in ways that looked disastrously painful.

Caroline, a horse lover, would normally have stopped and tried to find out if the animals were hurt, or if her magic could heal them – but the moment she realized she would not be skewered on those horns, the pain hit from her leg.

It was horrible pain, blotting out her thought, and for a second she swayed and took a deep, long breath, feeling as though there were no space in her mind for anything but the pain. Sweat sprang to her forehead, soaking her hair, plastering it to her skull.

She reeled. And then, through the pain, her gaze focused on the cage. Or perhaps it was the sound of the centaurs behind her, shouting something about Akakios.

Her eyes focused on the centaur in the iron cage, looking as though he would presently lose consciousness, his head inclined, his horse-body leaning on the cage bars. She must save Akakios.

It took all her will power, all her strength of mind, to force herself to walk. She remembered the story of the little mermaid who'd become a human princess at the pain of each of her steps being as though taken on knives. It felt to her now that every step she took on that leg was taken on knives. More, she could feel blood running down her leg to her ankle and sloshing into her shoe. She knew there was an important artery in the leg, and that she could be dead in minutes. It didn't matter.

At some time, perhaps when she was very small, she'd heard her father tell a war story. He'd said something about when you're in a war, you have a duty to fulfill, and it doesn't matter if you chose your duty or not, you must do it, even if it costs you your life – and that the pain and suffering to fulfill your duty don't matter, so long as you fulfill it.

She could no longer remember what the story was about, or whom it spoke of, but she understood this now applied to her situation. She had chosen to come into Fairyland to find and free Michael. If she wanted to fulfill that mission, she must help three people – or three creatures – who needed her help. Akakios was the second of those.

The task might not be of her choosing, but the mission was. If she died, she would die in pursuit of her mission.

Gritting her teeth against the unbearable pain, she realized she was using the sword to help support herself as she crossed the clearing. What an ignominious use for an eldritch weapon.

She found herself near the cage an eternity later. She couldn't have told exactly how she got there, only that she had. A moment of panic, through the stinging sweat in her eyes, as she realized she had no key to open that lock. And then in desperation, she raised the sword, and inserted it between the bars, and pried....

The cage door opened. Akakios jumped out. Relieved, Caroline let go a little of her iron will... and the unicorns snorted and reared.

"Lady," Akakios said. His arms were around her, unexpectedly powerful. In her confusion she thought that she shouldn't let a centaur embrace her. They were dangerous. They–

"Lady, let me take you out of here, before you lose your control over the beasts."

And then she was held in his arms, as he galloped to the edge of the clearing.

How odd, she thought. He looked much less young and helpless now that he was out of the cage.

The Duke's Duty

"Centaurs?" Seraphim asked. He felt shaken to the core at the realization that Gabriel had committed a crime, and a capital crime at that.

Oh, he'd known – hadn't he? – that Gabriel was in love with the necromancer. Seraphim had tried to tell himself it was no such thing, but it was not just Gabriel's refusal to form any other connections after he returned to Darkwater. There was also... the look in his eyes when anything relating to the debacle at Cambridge had been mentioned. Like a man driven into the desert and away from his heart's desire.

And yet, Seraphim had convinced himself it had been seduction. More, it had been seduction of one too young and innocent to know what was forward. And that the necromancer bore sole responsibility.

But if Gabriel had used a compulsion spell... Seraphim shook his head. No. There was no time to think about it now.

Gabriel might not be who or what Seraphim had thought he was – maybe. There was more to a man than the follies he committed in love. Seraphim's own father had committed follies enough in love, the siring of Gabriel being perhaps the smallest one. Which hadn't made him, as Seraphim had found out when he'd discovered Papa's secret papers and his even more secret activities, less of a hero, or less of an honorable man. Only children thought creatures came in perfect packages, all good or all evil.

Judging Gabriel's soul was not Seraphim's job, at any rate, something for which he would be eternally grateful. Judging him temporally might be, as his Lord and head of his house. But that was neither here nor there, as Britannia's legal system didn't apply here.

Instead, what was Seraphim's duty, left to him by his father, was to keep every member of his family safe, and at that Seraphim had been failing miserably. If someone were to be judged here, Seraphim would receive the harshest judgment of all.

So he sat down and asked the necromancer, "Centaurs?"

The man looked up and had the decency to give him an anguished look. "I thought there was no harm. Of course the king forbid anyone to travel into another world, even to rescue his daughter. I even understand the justification for it. The balance of power is such that the least magician in Avalon can control vast portions of other, less magical worlds. But the centaurs were not asking me to come to this world – or any world. They just wanted to know where the princess was. So I scryed and found her." He stopped and made a face. "I swear it was not till afterwards – that I realized that this must have meant they wanted to send someone for her. To rescue her?"

"Antoine," Nell said. It wasn't a question. She said it with decision, with absolute certainty. And Seraphim nodded and looked at Marlon again. "When did you realize it? And don't tell me it was just a thought. Something happened, something that told you why they wanted her location, and what they meant to do with it."

"Yes. Well—I checked later, and I found she was in our world. You see, they sent someone, an emissary of theirs, possibly a centaur, to find her."

"A centaur?" she said. "Antoine was not a centaur."

"You wouldn't have known," Seraphim said, cutting off her protest, and continuing as he saw her open her mouth. "So they sent someone to goad her into traveling to the kingdom. Why? In the name of what?"

"I don't know," Marlon said. "Except that I know my father is involved in it. As are the Blythes."

"The Blythes?" Seraphim asked, feeling suddenly frozen, as though someone had poured a bucket of cold water over him. "Of Blythe Blessings?"

"Yes," Marlon said. Gabriel made some sound and looked at Seraphim and Seraphim, feeling a headache coming on, could only think that he'd found the note in his father's writings that an alliance with Blythe's Blessings should be procured at all costs. He'd thought it meant… He reeled back a little. Had he been that wrong?

"For heaven's sake, man, what can all this cryptic stuff mean?"

"I don't know," Marlon said. "My exile made it difficult for me to investigate. All I know is that there is a plot and that you and your family have now got ensnared in it."

Seraphim cleared his throat. That much had also become obvious to him. And he'd let them be ensnared, even though they were his responsibility. He cast a look at Nell's profile, grave and attentive as she looked at Marlon.

Part of his confusion, Seraphim thought, had come from his attraction to her, the attraction he hadn't even wanted to acknowledge. Much good it would do him, he thought, to want the Princess Royal, the heir to the throne of Britannia.

It was time to stop being as foolish as Gabriel, and for as impossible a love. Perhaps it ran in the family.

But Gabriel wasn't the head of the family. Seraphim was. This would be as disastrous as his love for Nell. More. Nell was human and could be hurt.

Time to stop acting like a moon calf, and start protecting those who were his to protect.

Healing

How odd it was, Caroline thought, that Akakios had seemed so much smaller, so much younger in the cage. From the moment he'd got hold of her and galloped with her across the clearing, she'd known him for what he was. Young, yes. Probably too young to count as an adult in the world of centaurs, but some years older than she. She'd guess him to be nineteen or twenty, or maybe a little older. Strong with it, too, despite his injuries. He lifted her effortlessly, and his gallop faltered only once, when crossing the clearing, the type of almost tiny misstep that a horsewoman learned to identify as a sign of the mount's being tired.

He had deposited her amid the other centaurs, and then she'd let her control over the unicorns slip. She could hear them tramping and baying – an odd sound, unlike anything she'd ever heard before – in the direction from which she'd come, but the magic clearing where they lived seemed to hold them in their perimeter.

And Caroline, sitting on soft grass, beneath a canopy of trees, closed her eyes as the pain of her injuries hit her. An undefinable time later, she became aware of two people arguing loudly next to her.

"– already risked too much. I will not let you," the centaur chief was bellowing.

"In the great cause, I risked too much? What have you risked, father?" and though she'd heard his voice only once before, she was absolutely sure this was Akakios.

"Everything but my one remaining son," the king answered.

"Ah. And then it will all be for nothing, won't it?" Akakios said. "My brother's sacrifice, everything we've done to restore the balance and bring the land under control?"

The king sighed and Caroline thought there must be two sets of lungs at work there, because mere human lungs could not hold enough air for that long a sigh. "Let her go with someone else. Agapius or Thanos or… me, even. There is no rule that says you must be the one to go through the forest of dread to free the stranger."

"Just as there was no rule to say Athanasius must be the one to risk himself to bring back the princess to Britannia."

"And you know how that ended, you fool," the king said, his voice now bellowing out with a sense of outrage.

"He didn't follow the rules. He didn't make it public what he'd done and why."

"Something happened to prevent it," his father said. "You know he'd never–"

There must have been a sign somewhere, because their voice stopped abruptly and Caroline realized she'd opened her eyes, and was looking up at a bright blue sky through a canopy of leaves. She also realized her skirt was hiked up, and her petticoats with it, and had a moment of dreadful fear.

Looking down, she saw a very odd face so close to her that she let out a strangled scream. It was broad and dark, crisscrossed by scars, surrounded by straggly white hair, ornamented by an equally straggly white beard and, with all that, the possessor of the brightest, merriest pair of eyes she'd ever seen on any face.

It was the eyes that stopped her scream, and in the next moment she realized the smile that shaped the lips beneath the eyes was one of the kindest she'd ever seen too, and that the centaur – for it was a centaur – who was kneeling on the ground and had hiked up her clothes, was in fact doing something to her leg. The something had made the pain go away entirely.

Caroline half sat up and looked down. There were flasks of something green and herbal-looking on the ground. The elderly centaur had yet more flasks in a sort of sling across his middle, which had been fitted with little rings from which small bottles filled with varicolored liquids depended.

There was also a little pouch, from which the centaur now extracted a long roll of white cloth, which he started to wind about her thigh.

"Hello, Lady," he said, when he saw her looking. "I am Eleftherius and I am a healer. I have mended your thigh, and it should be strong enough to walk on in a very few hours."

She blinked at him. Her throat fell so dry that she thought she would die of thirst, but she remembered the injunction never to eat or drink anything in Fairyland. He gave her a smile, as though reading her thoughts. "I can take care of that, too," he said. "Of your thirst and your hunger, lady, but it is a dangerous game, and one that could cost you your life."

"My life?"

"Yes, for you see, if you don't feel it, you might not know when you've run through all your reserves and your body is dying. I can't make you not hungry or not thirsty, you see. I can only make you stop feeling it."

Of course, at his words, hunger had joined the torment of thirst, and now she couldn't think of anything else, couldn't do anything else, but obsess about when next she would get water or food. She had to be able to think. She'd done two good deeds. At least, she hoped freeing Akakios counted as a good deed. By the laws of fairykind, if she saved one more person, rescued one more victim in trouble, she should get her heart's desire, which was to get Michael out of Fairyland. It couldn't possibly take that long. "Do it," she said. "Whatever it is you can do for my present relief. I must be able to think."

The centaur selected a flask from the array at his chest, carefully tore out a piece of cloth, soaked it in something blue that smelled faintly of aniseed, and put it against the back of Caroline's hand. It felt cool and wet, and she thought it was very silly as a means of stopping hunger and thirst. But then there was a tingle of magic coursing through her, and she realized the liquid was more than some herbal medicine. The need to eat and drink vanished.

And then, sitting up fully, she looked down and saw the medicine on her leg was magic too. She should have known that. Such a stab wound as she'd had could not be healed that quickly.

She looked over to the side, from which Akakios's voice had come, and she thought that Akakios, too, though festooned in white bandages, looked more lively than he had before. "It was the iron cage," he told her, as she looked at him. "While we are not, like fairies or elves, or even dragons, incapable of touching or being near cold iron, and in fact many of us travel to non-magical worlds, iron will cloud our minds and hurt our bodies over time. And I was in it so long, concentrating only on making my bleeding slow down, that I would have died very shortly." His voice vibrated with a strong emotion as he said, "I owe you my life, Lady Darkwater."

"No," she said. And to his confused expression. "Lady Darkwater is my mother. I am Miss Ainsling or… or…," she reasoned, thinking that he was some sort of prince, for unless she was very wrong indeed, his father was the king of all centaurs. And if he was a prince, even of a different species, surely she ranked below him. "Or Caroline."

He inclined his head, a curtain of dark curls hiding a face that looked less pretty than it had when he'd been in that iron cage, but for all that not less attractive, with its beak of a nose and the intent dark eyes on either side of it. "Caroline," he said. "I owe you my life."

She didn't know what there was in that statement to make his father draw the sort of breath only a centaur's lungs could draw, seeming to gust on forever like an approaching storm.

Eleftherius the healer made a sound like chuckling, almost at the same time, only it was like chuckling and clucking your tongue all at once, and he said, his voice seeming to vibrate with some private joke. "I shall give you a bottle of this elixir, m'lady, the one that allows wounds to heal quickly. You and prince Akakios will, perforce need it."

"Yes," Akakios said. "Yes, thank you Eleftherius."

And at the same time his father said, "No. No, I tell you, he shall not go."

"Still fighting against the oracle, my king?" Eleftherius said with a chuckle to his voice. "What good is it, when it was the oracle cast at your wedding, before either of your sons was born?"

"They said–" The king said, then let his breath out, again with a sound like gusting. "They said there was a way out."

"Only if you're willing to let things lie as they are," the centaur said. "And for Fairyland to wither and the worlds unending with it. If you want to stop it, though, the oracle told you what the price would be." His voice sounded like he was repeating memorized lines. "You shall lose both sons, O king, and your line shall never again tread the glades of Fairyland."

Sarah A. Hoyt

The Lord's Duty

Seraphim felt as though his world had plunged into madness. First there was Nell's being the lost princess of Britannia. And she'd been in Britannia for over a year. And no one knew. That should have been impossible.

Princess, aye, and anyone of the blood, had more spells laid on them at birth than should be possible to contravene in any way. Safety spells, sure, but locator spells too.

And yet, someone had got her out of the royal nursery, surrounded as it must have been by locator spells and spy spells and discouragement spells. Someone had got her out and dropped her in the Madhou– on Earth. He was starting to learn that Earth was less of a madhouse than a world that moved according to rules Britannia wouldn't be able to understand. It wasn't the same as having no rules.

As far as that went, it made perfect sense. On Earth she would be out of the reach of mind probes and locator spells. But how had they got her out of the nursery to begin with? And how could they have dropped her back in the world without anyone noticing?

He found he was chewing the corner of his lip, while Gabriel, the necromancer and Nell continued talking around him. Half of his mind monitored what they were saying, but there was nothing new in it for him. Nell was telling them of her reading and was being told by Marlon, with insufferable, didactic patience, that her casting had been too broad to be meaningful… which Seraphim had known, he supposed, though he thought the casting had been useful nonetheless.

He could not doubt that Nell was the princess. It wasn't just the medallion, perhaps the last hereditary line of magical defense, which nothing short of destroying all of Britannia's system of magic could have stopped following her as an infant. It was also her resemblance to the queen. While a man might have bastards aplenty, and – had she resembled only her father – she might have been no more than a royal by-blow, queens were in a different position and not many had unacknowledged children. Oh, there were always legends, of course, but it didn't apply here, because now that he knew what she was, he could see the power she had as the unlikely blend of her parents' types of power.

No, Nell was the princess, right enough. The necromancer had found her, too, before this. But what did it all mean?

Out of the mess in his mind, a thought came, something Marlon Elfborn had said that made no sense. "Your father?" he asked turning to the man who had been explaining to Nell how spells should be cast. "You said your father and the Blythes were involved in this. What did you mean by that? Your name is Elfborn. You are a magical halfling of no known parentage."

The look that Marlon gave him was almost odd – half open mouth, as though a laugh had frozen halfway through emerging, and an arrested and yet somehow malevolent look to the eyes so strong, that Seraphim started to clench his fist in the ancient sign against the evil eye, before he realized the look was not really directed at him. Marlon's eyes might be turned in his direction, but he was really looking past Seraphim and at something or someone else entirely.

"I am Elfborn," he said, after a while, when he could get his speech, "because I am unacknowledged by my father, though I grant you, I could have forced him to admit to me, but the game was not worth it. I don't want people to know I have his blood in my veins. I would much rather not know I had his blood in my veins, if I could undo the knowledge."

"He is human, then?"

"Oh, yes," Marlon Elfborn said, and his voice echoed bitter and low. "He is Lord Sydell."

"Sydell!" Nell said, at the same time that Seraphim said, "The King's ears."

"Yes, indeed, and his eyes, and his secret hand too," Marlon said, and the malevolent look was back in his eyes.

"But…," Nell said, "I worked for him. I mean, after Antoine was captured, I was forced to work for him."

"Were you now?" Marlon said. "I wonder why, and what he planned that he had to wait for, thereby keeping you close and yet captive. I wonder – I very much do – what my dear papa can have been thinking, and why he didn't thrust you back to Earth as soon as he could."

"Because he couldn't." That was Gabriel, quietly. "Because her power wouldn't allow him to do so, not once she had touched the soil of Avalon. And that meant that he had to keep her subdued and hidden until he could… dispose of her more permanently. Which might very well be what all this is about."

"All this? The coil ensnaring your family?" Marlon asked. "My dear, I think that involves far more than disposing of her Highness. For one, you and I know all too well it involves Fairyland."

"But–" Seraphim said. "What are you two talking about? You can't mean that Sydell, the king's right hand or at least his left had anything to do with.... You can't mean the princess...."

But in his mind things were assembling in an all too clear pattern. Who could make sure that the princess's wards were perhaps not as strong as they should be – the king's spy chief and head of protection services. Who could make sure that any spells to trace or protect the princess were ineffective? – Blythe's Blessings, which specialized in that sort of thing and had been in charge of the business.

But why? If Nell stayed disappeared, the throne might – though it would take many many other deaths to do so – come to the Darkwaters, but it would never come to the Blythes.

Seraphim couldn't say that had been part of the plan, to kill everyone in the way until his house inherited and Honoria Blythe married him. He couldn't say that because it was nonsensical. So many deaths would need to happen that the amount stopped being serious and started being farcical. And beyond all that, they couldn't be sure he'd marry Honoria, certainly not back when Nell had disappeared. And beyond that, Honoria had brothers, and surely her father would want them to inherit if inheriting were to be done. No. That was not to be considered.

But something the Blythes had meant, and something they had done. And the snare into which Seraphim had fallen had scattered his family and might have been designed to kill him – and Nell – off world. In fact, now he thought about it, both their meeting and the trap set in Antoine's body, had taken them to situations where they SHOULD have died.

He took a deep breath and announced suddenly, loudly, "I don't think we'll be able to figure out anything more tonight. I think we should go to bed and sleep on it."

They looked surprised, but they did not argue. Which was good. He had no intention of sleeping on it. But he did intend to transport quietly to Britannia and have a long-delayed chat with Honoria.

Sarah A. Hoyt

The Ties

"Wait," Marlon said, as Gabriel headed out the door, after Seraphim and Nell.

Gabriel wanted nothing more than to continue heading out the door, to continue out and away, but he turned. "Yes?"

"I can't go upstairs," Marlon said.

"No. I shall ask her Highness if we can procure you a blanket and maybe soap and… other necessities you might wish for the night. Anything else?"

"Stay."

"Pardon me?"

Marlon's face animated with something near to a manic rictus. "Stay. It can't be any more comfortable upstairs for you than it is for me. You too are half-elf."

Gabriel frowned. It wasn't comfortable… not exactly. But he hadn't felt like his entire power was disintegrating, dissolving on Avalon's odd anti-magic field. "I wonder why," he said, then to Marlon's look. "It is not comfortable, exactly, Marlon, but it is not – either – the lethal effect it seems to have on you. I wonder what your mother was, what kind of magic mix you are? But I'm just half elf. I can go upstairs, and I can sleep, and I intend to do so."

Marlon opened his mouth, closed it. "I had hoped–" he started, though something, perhaps his preservation instinct, prevented his finishing that sentence. "That is, I thought you still had feelings for me, and I–" He took a deep breath. "We're in a strange world, one that is hostile to what both of us are, and I thought both of us could… that we could find solace or… or help each other."

And then something in Gabriel snapped. He would never be able to explain quite what it was, or quite what did it. He'd been a very young fool when he'd gone to Cambridge. Despite his early, rough life at Mama's hands, he'd been almost indecently sheltered when living with the Darkwaters, and accorded all the comforts of nobility with none of the responsibilities or liabilities. His position, as a child, somewhere between a servant and a member of the family, had been easier to support, since he'd really not been expected to do more work than Seraphim – and it had been the same kind of work, as they'd shared a tutor and learned the same lessons. But no one cared if Gabriel failed them, while Seraphim had been expected to excel. Not that Gabriel had failed them, but he'd felt no pressure to do well.

And servants had treated him with deference, but not the distance that isolated Seraphim. Not even with his being half elf. Not after that first year in the house when they'd realized he was not malevolent. And… and he'd been an altogether pampered little fool when he'd come to Cambridge.

The matter of what the cook at their house called "luvering" had never come up. Unlike the footmen and maids, and the anxiously fretting stable boys, no one seemed very sure for what sphere of life Gabriel should aim, when it came to a wife. He, himself, had thought – when he thought about it at all – that he would study for the law, and once he'd established himself he'd find a suitable daughter of a lawyer or solicitor or merchant.

He knew that wouldn't be easy. After all, no sane family would want to ally their name to someone who was half elf. On the other hand, he was also half-noble, and the connection, semi-acknowledged as it was, linked him indelibly to one of the oldest, noblest, and certainly most magical houses in Britannia. So the search for a wife would also not be impossible. Enough merchants would be willing to give a daughter to a man who was the by-blow of Satan himself for the chance to say "My son-in-law's brother, the Duke of Darkwater."

When Gabriel had thought of the future, before Cambridge, if he thought of it at all, it was into a vague vista of a comfortable home, a tidy wife, and maybe a couple of children. An ordered existence, quite different from what he'd endured while in Mama's custody.

The reason that, even though many servants his age were thinking of future marriage, his isolation didn't bother him was that after what he'd done to survive as a child, the idea of being touched, the idea of coupling with anyone at all – the idea of nakedness and intimate embraces – repulsed him with near-physical nausea.

And then there had been Marlon. It had been– Gabriel could still not explain it. It had been partly the friendship and the matter of like calling to like, so that when Gabriel had become aware that what he felt was more than friendship and that his interest had a physical edge, it was too late to draw back.

Then had come the horror of their parting, and for a long while Gabriel had thought that it was just Marlon – that Gabriel's wishes might otherwise be perfectly normal, or perhaps non-existent. But, through the years of separation he'd come to know better. Not that he'd risked such involvements again, nothing beyond the briefest of trysts. But he knew what he thought about and where his eyes were drawn.

So much for that. He also knew that as far as the heart went he still loved Marlon Elfborn. Would always love him. And forever. And that to involve himself with anyone else, of either gender, would be duplicitous, as well as – he felt instinctively – not far above his connections for pay in his very young days.

From his mythical picture of his future, he'd erased the comely wife who kept a tidy house, and, perforce, the two children. But that was just as well since, having failed at studying for the law, Gabriel was unlikely to ever leave the employ of the Darkwaters. At best, he could look forward to a future in which he became land manager, or, if Seraphim wanted him closer, butler. No position he wished to offer a wife. And thank all the fates, he did not need to have children. If ever the Darkwater family became desperate enough to count on his progeny, it wasn't a future in which he wanted to have children, in any way.

And thus things had been, until he'd gone back to ask Marlon's help. Only since then, since that moment, things had been shifting with him – slowly. Almost imperceptibly. First there had been Marlon's putting of a bind on him – as good as enslaving him body and soul and magic. And then there had been an accretion of thoughts, of actions.

Suddenly, looking at Marlon, he felt as if something had changed irrevocably. The long, slow slide of a few grains of snow on a slope had become an avalanche that had changed the landscape completely, leaving in its wake nothing but scoured land and flattened buildings.

Anger, resentment, betrayal, it all washed over him like a freezing wave.

He drew himself up straighter, and he heard the frost in his voice, when he said, "Marlon Elfborn, are you suggesting I spend the night here?"

Marlon looked surprised, surely not at the words but at the tone of them. "I thought—" he said. "Since I could not come upstairs… I thought you and I… We have a lot to talk about, a lot to … to understand about each other."

Gabriel took a deep breath. Even yesterday, if Marlon had received him that way… "We have nothing to talk about, sir," he said, very calmly.

"But– But you said– And when you… I mean, you said our very first… I mean, you put a compulsion on me!"

"Are you going to bring charges?"

"How can I? I am proscribed in Britannia."

"Very well then."

"But..." Marlon frowned, and as Gabriel turned to leave, surged out of his seat and grabbed at Gabriel's sleeve. "At least tell me why."

Gabriel pulled his arm out of Marlon's grasp. "I think you know why. Keeping Gypson in the attics and never letting me know what you'd done, regardless of your guilt over it, created your own situation. And mine too."

"But how could I know you wouldn't be repulsed and run screaming?"

"As opposed to what happened. You couldn't have known. But we were friends before we were anything else, and you should have suspected. You should have respected me as an adult and your friend. But you didn't. You still don't."

"How can you say–"

"You put a compulsion on me when I came to ask your help. You set one of the most infernal conditions you can set on a human on me. If you demand it, I have to obey you. How is that a relationship of equals or anything approaching friendship, let alone love?"

Marlon's eyes were oddly small, contracted with something that was fear and perhaps pain, too. "But– I had to," the last was a wail, emerging with the force of a two year old's self-justification. "Otherwise you'd have run! I couldn't stand to have you run again."

"Oh? I'd have run when I came to you of my own free will? Hunted and cornered I was, but I could have gone to any other world, anywhere else. I came to you. I trusted you. And what did you do? You put a compulsion bind on me. And you never even told me that you knew where the princess was, or... anything!"

Marlon's eyes now looked dark. He looked like.... In the gallery at Darkwater there was a painting of a duelist, painted on the eve of a duel – or at least the eyes had been done then. The man, a very young seventeen-year-old, was one of the past heirs of the Darkwater title. Only he'd never inherited because he was killed in the duel. Family legend said that he'd known that would happen – and the portrait confirmed it, with those bleak eyes that seemed to gaze out at never-ending darkness.

The same look was in Marlon's eyes. "How could I have known?" he asked.

"You couldn't. Human beings – and even creatures like us who are just somewhat human-like – can't know how others will react." And now Gabriel felt he had hit the crux of his anger, the center of what he'd come to realize. "People realize that other people too have the right to think and act of their own accord and that, should others not do what they wish them to do it is something they have to accept. People aren't puppets or toys." He narrowed his eyes at Marlon. "I was too young; I didn't realize it, but there's too much of them in you – too much of Fairyland. They are the ones who cast illusions and spells to force mortals to dance to their tune." He opened his hands in front of him. "Well, Elfborn. You have a spell on me, and you can call it, and make me your mindless slave if you wish – but that is all you're going to get. Do you wish to call the spell?" He waited. Marlon opened and closed his mouth. Gabriel crossed his arms. "Well?"

Marlon shook his head. His expression had gone unreadable, blank, like a statue or a wax figure.

"Is that no? Am I to assume you won't call the compulsion, then?"

Marlon took a deep breath. His mouth was raspy and grinding as it came out. "No," he said. And then, pulling on the threads of his own magic, which he'd set on Gabriel and snapping them with a broad gesture of his right hand. "You are free."

Gabriel took a deep breath and felt oddly cold, but also collected and perhaps more himself than he'd ever felt. "Very well then," he said. "Is there something I may bring you for your present comfort? Beyond a blanket and some soap and sundries?"

"No," Still the raspy voice. "No. Not… I don't need a blanket. I'll do well."

Gabriel felt disposed to argue, but the truth was he didn't want to come back anyway. Some tectonic shift had taken place within himself, and he wanted time and solitude to think about it before he talked to anyone, even Marlon. Perhaps especially Marlon.

"Very well," he said, and opened the door and closed it behind him. Outside, he took a deep breath of cool, clean night air.

Which was when the explosion hit, the force of it catching him and flinging him forward, away from the house, bodily, like a child flinging a lead soldier full force into soft soil.

Sarah A. Hoyt

Losing It

Seraphim came out of the basement with Nell, into the dark, soft night air. There was a smell that reminded him of when he went to the Darkwaters' home farm: rich soil and plants and something indefinable that said living things were growing all around.

He took a deep breath of the air. There was something different, too, something he couldn't define. He thought it was because this place was in the North American colonies. Though Seraphim had always meant to see them someday, it required money. Inside the world traveling to a different continent was hampered by matters of magic that made any jump across water difficult. So it had to be done the old way by ships, or the new way by carpetships, and either kind cost money and, more importantly, time, which the head of his family could ill spare.

"You're very quiet," Nell said. And he wanted to think of her as the royal princess, not the least because that would establish their positions firmly and help him discipline his mind and heart. But somehow, slim in those jeans that he could never think were women's attire, she seemed whimsical and young. At some level, she reminded him of the Shakespeare boys playing girls playing boys. Not that there was anything boyish about her rounded figure – or that he wanted it to be – but he thought she looked like a young girl trying to pass as a boy, a child playing comedy.

Hard to associate that with the court, and high birth and the pomp and circumstance of the occasions in which he'd met the royal family.

He said, in a contained voice, "Well, you'll agree that there is an awful lot to think about?"

"Doubtless," she said, but now she'd turned to look at him. In the dark, illuminated only by residual light from the windows of the house, and the far more distant moon, her face looked like something glimpsed on a crystal ball, when the image was just solidifying: there was the pure line of the jaw, the straight nose, her dark eyes looking up at him, anxiously, and her lips, a little quirked, as though demanding he account for whatever thoughts or plans he might have. She frowned at him, gathering those straight dark eyebrows over her nose. "But you're too silent. I wonder–" She paused, as if she'd cut her own thought off. "Is it their arrival?" She gestured with her head towards the basement.

The trained response, *Madame, I don't have the pleasure of understanding you* was upon his tongue, but he swallowed it, and instead said, trying to use the informal, almost familiar tone he'd been using with her before, "I'm not sure what you mean?"

"You've been easy with me," she said. "And not the duke, as you were recovering. I wondered, you know, because I've always seen you– That is, I get the feeling there are two of you, the duke and who you really are. And I think you've been yourself while you've been alone with me in the world. I suspect it's someone only your family knows, and probably not all of them. Now you're the duke again. You've gone elsewhere, closed yourself off. I can't read your thoughts in your expressions. Is it because they arrived? Surely it must be Mr. Elfborn's arrival, because your brother… he'd know you." But she hesitated a little when she said it.

And Seraphim realized that she was right. After thinking about what he hadn't done and what he must do, out there, in the underground room, he'd come to believe he must indeed act as the Duke of Darkwater and the head of his family. He cleared his throat. "No, it's just…" He took a deep breath. "I realized I've been a fool, letting myself get pushed around by circumstance, and never, never doing anything to find what is at the bottom of all this. I'm a witchfinder. That's what my father called what we do. We find the witches and the shape shifters before those who would harm them do. And here, like an idiot, after all this time rescuing people from just the sort of thing that has been visited on me and my family, I've let myself be caught in a trap, and I never tried to fight it."

She narrowed her eyes at him. "To give you your due, Your Grace, you were wounded and only half conscious through most of it." Then she smiled, taking the sting from the formal address. "Not that you'd ever accept it, would you? I think you're one of those who drives yourself harder than anyone else could drive you."

He made his features impassive, because if he didn't he was going to tell her just how hard it had been, just how early things had fallen on his shoulders. Instead he said, "Father was never truly reliable. I think I– No. perhaps I do him an injustice. At least half of his persona was to hide his work as witchfinder. But there might be more to it. I think his personality– He was very sociable, very… very joyful and full of life. The problem is that he was cut out neither to be duke nor to be a father. Oh, he was a good man, I think, in a way, in the sense he cared for those in the family, and he was forgiving of weakness, which he would be. But he was not… good at sustained effort. I think I took over the accounts at fourteen. Just watching the money flow out. And the loans Father took for carriages and horses and clothing…" He shook his head again. "And gifts for his mistresses. I remember being very puzzled at all the jewels he bought, when mother wore hardly any jewels." He shrugged. "So you see, someone has to drive me hard. I have to be reliable, and I have to be dependable, because there are people depending on me. If I let myself go, I could easily become like my father. I've let myself go in this whole matter, and look what a mess I made."

He saw her eyes turned to him, reflecting confusion and wistfulness, and he felt he could not let it stand that way. He'd never talked of this to anyone, not even Gabriel, but now he sighed. "Before… when I was at Cambridge… The reason Gabriel could get into that cursed coil was that I was distracted. You see, there was a young woman. At least I thought she was a woman, and young, the daughter of a healer."

Nell frowned at him, her eyes intent. "She wasn't?"

Seraphim shook his head and was glad that the dark hid the blush he was sure had formed on his cheeks. "No. She was a… You'd call her a siren, I suppose. Not a mermaid, but a magical being of the same ilk. We … I was very young and I thought I was in love. We became involved. I still don't know how I escaped, except she must have angered a very powerful man, possibly a rejected suitor.

"I was maddened, and she was feeding on my passion and my magic. I must have looked like someone in the last stages of consumption. If I'd had one more encounter with her, it would surely have been my last. Only when I went to our meeting, I… some magic hit… and I saw her as she was."

He remembered the blood red lips, the clawed hands, the thing that was more demon than human, and closed his eyes, trying to erase the sight. It would be with him to his last day. "When I recovered—" As well not tell her that recovery had taken the form of an uproarious drunk, and then days of recovery with Gabriel – how could he not have noticed how abstracted and… yes, and happy, Gabriel was those days – looking after him and force feeding him broth, before Seraphim's mind cleared. "When I recovered I realized I was as susceptible to lust and the madness of it as my poor Papa. I was no better than he. And later, when I found that due to my infatuation I'd missed Gabriel's own infatuation, his own danger, and that he'd gotten involved with someone as dangerous—" He hesitated. What he'd seen just now in the basement room made him not so sure his evaluation had been correct. "At any rate, someone I'd thought as dangerous as my own infatuation…. And I'd let him get involved in it, without noticing, without caring, I who had promised to my father to look after him! You understand? You understand I realized I have the potential to be just like

Papa and let everything go to ruin. And that's why I must not let go."

She gave him a worried look. "I don't think you could become like your father," she said, and her voice was soft, looking up at him. "Truly, I don't. Not if you mean his being irresponsible and letting go of things enough to hurt his family and let his duty devolve on you. I do think you could be easier, and take more joy in life, but I think you're also afraid of it. You shouldn't be. The duke is well enough, and I'm sure he's a fine man. But I rather liked Mr. Ainsling these few days, getting confused about how to use stoves, and struggling with safety razors."

"You like me incompetent?" he said, only half teasing.

"No. I like that you can laugh at yourself when things go severely awry."

He'd never be able to justify it. There was no justification. He was the worst of cads, the lowest of rakes, the most profoundly dishonorable of men. But what was flesh and blood to do, when she stood on her tiptoes, and put her hands on his shoulders, and kissed him?

It would have been well enough, he thought, after all, if she'd just kissed his lips.

Or just kissed his cheek. But the thing was, first she kissed his cheek, a hesitant peck and quite appropriate even between cousins as distant as they were. So he relaxed a little, as she looked up at him, her eyes dark and deep in the moonlight.

She said, in a little raspy voice, "Don't go indulging in any heroics, please? Not without me, at least."

He laughed a little at her rider, thinking that if he was going into danger, risking taking the princess royal along was like dragging a tasty lamb with him, while going to hunt wild wolves. He was still laughing when she said, "Oh, I like you like that," and stood on tiptoes and kissed his lips.

It was awkward. Odd, his lips still being parted in laughter and his being caught by surprise. He'd kissed women before, albeit not many. He'd kissed Honoria, very properly, when she'd accepted his proposal. This was all different and difficult. But when her lips touched his, his body had ideas of its own and before Seraphim could make use of his not inconsiderable will power, his arms had surrounded her gracious form, enveloping her, and pulling her against him so hard that she let out a little squeak. Even that didn't stop him, nor hitting her nose by accident as he drew her closer. His lips still found hers, and her lips were warm, with just a little edge of cold from its having been colder in the basement room.

She tasted of vanilla and coffee, and when their mouths met, it was not as though they were exploring, but as though they'd kissed already a thousand times, and now he'd come home, he'd found his proper place, and kissing Nell was where he was supposed to be, and what he was supposed to do, lifting her off her feet by the strength of his arms and feeling her heart beat frantic against him – or his heart beating madly against her. It was as though they were not separate anymore but one. More, it was as though they were always supposed to be one.

And then the light came on, sudden and harsh.

They jumped apart so quickly that it felt to Seraphim, much as being lifted out of a full dream into the awakening light of day. He stood where he'd been, or a few feet away, covering his mouth with the back of his hand, at the same time wanting to preserve the sensation of the kiss, and to hide it from other eyes, as though the kiss were a physical thing, there to be discovered, and turning in startled alarm to see… Nell's grandmother in the doorway.

"Are they settled?" she asked. "Did you solve the problem? Who are they?"

And Nell, looking ruffled, her hair all on end, said, "Yes, yes. They're the duke's half-brother and… and a friend. I'll tell you all about it," and started to walk towards the door.

Seraphim was going to burn in hell. He was going to burn in hell for taking advantage of an innocent, which she was. Oh, he had few illusions about her relationship with Antoine, but that had been different. She had thought herself a woman of Earth then, and the rules were different. The same could be said for her lack of shock at Gabriel's and Marlon's relationship. Seraphim hadn't yet decided if he liked that or hated it. After all, a wife who didn't swoon at the mention of the more carnal parts of existence might be very useful when it came to discussing things men dealt with every day. It might even keep a man from straying if his wife was his best friend, and if he could discuss everything with her.

But there he stopped short, because that was where he'd earned hell. He was thinking of Nell and wife in the same breath. But she was not his wife. She could not be his wife. She would not be his wife, even if he got his heart's desire. Future queens don't marry penniless dukes. They can't, particularly not in days when the health of the kingdom is at stake. Particularly not when the queens have been raised abroad and therefore must be more perfect and unimpeachable than ever normal princesses were. Any idea of love between him and Nell was forlorn, and he should never have encouraged it – and to give him his due her kiss had taken him completely by surprise. She must already have perfected the princely art of showing nothing in her face of what she felt. Either that or, of course, she was quite oblivious to the arts of flirting in Britannia and therefore had neglected to give him the right signals. He considered that a moment, then nodded. Most of what she did, normally, would brand her a desperate hussy in Britannia. Only she had not behaved that way in Britannia. But one thing was knowing what to avoid, and another what to show, to ensnare someone. And that last, he'd bet, she knew not. And it was as well, since the marriage of future queens was not a matter of romancing, but a matter of state craft.

All this ran across his mind as Nell went towards the door, up the creaking porch steps. He was ready when she turned back to look over her shoulder at him and said, hesitantly, "Seraphim? Are you–"

"I need to go up to my room for a moment," Seraphim said, and it was even true, curse Earth clothing. He needed time to compose his mind and calm his racing heart before he could face Nell and her grandmother and answer any questions the older lady might have – no, would have, if he had grown to know her inquisitive nature, and he had.

He walked past them, up the stairs quickly, refusing to look and see whether Nell's grandmother was staring narrowly at him, though he suspected she was. He tried not to hear their conversation either, though some of the words reached him. Fortunately they made next to no sense. He didn't think that Marlon and Gabriel were particularly happy – and what did their state of euphoria have to do with anything? Or why be said with such a tone as though it explained anything.

Down the hallway, into his room, and Seraphim closed the door, then took deep breaths. No, forget going back down and explaining things. If he saw Nell, he might lose control of himself yet again. It was the oddest thing. He'd never even felt like losing control with Honoria. No, perhaps that was not strange, since Honoria was an arranged match. A match he'd thought his father wanted. But he'd not felt like losing control with that opera dancer that he'd met while he was still at Eton, and whom he was sure was a prime article of virtue. Oh, he'd kissed her, and he'd have done more, if he'd had more money and not been a callow schoolboy whom she indulged in a kiss for a lark only. But he'd not felt as if he were plunging into the ocean, and over his head, and not in control of events. The only creature who'd made him lose control like this— Look what had come of that.

Seeing Nell again might not be a good idea.

And then there was the crazed Earth code. Nell would think she was supposed to go and brave danger alongside him, missing the fact that by being female she was more exposed, more vulnerable, and despite how much she might have worked for Sydell – Sydell was definitely on the list of people that Seraphim would like a long talk with – not as equipped for magical battle as she might think. And yet if Seraphim gave her half a chance, she'd insist on doing as much as he did. If not more.

His breath was now calm, and his mind clearer. He looked around the room. He couldn't take more appropriate clothes, because he had none. In a way, his very clothes would proclaim he'd been out of world, but he couldn't go gallivanting around Britannia in a dressing gown, either. He'd take what he had on, and steal, beg, or borrow more appropriate attire once he got there. If he read the situation aright, he was already so deep in trouble that he would hardly get in more.

He considered the pocket watch that had been his father's and bit at the tip of his tongue. He was starting to think there was some spell or tracking attached to that watch. For a year it had told him whom to rescue – at least if he used other instruments for more precise tracking. But recently it had sent him on wild goose chases or led him to traps. He thought someone must have sneaked in a spell beneath the reliable shell of the watch. How anyone could do that, who didn't have Darkwater blood – the watch being wrapped up in the family and the blood – he didn't know. Then again, if the rumors about Papa were even half true, Gabriel was just the only half-brother who lived with the family – not the only one, or even an anomaly. No, Darkwater blood might not be an obstacle, and magic didn't distinguish between legitimate and not. Only human law did that.

He pursed his lips, then thought that here, in this house, in the heart of a world most magicians couldn't brave, the watch would be safe enough. He'd leave it here and come back for it.

It was going to be hard enough to transport without taking a possible tracking device along with him.

Carefully, he built his spell. It was doubly difficult because he was transporting from the madhouse, and because he must keep it from the notice of the other magic users in the house.

Slowly, carefully, he stacked the symbols and the thoughts, the links and the power. Sometimes he felt as though he were trying to move a mountain.

By the time it was ready, his shirt was glued to him with sweat.

He closed his eyes and stepped into the portal. It seemed to him that at the same moment an explosion shook him, but when he stepped from Betweener, he was in a Britannia street – or rather in an alley that felt and smelled like London.

Just ahead of him, someone turned to look at him, and for a moment he thought it was Honoria. Same pale blond hair, same oval face. But then he realized that the face facing him, in total astonishment, was male.

And as the person tried to focus his eyes, with visible effort which – judging from the smell coming from him was due to gin – Seraphim recognized him.

"Damme, Darkwater," Honoria's immediately older brother Jonathan said. "Where did you come from and scare a man like that? And why are you wearing such odd togs?"

The Explosion, The Princess, and The Brother

Two women stood over him moving their lips. That's how Gabriel first thought of it. Two women. He could see a power signature around each of them, though one was markedly odd. The older one's. Not from Avalon. Different. Not from any world he knew, not even the many he and Seraphim had visited. He stared at her, narrowing his eyes. She was moving her lips in a way that indicated she was talking, but he couldn't hear anything at all. So she wasn't talking. Perhaps it was a spell.

It didn't look like a spell.

He looked at the other woman, still frowning. A small, slim, dark-haired woman, quite young and with that sort of bearing that people always said meant she had a lot of countenance. She had a large aura of power and there was something about her that he should remember.

Her lips, too, were moving, insistently, and now she reached over and grabbed his shoulder in a way that seemed over-familiar and moved her lips exaggeratedly. The other woman caught at her hand and pulled it away, but not before Gabriel had seen enough of her lip movements to have his mind piece them out. "Seraphim."

Like that it all rushed in on him. The girl was the long lost princess of Britannia, and she and Seraphim had come here, to the Madhouse, to seek refuge from attempts to kill them by sending them to hostile worlds. And Marlon….

He sat up and said, quite loudly, "Marlon! Elfborn?" He didn't hear himself, either. The explosion? His ears? He didn't remember hearing a sound from the explosion at all, but sitting in the garden, he turned his head towards the room he'd just left, and his mouth gaped open. The entire room – the portion of the basement that was visible just beneath the bottom floor, seemed to have blown out. The little lowered area where the stairs to the basement door had been had been blown entirely out, and the basement itself must have been blown out, because the foundation of the house looked askew.

The women were trying to call his attention, gesturing at him, but he had no idea at all what their gestures meant. He couldn't remember any sound from the explosion. He had no idea why he couldn't hear them. But his mind slowly assembled that the explosion had come from where Marlon was. Marlon!

He felt as though he'd just screamed Marlon's name, and it left his throat raw, but he didn't hear it.

He scrambled up to his feet, first at a shambling gait that involved his knees and his hands, before he found his balance, not so much walking as flinging himself forward, towards the little room, towards–

He found himself, tottering, at the edge of what was, reasonably, a crater. A black-scorched crater that extended under the house. One of the foundation beams must have been sundered or perhaps made askew, because the house was tilting downward there. But– But all there was where the little basement room had been was a vast expanse, coated with what looked like black glittering dust, as though a great flame had gone by leaving it quite scorched, carbonized, and covered in ice.

Which was… exactly what it was, Gabriel thought. It was not a physical explosion, but a magical explosion. Slowly, very slowly, he let himself down from his standing position to his knees, then back to sit on his heels. It was either that or fall forward into the crater and though it was fading fast, he could see now, narrowing his eyes, that there was still a fading magical field around it. What it would do to him, if he fell into it, was an experiment he'd rather not perform.

The older woman put her hand on his shoulder, and when he looked up, he realized she was really doing some sort of magic now. It was hard to tell what. Though her finger-movements were cabalistic, and her words seemed to be measured and ritualistic – from what he could tell of her lip movements, the fact was that what he could see made no sense. If someone had taken an Avalon spell and turned it inside out and sideways, he'd still have recognized it for what it was. This was rather more akin to what would happen if someone took an Avalon spell and threw out all the important points, leaving only the form and some of the incidentals.

He blinked. Then he heard and felt a loud pop. It was something he had experienced before, once, when his father had taken him up on a magical rug. It had been a foreign attraction brought to London by some Eastern rug merchant. They'd set up in the park, and for a shilling you could go up. Since the occasion coincided with a visit by the Duke to London, and since, when away from the house he treated both of them disturbingly alike, he'd taken both boys up on the magical rug.

Though going up had not made Gabriel quite deaf, it had made it sound as though all the sounds were very distant, and muffled and confused, too.

The effect had persisted upon landing, until his ears had given a loud pop, and suddenly he could hear normally. The same happened now, because he heard the girl– No, Her Highness the Princess Royal, say, "–Where His Grace has gone. His bed is undisturbed, but he couldn't have failed to have come at the sound."

Seraphim. He looked towards the princess. "Your Highness!" he said. "When is the last time you saw my brot– Darkwater?"

"Oh, please, call me Nell," she said, blushing a little, and then said, "So you can hear now. Grandma–"

"It was a quick healing spell," the older lady said. "Mr.–"

"Penn," Gabriel supplied automatically.

"Your brother and Nell came up, and Nell was explaining to me what had happened, and he excused himself and went to his room. We didn't think anything of it, assuming he needed to use the bathroom or something, and then–"

"And then there was the explosion, and he didn't come down, and he's in the affected side of the house, and I thought.... We called him, but there was no answer, and he doesn't seem to be anywhere." She looked towards what had been the basement. "What happened here? What caused this? And where is Marlon? Mr. Elfborn?"

Where was Marlon? For that matter, where was the furniture that had been in the room? Oh, surely it couldn't have resisted the force of the explosion, and some of it might be part of the carbonized layer all over the interior of the room. But not all. Even a magical explosion of this magnitude would leave behind debris. There would be pieces of sofa and table and– He swallowed hard at the thought of pieces of Marlon. A sense of irretrievable loss made him think he wasn't as much master of his heart as he'd like to think. "I don't know," he said. "It's a magical explosion. Have you ever–?" He'd thought he was too numb for grief, but the thought that Marlon had died, was gone forever, made him want to scream. He tightened his hands, until the nails bit the palms to restore some semblance of self-control.

"No," the princess said, then, quite shocked, "Is that ice over the walls?"

"Yes, and char too. But... I've never seen it either," he said. "But we studied them in school, Seraphim and I. It's... the explosions are possible only for people of very high magical power, when they do something that is really wrong. I...." He shook his head. "We were told, for instance, it could happen if two different transport spells, in two different directions were applied to the same room, at the same time." He swallowed again. Could that be it? Had Marlon and Seraphim said transport spells, both of them at the exact same time? But that would only make sense, given that the explosion was centered in the basement and that the ceiling above it seemed charred but intact, if they'd both been in the same room. And he was willing to bet they weren't. "Or two spells, both highly charged that contradict each other. But this…."

But this was destruction of a magnitude he'd not been taught in school. He'd been taught he might explode a table, or set fire to a chandelier. Even for that, enormous power was needed on both sides of the misguided spells. For this–

"Was it Mr. Marlon?" the princess asked.

Gabriel shook his head before he knew why, then caught the glimmers in the force field that told him it couldn't be. "No," he said, and to his own ears his voice sounded slow and incredulous, as though he were speaking nonsense and even he couldn't understand it. "No. There is dragon magic there and…."

"And?"

"Unicorn?" he said. And it sounded as crazy as it was. Unicorns were animals. They didn't set spells. "Marlon," he said. "Got caught in the cross spell."

"Is he dead?" from the princess, and she sounded like she was worried Gabriel would start crying or something. She need not be. He was not going to cry. Even though he felt as though he were drowning with the force of tears he couldn't shed, he was sure his face remained impassive. His grief was too immense for mere tears.

"I don't know," he said, simply, then added. "I hope not." And then because he must know. "And Seraphim? Where was Seraphim?"

"Two floors above," the princess pointed. "In his room."

"May I see?"

She nodded and led him upward. "You have to be very careful there," she said. "I'll stay here. I've braced that part of the house magically, and we think it will hold until we can get a construction company in to brace it properly and… and repair the damage, though what they'll think caused it, I don't know, but until it can be done, the floor will be unstable. So, I'll wait here, not to add unnecessary weight, and you tread carefully."

He refrained from telling her it was his dearest wish to do jumping jacks on an unsound floor, and instead walked slowly forward, on the creaking floor, to the door she had indicated.

The room was spacious, well furnished, and quite empty. He could see on the dressing table Seraphim's pocket watch, which they'd got from their father, and which was rigged to tell them when someone in another world was in danger. Over the chair of the dressing table was Seraphim's dressing gown. It looked like it had been washed and mended from what must have been interesting adventures.

Gabriel approached the dressing table, touched the dressing gown, not sure what he was looking for.

A shrill noise surprised him before he realized it was the watch giving alarm. Someone somewhere was in trouble.

They'd never figured out whose trouble precisely the watch picked up or why, for surely it couldn't be everyone in the universe in trouble for possessing magic at that precise moment. Given the multitude of worlds, there would be too many people in that situation.

He picked the watch up, flipped it open, and, lacking a proper scrying surface, looked into the mirror above the dressing table.

In the mirror, very clearly, he saw Seraphim. He had his back against a moss-grown wall and was surrounded by mastiffs.

Gabriel didn't think. Couldn't think. He pressed the right button on the watch and let the spell take him there.

Sarah A. Hoyt

A Matter Of Duty

Nell felt the magic from upstairs. It rang in her ears as something only a little less loud than the explosion that had left the room downstairs coated in glittering bits of magical dust, and which had forcibly bent the foundation of the house and thrown a grown man across the garden.

This explosion was more subdued, and came, inescapably, from the upstairs. But it was still loud. She was on her feet, from the kitchen table where she and Grandma had just sat down to continue – now changed – the talk the explosion had interrupted.

Grandma had just said, "You are an adult, and your own woman. I can't tell you what to do." Which of course, meant that Nell was too young to cross the street without someone holding her hand and that Grandma was very well about to tell her what to do, when this second explosion came.

On her feet, running towards the stairs, Nell realized, halfway up, that it had not been an explosion but an implosion – not a boom but a puff, as something vanished, something else flowed in to take its place. And it couldn't be just the disappearance of a man, or even two. No, something large had gone to cause that sound.

She slowed her steps over the unstable part of the house. She heard Grandma behind her, but it didn't bear stopping, not now.

The door to the room they'd given to Seraphim – had Duke ever been housed in such a ramshackle and casual way? – was standing open and creaking softly to and fro as though caught in a strong wind.

It did not surprise Nell, as she reached the doorway, that the room was empty – or at least that it was empty of the two men. The furniture remained there, in its proper places – but she didn't go in further than the doorway because a few inches in front of her nose, filling the entire space of the room, what looked like fiery dust motes flew, sparkling and dancing. She blinked at them, recognizing the markers of a very powerful spell, a shell-spell.

Someone or something had set a spell on this entire room, a spell that filled the room to the inner wall. Those spells were usually only built for important reasons, for a place where someone must do something. It was a compulsion spell on place, not person. And it was difficult to set, and could only be set by someone present.

That didn't disturb her as much as the feeling – as she watched the motes of light slowly fade – that she knew very well who had set this. There should not be a taste to magic, but there was: feel and a sense of the hand that had created a spell. It was akin to recognizing the hand that had formed letters, or the hand that had mixed a recipe.

She could not point to anything exactly, but she'd been near the man, and watched him create spells, and the spell created here was unmistakably Sydell's.

How could Sydell have come here? How gained access? True, she and Seraphim had been over the fields in the morning, talking while she showed him the places of her childhood. Where Grandma might have been was anyone's guess, but this place was defended and guarded. Grandma had done so from Nell's earliest days. Certainly she would not let anyone near who might be a danger. And Sydell had given off vibrations of danger from the moment Nell had met him.

She squinted around the room, without going in. The spell should be spent, and in fact, the glitter of it was dying by the moment, but you could never be sure. The spell had been set to cause someone to do something, and once the someone had done the something, it had slowly unfolded. That much was certain, that much not a problem to imagine. It was also no great stretch to know what the spell had caused the men to do. The two of them – or more likely Seraphim, carrying Gabriel along – had transported out of here in haste, probably somewhere the compulsion told them to go. That much was sure.

But if that had been the whole of it, there were other ways of doing it, subtler or stronger, all the way up to whatever had happened to Marlon. This was something else, something more targeted. No one did a full shell-spell unless there was a sequence of actions they wanted someone to perform. They were strong enough that often actions caused by them were repeated by the victim's ghost for eternity. It was said they were responsible for half the hauntings in Avalon.

She looked around the room. The spells were by definition dark and proscribed magic, since they robbed the victim of choice. They were often set to cause someone to do murder, but not only couldn't she imagine the men murdering each other – there was a limit to what even a shell-spell could cause you to do – but she couldn't see any blood stains on the floor. And there hadn't been enough time, since Gabriel had come up, for one strong and healthy man to strangle the other or vice versa. No. That was not what the compulsion had been. Then what?

Perhaps what had been intended had been precisely that the men should transport out. She suspected that on Earth it might be hard for someone of Avalon to physically seize and transport someone out. And the Darkwaters were both very powerful.

But something more there would be. Something to take along, perhaps? She looked around the room again, this time for belongings. Seraphim had arrived in this world in his dressing gown, now much mended and tattered, a pair of underwear that had made her grandmother marvel at the cunning arrangement of tying ribbons and grin in amusement at the lace with which people of Britannia bedecked all small clothes of the gentry, male and female.

The only other thing he'd brought, in the pocket of his gown, was his father's pocket watch, which she'd understood had some magic properties and which he and Gabriel used in their rescue missions.

She looked towards the dressing table where the watch had been, and it was gone.

And she stood there realizing the enormity of this: the two men whom Sydell had been trying to entrap from the very beginning; the men who'd been spied on, coerced, and finally accused falsely of murder so that the Duke's property could be impounded, had left this house carrying the one thing that Seraphim had brought into it, beyond his clothes. They'd left under strong compulsion set by the same person who'd been spying and conspiring against them.

The realization dawned and could no longer be avoided that the whole plot against them had been to seize this watch. Everything: their destroyed lives, the upended routines and livelihoods of all of Seraphim's retainers had been to get their hands on this pocket watch.

But that meant, surely, that the watch was not a normal watch. Petty thieves and burglars were not that hard to get in Britannia, and she was something of the kind in a much superior package – or had been while she was involved in Sydell's schemes. And she'd never been told to find it and seize it. So the watch must have anti-theft spells built into it, and probably could only follow someone of Darkwater name. And so this entire monstrous plot had been hatched to get hands on it.

She took a deep breath, blinked. And carefully, she thought the one word: idiots.

And then a sentence assembled itself in her head, as if someone else were thinking it, only the someone else was also her. She said it, in a whisper, as it came to her, "This has gone far enough."

She found she was out of the doorway, into the hallway, and across to the sound part of the house, where her room stood. "This has gone far enough."

Grandma came in as she was packing her clothes in the sturdy backpack she'd used for her youthful travels, before college. Not many clothes, but a change of underwear, a t-shirt, another pair of jeans, her first aid kit.

And wouldn't you know it, Grandma said again, and in exactly the same voice, "I will not tell you what to do; you're an adult."

Of course, that meant she was about to tell Nell what to do, and she did.

"All the intruders are gone," Grandma said. "It is all to no point for you to go chasing after them like a mad woman. You're back home. I had never expected you to come back, but now you're home. What need do you have to go involve yourself in the affairs of a world with which we have nothing to do?"

"I can't," Nell said turning around. "I have something to do with them. I am responsible."

It seemed to her that Grandma's face fell. She sighed. She approached the bed and mechanically started straightening the stuffed toys that had been there since Nell was little.

"Nell.... Perhaps I should tell you...."

There was something to Grandma's voice that made Nell look up. "Tell me what?"

"We... I am not... that is. You know I know magic, which is not natural on Earth, and I...."

Nell let go of her suitcase and gave her grandmother her full attention. "It has often struck me as odd, yes. Most human magic, on Earth – most magic on Earth – is not really magic, but yours is. What do you mean we are not...."

"There is a group of us. I won't tell you who or what we are because it would take very long and you probably wouldn't understand. I'm not sure I do, myself. I am not, however, from Earth. I belong to an organization... you could call it guardians. You know that Britannia in your – in Avalon – is closed against sending people to non-magical worlds. But not all worlds, not all lands are, and not everyone who travels to other worlds has benign intentions like your Duke's. So there is the organization. Think of us as Magicians Without Borders, if that helps. What we call ourselves translates as Guardians. When I was a young and idealistic girl, I enrolled and was sent to Earth. There's only myself here, and I couldn't keep the world safe, but I could at least find some of the magical intruders bent on exploiting the locals."

"But then—" Nell said. "Granddad. My father!" It felt to her as though her whole world were a lie.

Grandma shook her head. "No, they're real enough. I mean, they were from Earth. I fell in love with your grandfather, and I had your … adoptive father. But then—

"When he found you, I knew who you were. Or at least I knew you were royal and from another world, though the origin had been obscured. I found your name, which is why you have the same name in both worlds. And over the years I'd found out where you were from."

"Why didn't you tell me?" Nell asked. "Why not send me back?"

Grandma turned, holding a scruffy stuffed bunny between her hands. "Because I did a scrying. There is a very powerful magician on the other end. If you went back – If I sent you back— There was a very high chance you'd be killed." She paused. "Nell, I urge you to consider just staying…."

"Not now," Nell said, knowing Grandma would understand, as she did when Nell was very young, that what Nell meant was "no lecture now." Then she added, "Can you get me a couple of bottles of water and a package of crackers or cookies? I might need to go into Fairyland."

Grandma's eyes grew huge. "Nell," she said.

"I have to go. I'm responsible," Nell said.

"You are not responsible. He is a grown man and from another culture, and I know what time-traveling romances say, but– "

"No. Not that. I didn't mean I'm responsible for Seraphim. Seraphim is in trouble, yes. I might be to blame for it, yes, for things I've done to bring this about, but that is not it. And romance doesn't enter into it. Oh, I… I might… I have feelings for him, but that is besides the point," she added, as Grandma had been about to add that Nell was half-gone in love with the man. "He's not for me, on Earth or on Avalon. On Avalon because if I go there, I'll be the princess, and my marrying a matter of public policy and planning. On Earth because he could never come here and just be happy with me, and that is part of the reason I must go in and fix this. Seraphim is not just Seraphim, he is the Duke of Darkwater and the head of the second most magical house in the realm. Whether he lives or dies, and whether he's tainted by scandal or not, affects not just him, not just his family, but people who work for him, people who depend on him, and everyone who interacts with them. Who holds power over his house affects even more, as they're one of the houses responsible for the security of the royal family. The man is not a man, he's an institution, one of the threads that hold up the state-tapestry of Avalon. That I must save, restore, and make sure it's in his hands and not in much worse ones, and– "

"And?" Grandma said.

"And I must go back for the same reason," she said. "Whoever has used evil magic to remove the Darkwaters from here is also the person – or one of the people – who removed me from my birth parents. They want power, and it is essential they not get it. They are not good people. You came here to protect Earth, and I must go to protect Avalon."

Grandma had looked old, then, really old. Nell realized that this was when Grandma had accepted Nell would be gone again, and for good. It didn't matter that Nell had realized it at the same time.

Nell took off her clothes and threw on her prom dress, which, fortunately modest, could pass for an afternoon gown in Britannia, even if an odd one.

When Grandma came back with a box of Ritz and two bottles of water, Nell asked, "Was anyone here, today, in this room?"

"Only the ducting man," Grandma said. "He came to clean the ducts, like he does every fall."

"Was he… the same man?"

"Yep, Andrew, from the air conditioning place."

Nell only nodded. She knew Andrew. Had known him for years. Either he'd been replaced, not an easy thing to do, or….

"He might be—"

"A changeling," Grandma said. "He'd have to be from Fairyland himself, to mix dragon and unicorn. Besides, unicorns are the… thralls of the king of Fairyland. I will investigate as soon as I can."

Nell nodded and kissed Grandma gently on the cheek and told her, "I'll be back," without saying it would be for only a little while.

Then Nell hefted her backpack, stood in the middle of her room, and built her transport spell.

The cold of the Betweener singed her for only a moment. And then she was on the other side. But she didn't know where the other side was. She stood on a hill, overlooking a desolate plain, and yet it was hard to see clearly for a sort of grey, amorphous fog.

From somewhere at the bottom of the hill came a gloating voice, male, and awful, making her skin crawl, "So my darling nephew has come back!"

And then there was the snarling of dogs and the high-pitched scream of a young girl. Nell ran towards the disturbance.

Sarah A. Hoyt

A Ghost Of A Chance

Not all her equestrian lessons and prowess – and she was accounted a very good horsewoman by all her teachers – could have prepared Caroline for this moment.

Akakios had insisted she ride side-saddle upon his back. Only there was no saddle, just her sitting on the horse back of this creature who was – strangely – a young man in the front. In fact, he encouraged her – and blushed while doing so – to put her arms around his waist as she rode. "If we had a saddle," he'd said, with a smile. "It would not be necessary to hold onto me. Of course, if we had a saddle and I consented to be saddled, my father would disown me." He'd made light of it, and gave at the end an embarrassed chuckle, like one of the young men she met in drawing rooms who did not quite know how to address a lady.

After Caroline had arranged herself, as properly as it was possible on the back of a horse who was also a young man, he started walking at a pace, and they were quiet for a long while.

He spoke when she was just thinking that centaurs were very strange creatures and not at all as she expected, because while he smelled of warm horse – impossible not to when he had a horse's body and was moving – he also smelled of herbs and soap. His mane of dark hair, tied back, kept touching her face. They rode through a Fairyland glade strewn all over with little yellow flowers. The only path through them was a rocky, uphill way and Caroline wondered whether the grass and flowers wouldn't feel better on Akakios's hooves. Then she noticed how careful he was not to step off the path and shivered. One thing she'd learned, in Fairyland, was that what things looked was not what things were.

And then he said, "You must not resent my father, Lady. You see, he lost my older brother, his heir, in this mission. Athanasius left more than a year ago, and we have felt his death. So I have become my father's heir and now my father fears losing me."

"I do not resent your father. In fact, I don't know why I should. But what is this mission? Helping me through Fairyland? Surely your brother could not have been doing this a year ago?"

Akakios shook his head, "No. The real mission. Saving Fairyland and the worlds with it."

"How can you save the worlds? Save them from what?" she asked, but

– before he could answer – something appeared on the path in front of them.

Akakios reared, like a horse. She held on around his waist and screamed. She could feel his body tense as he tried to suppress what had clearly been an instinctive movement – the way the body felt and the reactions built into it. He put his front paws down with an appearance of deliberate force. He stammered. "Forgive, Lady– Forgive–"

But Caroline couldn't think of what he wanted her to forgive, nor did she say anything, because on the path, in front of her, looking translucent and yet somehow very real was her Papa, and her Papa had been dead for more than a year.

She wanted to say, "Papa," but as in certain dreams it seemed as though her voice was gone and she could not speak at all. It didn't matter at any rate, because Papa walked around Akakios towards her. Though "walked" might not be the most appropriate word, since he seemed not to move his legs at all. As he got close, Papa stretched a hand for her, but Akakios did something – Caroline wasn't sure what, but there was a hand lifted, and the singing of magic. What she could see of Akakios's face was very pale, like strained moonlight, and his lips looked almost gray and open as though he didn't have the strength to close them. He too said nothing.

And Papa's ghost spoke. "Caroline. You must go and save your brother. He has fallen into the most absurd trap."

"Michael?" Caroline asked, managing to speak though her voice came out tinny and too high and sounding not at all like herself. "I know, that's why I– "

Papa made an impatient gesture. "Yes, yes, that's why you and your mama came to Fairyland, a ridiculous endeavor if I ever heard of one, but it is not Michael I speak of. Oh, he's in danger enough, but it will not kill him, or not immediately. He's too valuable to the king for what he can get from Michael. No, it is your brother Gabriel who has just stepped into a great danger, and he'll be torn limb from limb in no time if you do not intervene."

"Gabriel!" Caroline said, because her mind had been nowhere near her half-brother, whom she thought safe somewhere else altogether. "Why would Gabriel be in danger?" Somewhere at the back of her mind was the thought that, after all, Gabriel was half-elf, and who else could better cope with the perils of this place?

"Do not try to get past my defenses," Akakios said, loudly, and put his hand up again, in between Papa and Caroline. "I do not know who or what you are, but you cannot get to the lady past me."

"I am the lady's father," Papa said, sounding amused. "As for what I am, I am the Duke of Darkwater – or I was. I suppose Seraphim has ascended, and I'm sure he's a better duke than I ever was."

"Papa!"

"You are not," Akakios said, "corporeal." His body braced like Caroline's pony when it was nervous, and Caroline, without thinking, ran her hand down his arm, seeking to calm him.

"No," Papa said, a glint of amusement in his eye. "I, too, fell in to a trap, much like Michael's. But fortunately, they don't know everything I know, and it left me freedom of movement… as long as I don't move my body. But Gabriel won't be allowed that. He won't be allowed to stay alive. You will find him where you hear the hell hounds bay."

Sarah A. Hoyt

A Friend In Odd Places

Seraphim looked in horror at Jonathan, and Jonathan looked back at him, raising an inquisitive eyebrow. "I thought you were exiled? I'm sure I heard something. Not that I didn't understand. I'd prefer to be exiled than to marry Honoria, and I don't say that just because she is my sister. Damn rum family we would be if I married my own sister, I mean, but all the same, even if she weren't my sister, I don't think I'd like to marry her, because she is– because she is–" he hiccupped loudly and said, in an ominous tone, "Damme if I don't think I'm going to shoot the cat."

For all Seraphim could imagine, it was quite possible Jonathan had come into the alley just for that purpose. After all, it made perfect sense to choose a secluded spot to throw up. But after a while, the honorable Jonathan Blythe, the back of his hand pressed to his lips, seemed to steady himself. "No," he said, meditatively. "Perhaps not."

Meanwhile Seraphim was thinking furiously. He'd known Jonathan since school, off and on. They'd attended Eton together and often found themselves thrust into the same circles. In such circumstances, it was impossible not to know a man's vices, such as whether he was prone to being sodden drunk in public. And that was not something he'd ever expected of Jonathan Blythe. Disorderly, sure, indiscriminately lustful and a devil with gaming. But drunk? In public? "Jonathan," he said. "Why are you drunk? How have you got in this state?"

He turned around and looked at Seraphim, and his eyes, though so much like Honoria's, yet had an animated expression to them that Honoria had never managed. Jonathan's eyes showed shock, surprise, and an underlying "tempting hell and the devil" sort of amusement. "Why, I got into this state because I would much rather be drunk than think about where the old gentleman and m'sister are going to get themselves. They think that they're using Sydell, but Darkwater, I tell you, no one uses someone who is half dragon-spawn."

"Who is what?"

"Sydell. Half dragon. Raised in a foundling home, till he was reclaimed on his father's death. Faith, didn't you know?"

"I begin to think, Jonathan, that I don't know nearly as much as I should. Can we go to your rooms in town? I believe we should have a good, long talk."

Sarah A. Hoyt

Little Necromancer Lost

"My rooms?" Jonathan said. Then he nodded suddenly. "Aye. My rooms. We can go there. I have some fine smuggled brandy that I–"

"Have had quite enough of?" Seraphim essayed.

Jonathan grinned. "Nonsense. I can tell you're not a Blythe. If you were linked to those mad people by family ties as I am, you'd know as I do that there is no such thing as drinking enough." He blinked in Seraphim's direction. "Have you considered, dear chap, that everything that has happened to you, even the royal seizing of your estates and the attainder of your title, does not compare in misfortune to being related to m'sister?"

Seraphim felt as though the world had whirled under his feet. "The attainder of what?"

Jonathan looked almost comically dismayed, a schoolboy caught in an horrendous gaffe. Which, in many ways was exactly what Jonathan was. An overgrown, bumbling, schoolboy. "Very sorry, Darkwater, that is–"

"That is, I don't actually have any right to that title any longer?" Seraphim asked.

"I'm sure it's all a misunderstanding. Or at least, not a misunderstanding, but you know, they mean to do it, only not–"

"Indeed," Seraphim said, and felt more than ever that they shouldn't, in fact, have this conversation in an alley. But it came to him, like a flash, that they probably also shouldn't have it in Jonathan's rooms. The Blythes might not suspect Jonathan of betraying them to Seraphim, exactly, but when someone was so unhappy with the course of events that he gave off his despair and anger like a cloud, his family couldn't avoid knowing it. Particularly not his very magical family.

But Seraphim's pockets were sadly to let. Particularly since these pockets weren't even, technically, his but belonged to the trousers he'd got from Nell.

The thought of Nell was not a good one. Their match had never been a likely thing, but now…. "Perhaps we can find a parlor somewhere that we can let for an hour or two," he said, "in some hostelry. A coffee room or something."

"At this time of night?" Jonathan said. "Unlikely. Everyone will see us coming and going. I'd think you'd not want to be seen. That is, I'd not want to be seen if there were a price on my head. What I mean is–"

"You can explain your meaning better shortly," Seraphim said.

"My rooms," Jonathan said, "are this way." And, with the cocksure certainty of the very drunk, he turned away from where the alley met the street and towards the other end, where it was blocked by rubbish bins.

Seraphim lurched after him, trying to stop him, but before he could get hold of Jonathan's sleeve, Jonathan tripped and fell – headlong forward.

From where Jonathan had fallen came a sound like someone wakening, and then a male voice – not Jonathan's – asked, "Who are you?" Even as Jonathan said, in a startled tone, but in the same vaguely polite way he'd employ to someone he'd stepped on at a ball, "Pardon me, pardon me. Exceedingly clumsy of me, dear fellow. That is– I do beg your pardon."

"I don't want you to beg my pardon," the other man said. "I want you to get off from on top of me. Where am I? Why have you brought me here? What kind of perfidious magic did you use to pull me–"

"Marlon," Seraphim said, "Elfborn."

Now Marlon surged off the alley's muddied ground, shoving Jonathan to the ground, and was on his feet, suddenly, his fists balled. "Darkwater. I should have known. You brought me here to get me away from him. How dare you? How dare you?"

"I beg your pardon," Jonathan said, mildly from somewhere near the ground, "But you should just call him Ainsling. His title is under a decree of attainder. I wouldn't wish you to commit a social solecism, old fellow. Who are you, anyway? Elfborn? Marlon– not the necromancer?"

Marlon cast the man a look over his shoulder, while Seraphim decided to ignore Jonathan entirely and instead to respond to the necromancer with withering disdain, "I did not transport you, if that's what you ask. Last I left you, you were talking to Gabriel in the room under the house. I went to my own room and decided it was time I stopped hiding and worked on solving our difficulties. I don't know what happened to you or why nor even who might have transported you here."

Marlon stepped forward, Seraphim was not sure why and never asked, because as Marlon surged towards him, the light from the street behind Seraphim hit the man's face, and Seraphim saw that it was covered with black residue, as though someone had coated it in coal. His expression must have shown his horror, because Marlon said, "What? Am I quite disfigured?" His hands went up to his face. Meanwhile Jonathan had stood up and blinked at Marlon, "No. It is magic explosion stuff– ice and – magic. It will come off. But it is the result of dragon magic."

"Dragon?" Marlon asked, and blinked.

Seraphim realized with a sinking feeling that the two of them, one drunk and the other possibly concussed – he couldn't imagine how Marlon could have found the time to be drunk, but he had been lying unconscious in an alley – could discuss this till the end of time, possibly loudly. And whether there was a price on his head or not, there surely was one on Marlon's. He let out air with an explosive sigh. "Jonathan," he said, keeping his voice low, "says Sydell is half dragon. Please, say nothing, Mr. Elfborn; there is no time for this. I believe there is a conspiracy afoot that has ensnared both me and my whole family, including Gabriel." He felt obscurely that he should despise himself for using the man's misguided affection, but a drowning man will get hold of any floating straw. "Jonathan seems to know something of it, and wants to go to his rooms, to talk, but I'm afraid his rooms might be magically spied upon."

Elfborn nodded. He didn't speak or protest, which at least spoke well for his intelligence.

He was quiet a moment, then gave a disquieting little laugh. "Well," he said. "I've been hiding for years. I can take you to the place where I've hid."

Seraphim bit off the question of how many corpses were hidden there too. This was the most unlikely ally and the most unlikely offer of help.

"If you must know," Marlon said, sounding stiff and forlorn, "Gabriel ended our attachment quite decisively just before… whatever this spell was, but…."

"But?"

"But I would like to see him and your family restored to a safe position. He's lost too much already, partly through my fault. And I… might even know something about this puzzle."

Seraphim wanted to say no. He wanted to turn back such tainted help. But he met Marlon's gaze and read in it concern and sincerity.

"Very well, then," he said. "We'll go to your… hiding place."

Battle Call

Akakios said, "I can hear them. The hell hounds. Lady, hold fast."

Caroline could not hold anywhere but to Akakios's middle, and she had to press her head close between his shoulders, feeling the horse body and the human move in unison, as they ran through.... She would never be able to say more about the landscape they crossed than that it was dark, with rocks and trees.

In her confusion, a fear assailed her that Akakios would set his hoof wrong and break it. She noted her Papa had disappeared, somewhere far behind. And then she realized that in this magical landscape, Akakios was better suited to run than she was. Nor would she be able to find her footing.

Akakios must have felt her fear, because he whispered, "Never mind, Lady, I was born and raised in Fairyland, and these glades are like daylight to me. I judge the baying is coming from out the walls of the royal palace."

It didn't calm her, except for her feeling it was kind of him to bother. She closed her eyes tight and tried to trust him, and she didn't open them again till he stopped abruptly, in a way that in a normal horse, and had she not had her arms entwined around his all-too-human upper body, would have sent her flying over the animal's head.

She heard a fearsome barking and snarling, and a voice crying, "Miss Ainsling!" and opened her eyes. She'd known Gabriel's voice before she opened her eyes, of course, and she felt torn between anger and fear. The fear because she could see Gabriel, up against a white, glimmering wall, surrounded by dreadful creatures the size of bears, who might be dogs, if dogs had teeth like daggers and eyes like burning coals.

And because, as Akakios stopped, some of the dogs turned towards them. Anger because Gabriel would call her Miss Ainsling if they were in public at all, and she would guess he thought the presence of a centaur constituted being in public. Or perhaps he was trying to spare the sensibilities of the dogs.

"Gabriel," she said, forcefully. "Come to us. We'll take you out of here."

It was only as the words left her lips she realized she'd spoken two impossibilities. First, how was Gabriel to come to them past twenty snarling, encircling hell hounds? And second, how would they take Gabriel out of here, when Akakios could barely carry her? And on perceiving her idiocy, she said, loudly enough to be heard over the dogs, "Oh, I am an idiot."

This surprised a laugh out of Gabriel, which went to prove, if anyone doubted it, that he was her brother, since her brothers always laughed at her.

And now she saw that he was holding a sword in both hands, a sword that appeared to be made of light. "Go back where you came from, you little fool," he shouted, apparently forgetting he was supposed to act like a servant in front of an anonymous centaur. "I'll keep them too busy to follow you."

As he spoke, he charged with his strange weapon, and the dogs that had turned towards her now turned to him, growling and snarling.

Akakios had already started edging them both away, and presently, with no seeming transition, the whole scene looked as though it were very far away and he had brought her to what looked and smelled like the middle of an orange orchard. The scent of flower was heavy in the air, the trees gave an impression of cozy protection, and it felt like a warm summer night.

"Oh," Caroline said. "How came we here?"

Akakios was looking over his shoulder at her and looked surprised for a moment. "We've not gone anywhere," he said. "Well, far enough for the creatures not to see it. I invoked a place, in my father's lands, where I often go to think. It is not–" he paused in exasperation, "physical. And yet it is. It's a place of the mind, a place of safety. We are also a little there, or at least our souls are, which means we won't be overheard by magical means, because the orchard is my place and casts its protection over me. Lady, that is your brother?"

"My half-brother," she said. "Gabriel. His mother is of the fairy. His father was my father."

Akakios nodded. "He is a valiant fighter," he said, "and we've heard the prophecy, of course; but Lady, where he is, and all alone, he will surely die."

She swallowed hard. She'd guessed as much since she'd seen him with his back to that wall, his sword of light barely keeping at bay the monstrous mongrels.

She knew the sword well enough. It was called Sword of Power, and men got taught how to create them in their elementary magic education. Women weren't, of course, because it was assumed there would always be a man by, ready to champion a lady with magical power.

Which was all very well and good, but being an untrusting sort, Caroline had made Michael show her how to do it.

She had even practiced with it, one summer, long ago. However, she had never made great use of it for two reasons: first, she hadn't been very good at it. Keeping up the sword shape required concentration, and at eight she was more likely to turn her head to follow a butterfly than to concentrate on keeping her fiery blade burning. Second, it took an enormous amount of power. An hour or two of holding that magical blade was like days at work and without food or sleep.

Granted that Gabriel was far more powerful than she was, how much effort did the sword take him? How long could he keep it going? Even if he was a powerful magician?

She imagined now that she saw in her mind's eye signs of fatigue. She hadn't been able to see his face, but she fancied that he dripped with sweat and that he hadn't swung the sword about with the vigor that he should have.

"Akakios," she whispered. "Can you command the sword of power?"

He seemed puzzled for a moment, then he said, "Aye. But, Lady, listen– "

"No, if you do it, and I do it, we can fight our way to him, can we not?"

And now Akakios laughed at her. "Lady, have you ever seen a horse harried and brought down by wild dogs? Never mind. We'd not make it. Before we got near my belly would be ripped open and we, both, devoured."

"Oh, you can't tell me we can't do anything," she said. "He is my brother, and Papa – whatever remains of poor Papa – insisted that I should free him. And indeed I should, Akakios, for without him I would have been brought to Fairyland when I was just a babe, and I– "

"No, Lady, listen. I can command the Sword of Power, and indeed, it will help us, but your mind must busy itself with something else. Remember how you got to me in that iron cage?"

"I don't have the horrid sword."

"No, I mean, the power of your mind, commanding the beasts."

"The unicorns? But that's because I am a virgin."

He made a sound that might have been a laugh or a sneeze, or rather, she suspected, a laugh hastily turned to a sneeze. His high cheekbones tinted a dusky red. "If that were the virtue, Lady, I warrant you I'd never have been taken prisoner. They should have told you then, and if not, I'll tell you, it is purity of another kind that counts: purity of mind, purity of intent, and purity of magic. My people came to you to rescue me, because you have those having been taken through the flames of dragon magic and having all impurities withered away. You must now, Lady, use your mind to control those beasts."

"But…" She paused. She could remember in her mind's eye the horrid creatures, and it seemed to her that she could remember their smell too, thick and gagging upon the air. "But they are… not unicorns."

"No," he said, a twinge of amusement behind his words. "Not half as smart as unicorns. But both of them are controlled by the mind of the king of Fairyland. and you defeated him once."

"The king!"

"Who else would you think? Yes, the king. Listen, I shall open a very small fissure in our protections. Extend, as it were, our minds beyond the orchard just a little. And you can see if you can command the brutes. If you can, I shall charge, holding the Sword of Power myself, leap over the heads of the brutes, and then we'll be by your brother and able to aid him."

She nodded and felt more than saw as he ripped, with his hand, in a quick pass, a gaping tear in the perfumed summer night into that other place: with the indistinct rocks and terrain underfoot, the white wall at Gabriel's back, and the snarling dogs.

Caroline reached out tentatively, trying to believe in her own power. Encountering the dog's minds was not at all like the unicorns'. One thing was to find a vacant mind edged all about with blood lust and the thought of violence. Another and quite different to step full body into a midden. The minds of the dogs were not like animal minds at all, but they reminded her rather of certain men she'd met – fortunately not many of them, though she suspected there would be more once she were presented to society – who stripped one with a single look and who seemed to be thinking the lowest, most revolting things to do to one.

Only of course, in this case there was no "seem" involved. She was in the dogs' minds, and the images assailing her made her gag. But she wrapped herself in the certainty that they could not touch her. Had not Akakios said that her power and her intent had both been burned pure? They could only make her feel impure and besmirched, and she would not let them.

It was easier said than done, but she thought of Gabriel dying because she went missish and let herself be scared away by lewd minds. And then she had it. She quieted the dogs, as one would quiet unruly animals. She thought strongly at them to be still and sit. She could feel in her mind as they obeyed.

She could also feel it would not last long. There was another mind controlling them, a far more powerful mind, and it was wrestling with hers and would soon overcome her.

And should Gabriel try to get out of his position, the other mind would surely overcome. And then Gabriel, without the wall at his back, must fall and be devoured.

She and Akakios must act fast before he were tempted to escape.

Before she could tell Akakios to do so, he was running. Words he shouted, which sounded Greek, brought the Sword of Power to his hands. He waved it frantically, dispelling any dogs' intention to attack them. And then he leapt.

Before they landed on the other side – it was a very long leap – he lost height. And as he lost height the other mind gathered control of the dogs. Caroline saw them leap up, snarling, and saw Akakios's sword cut down.

She screamed, sure they were lost, but Akakios kept his leap and landed, safe, on the other side, falling, however, on his knees on his front legs almost instantly.

His human body was panting and making a keening sound, but he was still brandishing the sword.

She judged, justly, that he didn't need her weight, and rolled off and said her own words to invoke a Sword of Power, and turned to stand by Gabriel's side, sword in hand.

She had been right – Gabriel looked tired and smelled of sweat and fear. As soon as she was off Akakios's back, the centaur rose on all his legs, his sword in hand, and laid about, covering the points she and Gabriel couldn't reach.

"Miss Ainsling, this is madness. What possessed you to get yourself trapped with me?"

"Only that you have yourself a fine defensive position, and that with three of us, perhaps we can fight free of this trap as you alone couldn't. And give over with the "Miss Ainsling," do. Akakios knows you're my brother, and I suspect centaurs are not so nice about classes."

Gabriel laughed. "Very well, Caroline, then, but you are wrong. Centaurs are particularly nice about classes. Well met, Prince, but this is a sad endeavor. How did you let yourself be lured into this by my scapegrace sister?"

Akakios, still sounding tired, said, "Not entirely by her, my lord. You see, we centaurs believe in prophecy."

"More fool you," Gabriel said, fighting. "I neither want my uncle's throne nor will I seek it. And I see you are cut about the legs."

"Not badly enough to warrant worry. One of the brutes got his teeth in, and another his claws."

"But Prince," Gabriel said. "I understand my sister has windmills in her head, but what do you mean us to do to get out of here alive? Have you any ideas?"

"At the moment, not a one, save faith something will happen." Akakios said.

And into that moment of calm a voice boomed, loud as the trumpet on judgment day, cloying with honey and rife with evil: "So my darling nephew has come back!"

The Knot

Seraphim didn't know precisely what he expected from a Necromancer's hideout. If there had been an image in his mind, it must have come from the dark illustrations in some children's book – supposing his mother would have let something that insalubrious near her children. Which she wouldn't have.

His mind insisted there should have been less light, cobwebs, and also there should be perhaps a smell of rot to go with the army of undead servants coming to bow to their master and tend his every desire. There shouldn't have been, he was sure of it, shelves lined with books he would have liked to read, a pleasantly untidy desk, covered in papers and notebooks that gave the impression of someone furiously working on something he enjoyed, and there certainly shouldn't have been comfortable sofas in faded, cheerful floral print. But most of all, he thought, there shouldn't have been, on one of the bookshelves next to the desk, at eye level, a misshapen porcelain dog, with a lopsided grin and mismatched eyes. There particularly shouldn't be that, because Seraphim knew where it had come from.

Fearing at any minute to come face to face with what remained of the unfortunate Aiden Gypson, not sure how to react to such a thing, and fairly sure that – in the end – he was being a moral if not a physical accomplice to necromancy, he concentrated on that dog, on that shelf. "That," he said, in the terrible voice one might use to impart news of dread catastrophe, "is Gabriel's."

As he turned to look at Marlon, he'd swear that, for just a moment, unholy amusement danced in the man's eyes. And for just that moment, Seraphim's hand started to curl into a fist, but then dismay succeeded amusement in Marlon's gaze, and he nodded once. "Yes. He gave it to me, years ago. He said he'd had it from a child. It's all… I expect to keep of him. Won't you sit down? I'll fetch tea."

Jonathan looked dismayed at this. "Tea? Have you no brandy?"

Saying in one voice, "If you'll pardon me, I believe you've had enough brandy," Seraphim and Marlon looked startled and grimaced at each other. Then Marlon left the room, and Seraphim was left with the unenviable task of trying to lead Jonathan to one of the cheerful sofas. This was easier said than done, because Jonathan had reached that point of his intoxication or the recovery from it, where every detail of a room or landscape is riveting and must be narrated as loudly as possible for the edification of oneself, as well as that of those around us.

Which was how, having pulled away from Seraphim, and towards a dark corner of the room, Jonathan said, "Good God. Is that him? His…" and probably under the impression that he had lowered his voice, "lover? The one he keeps as an undead catamite?"

And suddenly it all surged at Seraphim. The first thing that happened too fast is that Seraphim realized that in the corner he'd ignored, what he'd taken for unidentifiable clutter was, in fact, a human being, or what remained of one.

Aiden Gypson didn't look like a corpse, exactly. But neither did he look like a living human. More like someone had taken a human and replaced his skin and flesh with dried clay. Taking a deep breath, Seraphim could smell no decay, but all the same, it wasn't even a good necromancy job.

In proper necromancy, from what Seraphim had read, the corpse was preserved to look exactly as it had at the moment of death. Aiden's eyes were dry and lusterless, and his lips had receded, exposing teeth. He didn't react to their presence either. He was shuffling in place, little more than a flutter, which – Seraphim thought – was a permanent thing, and again a result of bad necromancy. Good necromancy could command the corpse so that it was in repose or moved in the same way as a human.

All this was instant, as was the realization that Aiden Gypson's soul – whatever remained of his individual spark – was pinned somewhere behind the body, and could feel what happened to the body. And then Seraphim felt ill. He had to swallow fast, so as not to be sick. Not good necromancy at all and how could Marlon?

All the sympathy he'd felt for the man when he'd unwillingly realized how much he cared for Gabriel dissipated. All the fellow-feeling of realizing he was, perhaps, not a monster, vanished. Instead, there was leaden dread and nausea.

Realizing that Aiden Gypson looked like Gabriel Penn – or at least that they were both the same type – only added to the dread.

The thought "Good God, had he meant to do this to Gabriel too?" crossed his mind at the same time that he realized that all this had been very fast and Jonathan was just now drawing breath to continue his narration.

It came at the same time as a flutter of silver and china, like someone trembling while holding a tea set on a tray, and he turned to look towards the door to the interior of the house, where Marlon stood, holding the tea tray. And at that moment, Seraphim felt his anger evaporate, and the dread with it, and, against his own will, sympathy rush in. Marlon had washed his face and changed, and should have looked more presentable. Instead, he looked as white and dead as his dead lover. Perhaps more so. His mouth moved, though no words emerged, and the lips seemed to Seraphim to form, "Not a catamite."

Jonathan looked towards Marlon too, and chuckled, a chuckle of high amusement, and said, "Far be it from me to say it is a terrible thing, if I've never tried it. It is illegal of course, but tell me–"

In a flash, Seraphim felt as though the real division in this room was not between himself and Marlon, though their tastes in bed companions might be very different, and though Seraphim could not possibly imagine taking a lover and making him a living-dead object.

But he understood the way Marlon both wanted to defend himself against the charge of keeping what remained of his lover for sexual purposes, and his dreadful horror of speaking of his private life to near-strangers. In an insane world in which Seraphim's life was more like Marlon's, he could imagine feeling that dread, that conflict of pressing needs.

On the other hand, Jonathan was something quite, quite different. He was, unlike Marlon or Seraphim, an uncomplicated man, who enjoyed carnal pleasures and took the world with hedonistic innocence. If he'd done something like what Marlon had done – or was accused of doing – he'd have done it for the simplest of all motives: to see what it felt like. And he might be pursued by the law, but he would not feel guilty.

Seraphim found that he had clamped his hand over the honorable Jonathan Blythe's mouth. "Not another word," he hissed at the brother of his erstwhile – was she erstwhile? – fiancée, in defense of the man he didn't even like, the man whom he, for years, had suspected of corrupting Gabriel. "Not another word, Jon, or so help me, you'll have to do with me."

"Why? I only want to know how it feels to–" Jonathan said, as Seraphim's hand lifted. The hand clamped down again.

"You're disguised, Jonathan. What's more, you're taking liberties. We are in Mr. Elfborn's home, and it's not for us to do him the gross injustice of accusing him of the worst."

"For heaven's sake," the irrepressible Jonathan said as soon as

Seraphim let go, knowing it was impossible to cover Jonathan's mouth forever and, faith, wringing his neck was probably one step too far. And besides Seraphim liked him, even though he disapproved of him.

"For heaven's sake," Jonathan repeated. "How can I accuse him of anything worse than necromancy?"

"Just so," Marlon's voice said, from the sitting area. "How could you? So let's establish that I'm a necromancer. I don't think that is a great insult, since I was proven to be so in a court of law, which is why there is a price on my head. Will you sit down, gentlemen?"

Feeling his back prickle as he turned away from the corpse, Seraphim did so, as did Jonathan following him. They sat, side by side, with Marlon sitting on a chair facing them. Marlon poured, asking civil questions about cream and sugar with the equanimity of any gentleman receiving friends.

"All very well," Jonathan said, as he held the cup of tea in both hands. "But I only wanted to know what it is like to tup–"

"Jon," Seraphim said. "Do you want to face me with pistols?"

Something like a suppressed cackle escaped Marlon, and Jonathan stared at Seraphim dismayed. "What? No. Good God, man. I'm no match for you."

"Good. Then please let's keep our talk to matters of the coil I and my family find ourselves in. And let's try to be civil to our host."

Jonathan looked baffled, but Marlon was giving Seraphim a long, appraising look. "Pardon me, Your Grace," he said, at long last. "I think I've misjudged you all these years. I never realized you were kind." He was still pale, and his face had a sort of rigid immobility that signaled, to Seraphim at least, that he was pushing himself beyond the boundaries of his comfort as he said. "And, for what it's worth, Mr. Blythe, I could not answer you in any way. I know as much about, how did you put it? Ah, tupping the undead as you do." His eyes crinkled at the corners, as though amusement crept through despite everything. "Perhaps less."

Jonathan looked astonished. He shook his head. "They said–" he started, then shook his head again. "Well, then, it's very strange, when you're already under sentence for necromancy, what else could they do to you?"

Despairing of explaining to Jonathan that there could be restraints on a man other than external, Seraphim looked at Marlon and said, "Pardon Jonathan. He's one of nature's own pagans."

"I see that," Marlon said, and something to his eyes told Seraphim that he did. He wasn't horrified or reproving of Jonathan. He was worried about where Jonathan's careening mind might lead, and also vaguely amused by such disregard for conventions and society, and perhaps a little jealous.

Marlon took a sip of his tea, set the cup down still mostly filled and said, "Now, for the matter at hand. We knew you and Gabriel – your whole family – were in a serious coil of trouble."

"You can say that again," Jonathan said.

"And you said…," Marlon hesitated, "that my fa– that Sydell is half dragon? How do you mean that?"

Jonathan blinked at him. "Why, I suppose in the usual way. His father slept with a dragon. Not that I blame him. It is said dragons are–"

"Eminently tuppable, yes," Seraphim said, anticipating what Jonathan would say, and feeling like he'd fallen into a mad dream. He didn't say these things. He didn't discuss these things with other people. But then partly that was because dukes didn't do that. And if he was no longer a duke, then he need no longer exercise restraint. But he was called to reality as Elfborn said, "I didn't know that," in a strained, sober voice. "How could I not know that? I didn't know he was raised in a foundling home, and how could I not, when I was raised in one?"

Jonathan made a dismissive gesture, drank down all his tea, noisily, and then extended his cup for more. Marlon poured, without looking, as though he did it automatically.

"Why should you? Unless you made a study of Sydell. And even then, you might not know it. He's taken great care to cover his tracks. I only know it because my father has known him from the time–" A hiccup broke Jonathan's talk, and he put the back of his hand against his mouth. "Pardon me." He took a sip of his new cup of tea. "—has known him from when Sydell was claimed by his grandparents, on his father's death, and so he remembers the scandal. M'father is maybe three years older than Sydell, but enough to remember, because Sydell was twelve or thirteen or some such when his father hanged himself."

Marlon's cup rattled in the saucer. His eyes were huge. Seraphim remembered, or thought he remembered, hearing that Sydell was Marlon Elfborn's father. It seemed an impossible thing, for one because Sydell was a perpetual bachelor, and it was rumored that he shared Marlon's – and Gabriel's – interests. But there had been that half started, "My fa–" and looking at him, now, Seraphim detected some resemblances to the king's left hand.

"Hanged–?" Marlon said.

"Oh, yes." Jonathan drank his tea, quite oblivious to the discomfort he was causing. "It's all the grand tragedy, you know. Worthy of an opera. My father says that old Marcus Sydell found out that his son was… that is, that he had, somehow, commandeered a dragon maiden out of Fairyland and that they were–" He hiccupped again. "—that they were involved, and he was furious, because he was trying to arrange his son's marriage, so he arranged for a banishing spell, restricting the creature to Fairyland. Costing the world, of course, but it worked." He frowned. "Or at least, Sydell had already been born, and his grandfather hushed it up and put him in a foundling home for magic children. Saint Patrick's, I believe, because they handle–"

"Half dragons, yes. And then," Marlon took a deep breath, "Sydell's father?"

"They don't handle half dragons well," Jonathan said, frowning. "Damme, what I mean is, no one but dragons handles them well. The discipline needed–"

"Yes? Trust me, well aware. But what happened to my– to Sydell's father?"

"What? Andrew Sydell? The father of the current Lord? He hanged himself."

Marlon blinked. "How?"

"In the usual way, I imagine. No, wait, I heard of it. With his belt from the entrance chandelier. Devilish thing, and his father was hard put to hush the scandal because, of course, all the servants saw it, what? But it can't be denied that all who… who get involved with Fairyland in that way lose their mind a little, and there it is."

"There what is?" This was Seraphim.

"Though he married his heiress, he was not happy, never had children, was taken with melancholy, and then hanged himself. I don't see what you want me to explain more."

Marlon was rubbing his upper lip with his index finger as though lost in a world of his own. At Jonathan's explosion, he looked up. "Nothing. You've explained things I've longed to understand my whole life." Then he looked towards the corner where Aiden Gypson stood. "And why some disasters… but that's neither here nor there. Tell us," he leaned forward. "Tell us in detail what my dear papa has been doing in this whole coil, for it's a knot we must uncoil."

"Your… papa?" Jonathan frowned.

"Sydell."

Elfborn had managed to stop Jonathan's mouth. Jonathan looked at

Elfborn in shock. "Sydell? You are…?"

"The result of a spell gone horribly wrong? Yes, I believe so. But let's move to relevant matters."

"It is a relevant matter," Jonathan said, aghast. "If you are… then what… then that was how he got access to–"

Seraphim's mind had put together things that he wasn't even aware of knowing. "That was how he got access to Fairyland magic, and managed to send the princess royal to another world, as well as use that magic, behind the king's back to… what? What does he aspire to, Jonathan? The throne of Fairyland or of Britannia?"

Jonathan frowned. "Why," he said. "Both, I imagine."

Sarah A. Hoyt

The Princess And The Precipice

Running in Fairyland, Nell thought, was perhaps not the brightest of ideas. Not that she knew much about Fairyland, but what Avalon knew – or thought they knew – it had occurred to her often that they were sure in knowledge they couldn't possibly have acquired in any rational way. Thus far, they were just like Earth.

In Avalon they said that Fairyland was a parasite universe. Somehow spawned when the universe had split due to some cataclysm at the dawn of time, it drifted in a time and place of its own, now touching this high-magic universe, now another, and vampirizing energy, magic, and emotion wherever it went.

Of itself, it was too low-energy to have a coherent organization or internal structure. Its only power, its only existence, came from the minds of men. That meant that it was a crisscrossing of ideas and thoughts, of legends and beliefs.

But before she could think, before she could realize the dangers of her location, Nell had run into the fog. Her mind was quick enough, and it had put together the voice and the circumstances of Gabriel Penn. Perhaps it was too much to be certain of this on so little, but she knew, she could feel that Gabriel Penn had ended in Fairyland and that he was facing a relative of great power.

She ran, feeling hilly terrain beneath her feet and moss-slippery covering on that terrain. The cold fog seemed to sting her throat as she ran, but she knew she must help this poor man. If it was true – and she could not doubt it – that she was the crown princess of Britannia, then all of this, somehow, gyrated around her. Had she never existed, this would never have happened.

It took a few moments to realize that she didn't even know if she was running in the right direction. The scream had stopped abruptly, and around her there was only silence, like being enveloped in cotton wool or wrapped in nothing. A doubt assailed her, suddenly: did she even have existence here?

And then she dropped.

There was no other way to describe it. Like in a dream of falling, it wasn't so much that the ground gave out under her, as it was as if there had never been a ground – as though she were one of those cartoon characters, running perfectly fine along ground that didn't exist, until they suddenly looked down and saw that there was no ground at all. And then they fell. And she fell.

Just as the image appeared, she banished it. Fairyland was shaped by men's thoughts, men's beliefs, men's fears. And women's too at that. And though she'd enjoyed the vintage cartoons as much as any other kid, on a Saturday afternoon, with a pack of DVDs, she had no intention of being caught in a world that expressed itself through dumb coyotes and Acme inventions.

She groped madly for something that would make sense of her situation and give her more than darkness and the sense of endless falling.

Stories ran through her mind – the princess and the pea, the herder of geese—but all of them were tainted with blood and pain at the heart and she thrust them away. Besides, she'd never learned them very well. They weren't in the weave of childhood on Earth. Not anymore.

And then she thought she had fallen through a rabbit hole.

Suddenly her fall had texture. There were earthen walls on either side, and here and there roots that had grown in from above. Before she had time to blink at it, she'd fallen into a little cave. No. A little room – with an earthen roof, but a wooden floor polished and covered by a Persian rug. There was a grandfather clock in the corner, a comfortable armchair in the other, and – over the armchair – a portrait of a white rabbit dressed in Victorian attire.

Her brain rattled from the suddenness of her fall, Nell blinked at the portrait thinking that now she had gone definitely mad. Then she looked at the table, where there was a plate with something that looked like pancakes, and a little metal flask. The pancakes had a note card in front of them, of the type that was used for fancy dinner parties, but on this one, instead of a name, were inscribed two words, the words she knew would be there: "Eat me." And the flask had one of those chains around its neck that liquor bottles had, and a little plaque inscribed with "Drink me."

Okay, she knew how this story went, and she got up and approached the table and reached for the pancake. Then stopped. From somewhere at the back of her mind came a confused recollection of things she had heard and read. Something about fairies not being able to bake, or use yeast, so all they ate was pancakes. In the story of Alice she had read as a little girl, what Alice ate was a cookie, but this was definitely a pancake, looking like the unappetizing buckwheat pancakes grandma had forced on her when she was going through that health-food phase years ago.

In fact, there was a theory that the UFO sightings on Earth were actually sightings of fairy denizens, under heavy disguise, and probably a little maddened by Earth's iron content. They also, inexplicably, had given the humans they wished to beguile some form of whole-grain pancakes.

Nell's hand was almost touching the pancake, and she glared at it. Alice, after all, had been led a merry dance through her adventures, and though she supposedly woke up at the end, was it true? The multi universe had truncated legends and confused, many-world stories. In some worlds things ended one way, in some another. She would never, ever, be able to think of the ending of Little Red Riding Hood in Avalon without stomach-churning disgust.

Persephone on one seed of a pomegranate had been condemned to spend half her life in Hades. What if the stories never told were that Alice kept getting pulled into Fairyland, into the mad world of upside-down riddles, for the rest of her life? And… forced to marry the king of fairy?

The idea came out of nowhere, but it put a chill up her spine. She was the Princess of Britannia. The heir to the throne of a kingdom where the throne meant more than state power, and land meant more than a lot of soil where you could grow things.

She barely understood how things worked, but she knew that there had been a ritual marriage between the mythical Arthur and the land. In Britannia Arthur was not mythical and the marriage might have been more than ritual. She didn't presume to understand it – she doubted anyone did. Like particle physics on Earth, it was the domain of a few, rarefied intellects, but it still affected how everything worked. And the kings and princes of Britannia – and to an extent every relative of the Royal line, like even Seraphim Darkwater – would have some of the land mixed into their very being, influencing every breath they took, every thought they had.

In the same way, the king – or princess – affected the land. If she ate this and belonged, even part time to fairy land; if she were married to the king of fairy, wouldn't that make Britannia a dependency of Fairyland? Fairyland could attach to it as a leech to an animal, and drink its fill, till either it killed Britannia or… Or all of Avalon burst.

She looked at the pancake, and then said, with bright malice. "I am a princess, after all. Alice wasn't. Shouldn't the offering be more suited to my status?"

And before her eyes, before she could even blink, the pancake changed into the reddest, most appetizing apple she'd ever seen.

Even knowing what happened to princesses in fairytales who went about biting beautiful apples; even never having been the type of person who longed for a good, crisp apple, Nell couldn't help feeling her mouth water.

Fortunately, she also felt a surge of anger: strong, blinding anger, affront that they thought she would be so easily tricked, and a blank rage that they dared – they dared do this to Avalon. She had never thought of it as her world before, and perhaps it wasn't, perhaps she was just its princess. But one way or another, she belonged – and she might be their last defense.

"Ah, no you don't," she said. Her voice echoed, unhinged and high in the small, proper, Victorian chamber, and it seemed to her that the rabbit portrait raised its eyebrows. Nell grabbed the apple, and threw it at it, hard, dead center.

The portrait exploded, bits of apple – far more than a single fruit could contain – and earthen wall flew at her, giving her barely the time to cower on the Persian rug, her hands over her head.

When she rose, shaking off dirt and pieces of apple, she was looking at a white, marbled hallway. From somewhere down it came the sound of working machines and a voice she thought she recognized said, "No, no. It is not supposed to work that way."

Sarah A. Hoyt

Between The Dogs And A Hard Place

"Only passing through, my Lord," Gabriel boomed back at the leering sort of voice that taunted him. "I want nothing of yours, and only what's mine."

"What's yours, I understand, is my crown?"

"No, only those mortals you keep captive here which are bound to me by blood or affection." As he spoke, he continued fighting. There was to him a sort of nimble lack of concern, a quickness of feet and wrist, as he cut at the hell hounds.

Caroline, beside him, tried to match his ability, and so busy was she that she didn't realize for a moment that Akakios hadn't joined them. While he could stand, it was obvious his forelegs pained him, and he could do no more than defend himself.

There was a long silence, and then the voice that Caroline couldn't identify boomed again, but said a word that Caroline couldn't understand, a word like liquid fire that seemed to scrape the senses as it fell. Behind her Akakios made a sound of outrage, but to Caroline's surprise, Gabriel laughed. His hair had come loose from its binds, and flowed around his head like brambles growing in a wild place. Somehow it made him look more elf than human, and his laugh was also more elf than human, seeming to hit some places out of her hearing range.

"Kind of you," Gabriel said. "But that is no offense. I might as you say be a human-lover and in thrall of the low magic creatures. Since I intend to live my life among them, I care not what your opinion might be. I care only to have my own returned to me."

"You cannot have them. I would not demean myself by dealing with such as you. You only seek to go behind my back and fulfill the prophecy."

This time it was Gabriel who answered in syllables of liquid fire. Caroline looked back at Akakios, who was very pale and looked unsteady on his feet, but smiled a little at her expression and said, "Ask not, Lady. Your brother wouldn't thank me to translate those words for your ears."

A snarl made her turn back to the fight, just in time to slice off the head of one of the hounds.

Her victory lasted only seconds. She was just wondering how come she, not an experienced fighter, had managed to kill one of the dogs, when the corpse on the floor became instantly whole and came at her again. She backed up. She now realized no matter how many wounds she inflicted, the dogs would keep coming at them, again and again and again, their number never diminishing.

That was why Akakios had said that no matter what happened, if they left Gabriel alone, then he would die here. But what would their having jumped in to help do, but increase the time he would survive? In the end, he must still, perforce, die. There was only one of him, and, all told, infinite numbers of these re-born dogs.

But then … "Akakios, you said he would die if we left him alone," Caroline said, "But what has our joining him ensured, but that we die with him, if a little late?"

"Well may you ask him, Caroline," Gabriel said. "The prince is a fool, and has brought you into an untenable position where you will do nothing but die with me. I do not wish to see you die, and anyway, Seraphim would find a way to raise me from the dead and kill me." He slashed forward, suddenly, earning them a little space and kicking the carcasses of dogs far away before they reconstituted themselves and came alive again. It seemed to Caroline that he had more strength here than on Earth, because these dogs were almost man-sized and he was kicking them easily. He looked at her, just a glance, his eyes wild. "It is me they want. Prince Akakios," the name was a shout, "can you manage, despite your wounds, to do the inverse journey of what you did? They'll close in on me when you leave, so you should have to leap a shorter space."

Akakios replied in the liquid-fire language this time, and Caroline thought it too must be those words that Gabriel wouldn't want her to know, except that Gabriel's answer back made it obvious it was something else, "You might not be disloyal, but you are stupid. I am not your lord or your sovereign, and dying for me will earn you nothing, and certainly not fulfill your prophecy."

This seemed to shut Akakios up, because he said nothing for a long while. Fighting as hard as she could and starting to feel not only her arms hurting with holding the sword of power, but her magic sting from the long-drawn-out-power needed to keep the sword going, Caroline wondered if Akakios was considering taking her out of here, and what she would do if he decided to do so.

Part of her wanted to leave. She was very young. She had never had a season. She'd never been allowed at grown up parties, and somewhere at the back of her mind was the idea that eventually, should she escape this, she would like to be married and have children, and perhaps get to travel a little and see the world beyond the isles.

It had never been a part of her plan to die at sixteen in Fairyland, defending her illegitimate brother.

On the other hand, if she left, if she walked away… she could imagine Seraphim asking her where she'd left Gabriel and what was the last thing that had happened to him. She could see the pain in Seraphim's eyes when she told him, and she knew she would carry the same pain with her her whole life. Gabriel might never have been acknowledged as their brother, but he'd been one of them and her friend her whole life.

And then there was the other side of it – that Seraphim would forgive her easily. After all, she was just a woman. No one expected of her gallant acts of self-defense, much less in defense of others. It was logical, because she was weak and she was young, and yet the idea infuriated her. She wanted to be able to protect Gabriel, who had so often protected her.

She'd just set her chin and decided that dying here was less painful than living a life considering herself forsworn, when Akakios tugged on her cloak. "Give me your cloak, Lady, do."

"My cloak?" Caroline asked, mid sword-swipe, wondering if the centaur had lost his mind. "What are you going to do with my cloak?"

"I cannot explain," he said. "Just give it to me. I promise not to harm it unduly."

"Do with it as you will," she said, without turning, loosening from her throat the pin that had held the cloak. She felt it fall from her shoulders and thought that it must be some arcane magic, particularly since Gabriel seemed to have anticipated what Akakios would do, and said, sternly, "Prince, this will not help."

"Perhaps nothing will help, Sire, but we must try."

There was… Caroline could not describe it. There was a sound that wasn't a sound, a whisper that wasn't a whisper, and a feeling like a small wind behind her, and Akakios let out with a small groan as if of pain.

When she turned back to look at him, he stood by the wall, and at first she thought he had shrunk. Then she realized the now-familiar Akakios face was atop a… human body, with her cloak wrapped around himself in the way the men of ancient Greece had worn a chiton.

She barely turned back in time to defend herself from a snarling dog, and would have been wounded, had not Gabriel come to her aid. "He is a fool," Gabriel told her, and for the first time looked truly angry. "He should get you out of here."

"If he got me out of here, I would not go," Caroline said, then shouted back, "Akakios, Prince, what do you intend on doing? How does this help?" She felt a little odd about his shape change. It was all very well for her to have ridden a centaur's back. Centaurs were a different species, and no one could consider them marriage prospects. But now he was, to all eyes, a man like all others. And she'd ridden upon his back.

She could almost hear Seraphim tell her this was no time to be missish, and Gabriel would probably say it too, if he thought of it, but she could not banish it from her mind, even as Akakios said, "My other form, Lady, doesn't climb too well. Or jump, like this, very easily"

And then she realized the wall behind her ended just far enough above for even Gabriel not to be able to reach up there. And she couldn't fully see Akakios leap, but he must have used magic to assist himself, because he'd jumped up and was holding to the top of the wall with his hands, then scrambling up with his feet. Before Caroline could fully get her breath, he was leaning down, almost from the waist down, and extending her both hands. "Lady!" he said. She got what he meant to do, and reached up. He grabbed around her wrists and pulled her up, with minimal assist of her feet scrambling up the wall.

When he hauled her all the way up, she threw herself, face first, onto a path that seemed to be fine white sand and run at the top of the wall, all the way up, like a widow's walk atop a fortification. Akakios's feet were twined around a marker on the other side of the path in a way that must hurt his injured legs, but he didn't complain.

She didn't need Akakios's prodding. She imitated him, then both of them leaned down.

"Sire," Akakios called down to Gabriel, now with his back against the wall again. "My Lord. Your sister can keep you safe a little while, if you give us your hands."

And Caroline realized what he meant, and bent her mind to stop the dogs. It took longer, this time, and was harder, but her mind was clearer if not stronger than that of the king of Fairyland. For a moment, the dogs stopped, as though frozen in their tracks.

Gabriel didn't argue. He must be very tired indeed, Caroline thought. Instead, he turned around and while she and Akakios each held one of his arms with both hands, he scrambled up the wall with his feet.

He fell half atop them, heavily, panting hard, then rolled off and lay on the path, still panting hard. "You are both idiots," were the first words he said.

"You're welcome, I'm sure, Mr. Penn," Caroline said with a sniff.

Gabriel took this cutting remark with a sudden and explosive laugh and sat up.

"I didn't say I wasn't grateful to you two idiots. Do you have any idea where you landed us?"

Akakios had sat up, also, and was rubbing at his ankles, which were bleeding from what seemed like giant dog bites. "I expect on the path to the king's castle," he said. "I will not shift if it's the same to you and if I can continue borrowing the cloak, Lady. The wounds are bigger as human, but they are of less consequence, and this is no path for a horse's hooves."

Caroline looked up and saw that they were in fact on the proverbial path that spiraled up the proverbial white mountain, to the proverbial fairytale castle, bright with pennants and flags. For a moment, it was so beautiful, it took her breath away. Then she remembered the voice of the king of Fairyland and shivered.

Gabriel, stretched, reached over, and touched Akakios's ankles. The wounds retracted, closed. In seconds there were only scars.

Akakios took a deep breath. "The king's touch."

"Or just very good elven power," Gabriel said. "Don't go saying stupid things, or we can't be friends anymore. I wonder why my ever-loving uncle dropped me outside this particular wall."

"He couldn't help it. It's the prophecy."

"Talking about the prophecy will also mean we can't be friends anymore," Gabriel said. "We could walk the other way, but my guess is the dogs will be waiting for us as soon as they can reach us. Also, I have a strong feeling Michael is kept up there," he pointed towards the castle.

"Then we'll go there," Caroline said, and thought how long it would take on this weary road. But at least there were no dogs. A nagging feeling told her there might well be something worse, but she ignored it.

Sarah A. Hoyt

Sugar And Spice

Nell was not stupid – or at least, she thought to herself, she tried not to be more stupid than she needed to be. And right then, she thought, it meant not going into those marble halls of Fairyland unarmed. So she reached blindly and found the neck of the bottle that had been labeled "drink me." Given that it was not the best of weapons, she should have brought a hunting knife or even a gun, though if her studying of magic in Avalon had meant anything, depending on what spells were on this place, guns might have behaved very oddly.

Well, she told herself. *Never mind that. Everything can be a weapon. After all, I can use this bottle to bean people on the head. And besides, there is a very good chance if someone annoys me enough, I can grab him and make him drink this. There is a good chance whatever is in here is as good as that apple.*

She blinked at the liquid, ruby-red and sparkling unnaturally, then walked into the marble hall. From inside it came the whir of machinery and she thought how odd it was that there would be machinery in Fairyland. Then closer, she heard the sound of many voices, all talking at once.

That was fine. She would find the voices. And she would figure out what they were doing, and what was happening with the Darkwaters, too. Suppressing a thought about what might be happening to one Darkwater, and what it might mean that her heart clenched at the thought of his being in trouble, she walked down the marble hall, thinking that it sparkled very oddly indeed. Marble and magic? It made an odd sound underfoot, too, as though she were walking on fresh ice on a winter morning at the farm.

Cautiously, wearily she turned a corner… and blinked again, as her eyes adjusted to the impossible.

The corridor stretched on, white and sparkling, and that was not the shocking thing. What was shocking was that to her right there was a door, and standing in front of the door – on either side – were clockwork soldiers.

They looked like something out of a Christmas play, all red uniforms and round faces painted with very red cheeks and large, black eyes. Their tall helmets were adorned with plumes. They held golden lances. And they were clearly, unmistakably tin, and had large wind-up keys sticking out of their backs.

As she took a step towards them, they both turned to stare at her and Nell's hair rose up at the back of her neck. It was their eyes. Painted eyes that were little more than black dots, should not be alive, nor follow one's movements. And they shouldn't have a sort of dreadful, intent expression.

She lifted her arm, pulling the bottle back, then let fly. It hit the helmet of the nearer tin man, then fell. It hit the wall and shattered, and liquid ran out, eating at the marble floor. The tin men advanced towards her. And now she didn't have a weapon.

And then she thought that food of fairykind was corrosive and possibly lethal to humans, then wouldn't it….

She eased the backpack strap off her left shoulder, let the backpack swing forward, all the while stepping back out of the reach of the tin men's golden lances. Without looking, she reached in, felt for the boxes of crackers, tore one open, got two crackers, and maneuvered the back pack onto both shoulders again. Then she held a cracker in each hand and ran.

The tin men started to swing the lances, but, of course, the problem of a tin man with clockwork innards is that they wouldn't react that fast, would they?

So they were taken completely by surprise as she shoved a cracker into each of their gaping tin-cut mouths… and ran past towards the door they were guarding. She wasn't even sure what would be behind that door, or why she should want to go there. But she knew for an absolute fact that she wanted to get past the tin men, and the door gave her something to interpose between her and those shiny golden lances.

She was barely aware of a sound of tinkle and whirr behind her, and then of tin objects falling – heavily. She didn't turn.

To her surprise, the door opened when she pulled on the handle, and she stepped into…

It looked like a Victorian scientist's mad dream. She had seen something like this on much smaller scale in the Darkwater's country residence. The place where the young Michael worked.

Here, it was bigger, and filled with more tin creatures. They ran huge, complicated machines; they sawed glimmering sheets of copper in half; they ran here and there carrying buckets of stuff.

In the middle of all of it, like a maestro conducting a complicated symphony, stood… she saw him from the back and swallowed, and opened her mouth to say, "Seraphim!" before she realized that while the dark curls were the same and the general proportions similar, this person was smaller – smaller even than Gabriel Penn, who resembled the duke in everything but size and height.

The word died on her lips, but she must have made some sound, because the young man turned around. He did look like Seraphim, but she now perceived he must be the same age as Seraphim's sister. He was as yet beardless, his skin pale and clear like his sister's. And his green eyes, so much a Darkwater trait, sparkled from beneath goggles of beaten copper and strangely shining glass.

He looked at her, his eyes wide open. "Who are you?" he asked. "And what are you doing here?"

And then she realized it wasn't just the glass that sparkled. His eyes were wide but empty, seeing but unseeing. They could see her, and yet they didn't, and she realized she would not be able to reason with him.

The realization came just in time, as his eyebrows drew together above his patrician nose, and he said, "You're not supposed to be here. There were guards." He frowned towards the open door, then looked at the people around him – no, the tin men around him, and lifted a hand.

Before he said anything, she knew he was going to order them to seize her. Also, she could see around him the netting of strong magic, and she knew the personality that had formed it. She also knew that though she might have powerful magic, she couldn't dent the magic of the king of Fairyland. She could control simple minds under his power, but not the mind of a fully reasoning and seemingly smart young man.

Then she thought this was a trap, like the *Alice in Wonderland* room. If she played by the rules, she would lose. The food of Fairyland… Okay. This was the equivalent, likely, of throwing the apple in that room. Before Michael Ainsling could order her seized, she remembered that people under spells were by nature slow and gullible. She said, aloud, "Wait. I came to bring you a message. Let me see…."

She swung the backpack from her shoulder, got a bottle of water from inside, and, before the young man could react to the strangeness of the packaging, pushed it at him, cap removed. "Drink."

He hesitated for a moment, and she thought that he was going to order his tin people to catch her. But his mouth was open, and he was holding the bottle. It was possible she couldn't do anything, but she had to try. Reaching out, she grabbed his wrist and shoved the bottle towards his face. Water splashed on him, a great deal of it bathing his face, but some must have gone into his mouth, because he screamed and lifted his hands to wipe at his face, and the threads of the golden spell-net around him snapped.

"Why did you do that?" he asked. "What are you–"

The bottle had fallen at their feet, and the water was gurgling out, corroding the marble. Michael looked at her, his eyes awake and intent for once. "You–" he said, and blinked. "Who are you?"

And then, with a startled look around "And where am I?"

Nell opened her mouth but never spoke. The ground behind her was crackling like egg shells, the tin people were converging towards them, and, suddenly, from the ceiling above, something fell. No. Someone. No. Several someones. She had the impression of three people, two male, one female, all dark haired. They fell between Nell and Michael. The ground gave way beneath them, and suddenly they were all falling, all of them, towards a darkness punctuated with pinpoints of stars.

Suddenly, as suddenly as they'd fallen, they stopped. It took a moment for Nell to realize they'd fallen on a black, huge, open net, and that the net was gathering at the top, like a sack closing. As this brought her in contact with the other prisoners: Miss Ainsling, Michael, Mr. Penn, and a young man dressed like an ancient Greek, it occurred to her to look up, to where the marble floor appeared corroded as well as fractured. Light from above shone through it, too. The sound of crackling under her feet came back to her mind and she said, "Sugar."

"Oh, no," Mr. Penn said. "I think it's quite all right to say 'shit' in these circumstances, Your Highness."

"No, I mean the floor is made of sugar."

"Ah," he said, his brow creasing. "Yes. My uncle is… whimsical. He derives–" Deep breath. "A great deal of power from the dreams of childhood."

And at that moment, as though on cue, the sickly-sweet, threatening voice came out of the big void beneath them, "By the rules, I had to let you find your brother, Miss Ainsling. I didn't say I had to let any of you go."

Sarah A. Hoyt

Very Unlikely Heroes

"But why are your family involved in it?" Seraphim asked Jonathan Blythe, frowning a little. "I can understand that Sydell…." Seraphim looked towards Marlon and managed, apologetically, "You'll pardon me, Elfborn, but truth must be told in some manner, and my own half-brother comes from similar background, and I understand that a lot of people raised in foundling homes, particularly those of noble origin, might resent the rest of the world that excludes them, no offense meant."

Marlon gave an odd, hollow cackle. "None taken, I'm sure. I could attest to some of that effect in myself, compounded by others…."

"Anyway, I could understand Sydell, ascended to power and pride, to need … more than mere mortal honors. But why your family, Blythe? They have all the honor of being one of the oldest magical families in the world. And they – unlike our family – aren't all to pieces, but have a handsome patrimony preserved through generations and augmented by a lucrative magical trade. They have nothing to gain from being involved in this."

Jonathan looked up at Seraphim. Seraphim was sure that his friend was still drunk, and also that he was still the same Jonathan he'd known since they were both children: a devil-may-care sensualist, more concerned with his pleasures and his experiences than with anything else. But Jonathan's eyes had gone very sober, very serious, and there was something uncommonly like shrewdness in their blue depths, something that made Seraphim uncomfortable. He'd always known that Jonathan wasn't stupid. But he'd also have sworn that Jonathan would rather endure any kind of hell than actually use his mind. Now, suddenly, he wasn't so sure. It was one more shift in his world, one more change from things he'd always known to things he perhaps should have thought more carefully about. Did he really know Jon Blythe? Did he really know anyone in what he'd thought his safe and familiar world?

"You'd think that, wouldn't you, Ainsling?" Jonathan said. He pulled at his lower lip, as though deep in some calculation. "The thing is, Seraphim, that in some ways you are a very naive man. I always thought that when we were at school, and you'd sit through the holy service, rapt, as though– never mind. I think you tend to believe the best of people."

"Oh, that's not true at all. I've rescued magic users from–"

Jonathan dismissed Seraphim's protest with a wave of the hand. "Yes,

yes. Other worlds, foreign atrocities and all that. That's not what I mean. I daresay that you know people do all sorts of horrible things, as who wouldn't who has read history? Even Richard the First, what he did to his brother, that Magical invisibility spell–" Jonathan shuddered. "I daresay you understand cruelty and meanness and even perhaps a very exaggerated sort of pride that requires more than its share of reverence. But that, Seraphim, is because those are the vices you can sort of see from your own position. Oh, I'm not saying you have them. I always thought you a rather good sort of man and, until the recent rumors, a dull dog." He dismissed any protest Seraphim might make with an airy wave of the hand. "I know, I know. Your father wasn't properly looking after the domains and all that. Understandable, but it made you a dull dog, anyway. It combined your penchant for looking after everyone and sticking your nose where it don't concern you with your excessive care of your name and family. Which means you never understood, never, for a moment, how most other people's minds work. No, don't interrupt me.

"I will confess that, like you, I never much cared for power and control over other people. You're not interested because you already had responsibility over other people at too early an age, and I'm not interested because I don't want to have responsibility, and it has always seemed to me the two are inseparable. But I am at least close enough to it to understand that other people want power and wealth, not because they need it, but because they can have it. M'father wants more power and wealth because Sydell wanted a partner in his dealings, and he contacted my father. And telling my father there were hundreds of worlds ready for the exploiting, devoid of magical defenses, and that someone – someone – could help pluck their wealth is sort of like telling me you have a cellar full of prime French brandy–" A bright look, as if something had just occurred to him, and he turned to Elfborn, "You don't, by any chance, do you?" And to Marlon's shaking his head, "Pity. But as I said, it's like telling me that and expecting me to say that no, I don't want to partake, because I've drunk enough."

Seraphim nodded. He didn't fully believe it. He wanted to tell Jonathan that there was a risk involved in this, that it wasn't as easy as sharing a cellar of brandy. But then … perhaps Jonathan was right. And besides, there was something scarier here. "But–" he said, as the full horror of it hit him. "But if they've been exploiting these non-magic worlds for decades, gaming their games of chance and their financial markets–" The idea was almost too monstrous to fit into words: the idea of all those non magical humans blithely exploited, with no chance of defending themselves. "—they must own several worlds by now."

"Very likely," Jonathan said, drily. He turned to Elfborn. "Sydell, I don't suppose there would be more tea in this house? If I can't have brandy.... You must know that I have a powerful thirst."

Seraphim noted that Elfborn didn't protest the name, though his eyes widened slightly at being called by it. He also didn't get up. Instead, he made a gesture and Seraphim felt the invisible threads of a spell do *something* to the tea pot, which returned to the table almost immediately filled with tea.

He frowned. Using magic for household tasks was normally disapproved of, but not because, as could be imagined, it weakened character or was gauche. It was disapproved of because any man who used his magic in normal household tasks every day would both shorten his life and keep his magic at a very low ebb, and magic after all was held to have a higher purpose. However, Seraphim noted, Elfborn had done it with almost no effort. The magic expended must be large enough to weaken a normal magician at least a little, particularly since he'd clearly bent space and time to bring tea back instantly instead of the more normal levitating of the tea things to the kitchen and making tea by normal, if magic-aided means. He narrowed his eyes. If Elfborn's power signature was smaller, there was no way of seeing it. Of course, his power signature was a confusing mess, a convoluted swirling of colors and places where odd power joined odd power.

Part dragon, part elf, part human – what *was* Elfborn? And could he be trusted at all? Seraphim didn't say anything of this, but instead helped himself to tea and said, "But still... I can see wishing to own other worlds, wishing to exploit their wealth, wishing to have power over their inhabitants, though I'd think that even then, once it's more than a world it can't be a matter of great–" He shrugged. "Never mind. Don't tell me again how naive I am, Jon. But what I don't understand is, why kidnap the princess? Why make an attack on my family? I can see that Sydell means to conquer both thrones, and I heard it from you that this is true – but I can't see how he gets there from where he is."

Which is when Elfborn's hand trembled. He said, "Oh, my God," and the teacup fell from it, shattering on the table, in a shower of shards and golden liquid. From his lips came horrible liquid-fire syllables that seemed to twist the ear and the mind upon which they fell. Seraphim knew it was elven language, because he'd heard it from Gabriel before, but this one, this one must be old and long encoded into a powerful form.

The effect on Jonathan was even more interesting. He put his cup down very carefully, then leapt across the small table at Elfborn, clamping his hand on the other man's mouth. "Not one more word. Not one more. Yes, you are right. That is it entire. But do not say it. What possessed you? Words of power! And those words. You might as well shine a beacon on us and call Fairyland's armies to us." He took a deep breath. "I am now going to remove my hand from your mouth. You will not say another word in elven. Do you understand me?"

Elfborn looked up at Jonathan and seemed to be having trouble believing this was the amiable drunk of moments before. At length, he nodded. Jonathan removed his hand and sat back again. Elfborn made a gesture and the shards of cup and the spilled tea vanished.

Seraphim looked at Jonathan, "You understand elven?"

"No. Well, not so much. There was this half elf who–" he stopped.

It was Marlon who broke in, with almost maniac cheerfulness. "Tuppable?"

"Very. She was… Ah never mind. She went back. But any rate, that I know that particular set of elven words has nothing to do with tupping. It's all part of Sydell's mad plan, and I've heard him quote it often enough," he glared at Marlon, "though never without the proper protections."

"I beg pardon," Marlon said. "I didn't think."

"That," Jonathan said, "is blindingly obvious."

"I don't have the pleasure of understanding either of you," Seraphim said.

"It's a prophecy," Marlon said. "I learned parts of it when I studied Intended History – that is history that–"

"I know what intended history is," Seraphim protested. "I'm not illiterate."

"No. Very well. As you know there are prophecies about almost every land, and the intent… it's like a spell that will almost for sure force it to eventually come true, unless a lot of mages take great care to avert it, and even then – if the prophecy persists for millennia and lots of people believe it and repeat it, it will gain force and will eventually…. You must know the king has mages working around the clock to stave off the prophecy about how 'From Albion's shores the lion's seed shall die.' I suspect that's what he thought was breaking through when his daughter vanished." He shrugged. "This prophecy is unusual because it applies not to a land or a race, but to Fairyland and… and all the universes." He seemed to run the lines in his mind. "I don't know how to say it prettily in English, much less in a way that you'll understand its magical force. Even in translation, the words have power, and speaking them–"

"Rather you didn't speak them, if it's all the same to you, Sydell," Jonathan interposed.

"No. Well, the prophecy is of a man, half elf, raised in human lands, who will come back and win the throne of Fairyland in a fair fight and take it unwilling and rule it... But it's an odd prophecy. The line is 'and in a day the might of Fairyland will be upended, the worlds stopped in their spinning.'" Lots of people think that this... tyrant king of Fairyland will destroy all the worlds. Others think it just means that magic will be changed in Fairyland. Others still– There are many opinions." He frowned. "I suspect my dear papa thinks though that he can cannibalize Fairyland to feed his power here, and rule here as a never-dying king." He frowned. "It would fit his pattern."

"Something like that," Jonathan said.

Marlon raised his eyebrows. "I see. Worse still. Very well. Now – what do we do about it? I suppose getting proof of this and taking it before the king's council would do nothing."

Jonathan shook his head. "They've had the king enthralled for years. From something I heard, Sydell raped and eventually sacrificed a dry– Your mother, Sydell?"

Marlon nodded. "That I've known since a highly illegal spell and a lot of prodding revealed to me who I was."

"Devilish," Jon said. "But the thing is, that gave them an open vein of power to Fairyland. They have half the court and definitely the king spelled. That's how they stripped you of your honors, Ainsling. If we showed them proof, nothing would happen. Or rather, we'd die very quickly."

"No," Seraphim said. He was seeing the horrible bind they were in. "Nothing short of killing Sydell will stop it, and if Sydell has that much power, I can't imagine– besides being against the law."

Marlon laughed. A startling, uncontrolled laugh, all elf. He grinned, and his teeth looked suddenly very sharp. "I'm not," he said, "within the law. And I'm not afraid of Papa's power. You want him killed? God – I didn't even realize it: I've wanted to kill him for years. Even if I have to die for it, it will be worth it. What have I to live for, anyway? I've lost–" a minuscule pause "—everything in the world worth living for."

"Wait," Seraphim said. "Merely killing him will do nothing, unless we have the proof we need of the conspiracy – and are in a position to present it to the king."

Jonathan slammed his cup down on the saucer, making a sound like a bell. "Damme. M'father has the records of his world-works under magical key and I might not be able to get them, but I'm of his blood and I'll try."

"What?" Seraphim said, shocked. "You can't mean that. If you expose him–"

"Yes, I do mean that," Jonathan said, and once more Seraphim had the impression he'd gone to sobriety through drunkenness and through madness to sanity. "You see, I was drinking because I thought somehow all this will explode in our faces. Sydell, once he seizes power, will let no witness live. And if he doesn't seize power, if it goes wrong, my family will be stripped out, root and branch. But the only guilty ones are m'father and m'sister. If I can prove it… If I'm one of the ones who save the throne of Britannia, we can save my mother, my house, and the young ones, who had no part of this." He let out a sudden cackle. "Damme, Seraphim, I'm becoming like you."

Seraphim took a deep breath. The casual attitude didn't disguise the risk the young man would be taking. He found himself in awe of Jonathan and a little out of step. Perhaps he really had never known Jon at all.

"Very well," he said. "I will then go to the palace – undercover, of course. Don't protest. Other than Marlon Elf– other than him, I'm the only one who might have the power to do it. I will collect the witness of spells from when the princess vanished."

"You can't do that," Jon said. "To do so, you'd need a connection to her. Damme, don't you think–"

Seraphim remembered her kiss on his lips, and took a deep breath. "I have a connection to her. No. Don't ask. I don't have time to explain."

Elfborn smiled as though seeing a design finally completed. "Very well, gentlemen. While you do that, I shall find my dear, dear papa and lay a trap."

Sarah A. Hoyt

A Fine Catch

Nell was scared.

She'd thought she'd been scared before, but she'd known nothing about what fear was. Yes, she'd left her home with Antoine when she was barely adult. She'd come to Avalon. But all of it had been understandable, if strange, to a girl who'd grown up with a grandmother who practiced some arcane arts and who read more than her share of fantasy books. Nell had cut her teeth on Tolkien – literally; her mother's copies of the books still bore the mark of Nell's teeth and gums along the edges – and then progressed to every kind of fantasy she could find by the time she was in high school. That into that mix there had also fallen a leavening of regency romances from the local library had given her the map she needed to navigate Britannia.

Some things it hadn't prepared her for. Nothing in her upbringing had prepared her, for instance, for the sheer material poverty of a world just starting into its equivalent of the industrial revolution. It had brought back to her that common-use objects: plates, cups, glasses, silverware, or even pins and needles, had once had to be carefully crafted and made by hand and were therefore expensive, and that their quality varied greatly. In the same way, she'd come to see that while the industrial revolution in Avalon was cleaner than on Earth, the machines being run by magic, not steam, it was still brutal and painful in many ways. But on Earth, when they told you about the children who worked twelve hours on looms and who had their little bodies twisted by having to get under and between machines, they didn't tell you about the system the machines displaced. They didn't tell you about rural poverty and squalor and of five-year-olds going out with sheep and goats in the cold and damp and staying out all day, or performing tasks that people on Earth would blanch to have even teenagers do without supervision. They didn't tell you of the accidents, the deaths. But most of all they didn't tell you of famines.

The new machines and the newfangled magical ways to improve the land meant fewer people working there, but fewer famines too, and the people came to the cities willingly, to work punishing industrial jobs that were, nonetheless, better than the farm jobs they'd left behind.

All that – the new society, the strange way of seeing things, even the way that, the moment they'd come to Avalon Antoine had been captured and held hostage by Sydell – should have scared her; and it had, as had her servitude to Sydell while trying to earn Antoine's redemption. But she had never been this scared.

At first she thought that she would have earned Antoine's way out. By the time she realized that wasn't possible.... She swallowed hard at the memory of Antoine's animated corpse. By the time she'd realized she couldn't save him, things had gone too far out of control for her to feel fear as such. She'd been too busy saving Seraphim and... and a fine muddle she'd made of that. Maybe that was why in the fairytales they never had the princess rescue the handsome hero.

But no, truth be told, the handsome hero had also made a muddle of it. At least, he wasn't here, she thought, in this net in which the rest of them were caught, spinning over what appeared to be an endless void, punctured with pinpoints of star light.

She closed her eyes and told herself – hard – that there was no net, no pinpoints. That she was free and near the throne room. But nothing changed. She could feel the threads of the net – thick, and made of what fishing line would be if it were as thick as mooring ropes – digging into her back. She could feel Akakios's bare feet digging into her side. And she could smell them all: sweat and fear and various grooming products.

Her eyes came open again. There was absolutely no point closing your eyes and pretending if you couldn't, in any way, make it true. People had pulled away from the center, by their weight creating niches in the net, which allowed them to spread out. Michael – she assumed he was Michael, since he looked like the changeling she'd first seen in Michael's workshop – sat sprawled, his back propped on the side of the net, his arms akimbo. His eyes had lost their vacant, shiny look, and his brows were now knit, over his nose, in a puzzled frown so reminiscent of Seraphim it made something within her ache.

Caroline and Akakios had backed away together. Nell noted they were holding hands, and cringed a little inwardly, wondering what Seraphim would think of that. A lady in Britannia had limited say on whom she wished to marry, and Nell would be willing to bet even a Centaur Prince would not be considered an eligible match.

A quick look at the remaining person, Gabriel Penn, lying still at the bottom of the net, looking up at the top where the net was gathered and held. It was nebulous up there, and Nell could not see how or what held it. "It will not disappear, no matter how much I think about it being gone," she told Gabriel.

He turned to look at her, and she scuttled back, alarmed. He looked... wild – she thought. His hair had now come completely undone, and there was an odd shine to his eyes: not like Michael's but more as though he were laughing wildly at some joke only he knew. In their situation, she couldn't imagine what that would be.

There was wild humor in his voice, a hint of suppressed laughter. "No, you wouldn't be able to," he said. Worse, his voice echoed in odd harmonics that she couldn't quite place.

Michael spoke before she could ask Penn what was so funny – not that she meant to.

"I was dreaming," he said. His voice sounded small and very young, as if he'd been a little boy, instead of a teenager. "I was dreaming about...." He made a face of deep thought. "There were machines, but... he... he– The King– He said that... He told me I'd have power, and I– " He burst into tears, and like that, the mad, laughing light went out of Gabriel's eyes. He seized hold of the threads of the net, dragged himself to where Michael was, put his hand on Michael's head. "Never mind. Never mind. It was all a bad dream. It is always best if you don't think of Fairyland as more than a mad dream. When they– " he took a deep breath. "When we get in your mind, it splits it. We're not the same as you are. We're not– "

Akakios said one word that Nell, without understanding it, knew meant King, or Sire, and then in English, "You know now that you must take your place. You have come to the prophecy."

The mad light was back. Penn, matter-of-factly wiped his younger brother's face with a handkerchief pulled from his sleeve, and managed to look tired, even as the mad light came back into his eyes. "I see the design," he said, "and the intent pulling me in, damme."

"Intent?" Nell said.

"The prophecy," Akakios said. "It said a man born of elf and human and raised on Earth would come back and become king of Fairyland, and– " an elven sound—"is the man."

"Mr. Penn?"

"Yes, that is my other name. It translates loosely as "Night Arrow." I haven't used it since... Never mind. The prophecy. I grew up with it. I think it intended me for the role. Stories that old, particularly in Fairyland, acquire a power. It pushed me. I did not want it but...." He made a face. "Never mind. It might have to be." He looked at Akakios. "I'm not sure I appreciate centaur interference, though."

Akakios' face went stern. "My father sacrificed his first-born and risks me for– "

"Oh, very well," Gabriel said, a king dismissing a pointless complaint.

"But how do we get out of here?" Nell asked. "And where are we?"

"I fancy we are between worlds," Gabriel said. "Not that way. There is air here, of course, but we're not quite in any world, anyway. Even if we got free, there would be nowhere to fall."

"Then– what?"

"I'll have to borrow power," he said. "I'll have to use the power of one not confined in this trap."

"What do you mean?"

"The king of Fairyland," he said, "can reach the magic of any of his subjects. I'll have to reach for one of them. But since I'm not yet the real king, it will have to be someone I know well. I'll use that magic to transport us out of here. And then, I think, curse it, I'll have to fulfill my destiny. But you and the others… Take them, Princess, and see them safe."

Sarah A. Hoyt

A Matter of Power

"One doesn't," the honorable Jonathan Blythe said, "simply walk into the royal palace. Particularly not–" he gave Seraphim Ainsling, lately the Duke of Darkwater a derisive look, and Marlon Elfborn, or perhaps Sydell, a puzzled one. "Particularly not, I say, when one has a price on one's head."

Seraphim raised his eyes at Jon, who seemed to suddenly have become all too sober, even if he retained his easygoing mannerisms. "Is there a price on my head, Jon?" he asked softly. "You said my title was removed, my property impounded – I presume – and I presume, as well, that I am under suspicion of murder, for I gather that's the excuse for all this, that unfortunate man who died on my estate? That I'm under suspicion of using illegal magic to kill him. But I've not violated one of those laws that put you under an immediate death sentence." Seraphim tried very hard to keep from sliding his gaze sideways at Marlon. "And even if I had, surely it would be a matter for the courts first? I am a peer of the realm. I might be tried in absentia, but surely I must be tried before I am condemned."

"Who said anything about laws or the realm?" Jon said. "Who said anything about trials, either? Or the death of the man on your estate? Sure, that's what they used to impound all you own and to discredit you in the eyes of the world, but if you believe that is what you're in real danger from, then you have no more wit than hair, and I wash my hands of you." He looked up, and must have read the plain incomprehension in Seraphim's eyes. "Ask instead why you were ever in danger – why there was a man on your estate. He was dead before he ever came to you, by the way. He has been dead for at least a year. And he was not, at that, exactly a man, but never you mind that."

"I am not sure what you mean," Seraphim said, and he meant it. He had no idea where this Jon Blythe had come from, who could spin plots and ideas that of course Seraphim had thought of, but only in the privacy of his own mind, and then quickly dismissed as too preposterous. It was impossible that a vast, shadowy network had been conspiring to ensnare him. Surely, what had happened to him was a series of spectacular bad luck, or else.... His mind stopped, because he knew for a fact that a royal princess had been whisked out of the realm, and Jon said it had been Sydell's and the Blythes' doing all along, but if it were so– "But why me?" he said. "Oh, surely, I was ... involved in many worlds, and they could have brought me to trial on that, since it violates the royal decree about dealings with other Earths, but what can that have to do with—"

"No," Jonathan said. "They couldn't have brought you to trial, because you know too much, and had they brought you in, the examining magicians would learn of it, and some of those are incorruptible old sots, as you well know."

"I?" Seraphim leaned back. He noted without thinking that Marlon had cleaned up spilled tea and broken porcelain and also that Marlon had poured Seraphim a new cup of tea and, having whisked from somewhere a glass decanter, was pouring an amber drop in it.

"Oh, brandy," the Honorable Jonathan said. "I say, can you—"

"No," Marlon said, drily. Then to Seraphim. "I think you should have what I've poured for you. It will help you."

"I—" Seraphim said, and obeyed automatically, though objecting, "I am not so much shocked as puzzled. I'm trying to think what I know that would give any examining magicians anything upon which to unravel a conspiracy. I know I have rescued.... This would be in the last month, I presume, since before that, they might know what I was doing but no one did anything about it."

Jonathan inclined his head. "They weren't sure what you were doing until my dearest sister accepted your offer last month. They suspected you might have taken over the role of witchfinder, which was your father's before it was abolished, of course. But they didn't know, and surely they couldn't prove it."

"The role of—"

"I see. Your father never told you?"

Before Seraphim could answer, Marlon intervened. "That part I know, though I didn't know you'd taken it over, have you, Seraphim?"

"I took over my father's work." The brandy might have been a bad idea, as Seraphim's head ached fit to split. "If that is what you mean. I never heard of an official role, but when my father... After the funeral, Gabriel, who was cleaning my father's room and disposing of his effects before I moved into it, brought me some very odd artifacts, and also a diary he found concealed in a cunning place only a person of my father's blood could open. Through it I found that though my father had many failings – and his failings were as real as his virtues – that his career hadn't been as deliberately ruinous as one would think. I mean, he still gambled. I think he was addicted to the rush of gambling, to be truthful. And he...." Seraphim smiled a little. "One can't deny that he left more by-blows throughout the district than any but the noblest of royal lines have ever managed to leave, which, considering he wasn't working on a kingdom scale, must be, I suppose, counted to his credit. But—" He paused. "But the truth is that most of the time he was away from us, most of his months of seeming neglect of his family, he was in fact occupied in rescuing unfortunates from worlds where magic is illegal. Gabriel and I… resumed his work."

"The work of the witchfinder," Marlon said, "of which your father was the last official one. And before you excoriate him for not living within his means, do keep in mind that he used to get a stipend for this work, and was used to a vast royal largesse."

"Oh," Seraphim said. Now his head was spinning and he knew this was naught but a mad dream. "But no one told me! Not even Mama."

"No, of course not. If she suspected what he was doing, better to keep it secret," Jon said. "But they would suspect you, particularly as your personality changed overnight after your father's death. So… when my sister accepted your so-very-kind offer." He grinned. "Remember she asked you for a lock of your hair?"

Seraphim remembered, because it had seemed such an odd sentimentality in Honoria.

"You didn't give her a lock of your hair, Ainsling?" Marlon asked, shock and amusement mingling. "Of all the crack-brained—"

"I thought nothing of it. One doesn't think—"

"No, of course not," Jon said. "You did an awful lot of not thinking, Seraphim. But that is why you can't walk into the palace. If you do, they will know you, no matter how you disguise your magical power or your physical body. They have a lock of your hair, Seraphim. They have a part of you and can trace your magic. They've already used it to send you on a tour of the worlds, I suspect, and try to get you killed. And I think the only reason we're safe here is that Marlon has made this proof against all but his own odd brand of magic."

"Of course," Marlon said, drily, but yet managing to convey the impression of having arrived at a momentous conclusion. "That is it precisely. My brand of magic. Neither human nor elven, nor dragon, but with hints of all of it. It is what has allowed me to survive in hiding this long." He looked up at Seraphim and grinned. "And it will now allow me to use it to disguise you. Because most of it doesn't come from Earth, they cannot trace it. Because I've long ago cut off the sovereign of Fairyland, he can't trace my power. We shall disguise you, milord duke, and you shall go, while we go about our several missions. And at the end of this you'll be a duke again in fact, and everything restored to its proper place." Something to his wry smile said there were things that could not be restored. "So. My magical power it shall be."

Sarah A. Hoyt

Blindly

There might have been more embarrassing things than finding himself being attired by the Honorable Jonathan and the publicly known to be non-honorable Marlon Elfborn, but if there were, Seraphim Ainsling would rather not experience them.

It wasn't so much the attiring, as Seraphim had dispensed with valeting too many times to need that material kind of attention, but the procuring of an old suit of Marlon's, a detailed discussion of whether or not the suit was too good and would draw attention and finally – but not least – that Marlon had re-sized it by frowning at it, with no visible magic expended, and no passes or magic ritual employed.

This was starting to worry Seraphim as much as anything else about this whole affair, and he'd ventured to ask Marlon, "How much magical power do you have – precisely?"

He got back a weirdly unfocused look and a shrug. "It's not how much power," he said. "It's which power. If I access my elf power, I have normal power for a half breed. That is what I normally allow to be seen. In the home—" He stopped and shrugged. "But there's also dragon power, I suppose. I used to have no idea what it was, but I suppose that *is* what it is. And there is human power, since my ancestors were noblemen and therefore magical. And I can draw from all of them.... Often do. I just learned early not to let it be seen, and to operate like anyone else. Part of the reason I felt– That is, I didn't have to disguise my power around Gabriel. Being of the royal blood of Fairyland, his is a match for mine." He gave a pallid smile. "But we'll not speak of it."

And with that, and a few comments from Jonathan, they'd let Seraphim go, attired in his borrowed suit, an unexceptionable suit of black wool with a white shirt, but not at all something that Seraphim would normally have worn. Whatever Marlon had done to dim Seraphim's obvious power signature, he'd done other things also. Looking at himself in the mirror, Seraphim found he looked... blurry.

"I made it difficult for anyone to focus on your features," Marlon had said. "Unless you wish them to." He'd hesitated. "While it's possible no one would associate you with the Duke of Darkwater, dressed as you are, they might, and you can't risk it."

"Features like mine are no great distinction," Seraphim had said curtly.

"My father made sure there were plenty of them about."

"Not exactly like yours," Marlon said. "Gabriel's comes the closest to that. And both of you are distinctive-looking enough, and both of you fugitives. But he told me, yes, that there were plenty of other bastards on your line." He'd hesitated. "Will you tell me, perhaps, why your father chose to shelter Gabriel, while ignoring the others?"

"I don't think he ignored the others, exactly." Through Seraphim's head had paraded a number of tenants, farmers, servants, all of whom bore a distinct resemblance to him and all of whom had been in some measure supported by his parents. "I think he left it to Mother to… to provide. Most of the time. He wasn't exactly heartless, just the least… that is, he didn't seem to think about his former paramours or … or their children, once he'd left them. But my—I think Gabriel's circumstances were what made him bring Gabriel home. That, or perhaps the fact that he did resemble me so much."

"I see."

"Why did you wonder?"

"I thought perhaps it was the fear of that untrained talent and what it might do. Or that perhaps Gabriel—but no, it will not be thought of."

Now, walking around to one of the innumerable entrances in the palace, Seraphim thought that he couldn't stop thinking of whatever might be driving Marlon's doubts. From the sound of it, he suspected Gabriel of something, or perhaps was afraid Gabriel had done something. For the life of him, Seraphim couldn't think what it might be, but he felt as though the last few weeks had pummeled his ability for disbelief. If someone had told him that Gabriel had committed some horrendous crime, perhaps including murder, Seraphim would merely ask whom his half-brother had killed and why.

But even in his present state, he couldn't imagine Gabriel doing anything heinous without dire need or without its being for a materially necessary purpose, and one that involved saving someone or something else, at that. He was, in fact, unable to imagine Gabriel being evil on his own and without need. He was, if truth be told, missing his brother horribly.

It turned out that Seraphim, who was used to thinking of himself as the pinnacle of society and free, might have been more limited by his position than Mr. Penn, who, as a gentleman's gentleman could very well go high or low in society, provided he didn't presume to mix with the toffs on equal terms.

For instance, Seraphim had no idea how to penetrate the royal palace and find his way to the princess's chambers. He might have been disguised so no one would recognize him, but surely not every bourgeois or clerk could enter the royal palace?

Turned out they could, to an extent. Marlon had indicated to him the service entrance at the back, and primed him with the name of a resident and told him to say he was delivering a message. So far so good. Seraphim had managed to go up a flight of stairs into a large salon.

And from there, he'd not managed to move, since each of the doors to the interior seemed to be guarded. What happened, perforce, was that each person in turn asked for the person he was supposed to see, and then when the person came out or sent word he'd see the visitor, the visitor was allowed in.

Here Seraphim stopped, because he had a feeling that if he asked for the man Marlon had named, the man might expect to receive a real message. And if there was a person in the royal palace for whom it was a habit to receive messages from a wanted necromancer, it was more than Seraphim wished to know. And the person, certainly, was more than Seraphim wanted to meet. Besides, from Marlon's expression, the name had been a throwaway one, used only as a means of passage….

That Marlon hadn't thought further than that had upset Seraphim momentarily, but then he'd shaken his head. No, he, himself, hadn't thought further than that. And it was his adventure. He had in the past gone into strange worlds and—

and there on the tip of his tongue was the name he could use to gain access. There was a young maid in the palace, someone he'd rescued from a world where even her small amount of magic was enough to get her killed. He'd brought her to Avalon where, after some adaptation and a lot of training by the housekeeper of the Darkwaters, she'd found a post in the royal palace.

Seraphim – feeling some trepidation at the act, even though Marlon had assured him that Marlon's power, continuously spun, would keep him disguised – approached the superior, uniformed footman at one of the entrances and asked if perhaps he could see Miss Valerie Arthur, whom he believed to be in charge of the East receiving rooms.

From the look the footman gave him, Seraphim deduced that Miss Arthur was far too superior a personage to involve herself with the likes of him. And then—

and then he was asked to give a name. If he gave his own, Valerie would see him on the instant, but even just his unusual first name was enough to get him arrested. So, shaking a little, he gave the name of his housekeeper as someone from whom he'd brought a message.

As soon as he spoke it, he was afraid that his housekeeper too was on the wanted list. She would have been, had it been widely known she'd turned a blind eye and helped place all these people coming from other worlds. But the footman asked Seraphim to wait, and then called over a runner.

What seemed like an eternity later, Valerie appeared. She came out into the room, looked at Seraphim, and obviously wasn't taken in by the disguise or the magical blurring. The later probably because Seraphim, after all, wanted her to recognize him.

She was a slip of a woman, smaller than Nell, with light-brown hair severely confined under a lace cape, and a completely unremarkable countenance that, nonetheless, suffused with pink at the sight of him. She went to drop a curtsy, but stopped it in time, running her eyes over his suit, and seeming to understand that he couldn't be here as himself. She opened her mouth in a silent O.

And Seraphim did the only thing he could do. He stepped forward, both hands extended, and took her little, cold hands in his and said, "Valerie! Do you not remember me? It is I, Joseph. My mother said I was to call on you and see how you were faring."

To her credit she rallied. She blushed further, looked at her hands as though she couldn't believe his, holding them, and then said, "Your… mother, to be sure. How kind of her. I have… a small… that is, there is a parlor where we're allowed to receive visitors, if we take care to keep the door open, but I– Well, it is a good thing I am taking a few hours– Please come, Joseph." In all confusion, she led him past the door into a shabby corridor. Seraphim could not correlate these worn hallways in need of a painting with the sumptuous parts of the royal palace he'd seen when he visited.

It also appeared to him, after a moment, that if Valerie were taking him to a receiving parlor, she was taking a very odd route, because they abandoned the plain and somewhat shabby hallway for even shabbier stairs, and went all the way up those to what appeared to be a level of servant rooms, then through a door almost hidden in a corner of the hallway, and up a set of distinctly old and uncared for stairs, into an attic that was filled with objects, swathed in dusty grey cobwebs, looming in the darkening gloom.

On the way he tried to question, "Valerie, where—"

But she'd put her finger to her lips and shaken her head.

Now she closed the door to the attic and turned around. "I wouldn't have done this," she said, "if I didn't owe you my life, but.... What are you doing here when you have a price on your head? What are you doing here obviously magically disguised? What can have possessed you to risk that?"

"I must," Seraphim said, "see the nursery from which the princess disappeared."

Her eyes went very wide then, and she stepped backward, as though looking for a place to sit. She balanced herself with a hand on a long discarded table and turned around. "Is it true, then? Was it your family who kidnapped her and who magically confused things so she was raised as the honorable Honoria Blythe?"

The Princess And The Power

Honoria?" Seraphim said. "No! I was– I suppose I still am– engaged to marry her."

Something in his reaction, possibly his genuine shock, seemed to reassure Valerie. She looked at him a long time, as though examining his expression, but her features relaxed. "I see," she said, at last. "There is a conspiracy, but it is not yours. I thought—" She ran a hand over her face. "But then, I thought perhaps it was because my magic is not of this world."

Seraphim had in turn managed to back against an old rocking horse and half-sit on it. He should feel, he thought, scared or outraged, or perhaps confused, but he felt nothing. Absolutely nothing. "Is that what we're accused of?" he said. "I thought it was murder…."

Valerie frowned. "It was murder at first, I think. It's very hard to think about it, but it was undefined, they said, and then…" She shook her head. "And then things changed." Her frown indicated deep concentration, deep thought. "Until you said that, I didn't remember it, and now it's hard for me to think about it. I think they first said you were accused of murder, and I think they couldn't… I think they couldn't locate the corpse. And then they said that you, and your father, and your whole family were guilty of conspiracy to kidnap the princess royal and, by magical means, make it seem like she belonged to another family."

"But why would we make her seem to belong to another family?" Seraphim said. "Would it not make more sense to keep her to ourselves?"

"No! Much was made of your offering to marry her, because, you know, if you married her… you'd someday be king. You could not marry her if you were her brother."

"No," Seraphim said. "But we have, or at least we had, friends and dependents, and surely any of them would be more reliable as marriage prospects than our rivals, the Blythes."

"Yes, but—" Valerie was visibly fighting something. "I think they did something – something magical. I'm not sure what, and even saying it makes me feel as though I might be going insane, because the amount of magic it would take… and for it to be undetected… but I think they did something to make us believe it. Because, despite all the changing stories, everyone has believed. And the king has recognized the Lady Honoria

Blythe as the princess Helena."

Seraphim groaned deep in his throat. Urgency came now. Not because Honoria had usurped the place of the princess, not because she would be the heir to the throne of Britannia if this went unchallenged, but because she had taken Nell's place. The idea of Honoria in Nell's place was unbearable and near-paralyzing. When he could think again he said, "You must take me to the nursery, Valerie, you must. Trust me, that's where the spell was first set, and if I can reach the center of the web, I can stop it."

She stared at him for a moment, then sighed. "It is only, Your Grace might not know it, but you are—"

"Wanted? I do know it. But I have a spell on me that makes me unrecognizable unless… unless I wish them to see me clearly."

She looked at him and frowned a little again. "I wondered why it made my eyes want to unfocus, but I'd guess I'm not getting the full effect, since you do wish me to recognize you." A little thought and she nodded. "Can you pretend to be here to measure the nursery? It is, of course, being completely remodeled since the prin– Is she the princess?"

Seraphim shook his head.

"I was afraid of that. In any case, she is engaged to be married and therefore the nursery must be remodeled, in the hop—"

"Honoria is engaged to be married? To me?"

Valerie looked down. "No, milord, to Lord Sydell. It was of course thought odd, his being old enough to be her father, and not exactly high enough in nobility… but he was the one who rescued her, and the king could not deny him her hand, their being sincerely attached."

Seraphim opened his mouth to say that from what he had heard and things he'd glimpsed at certain clubs, he found it hard enough to believe Sydell was Marlon's father, and the idea of his being sincerely attached to any woman was so unlikely as to border on the impossible. Then he realized he couldn't shock Valerie with any such implication, and felt a strong pang of missing Nell. Nell wouldn't at all be shocked. In fact, if Nell had any hint of it, she might blurt out what he was thinking without checking her tongue.

It would be, he thought, great fun to have Nell as a Princess Royal, even if it made any union between them impossible. Her solecisms and that irrepressible humor would set the palace on end.

But of course, he might as well wish for the moon. As far as Britannia was concerned, Honoria was now the Princess Royal, and his family the villains who had stolen her. It made no sense to anyone who knew anything of the tracings done at the time of her disappearance, but very few people remained clear on that, and a lot would never have been reported at the time. Just a strong spell over the people in the palace, and it would be carried off.

And the spell had to be in the room from which the infant Nell had been taken. Any further spell layered on the one that had hid the identity of her captors, any spell designed to make it seem like Honoria was Nell would need to be twisted into the original. He would go and he would pull it apart, if it was the last thing he did.

"Will you have the power to do anything," Valerie asked, "if you are spending it to keep the illusion over your features? And the illusion that there is no spell there?"

He smiled at her, though it felt like his face would crack. "It is not my power being used for that, and I suspect that the one spinning the illusion doesn't even notice the expending."

Valerie inclined her head. "Very well then. I shall take you through back stairs," she said. "Begging your pardon."

"I'd expect nothing else, and remember, I'm no longer a duke."

She looked like she would say something, then shook her head, compressed her lips and said, "Please to follow me, Your Grace."

Sarah A. Hoyt

Falling

Saying he'd use the power of a subject of Fairyland was one thing – finding power to use was another. Gabriel Penn, still Gabriel Penn, fighting against the encroachment of something alien and strange upon his mind, and knowing he was both himself and that strange thing and had always been, lay on his back at the center of the sack enclosing them all.

It seemed to him he was very alone despite his sister and brother, despite the princess and the centaur – Why was Caroline holding the centaur's hand? Damn the prophecy and damn its casual pulling of people into roles it had prescribed. Seraphim would– He cut the thought off.

If he gave in, if he succumbed to the prophecy's demands, he would not have to worry about Seraphim's wrath. He would not have to worry about wounding Seraphim's feelings, either.

It wasn't just that he would not be going back to Avalon – Gabriel's memory played over his years in the Darkwater household with a fond nostalgia that might have surprised those who had always thought of him as oddly out of place, neither servant nor family member. But it wasn't only that that he'd be leaving behind. Part of what made his time at Darkwater idyllic was that, away from his mother, away from Fairyland, he'd been able to pretend that he was human—just human.

Even his time with Marlon had been the same or close enough: they'd been pretending they were humans together, and it had been a lovely game, down to cleaving to human moral rules or at least to the extent of hiding and pretending.

But neither of them was human, and Gabriel was something more than a mere half elf. He'd tried to deceive himself for years that the prophecy was not really about him, that the cold, vast entity he felt, at the back of his own mind, the odd knowledge he had, the things he could sense were not – in any way – part of the fact that he'd been born to be king of elves.

He envied mere humans and their free will. He envied elves and their lack thereof. Created, as angels were said to be – though Gabriel had never met an angel and couldn't attest to it of his own knowledge – without free will, elves were bound to their fate like slaves to a master. They could rebel, but the rebellion either lasted very little, or it twisted the elf… like Gabriel's uncle.

But Gabriel was neither human nor elf, walking between the worlds forever. Which didn't mean he hadn't known what his elf fate was, or what he was meant to do.... He'd just thought his human half would help him escape it. And for a while it had. But prophecies were powerful things, especially in Fairyland. And there was more than one person – more than one entity – conspiring with the prophecy to bring him to the point and to make him obey.

And he'd run himself off his legs – he thought, going lax against the net, feeling the net dig into his back, and looking up at the nebulous dark where the net was hooked, probably to nothing more than a belief that something hooked it.

He glared at it, probing the fixings there. If he caused the net to fall, could he manage to catch everyone else in here in his power and transport them somewhere, possibly Earth?

Could he do that and arrange his own death? His mind flinched from self-murder, but it was the only way to avoid his fate; and oh, he wanted to avoid his fate.

But then he thought of Fairyland, and of the few glimpses he'd had of his uncle's mind, in recent days, and also of the complications that he sensed extended all the way to Avalon and maybe to Earth, of the Others that Seraphim and he had had to find, to rescue unfortunates from non-magic worlds.

Something very bad had been happening in Fairyland, and if his uncle continued holding power, it would only get worse. Gabriel had been taught, back on Earth, that Fairyland was a parasite world, feeding off other worlds, like a leech upon a healthy being. But his feeling, from the thing at the back of his head, was something else. Not something he could fully access or release without also releasing the... not-human personality back there, but he knew that somehow a healthy Fairyland was essential to all the worlds. As much as he would like to destroy the thing and make it burn, he couldn't. As much as his human half hated it, the slipperiness of it and its strange ways, he could no more destroy it than he could destroy his human family.

He narrowed his eyes, looking at the suspended net overhead. No. He couldn't kill himself or destroy Fairyland. Worse, he couldn't balk at the prophecy. If he somehow managed to get out of here without letting the thing in the back of his head out, it would still get out sooner than later. The prophecy would push him around and corner him, like a dog with a hare, until it had him just where it wanted him.

So, let the thing out, a little. Use it a little. Delay the evil moment as far as possible.

He said "Be ready, Princess," and was shocked at the odd harmonics in his voice, which seemed to echo with a weird force and bounce off non-existent walls. "When I release you, find your way home with … my siblings and this misguided centaur. Go home. Go home as quickly as you can."

She said something, but Gabriel couldn't hear it. He'd gone inside his own head, searching for the link to subjects of Fairyland.

It wasn't unexpected that he found doors barring him – metaphorically. The sacred groves rejected him, and the centaurs too, even though Akakios was his proof that the centaurs, too, were playing the prophecy and risking their lives and their prince to do it.

Magical fountains edged him off. There were no words, of course, but if there had been, they would have been the classical ones of "Turn away, turn away, for you are not of Fairyland."

The dragons turned their heads away from him, though he sensed they too were not quite refusing to take his side, but afraid of what the current sovereign might do to them.

And there hinged the dilemma. He could not fight his uncle for the royal position and the royal power unless he got out of here. But to get out of here, he needed the royal prerogative that would allow him to cut through the net and challenge his uncle.

It was a paradox, and he was bound more in it than in this net. His hands clutched futilely at the threads of the net on either side.

He'd need someone who was of Fairyland, but who had walked away, as Gabriel had. Someone who would give him the power to do this. He thought of his mother and shuddered. His mother… He'd never been sure if she loved him or not, or even if she felt anything at all. She'd been thrown out of Fairyland as a changeling at the age of five, and though she'd returned after, yet in her mind she remained a five-year-old child. She could break things without malice or intent, just to know what was inside.

No, in this strait, his mother was the last person he could trust.

And the first person? He tried to fight against the thought. All he could remember was that poor animated corpse against the wall. But Marlon had said that wasn't intentional. Which left….

Which left the ridiculous binding he'd tried to put on Gabriel when Gabriel had come back. But Gabriel sensed, in a way he couldn't quite think clearly about, that this was because Marlon had a horrible fear of being left, of losing those he loved. Perhaps not unwarranted. He'd never had many people who loved him back, from what Gabriel had gathered about his truly horrible childhood.

And despite that fear, he'd removed the bind and let Gabriel go.

Gabriel was imprisoned, but his mind and power were free. He searched through the worlds, finding Marlon's familiar mind-touch. Seen through the mind only, he looked younger and less defensive than Gabriel was used to – younger than Gabriel, in fact.

Gabriel had only a dim awareness of Marlon's surroundings: A house, a threatening presence. Heavens, was that a dragon? Was Marlon, then, in Fairyland?

He got the impression Marlon was … busy and in the middle of a knot of magic. But his response to Gabriel's mind touch was immediate. "Gabriel!" Marlon mind-spoke at him, recognition and gladness in his mental voice, and also the sort of total, shocked surprise that made Gabriel feel a little like he'd been unjust.

"I—" he said. He'd thought to demand and to order. But that surprise took the rug out from under his feet. He kept his mind and mental voice strictly human, and his request was framed in human words, "I am in trouble, Marlon, and I need to borrow your power to survive this."

"My… power?" Gabriel had a feeling of… not reluctance, but almost fear.

Gabriel let him see the net above, the people in with him.

"No chance of… waiting? An hour, two?" Again that not-quite reluctance, but almost fear.

"Uh, as you know… time in Fairyland."

"Oh. Yes. And Himself would manipulate it."

"Yes."

He almost heard Marlon swallow. For some reason the idea of ceding his power just now terrified Marlon, but on the heels of the swallow came an answer. "How do I do this? How can I let you have my power?"

"You recognize me as your sovereign," Gabriel said. "You pronounce your power mine to use."

"It is yours to use."

"No, in elven."

"Well, then," Marlon said and spoke the words, ancestral and inborn, at the back of every elf's brain, and he used Gabriel's true name.

It was like holding lightning. The shock of the influx of magic cut through Gabriel, as well as did, suddenly, a clear view of Marlon's mind, of where Marlon was. Or what he was doing.

Oh, hell. Not only had he just taken Marlon's power away during a duel, but he'd also pulled away his protections from Seraphim and someone else. It couldn't be helped.

His power pull would throw people about, too. That too couldn't be helped.

What could be helped was using the power to do what it should, and to keep his human self sane as the elf-self, unleashed by Marlon's fealty, in control.

It seemed to Gabriel as if all that was him stood in the middle of a black and blue hurricane of howling magic pouring out from his own mind. And the enemy was there, waiting.

He ripped the net with a wave of his hand and screamed at the others, as he tried to conjure stable ground for them to run on, "Run! Run on home. Run and leave me to my fate."

Sarah A. Hoyt

Unleashed

Seraphim felt the power pull before he could think where it had come from or what it meant.

In panic, he clutched at it, holding, as a forceful pull snatched it clear away. A pull stronger than any human could employ.

In that moment, he had a picture of Gabriel, of Caroline, of Nell, hurtling through space. No. Gabriel was jumping. But he wasn't Gabriel, he was… a creature. A giant creature, made of something not human flesh, but something crackling with energy and power. Yet undeniably Gabriel, with Gabriel's grimace as if he'd just realized whose power he'd pulled.

Only it wasn't Seraphim's own power, he realized with a start. It was Marlon's power. Marlon's power, which had served to disguise—

"Darkwater," the voice was Honoria's, raised in startled surprise.

Seraphim had been in the princess's nursery, looking around, amid a lot of other workmen and people outfitting the nursery for the next generation of heirs to the throne. The idea that those would be Honoria and Sydell's children made him want to shudder and abandon the world all together.

Something else that made him wish to abandon the world was the crisscrossing of power in the room. It would be invisible to most of the workmen and, he would guess, to all the people willingly admitted to that room, at least if Honoria had anything to say about it.

No simple household magician or maid would know any better, and those higher up who would be admitted would either be screened to make sure they knew nothing of malevolent magic, or else be within the conspiracy to lie to the king about his daughter.

But to Seraphim's eyes, to the eyes of anyone who had trained in dark magic – though not for the performing of it – the ropes of dark and filthy stuff across the room and forming a cat's cradle made him think that no one, not even Sydell's spawn, deserved to live in this room. Unless he was very wrong, it had taken human sacrifice and worse to create these, and Seraphim did not even wish to think about what the "worse" might be.

In his guise as a common tradesman, he'd been pretending to look at the drapes, and measure the walls, all the while trying to figure out where, in the center of this, the knot was holding the working in place.

For a working of this kind, to disguise and deceive people like the king who certainly knew better, it needed something material to hold it in the center. For this filthy a magic, probably a captive human – or supernatural – soul.

He had been working through the tangle of magical ropes, and thinking only of that, when Honoria's voice calling his title made him turn. In it, he'd almost lost the squeak from Valerie, which was not quite his name but might have been meant as a warning.

Seraphim's first impulse was to hide or fight, but he could do neither, and besides, both would be foolish. After all, he still had his power, and he still had his wits. At least, he hoped he had his wits.

In power and wits – he'd never deceived himself otherwise – he was Honoria's superior. What he lacked, of course, was the back up of several palace guards. But he'd been in worse situations, after all, and if worse came to worst, he could port out of here, to another world, and from that other world fight his way back here, to this moment, to confront Honoria again.

So he looked around and smiled at her, his best, dazzling smile. "Hello, Honoria," he said. "Or should I call you by the false name you've appropriated? Did no one ever tell you, Miss Blythe, that pretending to be the heir to the throne is treason and likely to lead to stretching that pretty white neck of yours?"

She didn't count on his coolness, he saw, and he immediately perceived he'd scored a hit when her hand went to her neck reflexively. It took her a moment to find her voice, too, and it came out squeaky and high. "How dare you? How dare you? After kidnapping me and giving me to a family not my own? After making me become engaged to you? After—"

Seraphim had taken note of the fact that the room had gone deadly silent, with every maid and servant hearing this, drinking it in. They wouldn't remember it, though. Part of the working in the room was to make sure that anyone in here would believe the story that Honoria had put about.

So he must still find the center of this – though it was akin to finding the tip to embroidery floss the cat had been at.

And at that moment, on that thought, he remembered Gabriel's method for doing just that. When Gabriel was young and still out of place in the household, Seraphim's mother, out of kindness, often called to him to help her disentangle the threads of embroidery floss. Gabriel's methods were unique. He would break the thread, anywhere, he said, then start rolling it, and when they came to another point that was raveled, fix them together by magical means.

Seraphim didn't have the need to do that here. He wouldn't be raveling this thread again.

So he answered coolly, "I don't recall making you anything, milady. I made you an offer, and you jumped on it eagerly enough." He grabbed the nearest thread, and, employing all his power, broke it.

Honoria's eyes widened, seeing what he was doing, though to the rest of the room it must look like he clutched at nothing.

"What are you doing?" she asked.

There was no appropriate answer for that, so he tried none. Instead, he yanked on the filthy thread with all his might, at the same time opening a very small gate into a world of fire, where he disposed of such things. He put the thread in it and started feeding it.

"Guards, guards!" Honoria screamed.

Seraphim ignored her. He was now pulling on the thread, with both hands, feeding it as fast as he could into the fire.

Ahead, he saw a knot in it and bit his lip, because it meant he'd have to cut it again.

Guards approached, running. There were guns pointed at him. Honoria was saying something about being wanted. Valerie, somehow withstanding the magic, was screaming a counterpoint.

But one thing Seraphim knew was that, by virtue of his birth, no one but the king could order him fired upon. Stopped, sure, but not fired upon. The guards were approaching cautiously. Cautiously because Seraphim must look to them like he was clutching at nothing, and a madman was always to be feared.

And then the knot was within Seraphim's hand, only it didn't feel like a knot, but like a tiny birdcage, of the sort that some people kept crickets in. Jumping out of the way of the nearest guard, Seraphim applied all his magic to breaking the cage so he could keep feeding the thread into the gate.

It resisted his efforts, and he thought of throwing it through the gate, cage and all, but….

A guard grabbed Seraphim's arm. "You'll come quietly your Gra– Mil– Mr."

And Seraphim, in despair, before the other guard, approaching, could use a magic-restrainer on him, put all his strength into crushing the cage.

It broke like glass, the shards biting deep into his hand, blood pouring down. It didn't matter.

The moment the cage broke, all the threads unraveled with a hissing sound like a raging fire. Anyone with magical power in the vicinity felt it like a flail upon the magical sense. Honoria screamed. Valerie covered her eyes. The guards let go of Seraphim, who stepped back, stunned, letting the remains of the cage fall from his wounded hand.

From the cage, like a fog, a figure emerged and materialized, and looked around with a puzzled expression before saying, “At last! It’s been such a long time in that filthy prison.”

Sarah A. Hoyt

The Tree, The Dragon, The Drunkard

There was a moment that Seraphim saw the creature clearly – a beautiful and stark-naked young woman with chestnut hair and… well, the odd thing was that while she was alive and looked like a lovely, vital young woman, all of her was chestnut-colored, and if one looked closely there was a hint of wood grain about her skin.

Seraphim, feeling as though an odd numbness were creeping up his arm from his palm, had no idea what he was seeing. The woman looked around, frantic. Put her hand to her chest and said, turning beautiful moss-green eyes first to one, then to another, all around the company of the room, "The Forest," she said. "I must have…."

An odd sound echoed, like fabric ripping, and in the middle of the floor, just in front of Seraphim, the boards heaved up, nails flying. One struck the guard who was holding Seraphim on the face, making an ugly cut. The man let go of Seraphim and started stepping back, as though he were not quite aware of doing it, till presently he'd backed up to near Honoria, as though looking for protection.

Honoria's face was a study in shock, her mouth wide open. Seraphim couldn't understand why her hair was whipping as if in an unseen wind, until he realized the magic unleashed from the thick, dark ropes had submerged the room. There was so much magic there, they were all in magic, like a fish in water, magic crackling and fizzling on their skins, magic making them stupid with the shock.

He knew that the spell that had held the various illusions together, down to the final illusion of Honoria being the princess, would be unraveling too, now the sacrifice had been taken from the center of the weaving.

The sacrifice… As though pulling the magic up into it, the woman had … Seraphim would like to say she had made an oak tree grow in the middle of the floor, only surely that was impossible, even with very great magic unleashed. And yet in the middle of the royal nursery, pushing aside the cradle, overturning the finely wrought rocking chair, upending the chests of clothing, an oak tree grew, here, far from forest, far from soil, far from brook, it grew and greened, loaded down with acorns.

The woman – nymph – sighed and eased into the tree, like a person easing into a soft bed. She backed into it and made a little "ahh" of relief. You could still see her, sticking out of the tree trunk, and she still looked human, glancing around with wide-open eyes. She looked at Seraphim and said, "You are not he," and then. "Good for you that you are not he. Where is he—my despoiler?"

Seraphim had the sense of her reaching back, searching through the world for…. He had a very bad feeling it would be for Sydell. It shouldn't be possible, and it wouldn't be possible, not for a normal, human magician. But if this was a nymph – a dryad?—then she would treat the human world as humans treated Fairyland: a not-quite solid overlay on reality, to be rifled through at will for what it might contain.

And then….

There was a sound as though of an explosion, and two men fell into the room. The odd thing is that though they both fell from about halfway in the air, and both landed awkwardly, when they landed they didn't seem to notice they'd dropped or that they were in a different place. Rather, they each rolled, and stood, and turned to each other again, ready to fight.

This was when Seraphim recognized Sydell and Marlon. His shock was not that, but that Marlon was losing and badly. There were multiple slashes on his arms and his shirt was so torn and bloody it was impossible to tell where he'd been hit or how many times.

The reason for this became obvious almost immediately. Although both of them held knives, Sydell was protecting himself with a magical shield while Marlon … appeared to have no magic at all. There was no aura of magic around his head. How could he have lost all his magic?

The puzzlement lasted only a second. After all, it did not matter where his magic had gone or why. All that mattered was that this was a very unequal duel. Seraphim didn't have magic to match Sydell's, but he had magic. He threw a shield around Marlon, just as Sydell's knife would have found his heart.

Both men suddenly noticed him. "You!" Sydell screamed, and ran at Seraphim, his knife ready.

And Seraphim, unarmed, seized on the only thing he had – the shard of the cage that had confined the dryad, which was even now in his hand, even as the splinters of it were making his palm throb like hell's fire.

He struck out with it, blindly, while using his other arm to deflect Sydell's blow.

His hand with the shard cut at Sydell's cheek, making oddly black blood bubble up and pour out.

A roar echoed. A feeling of scorching.

Before them in the middle of the room, steps from the tree, stood a vast red dragon with Sydell's expression in his irate eyes.

And Honoria, for reasons known only to her, was pounding on the dragon's wing with both closed fists.

Just when Seraphim thought things couldn't get madder, they did.

Another dragon broke through the plate glass window announcing, "I found you at last!" in words that were like roaring fire.

And Marlon looked Seraphim in the eye and screamed, "I gave him my magic! Your brother. Darkwater, I fear he's in a battle for his life. I can feel his struggle, through my fealty to him, and I fear he's losing."

Something Sickly, Something Sweet

Gabriel didn't know how he'd got back to Fairyland. He couldn't remember exactly how old he was, and he didn't know what he'd been doing just before he found himself here.

But there was no doubt he was in Fairyland. He recognized the mist around him, the weaving, writhing kind of fog that happened only when magic was involved.

It felt cold and clammy on his skin, permeating the sleeves of the too-small, too-tight suit, which should have been replaced years ago, when he was … six? seven? But which continued to be his only suit, even though his body had grown so much. His wrists showed, bony, exposed, and his hands, small, thin, covered in the scrapes and sores a sweeper boy accumulated keeping the crossing clean for the fine lords and ladies who didn't want to taint the hem of their clothing with horse droppings.

But he didn't know where his broom had gone, nor the last time he'd swept. He felt tired, as if he'd spent the whole day sweeping...but then why hadn't he gone home?

His bare feet plodded along the pavement he couldn't quite see through the mist, and his steps slowed down. Somewhere, up ahead was…. He couldn't remember, only that he was supposed to go there, that he meant to go there, but he didn't know why.

He shivered in the mist and wondered if his mother had locked the door because she was with one of those friends who paid money, and if he'd somehow wandered out so tired that he'd stepped, unwary, into Fairyland. But no, surely not. He'd been thrown out of Fairyland with his mother. He remembered it. And he had never wanted to come back.

A shiver ran up his spine at the memory of his last days in Fairyland, of what he'd had to do, how he'd had to find the will to resist, just to be thrown out.

Perhaps his uncle wanted him back? To serve as a source of magic and a– He cut the thought off, and continued walking.

If only he weren't so hungry. Starving, really, which shouldn't surprise him, since it had been his condition for most of his time in the Earth of mortals, at least since Mr. Penn had left Mama. But it surprised him, or rather, it felt unaccustomed to his body, as though he'd been well fed and well taken care of for a long time, and this discomfort felt like an outrage. It made tears prickle at the back of his eyes, and it made him feel scared and fragile in turns.

The smell of cake came from somewhere to the left, away from the path he'd been following. He didn't remember why he'd been following that path, and though he was in Fairyland and knew therefore that directions could change without warning, and that the image the smell of cake invoked, of a bakery window piled high with treats, was not true. All he could think was that the bakery near his mother's house sometimes threw out cake that had gone so stale that it could be used for no other purpose. He'd often found it in the rubbish bins behind the shop.

His steps changed almost without his meaning them to. The first disturbing change was that he felt as though the tendrils of fog had now become personal, intimate. They seemed to insinuate themselves into his clothes, attempt to crawl into his skin. The touch disturbed him, repulsed him. It felt too close, too… tight… too much of not letting him alone. It awakened memories he could not quite focus on.

As he walked on, still in fog, the smell of cake got stronger, and the light grew too. Quite suddenly, he was standing in a plaza amid shops. It was London, he thought, but not the London he lived in, with its decaying hovels, its narrow streets. Once or twice, he'd walked beyond his neighborhood and glimpsed something of this: clean facades, prim maids going about their business in starched, frilled aprons, and the window-shops filled with dolls and toys, with cakes and hams and all manner of good things.

The shop windows were there and laden, but there was no one in sight. The street was quiet, probably because it was nighttime. But in the center of the little plaza, a table was set with a sparkling white table cloth. On the table sat cakes and pies, and candy in big piles. The light pouring on it from the gas lamps above sparkled on sugar decorations and put a mellow gold color on the sweet buns.

Like Seraphim's birthday table, Gabriel thought. That first time. But when he tried to pursue the memory, it retreated before him, and he couldn't remember at all who Seraphim was.

Instead he approached the table, slowly, with the certainty that this much food, freely displayed, had to be some sort of trap. Even wild beasts knew that much.

He half expected it to disappear, but it didn't, and with his eyes fixed on a certain, particularly colorful, piece of candy, he imagined it melting in his mouth, sickly sweet.

But when he was almost within reach of it, the fog hardened like a prison and held him. "No," the fog said, whispering in his ear in a sweet, cloying tone. "No, little boy, there is a price."

Gabriel caught his breath in shock, on recoil of that voice, on memories that he couldn't reach, and yet that made him feel uncomfortable. "Please, sir," he said. "I'm just hungry."

And as he said so, it seemed to him he'd said these words before, and that what followed – He stepped back, recoiling from the sweets, but the fog was there again, not letting him run.

If the table weren't there, with its tempting sweets. If his stomach didn't hurt with hunger. If—

He felt willpower leave him and went limp in the grasp of the fog.

Through his mind, unbidden, came a voice, a glimpse of an adult in a classroom, standing by a chart that represented the worlds that touched Avalon and saying, "The power of Fairyland is in childhood. It reaches into this, feeds on it, in the manner of a leech or parasite. This makes Fairyland a parasite leech upon the worlds."

Gabriel had a moment of wanting to protest that it wasn't true, that the power direction was all wrong, and then he couldn't remember what it was all about. What a strange dream. He'd never been in a classroom like that. Classrooms like that were not for the likes of Gabriel Penn.

"Will you pay?" the fog hissed.

Gabriel looked at the table, at the candy. His stomach roared its hunger. How bad could it be? He had an idea that it could be very bad, but also that he'd survived it in the past. He closed his eyes. A voice came from somewhere in his memory saying, "An' you can do whatever you want with him, governor. No one will care. He's elf born and got only a crazy fairy mother. You can even kill him if it pleases you."

From somewhere too, came a memory that they'd almost had, but then Father had burst in and—

But the memory vanished as if it had never been, leaving only the certainty that it could be survived. But hunger might not be. When had he eaten last? How long could he keep walking with no sustenance?

He closed his eyes. He said, "I will pay."

And then the fog was on him, in him, touching every single pore of his being, while strange, alien thoughts poured into his mind.

Gabriel Penn found himself falling to his knees, while darkness and cloying sweetness consumed his mind.

Sarah A. Hoyt

The Weight Of The Crown

They'd no more hit the ground, running, than Nell realized she couldn't run on home. Even if she wanted to. She had no idea where "home" was, or for that matter which home she should go to: Earth, which she still thought of as home, or Britannia, where, supposedly, she'd first come from?

The place where they landed – running – seemed to be made of black shiny stuff, like really polished glass, and they were running along a corridor made of the stuff. It was hard not to slip, even in running shoes, and she worried that the less well-designed footwear of Avalon wouldn't be up to it at all.

The air that pumped into her lungs felt so cold it singed them. It was like walking in a snowstorm back in Colorado, the air icy and dry, and feeling like it burned its way down your nasal passages and made your chest hurt.

Nell tried to think – hard to do while running and hurting. She remembered again that most things in Fairyland were illusory and could be changed by the mind. She tried to think of running elsewhere – on a meadowland path towards an open portal to Earth, for instance – but nothing happened. She tried again, throwing her magic at it, and still nothing happened.

If she couldn't dent this "reality" imposing itself on her and her friends, then she must be in a type of trap like the net. And that meant… that meant they needed extraordinary magic to get out of it. She wasn't even sure that their running was taking them anywhere, or whether they were just running in place on a slippery, never-ending black-glass trap.

"I'm tired," a voice said behind her, and she recognized Caroline's voice.

"You shouldn't be," came the voice of the young man with her. "You shouldn't be. We gave you the magic potion that–."

"I'm tired," she said again. "And I'm thirsty."

And now Michael's voice came, sounding exactly like Seraphim's, only younger, at that age when male voices haven't fully acquired the depth of adulthood. "Lady, Miss, I don't think my sister can go much further."

Nell stopped and turned. Behind her, she heard her companions stop. She turned around to face them. There was Caroline, and a young man holding her hand, and she looked like she was going to faint, while he looked full of concern.

Michael, on the other hand, just looked pale, and was panting a little as if from the long run.

For a moment, something in the young man to whom Caroline clung called Nell's attention. He looked like someone.... The resemblance formed in her mind, fixed in disbelief and, finally, horror. Antoine. He looked like Antoine. But he ... he couldn't be.... And yet why not? Had not Antoine come from Avalon? Or from some other world that had connection to Avalon?

"Madam," the young man said, and his voice too echoed the memory of Antoine in her mind. "Milady, you see, my people gave Miss Ainsling a potion that should have prevented her feeling hunger, thirst, or tiredness. If she's feeling that, wherever we are, then something is leaching the magic and virtue of the potion she took. And nothing should be able to. I think, Lady, that this is a trap."

"Your people?" Nell said, more perturbed than she wanted to admit by the young man's resemblance to Antoine, even as she scanned the walls of the tunnel. She could now see it was not a tunnel but a box. There was more black glass at either end. Had it always been there, or had it appeared when the little group had stopped running? And if it had always been there, how had they been kept running in place?

"My.... My name.... The Lord—" Something that sounded like an elf name. "—whom you know as Gabriel Penn called you Princess.... Are you?"

"I am told I am the princess of Britannia," Nell said, miserably. She didn't want to be. More than ever, now, she didn't want to be. Back on Earth, when she'd been a young woman, fantasy adventures had seemed so romantic and exciting, but now all she wanted was to go back to Earth, go back to her job as a code monkey, and live a life of complete and ordinary lack of adventure.

His eyes widened. "My people," he said. "Have long been in search of you and... and of the real king of Fairyland. We've worked long and hard to find you. My brother—" He stopped for a moment, his voice gone watery, and Nell thought he had stopped to get his emotion under control before dissolving in tears. "My brother died in that quest. The prophecy said he would. I will, too, probably. The prophecy said if my father wanted to rescue both worlds he could do so, but it would cost him all his descendants. No more would those of his blood run in the woodland glades of Fairyland." The young man set his chin, all jutting angles, beneath a face still endowed with childhood softness and dark eyes swimming in tears. "He still did it. He still did what was right."

And now the hair at the back of Nell's head was trying to rise, and there was a feeling of dread, but she had to know, "Your brother's name was… Antoine?"

The young man blinked at her. "No, but he used that name when he went among men and didn't want to be known for what he was. His name was Athanasius."

"But… he used Antoine?" There was a distinct buzz in Nell's ears. Were the walls moving closer? "When he went among… men? What…?"

"My sister, Lady, do you have water? Your Highness?" Michael asked.

She got her backpack down and without thinking passed a bottle of water and some crackers to Caroline, then more to Michael. She continued staring at the Greek-looking young man. "Who are you? What are you? What was your brother?"

"My name is Akakios," he said," and I'm a prince of centaurs, only heir to my father, now my brother is gone."

She looked down at his very human bare feet, on the floor, "Centaurs?"

"We can change shapes." He sounded tired. "All centaurs are male. All our mothers are human. We don't become centaurs till we're five or six. And we can change back, though it takes some effort. Lady, the walls are closing in on us."

"Yes, I think so too," Nell thought, as in her mind the idea that Antoine had come to find her on Earth in service of some Fairyland prophecy, that he'd, in fact, sacrificed his life to bring her back to Britannia, put a whole other perspective on their involvement. He might have lied to her, and he might have had things in mind he wouldn't share, but he'd done what he'd done in service of an ideal and not because he'd wanted to seduce her. And he might have even loved her, for all she knew.

"It's a magical box," Michael said. "We must get out of it."

"Yes," Akakios said.

"It will take your power, you know," Michael said. "Because it can't be fully controlled, since your father didn't swear fealty."

"And hers," Akakios said. He looked at Nell. "Yours, Your Highness. You must use the power of your ancestors. Your connection to Britannia. You must be the one who forms the connection. The… the true king told you to run along home."

She didn't have time to instruct them to do anything. Their hands linked, and on one side Caroline's cold hand, on the other Michael's sweaty one, took hold of hers.

In the middle, Nell felt all their powers given to her – trustingly given. Michael's power, and Caroline's brilliant and dazzling power, and Akakios's all-odd shapes and yet reminiscent of Antoine's.

"Now, Lady, now."

And Nell, who'd been brought up to think that kings and queens and princesses were quaint things of the past, now tried to reach for what should be in her blood. For kings and queens and princesses long dead.

She felt as though a great weight rested on her. People thought that power over people was… power. That you could tell people what to do and they would. True, a lot of politicians thought so too, but those weren't the good politicians.

Public power wasn't glamour and glitz, ball gowns and being worshipped. Real kings, she felt, and, yeah, princesses too, served. They shouldered the burden because someone had to, and they used it to make sure the unthinkable didn't happen to those who trusted in them.

She felt the imaginary crown like a band around her head, but she knew what she had to do. Gathering all their magic, she thought about the palace in Britannia. It was by rights her home. They couldn't keep her out.

The glass box shattered with a sound like a note of music so high it hurt the ears. They were falling, hands still linked, from somewhere near the ceiling of a large room. A large room with a tree growing in the middle of it, two dragons, and a confusion of people.

The splinters of the cage, falling ahead of them, managed to hit the floor, where they stuck, vibrating, without actually hitting anyone.

And Nell fell in the middle of them, just beside Seraphim Ainsling, Duke of Darkwater.

Sarah A. Hoyt

Mirror and Crown

A surfeit of sweetness, a cloying lack of self. For a while Gabriel Penn was suspended in both, his mind more a memory of having a mind than a real thought, or real memories.

Then, from this place with no past, no future, no self, came the sound of footsteps, punctuated with the sound of a cane tapping cobblestones, not in the way of someone who needed help walking, but in the way of a dandy on the way to a concert or the opera.

That image – that memory – summoning up the very idea of memories and images and a world outside Gabriel's head—brought with it other images. He saw himself as an unfortunate fly, surrounded by a cocoon, suspended from a web, being devoured. He saw himself as a spun-sugar figurine dissolving in a puddle in between cobblestones, on a street more familiar than it should be.

He put his back to that street, to that memory. Like a man bracing himself against a physical object in order to leverage his physical power, he put his mental back to that street – the streets he remembered, the streets that he'd seen, just before—

He was in the middle of the look-alike London, empty as the real London had never been. It was raining. Rain guttered from the roofs, fell into the street, sang merrily along the gutters to join the other, overflowing effluvium.

Gabriel was an adult, and his clothes were soaked. He understood the necessity of the rain. The phrase "a bucket of cold water" ran through his head like a clue, but he didn't need it. He needed the feel of cold on his skin, the clammy feel of his soaked wool trousers clinging to his legs, the feel of that trickle of water running from his head down the back of his neck and his spine, under his already soaked shirt. He could feel his hair plastered to his scalp and his face. He imagined he must look like a drowned rat. But what he looked like didn't matter. He was not, in any sense of the word, somewhere physical.

He was in Fairyland. The thought crossed his mind, with all the strength and urgency of a warning, and was followed by another: he'd been damn near dying in a trap. He was in a trap still.

The awareness of this made him even more intent on the steps and the tap-tap of the cane approaching. He was in Fairyland. Only two things operated here: his own mind, and the mind of his uncle, his opponent. One of them would emerge victorious from this struggle, and it must be Gabriel. It must, because Gabriel was needed for Fairyland to go on existing. And Fairyland was needed… His thought cut off. He wasn't sure why Fairyland was needed. He suspected it was something he could not know until and unless he ascended to its throne. But he had a gut-deep intuition that it was needed. Else, why not have destroyed it, long ago?

So – where he was now, only two minds worked: his and his uncle's.

"Not… quite," an educated male voice said, and Gabriel spun around.

The man who stood between two buildings, as though he'd just emerged from an alleyway, was strangely familiar in a way that Gabriel could not place. He did not exactly look like Gabriel, but he was of the same type: dark hair, light eyes – in the man's case a greyish blue – features that could be considered beautiful but that were still, undeniably, masculine. And his build was also the same, tall and slender, with powerful shoulders. When Gabriel looked up from surveying the man to the man's face, he found the man was smiling. "Well?" he said, in the tone of someone who asks the answer to a riddle.

Gabriel frowned. "You must be spun by the king from my memories, but… I'm not quite sure…." Then he stopped. The man's clothing, too, was soaked, dripping with water from every fiber, even as rain continued to pour down to soak his hair and plaster it to his fine-featured face. The fact that he stood there, under the cold downpour, grinning and looking debonair, as though he'd just emerged from the opera, made everything worse, Gabriel thought.

As he watched, the man removed from his sleeve an immaculate white handkerchief hedged around with lace, and monogrammed with AG. Then, ignoring the fact that the handkerchief was as soaked as everything else, he mopped at his face with it, and said, "Do you like rain, O King?"

"I am not king," Gabriel said, and frowned a little, because if the man were his uncle's creation, then the rain would not affect him at all. The rain was Gabriel's and the weaker effect. To think his uncle might be pretending that rain affected his own creations was to go one step too far. Gabriel knew the sort of mental state his uncle was in – none the better as he thought he'd been in his uncle's mind and about to dissolve into it. It simply was not coherent enough for that kind of fiendish cunning.

So…

"Truly?" the man said. "Are you not? Then why are you here? What are you doing?"

"My uncle—" Gabriel said. "The kingdom– The prophecy—" He

couldn't quite find a coherent point to make his start.

"You know the kingdom of Fairyland goes by magic and power and the one who can hold it coherent and whole. Under those rules your uncle has lost it long ago—before your birth, in fact—and his continued holding of the nominal crown will destroy it and all of us."

"All of us—" Gabriel said. "You don't mean…. That is, you are one of us?"

An eyebrow quirked, and the man gave him a smile between puzzled and amused. "You don't remember me at all, Gabriel Penn. Do I look so different then?"

Through Gabriel's mind ran half-remembered lapses of judgment. There had never been very many, and none of them had meant very much or gone very far. He'd been too afraid of sullying the Darkwaters by contagion, particularly after his incident with Marlon and how close it had come to being public. But there had been the man who'd kissed Gabriel – and soundly too – when Gabriel had brought him his horse after one of the Darkwaters' parties. And there had been that man who'd stayed over and who'd—

But the thing was, the gentleman who'd kissed Gabriel had been so drunk, he'd probably not been aware that Gabriel was not female. Or else, he'd thought he was kissing Seraphim, something that made Gabriel smile even now. And the others…. None of them had looked like this man. Gabriel would have remembered someone who looked somewhat like him.

Something fluttered at the back of his brain, like a bird trying to beat its way out of a cage, and Gabriel frowned and shook his head. "I don't remember," he said.

This got him a broad grin with a hint of malice…. No, not malice, but malicious amusement, as though Gabriel were being particularly dumb and this delighted the stranger. An immaculate white hand was pushed forward. "Aiden Gypson at your service, Your Majesty."

Gabriel had got hold of Aiden Gypson's hand, which felt warm and smooth and alive in his, but the name made him let go of it and take a step back, with a strangled cry. "You're not– You can't be—"

"Why not?" he asked. "The problem is that my soul remains tragically attached to my body, because my soul isn't able to die… to transition in the way souls do when the body dies. And this is a place of the soul and the mind, so here I am wholly alive. What?" he said, at what Gabriel felt must be the look of frozen horror on his own face. "Did you think I didn't know? Did you think I was a passive victim? He never told you, did he? Of course he wouldn't. He's three parts foolish and one part– Never mind."

"He never told me what?" Gabriel said, his throat closing. "Marlon—"

"He never told you why he did what he did or why it went so horribly awry. You should be aware that it betrays bad judgment on Marlon's part. He clearly has a taste for cowards."

Gabriel was too shocked to be offended. "I beg your pardon?" he said.

"I said, Marlon has a taste for cowards. He picked me and then you in quick succession. And I, you see, found it impossible to bear the double weight of not being quite human and never fully fitting in. He came home to find that I had just killed myself – the idea that I'd died of an illness was his, and he was the one who put it about. Being a fool, he tried to bring me back. Only, I am, as much as he, elf born. My mother was a naiad who– Never mind. He couldn't quite bring me back, and once he'd done the magic – not being in full control of his own magic – he couldn't kill me. And so we came to my problem. I'm afraid," he said, and looked at the nails of his right hand, which Gabriel remembered as yellow and desiccated and protruding from dried flesh, but which were now white and buffed and carefully trimmed, "it will take the king's touch to set me free now."

"But … How does that make me a coward?" Gabriel asked, and wanted to protest it wasn't fair, that he would not be here if he were a coward, that he was here not out of his own ambition, but out of his wish to protect his family– that he—

"Well, King, if you aren't a coward, why would you spend so many years running from yourself? So many years pretending to be just human. So many years hiding and running. And why would you now choose to let yourself be killed by a madman who can barely hold his kingdom together rather than take what is yours – the crown and the strength and the life of Fairyland? Why wouldn't you acknowledge what is yours and make it part of you?"

Gabriel opened his mouth. "Because I'm not—" he started, but that wasn't quite true. He couldn't say he wasn't mostly magical, because he knew he was. The last few hours had shown that to him, if nothing else. "Because I can't—" but at the back of his mind he knew that wasn't true either. He could. It would just take… wanting it. Really wanting it. His uncle wanted Fairyland because without it he'd cease to exist. Gabriel must want it like that. He must, like a man at the races, take a final bet and stake all. But he still thought Aiden had no idea how vulnerable Gabriel was, how wounded. "You don't know what my childhood was."

"Don't I just! Do you think the orphanages for elf children are wonderful places, then? Has it occurred to you they might be worse?"

"Yes, but—"

"No, King. Know yourself for what you are. Then take your crown."

Gabriel blinked. He knew the man was right, and yet….

"First," Aiden said, his voice clear, "set me free. And then go to your battle with my blessings. What remains of me in this world, hopefully a very little and for a very short time, will go with you, as will all my good wishes."

"But I can't—" Gabriel said, and then realized that he could. He could see a tangle as though of loose threads behind Aiden, and he knew they were the lines of magic holding him to his body and the world. Elf magic. So strong that the setter himself couldn't break them.

He reached with his hand, tried to break them. Nothing happened. Then Gabriel took a deep breath and told himself he was the king of Fairyland, this was his loyal subject, and he could.

His fingers moved forward as though of their own accord and pinched the threads. For a moment an expression of utter relief painted itself on Aiden's face, then his fading form bowed and he said, "Farewell, O King," and he was gone.

Gabriel turned. He waved a hand. He didn't need the rain. He didn't need the street.

He narrowed his eyes to see the truth, the nebulous pathways of what remained of his uncle's mind.

A hallway of spun sugar seemed to form. Brittle and cloying, Gabriel thought. About right.

But he waved that away too, and willed himself to see clearly, to see the true form.

It was time he claimed his crown.

Sarah A. Hoyt

The Land, The King, The Magic

Nell couldn't make much sense of where she'd fallen. She was sure of only two things: There were two dragons in the room, and one of them was attacking Seraphim.

The second impression she got was that there were too many people, too many factions, a woman-shaped oak tree – or perhaps an oak-shaped woman-tree – growing branches towards one of the dragons, the other dragon reaching out a claw.

In the middle of all this, she was conscious of one thing: Caroline, and the centaur Akakios and Michael, all young, were all under her protection and her responsibility. In this room of intersecting attacks, she could not protect them—or not enough.

Across the room, Seraphim's erstwhile – or was she still official? – fiancée stopped pounding on the dragon wing and rounded on Nell, raising her hands in the initial invocation of power of every witch.

And Nell realized the crown she'd assumed – in effigy, as it were, to get here—still existed and still weighed upon her. If she were just a woman, any woman, as she'd thought, an Earth woman with some accidental power transported here she didn't know how, and living in a fairytale, then none of this mattered, and the safest thing for her to do was to transport out and to ignore Britannia and its troubles.

But not only had she been told, and shown, that this wasn't true. She could feel this wasn't true. She didn't know where this room was, but she could feel it was home. And she'd never had the title or honorifics of a princess, but she knew that she was the princess, the heir to the throne of Britannia. And she'd never been responsible for other people – save Antoine when he'd got captured – but she was now responsible not just for the people in this room, but for all the people in Britannia.

She wasn't sure what had been happening here, except she knew someone had kidnapped her as an infant and somehow kept her parents from searching for her – though they'd obviously missed her. And she didn't know how the intersecting currents of attack and defense in this room went, but she knew it couldn't be good to have two dragons and a tree-woman in a place her magic identified as home. And she didn't know what Seraphim had been doing, but he looked very odd, as though – as though he were turning into glass – and there was filthy magic spinning around the room, enough magic to make the entire world dissolve, were it unleashed further.

Nell hadn't learned anything about princessing, but one thing she did know: in Avalon, magic was more than a way of achieving this or that result; it was woven into the physical existence of the very world. And kingship was more than a political system; it was intertwined and woven with the magic, one of the pillars of the world, and the reason that her disappearance as true heir had been so dangerous.

She could only do one thing, and, her eyes fixed on Seraphim's fiancée across the room, lifting her hands to start an invocation that likely would blow up a room this full of magic, Nell did that thing: she raised her voice; she reached with all her being, she called with mind and magic and heredity. "I call the land. I call the land to my help."

From beside her came a smothered exclamation. She was sure she'd misheard, because dukes didn't swear like that, and even if they did, Seraphim wouldn't. She'd learned to know him on Earth, and she should know some expressions simply weren't in his vocabulary. "Oh, shit," was one of those.

But before she could think it through, the room shook. No, the entire building shook. Not as an earthquake, but as though the building rested on a rug that had been given a good shake by a concerned housewife. The building rolled. From deep within it, past the door to the room, came screams and the sound like something really large made of glass had shattered in a million pieces.

But Nell couldn't react, not even when Seraphim and the dragon vanished, and then Caroline and the centaur prince, and the tree and the man – Marlon Elfborn? – covered in blood. Not even when the other dragon roared, "Where did he go?" and bathed the entire room in a flame that wasn't a flame but something other, something that seared the mind and twisted the magic.

She couldn't move or say anything, even as Seraphim's fiancée fell to her knees sobbing, and as a man walking with the unsteady gait of a drunkard crossed the room in a shadowy, ghostly way that indicated he wasn't fully there.

Nell couldn't say anything, because in her mind was a voice. Or perhaps it was not a voice but… something… a collection of noises that assembled into words, as though someone had orchestrated the grinding of rocks over millennia, the growing of trees over centuries, the growth of plants over seasons, and the buzzing of brief insects on a summer day into something coherent and joined together, which formed words. "Yes?" the words said. And then "Daughter?"

Nell turned all her attention inward and tried to answer the call.

Suddenly, without a feeling of transition, certainly without passing through the Betweener, she was somewhere else.

Deep underground. Had to be. There were earthen walls all around; it was warm, and Nell was there, alone, at the center of it.

From somewhere came the sound of a beating heart – a very loud beating heart that, like the voice, seemed to be composed of all sorts of small, natural sounds.

And then the voice came again, "Approach," it said. And Nell did, walking forward into the twisting and narrowing tunnel, towards a glow of fire and a feeling of warmth.

Sarah A. Hoyt

An Irregular Man

The Honorable Jonathan Blythe had gone straight home. He found the house dark and cold, which it had been much too much of late—partly, he judged, because of his father's great ploy. The supposed princess having been raised with them, but exonerating them of all guilt in her kidnapping, was in fact a great social boon for his family. Mama and Papa, and even some of the younger girls, had been invited to parties every night.

What surprised him, though, was that there was no one waiting in the little room off the entrance hall, which usually had at least Mama's maid or Papa's valet sitting in wait for the Lord and Lady to come home. He walked in, and his steps seemed to resonate loudly in the empty house. He frowned. It couldn't be empty, damme. After all, the children would be in the nursery, perforce. They didn't go to parties. Little James was all of three years old. And the servants and nurses would be here too, would they not?

He walked, slowly, into the completely dark house. Rays of moonlight that shone through the magnificently tall windows in the wall of the entrance hall gave him his light as he found the marble stairs and walked up. Because his footsteps seemed lonely, he supplemented them with the tap of his cane.

Up and up and up, on a whim, all the way up to the third floor, and there, in the nursery, all was empty, all calm – the beds made, the children's toys neatly arranged. But his sweeping of the wall hooks that normally held the children's coats made him frown. They were, every one of them, empty. He quirked his brow and moved down the stairs.

And down there it was obvious that this too was deserted. More importantly, he couldn't hear any noise, not even from the kitchen, and it wasn't so late that the cook would have gone to bed. She usually stayed up late preparing the baking for the next day. Jonathan knew this, because he was known to go in via the kitchen entrance and get a tot of cooking brandy and a slice of day-old cake. The cook had never lost her fondness for the little boy whom she used to give currants and biscuits to. Now Jonathan thought about it, Mrs. Whimple, the cook, might be the only reason he bothered to come home most nights. He frowned at this but didn't dwell on it, beyond being sure that if he stopped coming, the cook would worry.

He wondered if anyone else would. But he thought – yes, he very much thought – that he was worried about them, too. Something had happened to render the town house this empty, and in the middle of the season.

He traced his steps back down the stairs and felt at the door. Someone had removed the knocker, as they did at the end of the season, to signal the whole family was gone from town.

They'd left without telling Jonathan? Well, that was hardly surprising. What was surprising was leaving so early, so… but now. The house was not totally empty. He could feel it wasn't.

He went upstairs, step by step, all the way up to the floor where his parents' rooms and offices were, and he stood there, and sensed. He wanted to be sure, for one, that what he was seeing was not an illusion, that he was in the right house, at the right time.

From Papa's office came the sense of someone living, and Jonathan headed there, tapping his cane along with his steps. He hesitated before the door, training and thought telling him he should knock or scratch, while everything else told him he should just open the door. It was probably Papa in there, or his secretary. And in there were probably the papers, the magic, the trace of the conspiracy that Jonathan had been seeking.

Jonathan opened the door and went in.

There was a mage light burning on the desk, and Papa sat behind it, with a pile of papers. A blazing fire in the fireplace was almost too warm.

Papa – who looked like an older and male version of Honoria – looked up, managing, perhaps for the first time since Jonathan had known him, to appear startled. "Jon!" he said.

"Papa," Jonathan said. A narrow-eyed sweep of the fireplace with his mage sight showed him that a lot of paper was burning there, and that the paper on the desk, which Papa was sorting, was overlaid with some sort of magic. It wouldn't show the wrong thing to the wrong eyes. "I see you're destroying evidence," Jonathan said, amicably, and went over to the corner cabinet where his father kept the liquor. He opened it, got a decanter, poured himself a glass. He was aware of his father's exclamation behind him but didn't turn around until he had a full glass of brandy and his cane and gloves firmly in one hand. He sat on the chair across from his father's desk and crossed his legs, resting gloves and cane on his lap. "I beg your pardon," he said. "But after I had shot the cat in an alley downtown, I lost most of the alcohol I need to think clearly. And all Darkwater and his friend would offer me was a damnable pot of tea. What?"

The What was at papa's look.

"Darkwater is in town?" Papa said. "I thought he might be. I could feel the situation turning and—"

"Suppose you tell me about the situation?" Jonathan said equably as he took a sip of the brandy.

His father raised his eyebrows. He shot a quick look at the fireplace. "How much.... What do you think the situation is?"

"I think that you and Honoria are somehow in business with Sydell. This is bad, Father, very bad. Inexcusably foolish to let yourself be snared into the plots of dragons."

"Ah. So you know that, but do you know what the plot is?"

"I know that you're doing business in other universes," Jon said and drank his brandy.

His father raised his eyebrows. "So you know that far."

"And I know that Honoria isn't the princess. Not half of it. There is no way the princess could look so much like you, Papa."

"Ah. Well, I never expected you to swallow that rasper. Though I trusted you to stay quiet."

It occurred to Jonathan that his father was a very dangerous man. Maybe as dangerous as Sydell. But somehow, Jonathan didn't feel at risk. "I've known you were running a smoky rig, Papa, for the last month. Why do you think I've been drinking so much?"

"How should I know? You've always drunk—"

Jonathan waved his hand. "How did it start? And why, Papa?"

"How did it start?" His father gave a hollow chuckle. "It started with your grandfather. He ran through the fortune like – Your mama says you resemble him, and I've often thought that was true, though now...." He narrowed his eyes and shrugged. "There might be a lot in of me in you, Jonathan. Though I'd never noticed it before. But if there is, you'll understand.

"When I inherited, the family was well-nigh destitute. Oh, we had the business, and the magic, and I could have built it back up in time. But I was married and I... I didn't want to spend my entire life laboring just so my heir could have a fortune to waste. So I started going to the forbidden worlds. The ones without magic. It's so easy to make a fortune there, Jonathan. It's not that magic doesn't work – though in one or two it won't except the residual we bring from here, and it will be lost if we stay – it's that they don't have magic there. Which means they can't detect it. Their financial markets are wide open. Their politicians will pay extraordinary sums for simple persuasion spells…."

"And?" Jonathan said. He could see the basic dishonesty of what his father had done but not enough to trouble him. "You made our fortune?"

"More than it had ever been, yes."

"And then?"

"And then Sydell approached me. He'd noticed what we were doing, and he gave me an ultimatum. I could stop – at that point it was very hard to prove what I'd done – or I could ally myself with him."

"And?"

"I couldn't stop."

"Why not? You'd made your fortune."

"But the power, Jonathan. The power. You have no idea what it's like to be able to dictate the fate of entire worlds when no one knows about what you're doing. It's better than being king."

Jonathan felt sick for the first time and for a moment was afraid the brandy would come back up. He stared at his father, his eyes impassive. Of all the things he'd never understood, the lust for power was the worst. His sins were pleasing ones: sleeping with this or that person or creature, drinking, eating. He could never understand the boys at school who enjoyed ordering others about. He could see they did, and he could see his father did too, but it was incomprehensible to him, and also vaguely nauseating. He remembered all the times at school when a bully had tried to force him to behave in a manner he didn't wish to.

"I see," he said at last. "So you dealt with the dragon."

"He wanted to replace the king. He wanted Avalon and Fairyland. I thought… I thought his madness was just that, and I thought…."

"And m'sister? How did she come into it?"

This got him a completely baffled look. "Your mama says your sister and I are alike. You know it is said the founder of our house was elf born, and your mama says both your sister and I have ice in our veins. I think… she's wrong. Your sister fell in love with Sydell. After that…." He shrugged. "Not that I understand it. The man is my age, and if rumors are true, he's never been interested in a woman, except the nymph he raped to get her imprisoned in the spell, years ago, the one who gave him his bastard. I thought…. I've been used to thinking that like his son's, his interests lay in another direction. At least for a while it was said that he kept various young men…." He shrugged. "I told your sister, and she accused me of lying. She fell in love with him head over heels, and… and he encouraged her. I think what attracted her was his power."

"His magical power?"

"That too, but his… power and his wish for power."

Jonathan gave a click of his tongue. "They do say girls fall in love with men who resemble their fathers."

His father looked startled but said nothing.

"So," Jonathan said. "Right now, you should be getting ready to be the foster father of the new queen. But you're burning papers. What happened that I don't know about?"

His father's eyes looked dull and odd. "She called the land."

"M'sister? Has she gone mad?"

"No, not your sister. How could she? The real princess."

"The re– She's in Britannia?"

"Yes. She came back some while back. A centaur brought her. Fortunately Sydell neutralized her and kept her where he could keep her power damped and her under his thumb. He tried to involve her with Darkwater so both could be condemned at the same time, before anyone looked too closely at her, but then…"

"But then?"

"It all went wrong," his father said flatly. "And she's called the land."

"Which causes?"

"Well, it gives her power, if she survives the challenges, to destroy all our spells, all our obfuscations. To prove who she is. Even now, the king has felt the call and knows his daughter is near and that she's not your sister."

"So you…."

"I intended to say it was your sister's plan, and Sydell's, which is true, and try to brazen out. If only evidence…." He looked up at Jonathan. "I intended to… I had caught, this afternoon, odd disturbances, and Sydell wouldn't answer my questions, so I sent the whole family to the country seat, and I—"

"Too late, Papa. Other people know. And Darkwater is in the world, and he knows, and…."

"I see," his father said. "Yes, I think you are like me. Underneath the bon vivant, you have ice in your veins."

Jonathan laughed. He set his empty glass on the side of the desk and slipped his gloves on. "Perhaps that's why I drink so much. It won't fadge, Papa. You know that even if there are no witnesses, dearest Honoria will talk. Yes, we could kill her, but Papa, I think there is another problem. If you survive this, you'll have to keep your nose clean, very clean. And I'll be watching, to make sure you don't do this again. Even if the thing with dealing in other worlds is lifted – since I think that was Sydell's idea – yet the king will monitor it, and what you've been doing will not be permitted. Would you be able to do that, papa? To give up the power?"

He read the answer in his father's eyes, even as his father said, "And you? Would you be able to take a house with a shadow on it and do any better for your brothers and sisters? And Jonathan, would you be able to resist exploiting those without magical power? You are like me!"

"Not entirely, Papa. You see, my wish has never been to rule others but to be left alone." He got up. "I'll bid you farewell. I trust you know what to do. I believe you have the necessary in your second drawer."

"Why don't you do it yourself?"

"Tut-tut, Papa. Judicial magicians."

Jonathan got up and walked out of his father's study. He presumed he'd have to sleep at his club, if all servants were gone.

He was on the second step of the stairs when the shot rang out from the studio and Jonathan was, suddenly, the only living person in the house.

Jonathan Blythe, Earl of Savage, stood transfixed for a moment. He'd like to say he felt nothing, but that was not strictly true. He felt no grief for his father, who'd never given him reason to feel anything.

But he felt a sure, unreasoning fury. If his father hadn't wanted to get rich in a hurry. If he'd not been addicted to power. If– Then Jonathan could have done what he planned since the age of twelve at least, and disappeared into a place where he was not known and had no responsibilities, and left his younger brother to inherit.

It wasn't possible now, and Peter would not have to shoulder the responsibility. Jonathan would spend the rest of his life living so impeccably, so above-board that he restored the family name.

He muttered a curse under his breath and left for his club.

But he'd gone no more than two steps outside when he realized this night was not a normal night for anyone.

Sarah A. Hoyt

Dragon's Den

Seraphim landed hard, on his shoulder. From somewhere he could hear water running.

I very much wish I would stop getting thrown around by magic, he thought. Then he felt more than heard the thud of a body falling near him. A very heavy body.

Aching, feeling as if his own fall had broken something, he twisted to face… the dragon. No… Sydell.

Somehow Seraphim was on his feet and turning to face the dragon. It was huge and swollen and monstrous, reddish-brown in tone, with wings like a massive armature, feet that each of them was as large as a man's body, toe nails that looked like the horns of some ancient beast. And yet, looking up, he detected in the huge face Sydell's expressions and Sydell's features.

Sydell had always seemed to him to be a smooth courtier, always ready to do what people expected. But beneath, a dark current ran, full of danger and … things Seraphim couldn't even understand.

The dragon showed the same duality, and a malicious… not delight. Though Seraphim supposed there was delight beneath the … fear?

"Welcome to the dragon cave," Sydell said, and it was horrible to see that dragon mouth shape the words, horrible to hear the well-bred accents in the gravel-like voice. "I don't know how that imbecile sent us here by raising the land, but I couldn't have planned it better. For decades I've been striving against your family. First your father… the king's Witchfinder, indeed. The corruption of a noble title to mean do-goodism in other worlds, and rescuing from their fate people who are no part nor parcel of our lives. Going in search of trouble, I call it. And preventing enterprising men from making a living in worlds too stupid to develop their magic systems.

"And then you, after we'd safely disposed of him. You – with the same nonsense, the same intent to rescue. And aided by that infernal creature, the exiled king, your brother. I don't think you ever realized how much of his power he lent you. No, you were so full of your position being the duke, being the important one, you never realized that he was feeding you magic, and that you were only able to do all you did by his eldritch powers."

The dragon grinned, and the grin was worse than the voice, displaying long, glimmering teeth, but more than that, showing a level of malice that Seraphim would much rather not have known existed.

"But here, Duke, here you are on your own. Just you and me, and no kings, no princesses, no one who will betray me or deflect me to save your sorry carcass. Here I kill you.... Or perhaps not. Perhaps I'd be convinced to spare you for a time...."

Seraphim's eyes had grown used to the gloom of the cave. It was an odd gloom, tinged with red, and it had taken him a while to realize the red came from a pile – a truly massive pile – of gold at the back. This surprised him just a little. Like most such things in legend, he'd always assumed the idea of the dragon treasure was a lie. It surprised him, too, because Sydell was not that old, and the pile of treasure had the look of something accumulated over generations, the result of pirate shipwrecks and historical rapine. Seraphim wondered where that treasure had come from.

But other things interested him more. There were... manacles on the wall, and from several of them corpses depended, half rotted, which explained the odor of must and decay in the air. But there were other corpses too, dead in a pile by the treasure and half eaten. In the light of Sydell's words, it was impossible for Seraphim not to notice that all the bodies whose characteristics he could discern were young and male.

Feeling his gorge rise, he wondered if decorating one's space in old lovers was a family characteristic of the Sydell line. Then he apologized mentally to Marlon. No. He might have his doubts about the man, and he might ... but Marlon, at least to his knowledge, had never viewed a tryst as the prelude to a snack. Certainly not, or word would have got about.

And that Marlon had maintained this dreadful place, unsuspected....

Seraphim swallowed hard again. It seemed to him at the back of the cave there was movement, and a human form, he didn't know whether bound or free, but he didn't want to think about it. Right now, compared to the mountain of dragon flesh, a human posed very little danger.

"Are you judging your odds?" Sydell asked, and the urbane humor in the dragon voice was almost more than Seraphim could bear. "Don't. You have no chance. Forget all your magical fights of the past. Without your... brother, you would never have had a chance. Do you wish to compound now?"

But Seraphim was still holding the black shard of the dryad's cage. And he'd be demmed if he was going to compound for a year, a month, or even a day of life, under these conditions and.... He looked around at the skeletons. No. He'd not been willing to marry Honoria for honor, and he'd not give in to a dragon's lust to preserve a few more … hours? days? weeks? ...of life. It wouldn't be much. He suspected what Sydell craved was power, and once you gave in, he was no longer interested. And even if it were not much, there were things more important than saving one's life.

He wasn't convinced everything was lost. Perhaps Gabriel had helped Seraphim with power, but that didn't make Seraphim helpless without it. And at any rate, he was a Darkwater, and his family depended on him. Power or not, chances of success or not, he would fight. For himself, for them, for what was right.

If he must die, let him die true to what he was.

He stepped back to achieve balance, his step unnaturally loud in the cave. From somewhere at the other end came a rustle and a sound of gold sliding. Human? Animal attracted by the remains? It did not matter.

Seraphim grinned up the mountain of dragon whose shadow dwarfed him. "Do your worst, Sydell," he said. "I'll see you in hell."

Sarah A. Hoyt

Rogue's Progress

It wasn't the ghost riders, riding madly through London, that scared Jonathan Blythe. After all, he'd had a decent magical education. He wasn't a fool, either. Ghosts are ghosts. Which is not to say that they can't do anything to you. Only uneducated fools would think so. Ghosts couldn't, of course, as such, touch you. They were on another plane. And couldn't interact with humans in the way physical objects could.

No, what ghosts could do, though, was trail magic. In fact, they couldn't help doing it. Crossing over from the other plane—whether they were true ghosts, caught in between the worlds, or just memories of past events, being reenacted in the present day—to manifest they required magic, and they brought with them a magic disturbance – a rift in the nature of the magical power that undergirded the world.

This was why on seeing a ghost, people would feel a chill and an eldritch fear. There was a disturbance in the magic, and it was impossible not to perceive it, even if you didn't have enough magic to name it.

But the more important point was that, once the magic had been torn, anything could come through it. Anything, including creatures that didn't normally inhabit the human plane of existence – things that were, or could be, physical. Things that weren't so well intentioned.

And London was now filled with ghosts. Jonathan was going to guess the ghosts of every person who'd ever died fighting or murdered in the land that London now occupied – Roman legionnaires and armored knights, women screaming and running in bloodied nightgowns, and through it all, in the middle of it all, every cavalcade who'd ever ridden through London – victorious or not. He was almost sure the ones in Roman armor, with plumes, were Arthur's cavalry when they'd come to London to install him. But there was also Essex's forlorn effort and John Lackland's last hope – riding disarmed and blindfolded, with their standards reversed, as they had on the way to their execution.

Jonathan swallowed hard, looking at these figures of defeat, not only at seeing so vividly brought to life that which he'd only before seen in history books, but also at the number of ghosts.

He knew what had caused it right enough. The land wakening would waken all who slept an unquiet sleep among the dead. But the land itself had caused a disturbance in magic, and now this….

It took almost no time at all for Jonathan to spot them. Demons, he supposed they should be called, although they weren't. Not really. Not the tempting demons of theology, at least. These creatures were barely sentient, little more than animated particles of evil.

But evil they were, walking lurching and rolling – they had varying forms – upon the land. Their forms gave one headaches, simply because they shouldn't possibly exist, and yet they did, claw and fang, and odd-colored eyes peeking out of unexpected places; fur and feather and something that was neither, in colors that made one nauseated just staring at them.

They were wrong. They smelled wrong, too, their stench following them. And they fell upon the passers-by, the late night opera-leavers, the prostitutes and their clients, the beggar children, with equal ferocity.

They didn't fall on Jonathan. He didn't expect it. Honestly, even creatures of the abyss had more sense than to fall on a trained wizard with years of practice, even if the trained wizard was Jonathan Blythe, who'd learned magic rather by default, and more to stop his masters badgering him than because he had any interest in it.

But gripping his cane – with its silver handle – in his hand, and frowning at the scene of mayhem around him, Jonathan was taken with a most unexpected sensation. He was sure – in fact, he could almost swear – that he was supposed to be doing something about all this. He heard screams from a group of crossing sweeper children who were trying, ineffectually, to defend themselves with their brooms against fanged purple horrors.

But, damn it all, he told himself. I am a rogue. Jonathan Blythe, only out for what he can get, if what he can get is a bit of tupping or some good liquor, at least. I am not a hero.

And yet, the growing conviction at the head of his mind, was that if he did not do something, he would not be able to wake with himself in the morning. His father's death didn't bother him – what? Far less ignominious and far less shameful than he deserved – but these children had done nothing but get caught at a bad time.

Sighing inwardly, he charged with his cane, swinging as hard as he could at the furry head and feathered one, at violet horror and red one, at horn and claw and fang.

The horrors recoiled, as the urchins, gaining heart, started swinging with vigor, sending the minor demons flying across the street.

Jonathan started forward, towards a group of besieged opera-goers, all female, all clustered and screaming, as demons pulled at their dresses and bit them. He realized the urchins were following him and, without looking, he said a careless spell endowing their brooms with demon-killing spells.

The screams of glee from the urchins as the demons exploded on contact told him everything he needed to know. They batted the demons off the opera-goers and flagged down a coach going too fast to accrue abominations, then charged forward, towards the next group.

He continued in this fashion, aware that he was gathering a growing crowd of followers, only because he was charging their weapons, until he met with a group coming the other way. They converged on a group of debutantes, just out from Almack's, screaming and crying as demons tore their pretty muslin frocks and bit their peaches-and-cream faces, and their rounded, perfect arms.

He'd seen a group of demons trying to drag one of the girls off, and he ran forward. His cane almost met, midair, with a fan going the other way. Fan and cane fell on demons at once, and demons exploded and burst. Jonathan's group of street urchins set to, clearing the road around, while the other chap's – no, girl's – followers, who appeared to be a ragtag group of prostitutes, did likewise.

And Jonathan, looking up, met with the brightest pair of green eyes, the reddest hair he'd ever seen, in the most impudent female face this side of a streetwalker's. He registered this impression, as well as the impression the girl was quality, if not wealth. She was dressed as a dowdy children's governess, in a black, very modest dress, which was all out of kilter with her beauty and her bold style. The fan she'd clearly bespelled to be lethal was chicken skin and drawn upon in jewel colors.

Jonathan set to killing demons again, but between one and the next, he removed his hat for a moment and said, "Jonathan Blythe, at your service, Madam, and you are?"

"Ginevra Elfborn," came a voice that matched the face, clear and loud, and well-accented.

"Elfborn," he said in some confusion.

"Elfborn and not ashamed. I am a governess at the orphanage where I grew. I was out for the evening to… well… and I came upon this!"

To… well…Those words set Jonathan's mind reeling. He was not going to ask, not right now, but the many things a woman like that could be doing out at night… well, he should be shocked, but he never had been a very regular man.

She caught the silence, he thought, and felt his thoughts.

"It is no use," she said, "your thinking a lot of indecent things. My mother was a swan maiden, you see; sometimes I need– Sometimes I need to be near water."

Jonathan realized that even as he was smiting demons, his face had split in a grin. He'd known a swan maiden once—

"Miss Elfborn. If you do me the honor, I'll escort you to the river, and help you kill demons on the way. That is, if you're agreeable."

He looked up for a moment to catch a glimpse of green-flashing, narrowed eyes, and a brief and surprised smile, "Indeed, Mr. Blythe. I shall be very pleased."

He'd tell her about the title later.

Sarah A. Hoyt

This Unwanted Crown

Nell advanced. It seemed to her that it had got unbearably hot, but she didn't feel it as heat, so much as unbearable confinement, touching the skin at all points. She got sweaty, too, instantly, and uncomfortable in ways she didn't even know people could be uncomfortable. It seemed to her she could feel every inch of her skin, she realized, startled that this was not normal, that in fact, most of the time, people forgot about most of their body. Just let it run on its own. Perhaps that was necessary to stay sane. You couldn't always be thinking of your left eyeball.

Then she thought these were very odd thoughts, and then that she must be dreaming. Yet she continued walking towards the glow ahead. There was a sense that if she were to get out of here and return to the world as she knew it – one of the worlds that made sense, at least, be they Earth or Avalon – she needed to go forward.

Only, as she got closer, the light seemed to grow dimmer. No, not dimmer, just more concentrated into strands, which seemed to drape all over, from ceiling to floor, like immaterial cobwebs. They gathered in three glowing cocoons at the end of the corridor in a sort of domed cave-chamber. It seemed to Nell that the walls of the chamber glowed gold, and also that inside the cocoons were three people – tall people with broad shoulders, though it was impossible to say whether they were men or women.

When they spoke, the voice that resonated didn't give her any idea, either, since it was a vibration, more than a voice. It gave the impression of a boom in the ears, but there was no sound.

"Daughter of the isles," it or they said. It was hard to tell if it was one person or all three speaking. "You come to claim your crown."

Nell spoke before she could stop herself. "No," she said.

"No?"

"No. I want no part of the crown."

There was a low thrumming. She couldn't tell if it was a thrum of disapproval. Then there was a question that almost managed to sound surprised and taken off expectations, "Why not?"

Nell had to think, because her words had come out before thinking. But as she looked into her heart, she saw that it was indeed true. She wanted no part of the crown. "I am not of this world," she said, and as the thrumming resumed, she said, "What I mean is, I believe I was born in Britannia. Someone… someone I trust said I was. But I am not of this world. I was taken while still very young to another world, to a world we call Earth, a world without magic, and that is my world and what I think of as home."

No thrumming, but the words came again, "And yet, that person you trust – perhaps love? – is in Britannia, is he not?"

Trust and perhaps love. Nell didn't have much experience with men. There had been Antoine, but apparently he hadn't been a man as such, just a lost centaur, carrying out some ancient prophecy. Then there was Seraphim. She had enjoyed her days with him. And perhaps it was love – maybe. She could imagine his moving back to the farm and living there, while they took some of the work from Grandma and did their best to make the place profitable and—

And it was totally impossible. He was a duke. Yes, he had brothers, and yes, perhaps he could leave and leave the inheritance to his younger brothers, but she was not stupid. While other dukes in the same position might do so, Seraphim would not. His family and his responsibilities were at least part of his being.

She shied away from what this might mean for her and for her family and for her responsibilities. "I… I am not for him. We're not of the same worlds. Our positions are so different." That was a justification, her unforgiving mind told her, for dereliction of duty. But why should she have this duty? She hadn't chosen to be born of this world, this kingdom, or this family. She hadn't been raised to them. She didn't want them. "I want to go back home and live there."

Another low thrumming, this one with a note of … yes, she was almost sure of it now. There were words in there. This low thrumming was a conversation between the people in those cocoons. "But you came to Britannia willing," a voice said, and it seemed to her this voice had what she would call an Irish accent, even though there was no sound as such, just a feeling. "You embraced magic willing. This is not normal on Earth."

"I was curious," she said, and then felt herself blush, fiery red. She knew she was blushing because her cheeks were even hotter than the chamber she found herself in, so hot she expected to smell burning flesh. "And there was a man. Or rather, he was a centaur. It is perhaps not known in Avalon, but women with… women who work in professions of the mind, on Earth, often have trouble… that is, men are not very interested in most of them. Or only some men. Most men who had been interested in me didn't interest me, and then there was… the centaur. He was interesting, and he took me traveling the worlds."

She waited. The thrumming resumed. "The centaur fetched you obeying a prophecy and gave his life for it. Does that not move you?"

"No. It is not my prophecy, and I did not want him to give his life."

"In fact," another voice said, one that sounded somehow older, "you have known or suspected for some time, perhaps from before the centaur fetched you, who you were and what your responsibilities were, have you not?"

"No," Nell said, in a little cry, then stopped. "Perhaps, but…."

"But?"

"It is crazy to imagine you're the princess of a lost world, and besides… and besides, I did not want it. Not after I saw the real Britannia, the responsibilities, the needs. Even with my fath– Even with the king in power, the heir would need to take up her share of magic. I've heard old people say the land suffers from lack of an heir. I– the heir would need to take up any future planning that involves magic and carry a burden that…. I do not want it."

The thrumming picked up again, this time sounding like a furious swarm of bees who were running rather hoarse. "In fact, you'd prefer to desert?" another voice said.

"Not desert. Not that," Nell said. "I wasn't raised to it. There are better people than I."

A long silence fell, and for a moment, for just a moment, Nell thought they'd now let her go, probably transport her all the way to Earth, and then she….

"Well then," the voices said altogether. "Look what will happen if you'll not take this unwanted crown."

In front of the cocoons of light, a mist formed, thick and glossy, like reflective fog. And upon the fog scenes formed and moved. People she knew, people she– Yes, she was sure she recognized Seraphim, and her heart leapt. Why on Earth was he in an underground chamber, trying to fight a dragon with what appeared to be a flint knife?

And then the scene shifted. And Nell screamed.

Sarah A. Hoyt

The Duke's Trial

There was blood on the floor, and Seraphim was dimly aware it was his blood, come from wounds suffered in combat with the dragon. In the same dim, distant way, he was aware that his body hurt. There was a claw through his shoulder, and the dragon's teeth had grazed his thigh. There were other wounds too. Seraphim didn't remember them all, and didn't think he had the strength to tally them.

It was enough that every part of him hurt, and hurt more when it moved. The hand he lifted, holding the fragment of the dryad's cage, might have been held down by weights. The legs that supported his body might have lost all strength. And pain screamed along his every nerve ending. It was enough that he felt more tired than he'd ever felt, so tired it took all his will power to stay standing and awake.

Blood soaked his clothes, ran to the floor, and became slippery underfoot. He was cold. It seemed to him the cave had grown dimmer. He knew it couldn't be true, and assumed this meant he was dying.

For some reason the thought didn't disturb him as much as it should. Perhaps because he lacked the strength to be disturbed. He wanted to close his eyes and to be done with all this.

And through it all there remained the dim but certain awareness that not only had he barely injured his foe, but his foe was enjoying this.

If the dragon had wanted, Seraphim knew, he could have ended Seraphim's life long ago. Instead, he chose to prolong it, like a cat playing with an injured mouse.

Seraphim could understand the behavior in cats. Instinct dictated it. Perhaps it dictated it in dragons too. They knew so little about the creatures of Fairyland.

Those that strayed into the ordered world of Avalon, they chose rather to immure and to make behave by human rules. Gabriel—

The thought of Gabriel brought a sharp pain in his mind, joining the physical ones. Perhaps it was true what Sydell said, that Gabriel had been the cause of Seraphim's magical strength and most of his ability. Perhaps it was true that without Gabriel, Seraphim would never have been able to evade the prohibition spells and go to other worlds and rescue people. Perhaps – as Sydell now said, his voice echoing funny in Seraphim's ears, while the dragon sprawled, smiling like a cat, across his pile of treasure – "You know, milord, it really was always your unacknowledged half-brother doing all the work, and allowing you to preen and strut like the useless peacock you are. He saved you from that siren. Even in the middle of his affair, he became aware of your peril, and he saved you. You didn't even know he stood in danger or of what."

But it wasn't that that upset Seraphim and caused the deep ache in his – for lack of a better word – soul. It didn't matter if he'd appeared ridiculous to Gabriel, or, indeed, to the world at large. What mattered was that he could not slay the dragon. And without slaying the dragon, he couldn't leave here. And without leaving here, he couldn't help Gabriel.

He'd been aware from a very early age that his father – hero to others, as he'd later been revealed – was not a responsible head of the family, and not capable of protecting them.

And so, Seraphim had joined with his mother in protecting both the family and their reputation: the ill-fated duel on Gabriel's behalf had been part of that. As had been the paying of fees and removing of entanglements from his father's name, and making sure that, whatever else he or the family went without, there was money for the younger ones' school fees.

But now – he remembered – Marlon had told him that Gabriel was fighting for his life, and if Seraphim knew the stakes involved, it was a terrifying enough fight – but Seraphim could not help him. Seraphim would die here, alone, and, more importantly, forsworn. His brother would die, alone, thinking Seraphim had left him to die. Thinking he was indeed unacknowledged and unaccepted.

The dragon head came in for a bite, and as it opened, Seraphim reached into the half open mouth and cut it across the tongue. The teeth closed around his arm so hard that Seraphim screamed.

From the shadows came the scurry he'd heard before. Seraphim dismissed it. It might very well be nothing more than the illusion of his dying ears.

The pain in his wrist was such that it was all he could do not to scream, and there was blood dripping between the dragon's jaws. Mine or his? Seraphim thought, but it didn't seem to matter. There was blood dripping down his forehead, across his eyebrows. He didn't remember getting cut there, but obviously he had. The droplets of blood that managed to make it into his eyes left a red curtain before his vision.

The dragon smiled across the arm he had captured, and let go. For some reason, seeing that his arm was still attached, with deep puncture marks across his forearm, but attached, seemed to make the wound hurt more.

"There is nothing you can do, duke. There was nothing you could ever do."

Seraphim tried, though he barely had strength left, to throw a spell-net at the dragon, but nothing came of it. Some sort of shield stopped it, before Seraphim could even see what it was, and with it went the last of Seraphim's magical strength.

"Your magic is now gone," the dragon said. "And you were never a physical match for me. Say you surrender and I might let you live… a while longer."

Seraphim gritted his teeth. He thought, yes, if he lived longer he might have a chance, but he remembered the bodies, the skeletons around him, naked, eaten. No. There would be no hope. Besides, he would live with the knowledge he'd let his family be destroyed.

"No," he said between his teeth, and lurched forward, and tripped on something that made a horrible metallic clatter.

He noticed, without much thought, that the dragon looked alarmed; then he looked down and saw a glimmer, a—a sword. It was gold and had cabalistic symbols on the handle, and Seraphim had a feeling someone – was someone alive in this horrible place, besides him and his foe? – had taken it from the pile of treasure and slid it across the ground at him.

All of this took a moment, and then he was – despite the screams of his body – grabbing the sword and running – running, though he was sure he'd die of the effort – at the dragon, and plunging the sword to the hilt in the dragon's chest.

Of course, given the relative size, a sword was more like a dagger, and the plunging of it into the dragon's chest brought only a scream of rage, but then….

But then Seraphim realized that the magical shield of the dragon seemed to be down, that the dragon was scrabbling ineffectively at the sword hilt with his claws, as though he couldn't quite grasp it.

Of course, it's spelled, Seraphim thought. It is a magical sword.

At the same moment in his mind was the magical tutor his mother had hired when he was very young saying, "If you ever have to strike at a dragon, plunge the dagger into his eye."

So he grabbed at the sword hilt, pulled it out and, feeling as though he was using strength he didn't in fact have, plunged it into the dragon's eye.

There was a scream – horrible and loud—and the huge body trashed around. In a spasm, a claw caught Seraphim across the middle, tearing his clothes and sending him flying, to hit his head against the wall, after which merciful darkness fell.

He woke with Gabriel looming over him, saying, "Wake up, milord. Wake up. We must get out of here."

Gabriel must have run mad to call him milord in these circumstances, Seraphim thought, but what he said was the first words on his mind, "You are alive, then. Good. I'm Raphael, and I—"

A hollow laugh escaped the man, and suddenly Seraphim realized it couldn't be Gabriel, because the accent was quite wrong, and while Gabriel might be mad enough to call Seraphim milord, he would not fake an accent in these circumstances. Particularly an accent that sounded remarkably like Nell's.

"You could say I'm alive, milord. Though many times I wished I weren't. Come, milord, we must get out of here."

Seraphim was suddenly aware that the ground was shaking and that pieces of rock seemed to be raining on them from above. Looking up, he saw that the ceiling had cracks and fissures and the rocks falling on them were pieces of it.

"It's caving in," he said.

"Yes, milord. Up. Come." The man was reaching for Seraphim, trying to make him stand, but Seraphim felt he couldn't.

"You go," he said. "Save yourself. I am done for."

Sarah A. Hoyt

The Land's Heart

Nell stepped forward, and the warmth enveloped her. At first it was almost too hot and too bright, and then....

And then she stopped being separate from the light and the heat, and she found herself in the spinning heart of everything: she could feel everywhere and everywhen, she was everywhere and everywhen.

In London, she was streets thronged with people, fighting odd threats. In the countryside, she stood on frost-crackling fields, while ghost riders ran and ravaged the sleeping farms, the silent homesteads.

Fairyland had broken loose and spilled into Avalon.

The part of Nell that could still feel and think felt a clutch at her heart, a fear that Gabriel had lost his battle and that this had always been part of the plan between the traitor in Britannia and the dark ones of Fairyland, that now the two would merge.

The part of Nell that now knew more, the part of Nell that was Avalon and whose mind went back through the ages, to King Arthur's time and before, knew this was nonsense. Not that it had been the plan. It might very well be the plan, but she knew better. Fairyland and the mundane world could not merge. They could only meet and annihilate each other. Easy enough for the forces of Fairyland to romp and storm through the lower-magical world of mortals, for a time. But then the lack of magic in Avalon would starve them, at the same time as they rampaged among the mere mortals.

And there was more. Fairyland powered every other world. Without it, magic would leach out of all other worlds. Its sickly state these last few years meant that it had already leaked out of the outer, most distant worlds, such as Earth. If this went on, then it would disappear from all other worlds, and eventually life would go with it. And if this night Fairyland spilled into Avalon and Avalon into Fairyland, it would all burn itself out in a moon.

But the land had its strength. What it lacked was a will and a mind. And that – Nell thought – wasn't right. She felt the connection that should link the land to the king. She was not – yet – the Queen of Britannia. The land should be linked to the man she must learn to think of as her father.

Nell followed the link in her mind and found the place where it was cut by a dark, dank stuff like mildew that had eaten at the quick, living magic.

It was as though Nell's heart had plummeted down around her feet. She could not solve this, and get the king – her father, she must think of him as that – to take over the battle. For now it was her battle, and then – and then she would make sure the king received the power. It was too early. She did not want to wear the crown.

But all the same, she must lift the sword, symbolically and in truth, the sword of power in the land.

She felt it in her hands, that legendary sword that had been Arthur's and the first Richard's, the sword that took form and substance now and then, but which was forever and always a sword of the spirit.

It was heavy, here at the heart of the world, and it was a symbol, more than a real weapon. Nell lifted it.

Against the growing invaders, against the dark armies, against the creatures of ill-defined magic and ill-disciplined force, she lifted the sword, and with it raised the strength of the land, and she called, "Fight!" And she screamed "Arise!" And she commanded, "Defend!"

From every sacred grove and every cleanly hill, the power of the land, the power, rose, and the magic grew. The invaders, surprised, fell back in disarray, clambered back in fear. They wouldn't be banished, not completely, but they would not rampage. They held in tight circles, defensive, embattled. And around them the magic of the land shimmered and sparkled.

Sarah A. Hoyt

A Fighting Title

Seraphim became aware that he was being dragged over the rough floor. He tried to protest that he should be allowed to die in peace. It seemed to him peculiar that the odd man from the dragon den should insist on dragging a dying duke along with him.

Only he wasn't a duke anymore.

And from somewhere anger came. He'd not asked to be the Duke of Darkwater. He'd not asked to be the first-born of the previous duke's large and irregular get. He'd not asked his father to die early and to leave Seraphim in charge of an encumbered inheritance and younger children who depended on him.

And, most of all, he'd not asked to find his father's secret papers, not to feel obliged to rescue the unfortunates that his father could no longer help.

He had asked for none of this.

And now, now that he must die for it, some lunatic wouldn't let him alone.

He moaned loudly, and there was a moment of hesitation, but then the dragging resumed.

Seraphim became aware that the ground was shaking beneath him, that his arms hurt as he was being dragged, and that – and this part galled him – someone was shoving quite an unreasonable amount of magic at him, pushing and forcing it past Seraphim's weakened defenses, forcing Seraphim's body to heal itself.

It was an odd magic, not untrained, but strangely structured. Instead of healing Seraphim it was forcing him to heal.

Now, there was somewhere –

Seraphim had seen that magic somewhere, felt it somewhere. As his body started to recover, his mind pursued the mystery and found in its unraveling enough incentive to wake up more fully. There, there, the taste of it, the force of the magic.... He knew that type of work.

And then it hit him. The Madhouse. No. Nell's world. Earth, they called themselves – though, of course, every unaware world called itself Earth – the world without magic. People from it always learned magic backwards and sideways and did things by methods no sane trained magician, let alone a teacher of magic, would think right. It was as though an entire world had decided the way to build a house was to start with the roof.

And yet, the misbegotten, scrambled magic worked, after a fashion. Not well, on Earth, but pretty well everywhere else.

He had woken now, enough to feel his whole body. The annoyance of being dragged, the rough stone tearing at his skin, all of it combined to bring his eyes open.

He was still in the dragon cave. Rocks were falling from a cracked ceiling. Through the fissures, he could see glowing red lava and what looked like fires of hell. He wondered if they were beneath a volcano now coming awake, and wondered how long till glowing lava dripped through and incinerated him and his—strange savior.

He looked up the length of his stretched arms to where a man who looked much like Gabriel was walking backwards while pulling on his hands.

"Stop," Seraphim said. "Stop."

"I'm not leaving you here," the young man said. "Not on your life. But I can't do transport. Never learned how. So we must get out this way. I think this hallway will—"

"Stop," Seraphim said, and as the only way to avert this humiliation of being dragged along like a sack of rocks, said, "I'll stand. I'll stand."

His hands were let free, and he did manage to stand, unsteadily, on legs that felt as though they were made of running water and insufficient willpower.

The man who looked like Gabriel stepped back, rapidly, as though even wounded Seraphim might wish to, and be able to, take a swing at him. Seraphim focused a swimming vision on the man and said, "Thank you for healing me. Are you from Earth?"

He got back a surprised, feral smile, a fugitive thing. "I am from Earth, milord. I am– I was lured here, on my insufficiently tutored magic, and I—" He closed his mouth on visibly unsaid thoughts, as the ceiling above gave a loud crack, and rocks fell all around. "Milord, can you run?"

"No," he said. "No." He felt himself swaying on his feet. "A transport spell might be easier."

He reached for the man's hand, because he didn't think at this moment he could transport anything he wasn't actually touching. The man's hand felt too hot and rough. Seraphim started saying the spell, wondering if he could in fact make a transport spell. He wished them out of this hole, out of this horrible enclosure, and into a safe place. He didn't much care where just now.

"Use my magic, also, milor'," the man said, and Seraphim gratefully found it accessible, even if strange, and ignorance-twisted, and he made use of it, weaving his transport spell rapidly, turning it so that it closed finally with a resounding thud.

And then—

In a moment they were out of the cave, the heat, the threat of cave-in; and cold rushed in upon them. They were in a vast, white clearing. Seraphim realized, in shock, that there was snow all around, white snow, sparkling and reflective like ground glass.

In the middle of the clearing was what looked like a tomb, stone and sculpted, beside which a heavily veiled woman mourned. Atop the tomb, where normally a pious, joined-hands statue lay, there lay a man.

"Father!" Seraphim said.

Sarah A. Hoyt

King and Kingdom

It was dark and dank, and smelly. Gabriel's first thought was that he was within a rat's warren, or another such passage, built by creatures who, by night, live from the bounty of humanity's building.

All Gabriel's wishing this away didn't work, and though he ordered with all his kingly might, he realized it would not go away. Dark, and dank, and suffocating, the twisting paths led, by crooked paths like the random weavings of worm upon wood ever downward, ever tighter.

I can't wish it away, he thought, because this is the true thing. This is what is beneath all the spun sugar, all the mechanical soldiers, all the cloying, false sweetness was just that, false. This is what underlay Fairyland, a narrow complex of tunnels getting every smaller, ever tighter, like something a creature would spin while getting away from light and from life, and perhaps from sanity.

The tunnels got progressively narrower, and their surface had a weathered look, which puzzled Gabriel, because what was there to weather them here, deep in the heart of a magical kingdom and away from everything that might touch them? There was no rain in Fairyland, no currents of deep rivers.

No, Fairyland was all a thing of the mind.

Shortly, the tunnels got so narrow that Gabriel was walking them hunched forward, his head bent. They smelt of rats. It was a smell Gabriel knew well from his wretched childhood, a smell that made the hairs rise up at the back of his head, that made the bile rise up at the back of his throat.

He felt as though he were back there, in the narrow rented lodgings, lying in the dark, covered by the thin coverlet that somehow seemed to make one feel colder and to confer no comfort, waiting for the sound of feet behind the soffit, for the smell of rats, for the horrid feeling of their feet running across you.

Once, during a cold winter night, a rat had bit him on his toe, and it had taken forever to heal.

But there could be no smell of rats here; and yet when Gabriel tried to banish it, he couldn't. There was nothing there but the smell of rats and the narrow tunnels, and everything that was powerful in him told him these could not be altered because they were the true thing.

It took him a while – and by this time he was on hands and knees—

for him to realize why this was the true thing. The smell of rats was how his mind translated poverty. And Fairyland was poor. Fairyland had defaulted, to Gabriel, to its ultimate existence without disguise: poor, narrow, ever tightening and ever more convoluted. A dark place, spinning ever tighter.

It came to him that when it was so tight it would barely fit him would be when he would find the present monarch. It came to him that his teacher had been right. Fairyland was a parasite among the worlds, floating free and sucking life and magic out of everything it touched.

How could he want to be the monarch of such a thing? How could anyone but a madman want to rule a parasite-land.

But no. An instinctive recoil, a knowledge deeper than was possible to have from his lifetime, spoke to Gabriel out of the depths of racial memory. This was what Fairyland was now, yes, because it had a madman at its center, a madman who had been ruling it for centuries, and who had spun off all his own magic, so that he need now feed off other worlds and off unfortunates kidnapped for the purpose, as Michael had been. Gabriel's stomach lurched at the knowledge that there had been many others, adults and children alike, who had been used for this purpose, and who had not been rescued until they were but dry husks, sucked of magic and life.

And at the same time the king had needed to suck dry the magic of other worlds – which was where his mad pact with Sydell came in. If Sydell were king, he'd promised, the king could have the choice of magic from Britannia, the magical core of Avalon, until there was no true magic left there.

Gabriel shook his head. It was not supposed to be like that. He knew, knew with his whole being. There had been other kings, and things had been different then.

When a strong king stood at the center of Fairyland, he generated magic that fed the whole land and that in turn fed magic to every world that connected into it.

Gabriel, now crawling into the very narrow, very deep darkness at the heart of Fairyland, thought "But that would mean you wouldn't be you, any longer. It would be an organic thing. Humans call it king, but it isn't, not really. Generator, perhaps. Or… or servant." The thought of how many years he had been a servant came and went in his mind without his protest. He hadn't liked it, but it was far better than his years of hunger, his years of despair.

And then he thought that this would be worse. Not servant-servant, but a service that reached into your mind, into your heart, into your very being.

He'd stood by the side of ballrooms and watched the couples, and kept an outwardly respectful appearance while keeping his own thoughts, while meditating on the shortcomings of the people around him, and finding their folly funny.

This indenture would allow no such relief. Once he became Fairyland's … ruler for lack of a better word...he'd have to keep on with it. Everything he did, everything he thought, would reflect itself upon the land.

Any love, such as mortals knew love, that he might have, would have to restrain itself to time away from Fairyland, and those would have to be very brief, very limited moments; or else Fairyland would feel his absence and reach out for someone else – for something else that would feed its magic.

Gabriel knew of a certainty, suddenly, that there had also been other dark kings before. Here at the heart of Fairyland, the instinctive knowledge of Fairyland's history was impossible to avoid. The land knew, and, knowing, communicated itself to him. There had been other kings, worse even than this one, kings who had forced the land to reach outward and enslave humans to its will, and demand human sacrifice to feed itself.

There had also been kings who'd send their beings forth to kill and commit mayhem, to harvest life to feed Fairyland.

Fortunately, Gabriel had had a very moral upbringing, despite his father's failings and his mother's irregularities. The thought passed through his mind and made him smile, but it was followed by the thought that there was nothing fortunate about it. He wouldn't be able to convince himself that it was right and just to leave Fairyland to gratify his whims, or even his dreams, for long enough to cause it to go out of control. His uncle had left Fairyland in pursuit of his obsessions. That those obsessions were judged by humans to be vile made no difference at all to what they did to the land. Gabriel's own dreams might be considered by some to be vile, also, but—

A thought of an almost discarded – almost but for their renewed acquaintance – youthful dream of living in Marlon's lodgings, of growing old with him, in the quiet house filled with books, now that the ghost-lover was gone, came and went. He thought of Marlon, at sixty, that flame-bright hair gone pale, sitting by the fire, reading, and then released the thought.

It would likely never have been like that for them, anyway. And at any rate, Gabriel knew better. You couldn't just not do your duty and collect all the rewards of doing your duty. He couldn't simply wish that Fairyland be healed and not step into the role of king. He was the only one who could heal Fairyland, and anything worth having was worth paying for.

Anything that big was worth dying for.

He was now crawling through a tunnel so narrow that he could barely breathe. It couldn't go on much longer. His uncle must be somewhere ahead. Should he go forward? Or was he unwilling to pay the price?

Ahead, in the dark, he saw red, glowing eyes, like a trapped rat's.

He thought back to an Autumn day in Darkwater, walking in the garden, and seeing the gardener pour something into a hole. He remembered the day so clearly – it had been shortly after his father had brought him there – that he could feel the strange comfort of the woolen overcoat, the softness of the muffler around his neck, and feeling quite odd in these clean clothes, and in the half-deference the staff gave him – because everyone knew whose get he was. Even if they were in fear of his fey nature, there was no denying, with that face, he was the lord's son, and therefore they'd called him Master Penn and touched their hats at him.

And the gardener had done just that and said, "As it is rats, Master Penn, and they've been going all under the forcing houses, the way to get rid of them is to stop all their entrances and exits with pitch, and to let them starve."

He thought, I'm stopping the entrance and the exit. And then realized he was wrong. Yes, this tunnel was Fairyland, and his uncle's mind was at its end, starved and stoppered. But to starve him – to stop his exits.... It meant cutting off his food – cutting off... his access to Fairyland, stopping everything he was, and everything he could be.

"Yes," Gabriel said, and reached for the threads leading from his uncle to everything that was Fairyland.

It came to him the only way to cut those threads was to attach them to himself. To make himself the center, the spin of them. To let them eat him alive.

"Yes," he said, though it felt like his lips had gone ice cold with saying it. Tears tried to spring to his eyes, but it was too late. Everything in Fairyland that needed feeding – and that was everything – attached to him: to his mind, to his body, to his essence.

He felt more than heard a scream from his uncle, the scream of a starving creature. Gabriel had starved. He felt a pang of pity.

But then he thought of the spun sugar, the cloying sweetness, the adults – and children – enticed, like wasps to a poisonous trap. Not let go till they were quite dead.

And he pulled the rest of Fairyland to him.

He heard a shriek as all the force went out of the old king. If his father hadn't, however belatedly, done his duty, Gabriel wouldn't be alive, and wouldn't be here. Well, Gabriel was his father's son and late to his duty, but he meant to fulfill it, so that others might live.

And then Fairyland exploded outward, into groves and rivers, into sacred glades and centaur meadows.

And Gabriel was in a white room, in the middle of a white palace, on a throne made of crystal, looking out over a vista of the realm that owned him.

He closed his eyes and bid farewell to his humanity.

Fire and Flood

After the Dragon flame came and seared away… Caroline didn't know what...she felt that for a moment she saw the whole royal nursery illuminated from the inside, like the words of the scripture about the day of judgment when the secrets of every heart shall be laid bare.

She herself was not affected. She'd come through dragon fire once, and she felt like there was nothing left to burn, and she turned to Akakios and saw him, for a moment just as he was, young man and centaur both and something else, something that might be his soul – something shining and… something she belonged to.

It was hard to put in words that which was not designed for words, not even those spoken only in the mind. She reached back her hand, in the flood of fire, and found his hand reaching for hers, warm and alive and very human.

And in the next moment the dragon turned on the sobbing woman who'd been – perhaps still was – Seraphim's fiancée, and concentrated the fire on her.

Honoria screamed and fell to the ground on her knees. Just as when inside Akakios Caroline had seen his true essence, Honoria's looked smaller, and sad, and defenseless – at least for a moment. And then that seemed to shrivel away and leave nothing….

The dragon looked at her with a pitying look, and then it shifted. Where it had been there was a woman, the woman that Caroline had helped in the glade. But her eyes were even sadder now, and she looked around and then fixed on Caroline, "You," she said. "You are kind. Get someone to minister to this unfortunate. She is bearing the child of a dragon, and she is not whole."

The dragon shifted again, "But now I must go," she said. "The new king will require my attendance."

Caroline had barely the time to blink, and the dragon was gone, not through the window, but transported. Honoria remained on the floor, crying, and Caroline wondered with horror whether her being asked to look after Honoria – and her child? Caroline blushed at the thought – meant that Seraphim would have to marry Honoria after all. How else could Caroline be expected to look after the woman, if they were not to be related?

But she didn't want Honoria to marry Seraphim. If she was pregnant, then she must have behaved – as Mama would say – like a very abandoned female, and with Sydell, yet, who seemed to be at the heart of all this.

She didn't even know if Seraphim was alive, and she feared very much that Seraphim would consider it his duty, too, to look after Honoria and her baby, though it were none of his. But her heart turned within her. She didn't even know if Seraphim were still alive. He'd been transported with Sydell-who-was-a-dragon. Where would he be now?

Sarah A. Hoyt

A Time To Choose

Marlon would never be able to tell exactly what had happened as the dryad who was his mother transported him out of the room.

There was a time of infinite slowing, it seemed, when he saw life from the heart of a tree, a creature almost immortal – and full immortal in Fairyland – straining years through the measure of growth rings and sunlight, viewing humans as nothing but passing, ephemeral creatures, the kind you could ignore. They wouldn't be around very long.

His human senses, such as he retained, offered him a mingled green view, a passing scenery of centuries, of buildings being erected and collapsing, and none of it mattering very much.

The tree he was – he thought after a while that what was really happening was that he was sharing his mother's memories – was in the center of a grove, surrounded by brothers, and sisters, just like it. He felt their thoughts, as slow as his – hers? – and just as close as his own. They were one, that grove of trees. Just enough individuality to be unique, but enough community that it was like being one of a group of twins, with that communication it was said twins had, where they could guess each other's thoughts.

He felt the love and joy of the creatures around. And he thought how cruel, how inhumane of his father, to have separated his mother from this for more than two decades.

It wasn't that a human could have withstood such magical, solitary confinement well, but that a dryad couldn't stand it at all. They weren't meant to be alone, but to live in a grove, roots entwined, a small part of a living whole.

And then the voice came, like a dream. "This too you could have, my son. This too you could choose."

He stood still, within her consciousness. He felt the bark – as it were – form upon his body, as his outstretched arms became branches.

It should have felt terrifying, but it didn't. It was more the feeling of coming into your own house, of closing the door after yourself, of entering a space where you were safe and nothing could harm you.

But that wasn't true, was it? He stirred, and felt as if the bark upon him cracked. He felt his mother's mind, rushing to still the panic, but the panic wouldn't subside.

His mother had been safe, like this, covered in bark, in a woodland glade, but the dragon had reached in and despoiled her, and taken her away to enclose in an evil spell, animating it and giving it strength. He wouldn't be safe.

"The dragon could do so with the connivance of the king," she said. "But there will be a new king now."

But the dragon within Marlon was now alive and awake. Or if not the dragon – he didn't think he, himself, could actually turn into a dragon—but there was dragon in him. And no wonder all his life he'd been caught between two natures, never sure what he was or what to do, both the dragon and the tree that burns, both the rooted communal being and the individual who longed to nest upon cold treasure.

But if he became the tree, wouldn't the dragon rebel?

And the human too?

And then he felt his power rushing back to him.

He'd given his power to Gabriel for his final fight. If the power returned to him, it could only mean one thing: Gabriel was dead.

Bark and quietness went flying, and the sacred stillness of the grove, as Marlon screamed, "No!" and his scream shattered the illusion and left him – cold and alone – in the middle of a whirlwind of magic.

Rings on her Fingers

Nell, in the space she was in, in which she was not Nell at all, pulled up all the defenders of the land, waking long-dead warriors from their graves and bringing up the force of the land against the intruder.

Suddenly she felt a force join hers, and a polite voice she knew well say, "This too I shall take from you, Princess. I shall manage my own."

She recognized Gabriel Penn's voice, and in the next second, the forces of Fairyland were pulled back, and the land of Avalon was left without intruders, but more, she felt as though suckers had been attached to places of power, and were now being detached.

"My predecessor," the exquisitely polite voice said in her mind, "was not strong enough to hold Fairyland, and he let it become a parasite upon other times and other places. I will not continue that practice."

The feeding lines pulled back from all the places where they had been attached, and the magic of the land surged, luminous and clear and pure, so much magic.

In the center of it, Nell let it wash over her like a cleaning tide.

Once it was past, once the blinding light of it was gone, she pulled at the severed ends of the magic that had once knit land and king, the magic severed by Sydell's crime and Sydell's dark magic.

In a land in which the king is part of the magic of the land, and part of the heart of it, it shouldn't be possible for an intruder to come between them, and to turn the king deaf to the land and the land against the king.

That it had happened at all had required unusual perfidy and dark treason, and a man endowed with the magic of two worlds.

Nell pulled back the threads that had gone into Fairyland, through Sydell's dragon-nature, and knit together the ends of the king and land.

For a moment, she was caught in the middle, as the land surged to its rightful sovereign, like a child long separated from its parents.

And then suddenly, with the surprise of something you know is coming, but which has been so long in arriving that you think will never now come through, the burden was lifted from Nell's shoulders, the land from her mind.

The spinning around her of wishes and wants not her own, of places and beings that were, for a moment, like a part of herself, left her shaking. It was a relief, but the sort of relief one feels when a long illness ends in a quiet death.

She reeled under the blow of the withdrawal of power, and she, who had been multiple and ubiquitous, was suddenly just Nell, in a small body, and all too human.

She was also, she realized, in the royal palace. At least, the hallway in which she found herself looked like an engraving she'd seen in a book about the royal palace of Britannia.

Facing her was an elderly couple. Though they were dressed like the upper class of Britannia, it took her a moment to realize they were the king and queen.

A king was, after all, supposed to be on a throne, and surrounded by majesty and might. Not in a hallway, looking surprised, and clutching at the hand of his equally-surprised looking wife.

But the majesty hit Nell immediately afterwards. She knew the power she had held, all too briefly, belonged by right to this man. She could feel him – even at the same time that he was just a middle aged man, in a restrained dark suit, being the land, and keeping all the places of power flowing through himself and to the land, defending all magical borders, clearing all magical snags, keeping the land in good order.

And he did it without letting his emotions affect it, without letting his real life intrude. She'd never be able to do it. Never.

She realized she'd said all this aloud when the man's tired face – how tired he looked...no, how ravaged, as the land that has endured the scouring wave of a tsunami will look ravaged and stripped of life and joy – essayed a small smile. "You learn," he said. "You learn. And I didn't do so well myself, daughter?" the last was said tentatively, as a question.

Nell swallowed. She felt the grime of the cave on her hands. She knew her hair was a mess. She was wearing jeans, which must seem very odd to Britannia eyes.

She was facing the king. And she didn't feel in the least princess-like.

"I'm not going to force you to take the crown, you know?" the king said. "I'm not even going to force you to stay in Britannia. The land would be better for you, but God willing there will be time for me to train another successor. There are some cousins—"

For a moment there was immense relief. It was like having the land lifted from her shoulders. There was freedom. The door was open.

Nell could leave. She could go to Earth. She could go back to her normal life. She'd had her adventure, as grand, as important as anything she could have dreamed of within the pages of a fantasy novel. She'd had Antoine, who turned out not to be a villain at all, but a noble centaur prince, sacrificing himself for his kind. And if he'd also tried to attach the heiress to the throne to him, who could blame him? He was a prince. Giving up a throne for a throne, and a position of power for a position of power, seemed only fair.

She had met Seraphim, and she'd known he could love her, and she could love him. She'd seen palaces and hovels and strange worlds most humans couldn't even dream of.

Now she could go home, and settle into life at the farm, the life she'd thought she'd have when she was a little girl.

It was a relief, a great freedom, an inestimable gift. She had had adventure, and now she could have her life back.

She opened her mouth to speak, and only then she caught sight of her mother. She couldn't be anyone else – she looked like Nell herself, only aged, both by time and by a broken grief.

Catching her mother's gaze, Nell knew the queen had mourned the daughter she'd lost, the daughter she wasn't allowed to search for. She read in those eyes the loneliness of years, when the queen had tried to imagine how her child was growing up and how – the longing of the empty arms to hold the child she'd held all too briefly.

And now in them she read the resignation to let Nell go, if Nell must go, and a sort of sadness for the future she would also miss.

She looked back at her father, and beneath the regal look she caught the same fear, the same pain. The king and queen Nell could have refused. The throne she could have ignored. But not the longing in her parents' eyes. They'd missed her growing-up years, but they might yet see their grandchildren grow up. Would, for sure, see them grow up if nature allowed, because princesses don't decide their own marriages.

Farm and normal life vanished. She was the Princess Royal of Britannia, and one day she would carry on her shoulders the burden her father now carried. And her son or daughter would carry it after her. She was not Nell, herself, alone, but a link in an immutable chain, forged before her birth and extending well into the future.

Slowly, slowly, she sank to her knees. She inclined her head. "Sire," she said. "Father. I would like to be allowed to resume the duties I should have had, and to learn to carry your burden one day."

There was a moment of silence, and then, to her shock, to her trembling surprise, the king and queen were pulling her up, hugging her, being human and warm and parents. The queen was crying, convulsively, a seemingly-unstoppable spasm.

"My dear," the king said at last. "Cecilia. There is nothing left to cry for."

"I know," the queen said. "But sometimes we cry for joy." From her sleeve, she took a handkerchief and dabbed at her face and then, with what seemed to Nell near-miraculous self-control, she took a deep breath, and the crying stopped. She smiled tremulously at Nell. There was a smudge on her cheek where Nell had kissed her, and Nell's handprint was on the king's shoulder.

The king and queen looked at each other and didn't seem to notice.

And then the queen called out, "Come and bring my daughter some suitable clothes, and prepare a bath for her. The princess our daughter has come home."

Duke and Duke

The man on the tomb woke and sat up, and Seraphim realized that, while it was his father, it was his father as he'd never before seen him. He'd supposedly died only a year ago, but his hair was all white, and his face lined. Yet his eyes had the same carefree, roguish shine Seraphim remembered.

And Seraphim's mother looked up. It was she who'd stood by the tomb.

"Your father guided me here," she said, "when I was lost in the paths of Fairyland. His projection… his spirit, found me and brought me here, where his body was. Here, where he could keep me safe."

"His… body?" Seraphim said, approaching.

Into his half-unbelieving ears, his father poured a tale of how the old king had kidnapped him, to use his magic as fuel for Fairyland. "He left a changeling to die in my place, an aged fey in my form."

"But why?" Seraphim said, striving not to show that in fact this was the final blow. He'd had pride stripped from him, and love too – because he knew better than to think he could aspire to Nell – and now his title, the title he'd resented but strived to deserve, was taken from him too.

And the heart could not stand it. But it had to stand it. This too he would endure. This too he would survive. His father was the duke, and Seraphim would return to being a dutiful son. It wasn't as though he had illusions about the Duke's ability to actually perform his duties. It wouldn't do. No. The Duke would be the Duke, and Seraphim would retreat to the obscurity of managing everything – at least what Papa didn't squander. The Duke would, Seraphim supposed, resume his duties as witchfinder. And Seraphim would have the estate management and the books to balance. And in the fullness of time he'd find some nice, steady girl to marry – with Papa's consent – and produce children for the succession.

It was what would have given him great joy, even a year ago. But now…now he'd have to do it alone, without Gabriel's supporting presence. And he'd have to learn again the quiet ways of keeping Papa in check.

He looked at his mother, saw her looking at his father, realized that – despite all his faults, his roguish inability to keep himself to her only – she loved him. She was glad he was alive. Seraphim ought to be glad for her.

But Seraphim's father was looking at the young man with Seraphim, and Seraphim realized it must seem very odd, since they were both mostly naked and looked like they'd crawled through a furnace. He opened his mouth to explain. "This is Raphael. I don't know his sur—"

"His surname is Ainsling. I met his mother on Earth," Seraphim's father said. "Barbara, before I met you. I was trying to forget—" There was a pause. "His mother died giving birth, and his aunt took him to raise. I have… visited. But he disappeared. Two years ago. We thought—"

The young man nodded. "I was lured with, of all things, a job advertisement. Sydell…"

"Ah," the duke said. "Ah." Into the silence poured all the horrors that Seraphim could well imagine, of two years in that cave. He'd never ask the man – his older brother? – what it took to survive, in that place where so many were now skeletons. There were things you can't want to know, even if someone else had to live through them. And besides, Seraphim's all-too-vivid imagination told him he didn't want to know.

The angel names given his children were something he must get out of Papa and soon, though they might not mean any more than a personal eccentricity. But right then there was something more pressing, "You're older than I," Seraphim said, in a controlled voice. "That means you're the heir."

"Not for all the tea in China," the man said.

"Nonsense, Seraphim," the duke said. "His mother wouldn't marry me…. And then I met your mother."

Seraphim was going to ask more – about Raphael's mother and who she was and, given the man's resemblance to both himself and Gabriel, whether his mother too had looked like the fairy princess who'd captured the duke's heart. But all sound stopped on his lips.

A centaur had galloped up, and now crouched upon its front knees, in the way centaurs did, that passed for bowing. "The king of Fairyland," he proclaimed, "wants to speak to all of you."

A Moth To the Sun

Marlon found himself, suddenly, in an immense, white hall. Confused he looked up. Shocked, he said, "Gabriel!"

Gabriel sat on the throne of Fairyland, a throne of crystal and light. And yet, he wore the clothes he'd worn as the servant of the Darkwaters – a somber suit of good stuff, nothing too expensive, but respectable enough – and looked just like the old Gabriel.

He might have been the incoming student, sitting quietly in Marlon's lecture, so many years ago. Oh, older, perhaps, but the same cursed green eyes that had looked up at Marlon's with an odd sort of hopelessness, now looked down at him from the throne.

Gabriel smiled, a smile that looked sadder than his eyes, and said his real name, in the elven tongue, in liquid syllables that the human tongue couldn't hope to pronounce, then added, "But you may call me Gabriel." The sad smile again. A deep breath. "You saved me. By giving me your magic, unquestioningly, at the right time. You saved me, and you let the prophecy happen. In exchange, I can give you—" Another deep breath, and those despairing eyes gazing into his. "I can offer you a title in Fairyland. Pick what you want. Duke or Marquis, or what you wish. Only… Only stay, Marlon. Stay in Fairyland and be of us."

Marlon looked up. The ice-looking throne, and Gabriel upon it, looking as he always had. And then he saw the trap. There were always traps in Fairyland. One had to watch for them. And to expect plain dealing from its kin was akin to expecting dryness from a rain storm. "Gabriel," Marlon said.

Gabriel looked as he'd always done, but he wasn't. He'd pulled his majesty back into himself, to appear inoffensive and mortal. He had chosen his old clothes to lull Marlon into believing nothing had changed. But Marlon's magical eyes could see the tendrils of power infiltrating and expanding everything, twisting and writhing through all that was Fairyland, which was to say the heart of magic, slowly expanding through all the universes.

The power, so immense, on that throne, was not something that Marlon's all-too-mortal mind could even comprehend.

If he stayed, if he continued to love the small part of it that was Gabriel, Marlon would be consumed as surely and as completely as a moth in love with the sun.

He felt as though his heart were being pulled from his living body, but he had once already tried to hold onto a love that could no longer be, and through it created a living hell for what remained of the man he'd loved. He bit at his lower lip, a quick glance of pain, to recall himself to reality. "I can't, sire. I can't, milord. I am not wholly of Fairyland, and I have duties. For if you are here, my natural father must be dead, and I must – I believe I am the last of the line."

He felt as though something had snapped. Gabriel had been holding onto one last forlorn hope, Marlon realized, and, being the king of Fairyland, hadn't been able to prevent himself from holding out one last enchantment, a magical trap to convince Marlon to fall in on the side the king wanted.

A long silence, and then Gabriel laughed, a laugh that sounded surprisingly like his old laugh, but that echoed in strange harmonics that resonated with the magical parts of himself. "I should have let you keep the slave spell on me, my friend," he said, softly, amusement and sadness mingling in his voice. "Then they couldn't force me to be what I must be. It cost me more than you can guess, to give up that mortal life—"

He was silent again, and when he spoke, it was with the force, the majesty of the sovereign of Fairyland, "Go then from us, Lord Sydell. Yours is an old and respected title. May you bring it the honor it should have had. We shall speak with our brother the mortal king of Britannia to end your exile and give you what is due to you."

And with that, Marlon was alone in his lodgings. In the corner lay something. He didn't need to look closely to know that what remained of Aiden Gypson had also left him.

There was relief in it, of course, and joy too, for Aiden's sake, but he'd never known he could feel so thoroughly, so unutterably alone.

Paying Dues

Seraphim found himself before the throne of Fairyland. It was hard to tell exactly what the room looked like. It seemed to extend in all directions, and be full of people, but if you turned your head, all you saw was white marble pavement extending till forever.

Gabriel sat on the throne, only it was not Gabriel. Not the brother that Seraphim had known, the friend he'd shared his adventures with. Instead, it was something … not human. There was the human there, but submerged, like the dark shadow at the center of a light.

Dark wasn't exactly right, either, since Gabriel seemed to be attired in something that might well be woven crystal and light. And yet, his expressions were those that Seraphim knew.

There was gladness and relief at seeing them, at knowing they were alive and well. There was amusement and affection in his look at his father, and affection and slight sorrow in his look at Seraphim, and a look at Raphael that told Seraphim that Gabriel at least knew very well what the man had had to do to survive in the dragon's den, and didn't like it any better than Seraphim liked his own imaginings.

They stood staring at Gabriel. Belatedly, it occurred to Seraphim, they ought to bow, but then Gabriel was speaking to their father. "Father," Gabriel extended something. It was a small, circular silver object, and it took Seraphim a moment to realize it was his father's pocket watch. "It might have kept you from being killed," Gabriel said. "But might I say it is a bad place to keep a soul? I would take it now into yourself, sir, and trust in more mundane protections."

And their father, who had never in his life looked embarrassed, now managed it. He said, "Well, with Sydell on the prowl… Well…."

"It was almost captured several times," Gabriel said. "And then it was lost and it took me all my power to retrieve it from where it was fallen. Take it, sir. The rest of us carry our souls with us, and, you might find, it helps you act more human, more humanely, than you have done."

Like that, and while their father did something with the watch, he turned to Seraphim, "You will resume your duties, brother," he said. "And I have not forgotten how difficult those were, because of the lack of funds." There was a gesture, and then, from the dark, something that was no more than a sketch of light – with wings? – put a large trunk in front of Seraphim. "Those, my brother, are for you, and for the education of the young ones, Caroline and Michael, and I assume the education of prince Akakios, too, who barred himself from our world through his choices. You will have to provide for him, and I'm providing for you."

"Fairy gold?" Seraphim asked.

A laugh that was much like the old Gabriel's. "No. We do know, in our long lives, of gold that was buried and forgotten. That's all this is. It will be transported with you, when you go. May you use it in health and for your house's honor, Duke."

Seraphim blinked. "I am not—" he started but didn't finish. There was the sense of his mother's arm, clutching at his father's, the sense of something that wouldn't be said, but that his parents had talked about long before he'd seen them again.

"Ah, I have no intention of resuming the position," his father said. "Just reversing the succession. Parliament. A whole lot of bother." He cleared his throat. "Your mother and I… That is, I have identities and lives and… sometimes property in other worlds, and I only strayed because your mother couldn't go with me, and now—"

"I shall make paths through Fairyland free to you," Gabriel said. "So you can cross wherever you wish to go."

Seraphim thought, suddenly, that he was the most despicably inconsistent of creatures. He'd thought he wanted his title and his responsibility back. He'd thought—

But now it fell on his shoulders like a crushing burden; he realized even the gold at his feet was not enough to make up for the pain in his heart, for the loss of Nell. And that the Duke of Darkwater could even less afford to break decorum than Seraphim Ainsling could.

Gabriel had turned to the other man. "And you my friend, when you arrive at your place, on Earth, you shall find in it those bits of the dragon treasure that will be of use in your land. Go from us, and strive to forget the years the dragon ate."

Raphael disappeared, and Seraphim's father, his arm around his wife, turned as though to go, and Seraphim said, "Wait. Why the angelic names?"

The duke looked puzzled. "I thought they would protect you. I thought you'd need it."

"Likely," Gabriel said, amused, as the old duke and the duchess vanished.

"I wonder," Seraphim said, "whether there is a Uriel somewhere."

"I wouldn't bet against it," Gabriel said.

"I am going to miss you," Seraphim said.

"I will miss you too," Gabriel said. "As much as I can miss anything. As much as I can remember, brother."

Like that, Seraphim found himself standing in the middle of his bedroom, in the closed-up house at Darkwater. There was a very large trunk at his feet, which he was sure was full of gold – gold that couldn't begin to compensate for the loss of a mother, or a love, or even a brother.

But the Duke of Darkwater didn't cry. He presumed now, with Sydell's plot unraveled, he was no longer hunted. He must get his servants back, and his family. And he must see to Akakios's settlement and education. And he must see to Caroline's education too. And Michael's. And he must, in the fullness of time, pick a bride.

The Duke of Darkwater had a lot to do. Crying was the one thing he couldn't give time to.

Breakfast In Family

I don't understand," Caroline said, pettishly, over the breakfast table, "why I must go to boarding school. Or why Michael must go to a different boarding school."

Perusing the paper in front of him, with unseeing eyes, Seraphim said, "Because there are no schools that take both boys and girls. Because now that Mama is no longer with us, you must learn things of deportment and dress that I am simply not qualified to teach you. Because you will eventually be presented and have to maintain your status, so that you can marry Akakios when he comes of age."

"I don't understand either," Caroline said. "Why the king made Akakios a duke. He is a prince."

"Of centaurs, which don't exist in our world. The prophecy bars him from Fairyland, and he can't turn into a centaur here. So, we are paying for his education, and the king has made some sort of exchange with Fairyland, which has created him an earldom. You will be well provided for."

"I don't want to be well provided for if it means going to school and only seeing all of you on holidays."

Seraphim didn't answer. His eyes were fixed on a picture in the front page of the paper.

"And I don't understand, either," Caroline said. "Why Nell must marry the nasty Prince of Lombardy. And I don't care if everyone thinks it's so romantic. It's not. I saw at her coronation as princess how she looked at you. And I saw how she looked at you when you were officially created the king's witchfinder. It isn't right for people to marry people they don't love."

"Sometimes," Seraphim said, "it is their duty." He had tried to do his duty. He'd offered to marry Honoria. It had only got Jon to laugh in his face and say, "For a mad woman, clean out of her head, who needs to be led around by her hand, and have everything done like a toddler, my sister attracts a lot of marriage proposals."

"A lot of—"

"I saw Sydell this morning," Jonathan said. And to Seraphim's face. "The son. The one we knew as Marlon Elfborn. I understand he was your brother's—" For a horrible moment, Seraphim feared that Jon was about to say something graphic that involved the word "tup," but he seemed to be a different Jonathan these days. "Well, never mind that. He offered for Honoria, and I accepted."

"But—"

"My dear Seraphim," Jonathan said. "The child she carries is his half-brother. He feels obliged to look after her and the child. And it is succession for him. And unlike you, he will not feel the need of a woman for his present comfort." He grinned, the impish grin of the old Jonathan Blythe, even though he sat in his office, and wore a mourning armband for his father, who had blown out his brains in this same office. "My dear Seraphim! He made me the most stiff-lipped speech, about his duty and how one isn't put in this world only for one's own pleasure." A deep sigh. "He could have been you. As though I didn't have duty enough in my own life. It is all very depressing."

It was all very depressing. If Seraphim had been allowed to marry Honoria, at least he would have had an excuse for how barren and empty his life was. Duty and more duty. It was all duty.

Sarah A. Hoyt

A Visitor

Lord Sydell sat in his office, looking out the window over his lands. From where he sat there was a copse of trees visible, turned all the autumnal colors.

He got up and paced to the window. His son – well, the one the world would always know as his son – had been born yesterday, a healthy lad, more human than Marlon himself and perhaps more stable, since there was nothing of dryad in him, and the dragon was very little.

Marlon had felt it incumbent upon himself to keep the child from the homes for magical orphans, to keep him from opprobrium and shame. He would be brought up as the legitimate son of the son, and he would grow with an adoptive father who would, Marlon thought, be very able to love him, despite everything.

It would be interesting to see a child growing up, to teach him to fish, to read him books.

For now, there was a nanny hired, because the little tyke's mother wasn't capable, even, of looking after herself.

He'd been told she would not last long, and he mourned that. Though she was a shell of a woman, his duty to her, the supervising of her nurses, the daily visit to her chambers, in which he reassured her that all was well and she was safe, were anchors in his life.

Now the child and having the child raised as normal, as average as possible for someone with dragon blood, must be his anchor. The one anchor he wanted he could not have.

He had this: the title he never wanted, the lands he never coveted, the child he hadn't sired. On his grounds, too, he had Aiden's grave. He knew no essence of Aiden remained behind, but he visited the grave in the evenings, and it gave him the solace of memory of a time not so duty-bound.

He heard a sound behind him, the clearing of a throat, and turned around, sure it was his butler, Miller, with some minor point of household etiquette.

Instead, he found himself looking at familiar features, familiar dark, curly hair, familiar green eyes. He looked wholly human, though he was wearing clothes a little better than those expected of a servant.

"Gabriel," he said. And then, "Is it really you? How is it possible?"

"It is really I," he said, and there were almost no magical echoes in his voice. "Not for long. A few hours. Now and then. But once you learn to control it… I can be myself. On Earth, I can be myself. Now and then. For a few hours. If you would—"

A long time later, Marlon said, "You're not going to do something foolish and pretend to age along with me, are you? Because it won't fadge, my dear. I'd know. And it would be worse than—"

"You won't age very fast," Gabriel said. "You have too much fey blood for that."

"No. But I will age faster than the eternal king of Fairyland."

Gabriel sighed. "Yes. And no, I won't pretend."

Marlon squeezed his hand. It felt warm and alive and human, and a little calloused, as it had been. "Good," he said. "Good."

Sarah A. Hoyt

For Love

She couldn't take it. She couldn't endure it. One more official portrait with Louis Hess, the Prince of Lombardy, and she was going to go completely insane.

Nell could take the lessons in magic, the lessons in managing a kingdom, even the lessons in deportment and attire, but she could not endure pretending to be in love with someone while her heart was breaking for Seraphim. Not that there was anything wrong with Louis. At least, not that she knew.

"I wasn't in love with your papa when we married," her mother told her, while they looked over the wedding clothes, one more time, on the eve of the wedding.

Nell sighed. Her mom looked up at her, and Nell had the impression there was laughter behind her eyes, though she looked grave. "But I wasn't in love with anyone else, either. And I've seen the way you look at Darkwater."

Nell made a dismissive gesture.

"The thing," her mother said. "Your marriage to the prince of Lombardy was decided before you disappeared and your father couldn't stop it or go back on his word."

"I know, Mother. We've been over this."

"Yes, well." Her mother smiled. She went to a corner and came back with a valise. "Look, your father can't break the contract, but it doesn't mean it can't be broken. And once it's broken, it can't be put back together. We've made arrangements…." The smile turned into a grin. "We've not waited and prayed to get our daughter back all these years to see her made unhappy. Go, Nell, seek your happiness. We will be ready to pardon when all is done."

In The Night

"Milord, there is a gentleman wishing to speak to you," the footman told Seraphim, who looked up from the ledger he'd been frowning at, without seeing it, for hours. The room was too quiet. The house was too quiet, now that he lived here alone. And there was no shortage of money and—

And Nell was to be married tomorrow, and forever out of his reach. Not that she'd ever been in it.

"Yes?" he said welcoming this distraction.

"He is at the door, with a carriage."

"What?"

"He says the Princess Royal has had a horrible accident, and she wants to see you, she wants you at her bedside before she—"

"Nell!" Seraphim said. This was worse than the idea of her marrying. He got dressed in his coat, and his hat; he got his cane, all in a rushed dream. He ran down the stairs.

The young man waiting at the bottom was vaguely familiar as one of the king's secretaries, which surprised him, since he was wearing a driving cape, and the attire of a coachman. But he supposed that, even in extremis, the royal family must keep these things private.

"She asked that you come, Your Grace," he said.

"Of course. Of course," Seraphim said, plunging into the open door of the carriage.

The carriage was dark. There was no lamp lit inside, as there would be normally, but he was too panicked to worry, and then, when he thought to worry, his eyes had started to adapt, and the carriage was bowling along at a fantastic speed over cobblestoned roads, rocking so hard he was afraid it might tip.

But his eyes had started adapting, and he could see, sitting opposite him, very pale, very composed, Nell in a traveling dress and hat.

"Nell!" he said. "What is the meaning of this?"

"We're getting married," she said. "There is a priest waiting to marry us at Canterbury, in the dead of night."

"What? But— Nell, you can't be eloping with me!"

"I'm not. I'm kidnapping you and marrying you." Her little face was very serious.

"But… my dear… your duty…"

"I will do my duty," she said. "But Mama said it is no part of my duty to sacrifice my heart for an old treaty."

"Lombardy will take offense."

"Well, then let them." She looked at Seraphim very seriously. "We'll send Jonathan Blythe to them. They'll end up believing this was all their own idea."

Seraphim opened his mouth, closed it. He thought of his lonely study, his lonely life. "My dear, we can't, we—"

"Seraphim Ainsling – if you don't want to marry me, tell me now, and I will order the carriage turned around."

He opened his mouth. He closed it. "You know very well I can't tell you that."

"Very well. We have an hour before we get to the chapel." She smiled at him. "And it's a very long time since you last kissed me."

Sarah A. Hoyt

Sarah A. Hoyt was born and raised in Portugal and lives in Colorado. In between the two lie many years and several interesting jobs ranging from professional steam ironing to work as a multilingual scientific translator.

She has written science fiction, fantasy, mystery, historical mystery, historical fantasy and fictionalized historical biography. She also writes under the pen names Elise Hyatt, Sarah D'Almeida and Sarah Marques. When not working, she likes to spend time with her two sons, her husband, or a variable clowder of cats .

Made in the USA
Lexington, KY
01 September 2014